REBECCA TOPE is the author of three bestselling crime series, set in the stunning Cotswolds, Lake District and West Country. She lives on a smallholding in rural Herefordshire, where she enjoys the silence and plants a lot of trees, but also manages to travel the world and enjoy civilisation from time to time. Most of her varied experiences and activities find their way into her books, sooner or later.

*rebeccatope.com*

*By Rebecca Tope*

## THE LAKE DISTRICT MYSTERIES

The Windermere Witness • The Ambleside Alibi
The Coniston Case • The Troutbeck Testimony
The Hawkshead Hostage • The Bowness Bequest

## THE COTSWOLD MYSTERIES

A Cotswold Killing • A Cotswold Ordeal
Death in the Cotswolds • A Cotswold Mystery
Blood in the Cotswolds • Slaughter in the Cotswolds
Fear in the Cotswolds • A Grave in the Cotswolds
Deception in the Cotswolds • Malice in the Cotswolds
Shadows in the Cotswolds • Trouble in the Cotswolds
Revenge in the Cotswolds • Guilt in the Cotswolds
Peril in the Cotswolds

♦

A Cotswold Casebook

## THE WEST COUNTRY MYSTERIES

A Dirty Death • Dark Undertakings
Death of a Friend • Grave Concerns
A Death to Record • The Sting of Death
A Market for Murder

a&b

# The Windermere Witness

## REBECCA TOPE

Allison & Busby Limited
11 Wardour Mews
London W1F 8AN
*allisonandbusby.com*

First published in Great Britain by Allison & Busby in 2012.
First published in paperback by Allison & Busby in 2013.
This paperback edition published by Allison & Busby in 2017.

A CIP catalogue record for this book is available from
the British Library.

10 9 8 7 6 5

ISBN 978-0-7490-2255-6

Typeset in 10.5/15.5 pt Sabon by
Allison & Busby Ltd.

The paper used for this Allison & Busby publication
has been produced from trees that have been legally sourced
from well-managed and credibly certified forests.

Printed and bound by
CPI Group (UK) Ltd, Croydon, CR0 4YY

*For Vronny –*
*hoping we're still friends after*
*two weeks in a car together.*

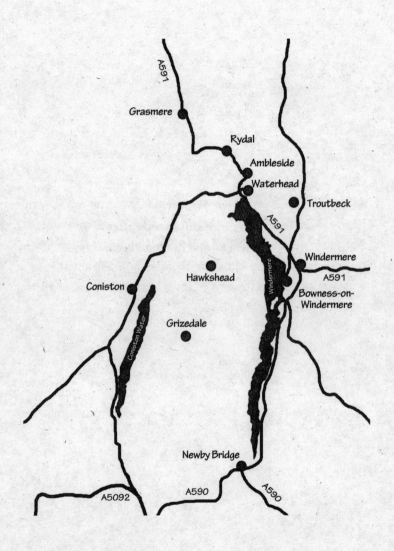

## Author's Note

Most of the places mentioned in this story are real – the hotels and monuments and some shops. The private houses, however, are products of my imagination. I have taken liberties with the buildings of Troutbeck in particular.

I am grateful to Michael Jecks and Tony Geraghty for information concerning guns.

# *Chapter One*

What a day for a wedding! Sheets of rain sluiced across the windscreen, giving the wipers a harder task than they were equal to. The road ran with water, so it resembled the lake that lay a few yards to the right. The turning into the hotel was ahead, somewhere, on a pimple of land jutting into the lake. On a bright day, it would be a stunning venue for a wedding; the photos spectacular. Today it would be madness for a bride to venture outside in silk and lace and expensively wrought hair. The many thousands of pounds that must have been spent on the event would do nothing to mitigate the disappointment, if Simmy was any judge. There would be huge umbrellas on standby, of course, and other tricks with which to defy the weather, but rain on this scale would defeat every attempt to save the day.

Behind her, the back of the van was filled with scent and colour, conveying all the layers of meaning that went along with flowers. She was confident that her work would meet all expectations. She had laboured over it for a week, selecting and matching for colour, shape and size. The scheme was a rosy peach ('Definitely not peachy rose,' said the bride with a grin, when she and her mother had come to talk it over) with scatterings of rust and tangerine to echo the autumnal colours outside. Colours that were muted to grey by the rain, as it had turned out.

The hotel's facade was a pale yellowy-cream on a good day. There was a confident elegance to it, despite the lack of symmetry. The older part boasted a columned entrance that Simmy suspected might be a loggia, officially. She had been profoundly impressed by the whole edifice, on a previous visit two months before. The chief element in its reputation, however, lay in the setting. The lake itself was the real star, and the various architects who had created the Hall had had the good sense to realise that. All the ostentation lay indoors, where no expense had been spared in grand ornamentation.

She parked the van as close as she could get to the humbler entrance where deliveries were customarily made. A team of hotel staff was on hand to assist, and within the hour, the centrepieces, swags and two monumental arrangements had been set into position. During that hour, Simmy lost herself in the creative process, immersed in colour and form that were intended to enhance the romantic significance of the event. She gave brisk instructions to the people detailed to work with her, their tasks restricted to pinning and tying, fetching and carrying. The florist herself attended to everything else. Everything fell perfectly into place, exactly as she had envisaged. Clusters of red berries to suggest fruitfulness; luscious blooms for sensuality; some dried seed heads for permanence – she loved the understated implications that few, if any, wedding guests would consciously grasp, and yet subliminally they might appreciate.

'Just the bouquets and buttonholes now,' she told her helpers. 'Where do they want them?'

The bride's mother was telephoned, and Simmy was asked to take the flowers to the suite upstairs. In the lift she balanced the large box on one hand and thought briefly about weddings. Just as births and funerals conjured a kaleidoscope of personal memories and associations, a wedding always called up comparisons with others one had experienced. In her case, it was her own, nine years earlier.

She was on the third floor before she could get far in her rueful reminiscences. Room 301 was awaiting her, the door already open. Inside was a flurry of female activity, half-naked girls with hair in rollers, a heavy atmosphere of near hysteria. 'Flowers,' she said, superfluously, looking for a familiar face. She saw herself reflected in a gold-bordered full-length mirror – a misfitting figure amongst all the froth of silk and lace, dressed in a blue sweatshirt and jeans. Her hair was untidy, her hands not entirely clean. She had given no thought to her own appearance, which made her a complete alien in this room where appearance was everything.

'Oh! Let's see!' And there was Miss Bridget Baxter, soon to be Mrs Bridget Harrison-West, fumbling at the lid of the box in her eagerness.

Simmy carefully set it down on a marble table beneath the window and lifted the lid. 'I hope they're what you wanted,' she said.

The bride met her eyes with a direct blue gaze that would instantly endear her to the greatest misanthrope alive. 'They're

11

fabulous!' she said. 'Look, everybody! Aren't these gorgeous!'

'Keep them cool, if you can,' Simmy advised. 'Probably the bathroom would be best.'

The enormous room swirled with bridesmaids and long dresses hanging on a wheeled rail. There were two big sofas, on one of which sat a young girl, intently fiddling with her fingers and apparently muttering to herself. It could only be the smallest bridesmaid, traditionally referred to as the 'flower girl', and as such, Simmy felt herself justified in making an approach. She sat down on the edge of the chintzy sofa.

'There's a special bouquet for you to carry,' she said. 'Do you want to see it?'

The child shrugged, but flashed a quick smile that seemed friendly enough. 'If you like,' she said.

'This is all a bit . . . *daunting*, isn't it?' Simmy sympathised, with a glance around the room.

'"Daunting"?' the little girl repeated with a puzzled frown.

'Overwhelming. Stressful.'

'It's a wedding. This is what they're like. I went to one before.'

'Did you? Were you a bridesmaid then, as well?'

'No. They were all grown-ups that time. Thank you for the flowers.'

Simmy felt subtly dismissed, by a child who was probably accustomed to being attended to by people paid to do it. She smiled briefly, understanding that there was no further role for her.

There was a smell of lavender soap and warm ironing. Ms Eleanor Baxter, mother of the bride, was nowhere to be seen. Simmy was not sorry to miss her. When choosing the flowers, she had been a disconcerting mixture of autocratic boredom and penetrating exigency. The flowers had to be right, because this was a wedding, but weddings were actually a tedious necessity that she very much wished she didn't have to bother with: that had been the general message that Simmy picked up.

'Look at that rain!' cried one of the girls, standing by the window. 'The lake will overflow if it goes on like this, and we'll all be washed away.'

'It's a disaster,' said Bridget cheerfully. 'I knew this would happen.'

'But last weekend was so *lovely*!' moaned the girl. 'Warm and sunny, and lovely. How can it change so quickly?'

'That's England for you,' said Bridget. 'It's all Peter's fault, of course. He wouldn't miss his sailing, even to get married.' Everyone within earshot laughed, causing Simmy to suspect that the reality was something rather different.

She made her departure, with a murmured good-luck wish. Not that it was needed. Miss Baxter, spinster of the parish of Windermere, was so comprehensively blessed that a rainy wedding day would hardly dent her faith in her husband, or in the world. Although the florist had been given no special confidences, she did happen to be acquainted with the bride's hairdresser, who had. 'She loves him, Sim. They've known each other for years, and he always said he'd marry her the moment she was old enough.'

'Don't you find it the weeniest bit creepy?'

'Why? Because he's twenty-five years older than her? No, not at all. It's lovely that he's waited all this time for her. It's like a fairy tale.' Julie was a romantic creature, and Sim saw no cause to undermine her illusions. Besides, from the glimpses she had gained of Bridget, it seemed she would wholeheartedly agree with her hairdresser.

The wedding was scheduled for eleven, which left an hour and a half for Julie to work her magic. 'She wants the whole works, with tendrils and pearls,' she'd gloated. 'I can't tell you how much she's paying me. It's embarrassing.'

Simmy had felt no envy. The proceeds from the wedding flowers would keep her in business for some time, and do her reputation no harm at all. There was every chance that the hotel would recommend her more often, now she had been selected for the Wedding of the Year. The pictures in the gossip columns would cement her position, with any luck.

Outside, the van was about to be joined by others. Two vehicles were making a stately approach down the lesser driveway, and Simmy realised they would want her out of the way. She would do best to leave by the main entrance. As she drew level with the loggia, she saw that a knot of men had gathered, under huge umbrellas. Somebody amongst them was smoking. They looked like a clump of bullrushes growing beside the lake, their seed heads exploding in black arcs, silhouetted against the water behind them. They were laughing together as if the weather meant nothing to them. Too soon for wedding guests, surely? Family and close friends would be staying at the hotel; others would arrive in relays – some for the ceremony, some for the wedding breakfast, and another batch for the obligatory evening disco. Getting married at eleven meant a marathon fifteen hours or more, these days, albeit with lengthy interludes during which nothing happened. Simmy remembered it well.

The jocular group eyed her van as she drove slowly past them. One individual detached himself and flapped a hand to stop her. She opened the window on the passenger side and heard one of the others call out in puzzlement – 'Hey, Markie, what're you doing?'

'You're the florist,' he said, with a glance at the stencilled logo on the side of the van before peering in through the window. 'You live in my house, in Troutbeck.'

She stared uncomprehendingly at him. 'Pardon?'

'I was born there. We moved away three years ago. The new man didn't stay long, then.'

'Mr Huggins? He lost his job, apparently, and had to go to Newcastle to find another one.'

The boy shrugged. 'It's a nice house. I hope you're happy there?'

'It's lovely,' she said.

He smiled, and changed the subject. 'Did you bring the buttonholes?'

'I did,' she nodded. 'Why?'

He was very young, perhaps not even eighteen. Simmy suspected she was more than twice his age – not that this detail seemed to deter him from flirting with her. 'I hope mine's the nicest one,' he grinned.

'You're not the best man, are you? It's my guess you'll be one of the ushers.'

'The *most important* usher,' he corrected her. 'I'm the bride's brother.'

*Aha!* thought Simmy, remembering the gossip she'd heard about the family. The coincidence of the Troutbeck house

15

gave her a sense of fellowship with him, and she tilted her head teasingly.

'Well, I'm sorry to tell you the buttonholes are all the same. Won't you get wet, standing about out here?'

'We're waiting for my pa. He'll need an escort to give him the courage to go in. We can't just let him turn up without a welcoming committee. He's due at any minute.'

'I see.' *Pa*, she concluded, was father of the bride, the very much divorced one-time husband of Eleanor, Bridget's mother. George Baxter had been married twice since leaving Eleanor, and was assumed to be not finished yet. And that made the effervescent Markie, even if he was brother of the bride, deserving of no special treatment where buttonholes were concerned. 'Is that the groom?' She peered through the rain at a moderately handsome figure with broad shoulders and full lips.

'Peter – yes. He's a good bloke. Known him all my life.'

'So I gather,' she said recklessly.

'Talk of the town, right?'

'Wedding of the year,' she agreed. 'I've heard the whole story.'

'No, you haven't,' he corrected her, with a sudden change of expression. 'You haven't heard a word that's true, I can promise you.' The word *dread* flashed through Simmy's mind, only to be dismissed as far too dramatic. Even so, the boy plainly wasn't looking forward to the arrival of his pa.

'Stressful business, weddings,' she offered.

'Too right,' he agreed. 'I'm never going to forgive Briddy for this.'

'Well . . .' she put both hands on the steering wheel, 'I should get out of the way. My part is finished.'

16

He seemed reluctant to let her go, glancing back at the cluster of men. Only one of them was watching him – a tall man in his early forties, with brutally short hair and a green waterproof jacket. His egg-shaped head looked all wrong without a decent covering of hair. 'That's Glenn,' whispered Markie. 'Peter's best friend.'

'The best man,' Simmy nodded. 'Is he worrying about his speech?'

'Not so's you'd notice. He was drinking till four this morning, apparently, but you'd never guess. I was legless by midnight. The other chap is Pablo. He's Spanish.'

'And under the loggia?' She had only just noticed another man, sitting in a wheelchair out of the rain. Once glimpsed, she could not take her eyes off him. He was also watching Mark with lowered brows.

'Oh, that's Felix. Peter's cousin.'

'Really? I don't think he was in the stories I heard about you all.'

'He ought to have been. Broke his back falling off Castle Crag, a year ago. Dreadful business. But he's being totally heroic about it. They all say so. Peter wanted him for the best man, obviously, but he flatly refused. He's getting married in the summer himself.'

Simmy dragged her attention away from the damaged man and smiled a vague acknowledgement of Markie's innate politeness in keeping her abreast of the personnel. 'Shame about the rain,' she said. 'It's not slacking off at all, is it?'

'It'll stop at eleven-fifteen, that's official. Nothing to worry about.'

'Really?'

'Yup. Glenn's got a hotline to the Met Office, or something.'

She revved the engine. 'Have fun, then,' she said and drove away.

The two-mile drive to her shop involved negotiating crowds of disconsolate visitors in Bowness. Despite Saturday being 'changeover day' for self-catering as well as most of the guest houses, there were plenty of exceptions to this rule. They came in caravans; they stayed in hotels costing anything between £50 and £250 per night; they thronged the B&Bs, such as the one her mother ran in a quiet backstreet in Windermere. The lake cruisers still plied up and down from Lakeside to Ambleside, doing even better business than usual, in the rain. Stuck in a traffic hold-up close to the jetty, Simmy watched a large ship approach. Even after nine months, she still found them incongruous on a freshwater lake, albeit ten miles long. Like an overlarge toy in a bath, it struck her as wasted when it should be taking people across the open waters of the Adriatic. But there was seldom any difficulty in filling the hundreds of places aboard, and nobody else appeared to share her slight sense of absurdity.

'Persimmon Petals' was in the main street of Windermere. While Simmy was at the hotel, her teenaged assistant Melanie was holding the fort. Melanie lived on the eastern edge of Bowness and attended college at Troutbeck Bridge, taking Advanced Level Management for a year, aspiring eventually to become a hotel manager. The timetable contained enough gaps for students to find paid employment around the town, and Melanie worked at the flower shop for fifteen hours a week. She talked a lot about 'the hospitality industry' and its innumerable ramifications. Simmy could often not understand her.

'Everything okay?' she asked, having located Melanie in the back of the shop. Her large figure was generally easy to spot. As tall as Simmy, she had a generous covering on her bones, and a big round head. She also had no sight in one eye, thanks to a fight with her brother when she was four.

'Fine. How's the bride doing?'

'She's disgustingly relaxed and cheerful. Doesn't care about the weather. Loves the bouquets. Julie's going to be in her element. I was a bit surprised that she hadn't got there yet, but nobody seemed worried.'

'You haven't heard, then?'

'What?'

'Julie won't be doing it. She's broken two fingers.'

'*What?* But none of the wedding people seemed to have heard – they'd have been in far more of a flap if they had. How do *you* know? What happened to her? I only saw her on Thursday.'

It was a daft question. Everybody knew everything in Windermere. Behind the throngs of tourists, there was a small core of residents, both dreading and yearning for the few quiet weeks after Christmas when they could breathe more easily and compare notes as to how the year's business had been.

'Graham Forrest came in for some roses, five minutes after you left. He's lodging with Doreen Mills now, in case you didn't know. And she's Julie's aunt. It happened yesterday. She trapped her hand in a hairdryer, somehow. It "jackknifed backwards", that's what Graham said. Lucky it wasn't a customer. She'd have been sued. You'd think—'

'Yes,' said Simmy hurriedly, hoping to avert a short lecture on health and safety. 'Right. So who's going to do the hair? Will they still *pay* her? My God! This is going to wipe the smile off young Bridget's face.'

'Yeah,' said Melanie, her expression mirroring Simmy's own mixture of concern and thrill at this unexpected setback in the life of the local golden girl. Except, even this might not seriously upset her. She could get married with her hair in a simple chignon, and the sky would not fall. 'They've sorted out somebody else, I suppose. The hotel will have a list. They always have a contingency plan.' She spoke proudly of her chosen profession. To Melanie, floristry was a poor lightweight line of work. She made no secret of the fact that she was only there because there'd been no other choice with the right number of hours.

'But it won't be the same. And the *photos*,' Simmy said. 'She's got to have proper hair for the photos.'

'They're sure to find somebody else,' Melanie insisted. 'Julie's not the only hairdresser in town.'

A fussy customer occupied the next ten minutes, but Simmy's mind was not on the job. Poor Julie – she must be feeling wretched, not only because of the wedding, but because fingers were painful when broken, and extremely necessary for any sort of work. 'Which hand was it?' she asked.

'Oh, the right. First two fingers on the right. She won't be able to do anything for weeks.'

Outside it was still raining. The deep grey-brown of the local stone had turned black from the soaking. The big building at the top of the street looked like a looming battleship. 'Shirley C's got a great big puddle outside,' she observed. The biggest shop in town was another incongruity that Simmy still had to wrestle with. It sold lingerie, with the long street window full of plastic torsos modelling knickers and corsets for every passing visitor to admire. How it managed to survive, nobody knew. *Thriving mail order business*, some know-all suggested. The sheer brazen take-it-or-leave-it attitude was what struck Simmy most powerfully, seeming typical of the whole approach to life in the region. Nothing was done for ostentatious show – the stone walls were simply there to keep the sheep in; the houses were made of the same material as a matter of course, but if someone wished to add stucco nobody objected. It all worked out quite peaceably, because the fells and the lakes were of so much greater interest and significance than any human activity.

The wedding remained at the front of her mind for the rest of the morning. At eleven-fifteen, she gave up all attempts to concentrate on the work in front of her, and went back to the street door to examine the sky. Markie Baxter's predictions came back to her – that it would stop raining at exactly this time, which would be more or less exactly the moment when Bridget and Peter became man and wife. Assuming everybody presented themselves punctually, of course. That, in Simmy's experience, seldom happened.

The puddles and rivulets in the street were deterring most would-be shoppers. The beck alongside her mother's house would be frothing and scrambling in full spate after so many hours of downpour. The lake would be lapping at the jetties and piers along its shores, and creeping closer to the hotel that had been built so hazardously close to the water. Had it ever flooded, she wondered? It was hard to see how it could have avoided it, in the two centuries since it had been built, and yet she had heard no local stories of inundation.

As she watched the little town centre, she realised that there were faint shadows being thrown by the few shoppers as they walked along the shining wet pavements. Umbrellas were being closed, and chins released from enveloping collars. 'Mel – it's stopped!' she called back into the shop. It was like a tap being turned off, and she marvelled at it.

'What did you expect?' came Mel's voice behind her. 'The Baxters and the Harrison-Wests between them are more than a match for the weather gods. Nobody would dare rain on their special day.'

'The boy, Mark, said it would stop at eleven-fifteen. It's like magic.' Simmy still couldn't credit it.

'What boy would that be?'

'Mark. Markie – whatever they call him. Her brother, isn't he? He stopped me for a chat as I was leaving.'

'Half-brother, Sim. He's her half-brother. Don't you know the story?'

It was a question she must have heard a hundred times since relocating from Worcestershire. Everywhere there was a story, a piece of local history that she was expected to have absorbed within weeks of arriving. 'Different mothers?' she ventured. 'But they can't be more than a year or two different in age.'

'Less than a year, actually,' grinned Melanie. 'There

22

was never any secret about it. Poor old Eleanor just had to put up with it.'

'But I thought she divorced him?'

'Not until the children – that's Markie as well as Bridget – were old enough to cope with it.'

'Why would it affect Markie? What difference did it make to him?'

'I'm not sure, exactly, but everyone says there were major changes to both their lives. Once George had gone, both Eleanor and Markie's mother would have been on the same footing. The balance of power would shift.'

Simmy did her best to imagine how it would have been. 'So how old were they, then?' she asked.

'I don't know exactly, but they weren't babies. And then it was *George* who divorced *Eleanor*. He'd fallen for the Plumpton woman by then, and wanted to marry her.'

'Lordy, Mel – it's like something out of Noel Coward.' Except it wasn't really, she acknowledged. It was all quite commonplace in the present day. Mixed-up families, with no two children sharing the same two parents, and everybody more or less amicable about it. It was she, Persimmon Brown, who was out of step. She was the one who could not find it in herself to forgive or forget or cease to wish every sort of hell onto her one-time husband, Tony.

# Chapter Two

'P'simmon!' warbled her mother. 'What are you doing here? I'm knee-deep in sheets, look.'

Her mother was the only person who used her full name, and even she omitted a couple of letters, pronouncing it in her own unique way that made it sound oddly Irish. When asked repeatedly to give a rational account of her choice of such an outlandish name for her baby, she always said, 'You were bright orange when you were born. You looked just like a persimmon. How could I resist?' But nobody in England knew what a persimmon looked like, Simmy argued feebly. The name was ridiculous. 'So change it,' challenged her mother. 'Maybe you'd have preferred to be Apricot?'

Simmy would have preferred Liz or Jane or Emily, when she was eleven, but gradually she came to appreciate some aspects of her name's uniqueness.

Teachers had been crass about it, baulking at this unknown name when Kezias and Chloes and Zaras went unremarked. *Per*simmon, they would cry, making it sound awkward and unbalanced. Even Per*sim*mon was clunky. Nobody ever got the hang of P'simmon.

'I did the wedding flowers at Storrs Hall,' she said. 'Julie's broken her fingers. She can't do the hair. It stopped raining at exactly eleven-fifteen, like magic. Did you have a lot in last week?'

'Full to bursting. Daddy had to go foraging for eggs at ten last night and I had him waiting table this morning. You know how he hates that.'

Simmy knew better. Her father made a complex private game out of serving breakfast to their guests. He had a mental list of a dozen or more snippets of local information, which he issued on a strict rota basis. He would subtly steer any conversation around until he could deftly slip in the fact that Mountford John Byrde Baddeley would be for ever turning in his grave at the memorial they'd built for him. Or that Lake Road had once been the main highway through Windermere, choked with traffic for centuries. Now it was silent and still and very much improved.

'He doesn't mind, really,' she argued mildly.

'He likes the money.'

The house had five guestrooms. When it was full, earnings reached three hundred pounds a night. In the summer peak, they might all be full every night for weeks on end. By any standards, the money was significant. The fact that Angie Straw was an unreconstructed hippy who found the normal rules of B&B-hood completely impossible to adhere to, seemed to matter little. She had a dog and a cat which might appear without warning anywhere in the house. She allowed guests to bring their own dogs, and kept a constant stack of patchwork cotton bedspreads for them to lie on. 'People always say it'll sleep on the floor, but of course that never happens,' she laughed. The useless extra cushions that so many landladies heaped onto the beds were absent from her establishment. She gave people real milk in little jugs that she collected from small potteries across the country. There were no televisions in the rooms. Instead she had erected a substantial bookcase on the landing and invited people to help themselves. She let people smoke in two of the rooms, and smoked unashamedly herself. This last got her into the most serious trouble, but her website made a feature of it, and earned her a steady stream of relieved customers as a result.

'You wouldn't believe how many people like their dogs and fags so much they never go away unless they can take them along,' she said. 'They think I'm wonderful.'

The legal implications of allowing people to smoke simmered ominously in the background. Simmy was fairly sure that it would only take one complaint to bring the authorities down onto her mother's head in an avalanche of litigation. But she had no hesitation in supporting the right to allow anything in your own home. The smoking ban had gone ludicrously beyond what was reasonable and the sight of sad little groups of smokers standing outdoors in all weathers always gave her a pang.

'Bridget Baxter's married by now, then,' said Angie. 'Peculiar business. Who's Julie?'

'The hairdresser. I suppose they knew about it when I was there, but nobody said anything. All the girls had rollers in and Bridget seemed amazingly relaxed.'

'Probably stuffed to the eyeballs with Valium. Nobody uses rollers any more, do they?'

'I think she's going for a retro look. All bouffant.'

'Dangerous in the rain.'

'The rain stopped. Markie said it would, and it did.' Simmy was still wondering how that had happened so predictably. 'Amazing.'

'Markie?'

'Bridget's half-brother,' Simmy told her, with her newfound knowledge. 'Only a year younger than her. All rather scandalous.'

Angie tossed her head impatiently. 'Not interested,' she asserted. 'Not my kind of people.'

It was true that Simmy's mother tended to focus on higher matters than the local gentry. She read literary biographies and watched old French films and never gave up trying to persuade everyone else to do the same. Unusually for a B&B she provided a sitting room for the guests containing a TV and DVD player, with a stack of discs that only the most dedicated film buffs could be expected to watch. There were also games and jigsaws and about five hundred more books, additional to those on the landing. The surprise was that these eccentricities were received with acclaim. 'Beck View' was suspected to be the most popular and successful establishment in the whole of Lake Road.

'Can I have lunch?' Simmy asked. 'Is Daddy going to be in?'

'He is. We're having sausage bake with spaghetti,' her mother informed her. 'I've got a new lot of people due at three, the pests. It clearly says on the website that we don't want anybody before four, but they always think I'll make a special exception for them.'

'They're right. Couldn't you say you'd be out? Can't they find something else to do for an hour?'

Angie shrugged. 'We've been recommended by some friends of theirs, apparently. I didn't recognise the name of the friends, but they sound all right.'

'Not really pests, then?'

'It depends. You can never be sure. They'll go out for an evening meal, anyway.'

'No wonder you can't remember their friends. There must be hundreds who've stayed here over the years.'

'Thousands, actually. And I do usually remember them if I see them again. Although there are some who make no impression whatever.'

At thirty-seven, Simmy conducted her own life well out of sight of her parents. She had bought a small stone house halfway between Windermere and Ambleside and made sure she didn't visit Beck View more than once a week – often less than that. Catching up with news was generally done over lunch, as it would be today.

Except that the comfortable family meal never took place. Five minutes before the three of them were due to sit down together someone rang the doorbell. Angie asked Simmy to get it, and she found Melanie on the step. 'Something's happened down at Storrs,' she gasped. 'Somebody died.'

Simmy visualised an overindulging uncle succumbing to a coronary and knocking trays of champagne flying. Melanie's excitement, always quick to flare, struck her as excessive. 'Oh?' she said. 'And that warrants leaving the shop, does it? Couldn't you have phoned me?'

'It's the boy – Mark. He drowned in the lake.'

'No!' Simmy's insides cramped with a sudden involuntary horror. 'Was he boating? Surely not. He was an usher . . .'

'I think we ought to go down there and see,' Melanie insisted. 'You spoke to him today. They'll want to know what he said to you. They want you to be a *witness*.'

'Don't be stupid. Of course they don't. Why me, when there must be hundreds of people who've seen more of him than I did?'

Melanie's dimples appeared as she manifested extreme exasperation and her sightless eye stared insistently. 'Sim, listen,' she urged. 'There's more to it. Joe called me just now. It's terribly serious. The Baxter man has gone berserk, accusing everybody in sight of killing his boy. Joe says Markie never showed up for the wedding at all. He must have been in the lake all morning. So when I said you'd seen him, Joe said you had to go and make a statement. He said I should fetch you and take you down to the Hall.'

'Joe,' Simmy repeated, dazedly. 'The policeman, you mean?'

'*Yes*. He's my boyfriend, in case you've forgotten.'

'He shouldn't have told you about it, should he? Is he allowed to do that?'

'He knew we did the flowers. We're *involved*, Sim. This is a *huge* thing to happen. The Baxters and the Harrison-Wests, for God's sake.'

Simmy began to imagine the headlines and the gossip, and felt icy rivulets flowing through her body. But still she was far from grasping the central import of Melanie's news. Standing there on her mother's doorstep, her jaw working erratically as she attempted to speak coherently, she wanted nothing more than to close the door in her assistant's innocent face.

But she could not do that. 'All right,' she said. 'I'll go and tell my mother. Give me half a minute.'

'Bring a coat,' said Melanie, with a maternal touch that would never have occurred to Angie. 'It's turning colder.'

The van was still parked behind the shop, so they walked briskly back to collect it. 'Why didn't you drive here?' Simmy grumbled. 'If there's such a great hurry?'

'I told you, I haven't got the motor today. I came on the bike. And you won't let me drive the van, remember?' This was a sore point with Melanie, who was unmoved by arguments involving the price of insurance.

The convolutions of Melanie's transport arrangements had never properly registered with Simmy. She shared an elderly Fiesta with an older brother, a liability in Simmy's view, which regularly refused to start. For backup, Melanie used an expensive bicycle that she resisted as much as possible. Melanie was not really built for cycling. 'Did you?' Simmy puffed. 'In all that rain?'

'I did. It was horrible.'

'Must have been. Gosh, you never realise how steep this hill is until you try to walk up it quickly, do you?'

'Nearly there,' Melanie panted.

The van, with its cheery floral logo, seemed an incongruous vehicle in which to arrive at a police investigation, but there was no choice. They were through Bowness and on the final stretch down to Storrs within a few minutes. The whole scene was completely transformed from that of a few hours earlier. None of the festive merriment of a wedding was to be seen. The lapping waters of the lake struck Simmy as almost voracious, gobbling up poor young Markie for no reason at all. What in the world could have happened to him, she wondered, when he had been so happy and relaxed, apparently moments before meeting his death? Except, she corrected herself, he *hadn't* been all that relaxed. He'd been worried about meeting his father, impatiently waiting out in the rain.

The last of the rain clouds had slipped away to the east, leaving a pale blue haze overhead. Simmy glanced at her watch, in an attempt to calculate how much time had elapsed since she was last there. It was a quarter to two – four and a bit hours, in which the lives of a dozen people or more must have been permanently changed. The memory of the little bridesmaid twiddling her fingers on the sofa came unbidden to her mind. Was she a cousin, perhaps, or somebody's stepdaughter? Had she known and loved the charismatic Markie? Would anyone manage to explain to her that she was never going to see him again?

They had to park on the roadside and walk down the hotel's drive, having explained themselves to a policeman at the main gate. There were people everywhere, some with obvious TV cameras, and vehicles almost blocking the road that continued down to Newby Bridge. The hotel's lawn was suffering badly from the heavy traffic across it, so soon after the rain.

Inside the hotel, the staff were plainly pulling out all the stops to maintain a calm front, while cooperating fully with the police. The magnificence of the rooms made their task a lot easier. The building seemed to be saying it had seen every sort of upset before, many a time, and this latest episode was not going to change anything. People might shout and bustle and throw accusations, but the Hall would drift serenely on, its gaze on the forested slopes across the lake, and keep the whole business in perspective. Simmy took a moment, as she was escorted towards a room somewhere to the left of the main entrance hall, to appreciate the fabulous rotunda with the gallery running around it, like a replica of St Paul's Cathedral. Would whispers run around it, like its more famous forebear, and reveal the secrets behind the death of Mark Baxter?

Her strongest feeling was one of being an interloper, an unjustified intruder, there under false pretences. She was, after all, a humble florist, with no claims at all to special insight of any description. At some point, outside the Hall, she had been parted from Melanie, who had said, 'See you later,' before melting away. Simmy could not help feeling that Melanie would make a far better witness; that she had a firmer grasp of what had been going on.

She was shown into a room which contained seven or eight people sitting at tables. As she focused more carefully, she saw they were in twos, and that notes were being taken. The room was more than large enough for the pairs to speak privately without being overheard. A man with a long head and small eyes behind spectacles appeared to be waiting for her. Her escort was a young constable, who said, 'Mrs Brown, sir. The florist.'

'Ah! Yes. Thank you very much for coming, Mrs Brown. It's a big help for us if people can come and see us quickly, while everything's fresh in their minds, as it were.'

She raised an eyebrow at him, and waited to be invited to sit. 'Sorry,' he realised. 'I'm Detective Inspector Moxon. Do sit down.'

She glanced around the room, wondering whether all the other interviewers were of such senior rank as hers. It seemed highly unlikely. She recognised none of the interviewees.

'I still don't know what happened,' she complained.

'That's what we're trying to find out. But first I need to make a note of your full name and address, and phone number, if that's all right.'

She gave them automatically, trying to quell any temptation to make difficulties. In the back of her mind, her rebellious mother muttered about databases and unwarranted storage of personal material.

'Thank you,' he nodded. 'Now, I expect you'll understand that we need all the help we can get. We've asked you for interview, because I have it on the authority of a Constable Joe Wheeler that you were here this morning, with the wedding flowers, and that you spoke to the young man, Mark Baxter, as you were leaving. Is that correct?'

'Yes.'

'What time would that have been?'

'When I spoke to him? Something like twenty past nine, I suppose. I got here just after eight, and spent an hour arranging the flowers in the room they were using for the ceremony, and the banqueting room. Then I went up to the bridal suite and delivered the buttonholes and bouquets. I was back in Windermere at about a quarter to ten.'

'A five-minute drive?' he frowned gently.

'I got stuck in Bowness. There was a coach and quite a few caravans coming and going. It might have been twenty-five past nine, perhaps, when I saw Mark. We only chatted for a couple of minutes.'

'Had you ever met him before?'

'No.'

'What did you chat about?'

'The wedding. He seemed excited to be an usher. He wanted the best buttonhole and I told him they were all the same.'

'Did he say why he was outside?'

'Waiting for his father, he said. There were three or four other men waiting with him.'

The inspector's little eyes brightened. 'Indeed? And did you know any of them?'

'No, but Mark told me their names. One was the best man, Glenn, I think. Plus the groom and a Spanish man called Pablo. And Felix, of course. He's the groom's cousin – in a wheelchair. You'll easily confirm that. They were all quite a lot older than Mark. I think one or two of them were smoking. They had big umbrellas. It was raining hard.'

'So there were four of them?'

She paused to think. 'Five with Mark.'

'Did it seem strange that he should speak to you? Didn't you get wet?'

'I was in the van. He waved me down as I was leaving. It *was* a bit funny, I suppose. One of the other men shouted after him, asking what he was doing.'

'Did *he* get wet?'

'He must have done. He didn't have a brolly of his own. He put his head in through the passenger window. He was very young. I imagine he was just a bit bored with all the waiting about, and wanted someone to talk to.'

'But . . . forgive me, but *you* are quite a lot older than him as well. Why couldn't he have talked to his male friends?'

'I have no idea. I can only make wild guesses, which I don't expect would be very helpful.'

'Impressions, however, might be useful,' he argued. 'You have to understand how little we know. We build up a picture out of a lot of small details, from various sources, in the hope of reaching a solid conclusion.'

She said nothing, still absorbing the fact of the boy's death, and failing to attach much significance to anything other than that. Nobody had uttered the word *murder* as yet, although she remembered Melanie telling her that Mark's father had been hurling accusations.

'So?' coaxed the inspector.

'Um . . . ? What was the question?'

'How did he seem to you, really? Excited, bored, on the edge of the group he was with – that's what I've got so far. He was waiting for his father. Did he seem eager to see him?'

The fleeting expression she had observed on Mark Baxter's face came back to her with a sudden jolt. 'No, I don't think so. He seemed a bit scared, actually. Or *jittery*, maybe. Wanting to get it over with. I don't think he knew the others very well, being so much younger. But people are often like that before a wedding, aren't they? Especially a great big one like this.' A thought struck her. 'They *did* get married, didn't they? All this didn't make them cancel at the last minute?' An unworthy anxiety that cancellation might jeopardise the payment of her bill crossed her mind. *No*, she told herself, *they'd have to pay me, whatever happened.*

'They got married,' he told her with a tight smile. 'Minus one usher. It didn't seem enough of an omission to warrant any delay.'

35

She grimaced. 'They must feel terrible about that now.'

'I imagine so,' he said, with an invisible shrug to indicate that this lay beyond his sphere of interest.

'And what an awful business for the hotel,' she went on, as more and more repercussions flooded her mind. 'You've already made a frightful mess of their lawn.'

'You're not from around here, are you?' he said suddenly.

'What? No, I'm not. I moved here earlier this year.'

'From where?'

'Worcestershire. But I was born near Manchester. We've moved about a bit. My parents run a B&B in Windermere now. I came to be near them when my marriage broke up.'

'Do you have children?'

Normally the question was brushed aside with a quick 'No' and a change of subject. But this was a police detective, and answers had to be given more carefully. She met his eye and shook her head. 'We had a little girl who was stillborn,' she elaborated. 'Nearly two years ago now.'

'I'm sorry,' he said, with something that looked like real emotion. 'That must have been hard.'

'As you'd expect, more or less. We're not a very prolific family. There are compensations.' She held his gaze steadily. 'I mean it – there really are.'

'Good,' he nodded. 'I'm glad to hear it.'

'Have we finished?'

'I think so, yes. I should have told you sooner that this is a murder enquiry. First indications are that Mr Baxter was killed by a blow to the head and his body deposited in the lake. Two people found him during a search after the wedding ceremony had been completed.'

'What time was that?'

He gave her a look that said *All right, I'll let you ask me one question, and only one*. 'About eleven-forty-five.'

She glanced around the room, and then at her watch. 'You moved quickly,' she said. 'Setting all this up, and getting me down here. I'm amazed.'

'Constable Wheeler can be thanked for the last part. He knew you'd done the flowers and were here this morning. He called your assistant who said you'd spoken to Mark. He suggested she bring you down for interview right away.'

'Yes,' she said, still half dazed. 'I know. But even so . . .'

The detective smiled. 'Were you always a florist?' he asked, in something that felt like an attempt to send her away in a lighter frame of mind.

She hesitated. 'Market gardener, originally. It's a long story.'

A man across the room was half turned on his chair, watching Moxon closely, plainly waiting for a chance to interrupt. 'You're wanted,' said Simmy.

'Ah!' he nodded a quick thanks for the alert. 'Thank you again. I might want another chat with you at some stage.'

'Right,' she said, and got up from her seat. She wanted to protest loudly to somebody, somewhere, that the boy should not be dead, that she should not have spoken to him, and that bad things should definitely not happen to innocent young souls.

# *Chapter Three*

She wandered out of the hotel, hoping to see Melanie waiting for her. The shambles of the wedding was increasingly evident, with groups of finely dressed guests hovering uncertainly on the lakeside. There should be a major banquet underway by this time, with champagne and speeches and gaiety. Whatever might have happened to Markie, people had to eat, and the planned schedule presumably somehow had to be adhered to. The additional staff employed by the hotel would be in the kitchen and its adjoining rooms, wondering what to do. The main players would be required to speak to the police, the parents of the dead boy too flattened to play their wedding roles. Except, his mother was unlikely to be present. George Baxter was unlikely to countenance the presence of both her and his first wife, Eleanor. Where was she, then? Did she know what had happened?

The ambivalence of all weddings was a familiar theme for Simmy. Serious and silly, portentous and frivolous – the excesses inherent in the celebratory aspect overshadowing the profundity of the emotions and the public commitment. Hapless registrars did their best to conjure the more solemn implications in the midst of froth and flowers. As a florist, Simmy understood that she was assumed to be on the side of the froth. She was expected to focus on matching shades of peachy pink, and the exact drop of a swag of autumn leaves – and she diligently fulfilled such expectations. It was a job, a profession, for which she had studied and passed exams. Few people grasped that a florist had to listen to stories of sudden deaths and inconvenient births. They had to take enormous care over wording on cards and timing of deliveries. The wrong flowers could cause decades of offence. They were invisible but crucial bystanders at the major life events that overtook every family in the land. Where a wedding demanded far more labour than any other occasion, Simmy was fully aware that the really important work lay with a funeral.

And young Markie Baxter was going to have a very big and very public funeral one of these days.

There was no sign of Melanie. The massive hotel gave plenty of scope for getting lost, with the so-called service wing as large as a substantial mansion in its own right. Mel knew many of the staff, having been at school or college with them. Her best friend was married to the deputy manager and her cousin was in charge of the team of chambermaids – most of them from Eastern Europe. The world of a major four-star hotel struck Melanie as intensely glamorous, and fuelled her eventual goal to work in one. She regularly reminded Simmy that her participation as a part-time assistant in a florist's shop was purely temporary and expedient. Simmy received these reminders with mixed feelings. She liked and trusted Melanie, but she knew there were plenty more where she came from, and the prospect of a succession of assistants was actually more appealing than otherwise.

An odd pair of people caught her eye, sitting on a damp rustic seat under a tree at the edge of the lawn, holding hands. It was Eleanor Baxter and the little flower girl from the bridal suite, their heads bowed in a strikingly similar attitude. Automatically, Simmy went towards them, drawn by the stillness and sadness coming off them like steam. Were they grandmother and grandchild, she wondered confusedly? Surely not – Eleanor was barely fifty, a slim and glamorous mother of the bride, taking up the role with an aggressive zest that Simmy had found difficult. She was unlikely to be this child's grandmother.

Wishing she had paid more attention to the gossip about the family, she met the little girl's eye and smiled tentatively. 'Hello,' she said.

Woman and child stared at her with barely veiled hostility. She couldn't blame them, when she thought about it. What was she doing? Whatever did she plan to say to them? 'I'm so sorry,' she floundered. 'What a terrible thing to happen. I mean . . .'

The older woman scowled blackly. 'Please be quiet,' she snapped. 'We were hoping to be left alone for a while. Lucy and I have no part to play at present.'

Belatedly, Simmy realised that there was every chance that the child – who appeared to be about six – had not been told anything specific about what had happened. What *did* you tell a child, who thought she was at a wedding and turned out to be embroiled in a murder?

Lucy huddled against her companion and swung one foot agitatedly. The peach-pink outfit made her look like a doll. An expensive doll with a china face. It was difficult to believe she was a real individual with swirling emotions. As youngest bridesmaid she had been a sort of mascot, a point of endearing innocence in the wedding pictures. Now she was a vulnerable embarrassment, who ought to be taken home by somebody.

'I'm sorry. Is there anything I can do to help?' Her sincere intentions must have come through in her voice, despite being totally unable to think of any assistance she might usefully supply.

Eleanor Baxter looked up at her thoughtfully. 'Do you live locally?'

'Well . . . yes. A couple of miles the other side of Windermere. Why?'

'Would you take Lucy for me? They won't let anybody else leave until they've asked all their questions. And we *are* supposed to be having a wedding breakfast. God knows whether that's going to happen now. It seems impossible, either way.'

Simmy gulped. Modern protestations rose to her lips, the most daft of which was *But I haven't had my CRB check*. Didn't the child have a mother somewhere, or a nanny? How was it possible that she could be handed so readily to a total stranger?

'Where's her mother?' she blurted. 'That is – who *is* she?'

Again the two pairs of eyes stared at her. '*I'm* her mother, you fool. This is Bridget's little sister. I thought everybody knew that.'

'Oh! I'm so sorry. How stupid of me. But . . . she doesn't know me. You can't just . . .'

Lucy remained passively on the seat and awaited her fate.

'Of course, it was an outrageous request,' said Eleanor stiffly. 'But things are rather desperate, as I expect you can see. The fact is, Lucy has never been very interested in the

41

wedding, have you, darling?' She nudged the child, who shook her head. 'She's not really the bridesmaid type, but of course Bridget wouldn't listen to anything like that. She thinks everyone's as mad about weddings as she is. There are hardly any other children here – just a pair of teenaged boys. It would be doing her a great kindness. You might take her for a walk in the woods, something like that.'

'In that dress?'

'Ah. The dress is a difficulty, of course. Do you have children? Might you not find some clothes for her?'

'Surely she has some of her own, in a room here somewhere?' Lucy had been wearing something casual earlier in the day, Simmy remembered. 'Where are the things she had on this morning, when I brought the flowers?'

Eleanor sighed. 'I suppose I could go and fetch them. We're on the top floor.' She looked hopefully at Simmy, who stood her ground. No way was she going to start running errands inside the hotel for a woman who had full use of her own legs, murder or not.

'Don't worry. My mother has a collection of children's clothes. We can go there.'

'Oh?'

'She runs a B&B in Windermere. She's discovered that it's easier to supply emergency clothes than let people try and do some washing.' This summary concealed a great slough of painful experience associated with dirty clothes and American insistence on total cleanliness at all times.

Eleanor smiled tightly, as if it pained her to hear such disclosures. The dead boy, Simmy reminded herself, was the son of Eleanor's one-time husband, by another woman.

42

There was no term for it – 'stepson' assumed the father had married the mother, which George Baxter had not done, if Melanie could be believed. There was no reason to think Eleanor had felt warm towards Markie – but neither could it be assumed that she had resented or hated him. Nothing could be taken for granted. 'Perhaps you should give me your name and a telephone number,' Eleanor said.

Simmy extracted a card from her shoulder bag. It introduced her as 'Persimmon Petals' with address and phone number, and a tiny line that added 'Proprietor: P. A. Brown.' She rummaged for a pen and added her mobile number. 'My name is Simmy Brown,' she said.

'Simmy?' Eleanor rolled her eyes with no attempt at subtlety. 'Are you telling me your Christian name is Persimmon?'

'I'm afraid so. But I go by Simmy.'

'I'm not sure I should let Lucy meet your mother in that case.'

It was a joke, of a sort, and Simmy took full advantage of it. 'She is a bit overwhelming,' she admitted. 'But very good with children. She's got a room full of games. Lucy might like to spend the afternoon there. I haven't got anything for her to do at my house.'

'No children, then,' nodded Eleanor. 'That's a shame.'

Twice within the hour she had been reminded of her failure, her lack. It was almost too much. 'I'll have to find my assistant. We came in a van. There's no child seat. She'll have to sit on Melanie's lap. It's probably illegal.'

'Probably,' Eleanor agreed carelessly.

Lucy had slowly perked up in the course of this exchange.

Simmy detected a spark of interest that suggested a lurking spirit ready to be rekindled. She began to suspect that what she had seen thus far was in no way representative of the true nature of this small girl.

'All right, then,' she decided. 'You can find us at Beck View in Lake Road. It's a big house, with a sign outside. On the right as you approach from this direction. We'll wait for you, shall we?'

'Thank you. I'll be sure to come for her by six. At least – somebody will.' She sighed again. 'It might be her father, if they won't let me escape from here by then.'

'Dad?' chirped Lucy, speaking for the first time. 'But he's in Ireland.'

'Is he?' Eleanor blinked her confusion. 'Are you sure?'

The child nodded emphatically.

'Oh, yes, I remember now. We're supposed to stay the night here, aren't we? God, this is such a bloody mess, Luce. I knew it would be awful, but this is ridiculous. That wretched boy . . .' She stopped herself with an effort.

'Simmy?' came a new voice. 'What's going on?' Melanie came into view, around the dripping autumnal branches of the tree. 'I've been looking everywhere for you.'

'This is Lucy,' Simmy introduced. 'We're looking after her for the rest of the day. I thought I'd take her to my mother's. Are you coming back now in the van? It would be helpful if you did.'

To her credit, Melanie made no objections and asked no questions. 'Okay,' she said. Even when they were packed into the van, she was still just as restrained. Perhaps, thought Simmy, as one of a large family, it seemed quite

44

normal to her to take charge of a strange child when the need arose. As for Simmy herself, the situation became increasingly alarming with every passing second.

Angie took one look at the frothy silk dress and shook her head at the crazy ways of the world. 'You poor thing,' she sympathised. 'That looks horribly uncomfortable. I've got a very nice brown tracksuit in my treasure chest, just your size. Come and see.'

She led Lucy into the cluttered back sitting room, and opened the wicker basket where she kept assorted clothes. The tracksuit was produced effortlessly, and Simmy could see that it was perfect for the occasion. A rich dark brown velour, with elastic at ankles and waist, it slipped onto Lucy as if made for her. The instant transformation was like magic. The little girl moved her arms experimentally, and gave a little skip. Before Angie could rescue it, Lucy had kicked the peach-pink dress in disgust. 'And my hair,' she said. 'It's tight.'

She had been coiffed into a wispy topknot, with corkscrew tendrils around her ears. 'Who did the hair?' Simmy asked, before she could stop herself. 'It was supposed to be my friend Julie, but she had an accident.'

'A man,' said Lucy disdainfully. 'He called me *duckie*.'

'Tch,' said Simmy, with feeling.

'The flowers were nice, though,' Lucy said, as if Simmy might need consoling. 'They were the nicest thing of all.'

'Thank you. Didn't you like the rest of it, then?'

'Not much. Too many people.'

'I know what you mean.'

*Don't ask too many questions*, Simmy ordered herself. If there was one thing she could remember about being six, it was the annoying habit grown-ups had of asking about school and recent holidays and none of the things that were really interesting. She also reminded herself that it would be unethical to quiz Lucy on events of that morning. Hadn't there been something in a famous novel about that? She thought it might be a Henry James, much of whose work she had read with unnatural pleasure at the age of seventeen. 'Nobody your age likes Henry James,' her mother had objected. 'Hardly anybody of *any* age does, come to that.' Simmy had thought it wonderful, all the same.

'Do you know how to play Downfall?' she asked hesitantly, scanning the shelves of board games in the room.

'I'm hungry,' Lucy announced, with a shade of reproach. 'And *very* thirsty.'

Simmy laughed in a little shock of realisation. 'So am I, now you mention it. I suppose we both missed our lunch. I haven't had anything since breakfast, and that was early. And I only had toast.'

'I had sausages,' Lucy admitted.

This was not a doll after all. It was a human creature in need of sustenance, and warm clothes and reassurance. There might be lavatory issues and unknowable routines. Great kindness was called for. Simmy looked to her mother, with a fragile hope of rescue.

'Cold chicken, bread, apples, coleslaw,' she listed, without enthusiasm. Angie, like her daughter, was tall and lean. She wore narrow spectacles, over which she liked to glare, like a schoolmistress. 'We gave your spaghetti to the dog. You might remember that you rushed off two minutes before it was due to be served.'

'We can make chicken sandwiches, then,' said Simmy. 'Thanks, Mum. Come on, Lucy – the kitchen's down this passage.' She led the way to the well-appointed room that always made her think of a small factory, with the two large cookers and stainless steel sinks, flanked by a massive fridge and humming dishwasher. Producing a full English breakfast for up to ten people at a time required an industrial level of efficiency.

Her father was at the table, doing a crossword. He looked up, patently ready for anything. 'Well, hello!' he twinkled. 'It's a little girl. I like little girls.'

Lucy gave a little huff of acknowledgment, apparently assuming that everybody liked little girls.

'This is Lucy,' said Simmy. 'She hasn't had anything to eat since breakfast.'

'Or you,' said Lucy, in a proud show of generosity. 'I had sausages.'

'And thirsty,' added Simmy. 'We both need a drink.'

There was a shelf full of cartons of fruit juice in the fridge. 'Apple, orange or pineapple?' Simmy asked the child.

'Pineapple,' said Lucy.

'Pineapple, *please*,' said Simmy's father automatically. 'Politeness costs nothing, but works wonders for oiling the cogs of social exchange.'

'Sorry,' said Lucy, easily. 'I forgot.'

Angie had not followed them into the kitchen. Simmy brushed away a suspicion that she had transgressed in her mother's eyes. To accept the commission of minding a small scion of the wedding party ought to have struck her as a pleasing piece of spontaneity, a sign that her daughter was less unlike her than she often believed. Instead, coming on a busy Saturday it was an annoying imposition. Angie was not so much maternal as businesslike in her approach to children. She thought she knew what they liked, and what their basic requirements were, and left the rest to the experts. It had been obvious from the start that Lucy liked and trusted her.

'People due at three,' said her father, cocking his head at the clock on the wall. 'Bad timing, petal.'

Simmy was stunned to discover that it was already ten minutes to three. Her inner clock had stopped around half past one. 'No wonder we're hungry,' she said. 'I can't believe it's gone so fast.'

'Funny old day.'

'To say the least.'

She made sandwiches, which Lucy ate without fuss or mess. Given a chance to examine her more closely, Simmy diagnosed a robust individual, both mentally and physically. There were no vapourings about butter or onion or having the crusts cut off. There was ample flesh on the little skeleton, too. Lucy enjoyed her food, it seemed. She would probably have made short work of the wedding breakfast, given the chance.

Her total ignorance as to Lucy's home situation was a gnawing frustration. It made conversation almost impossible. Plainly it was taboo to mention the deceased Markie, for a start. But perhaps there were other relatives it was safer to introduce. 'This is my daddy,' she explained, belatedly. 'His name is Russell. Did you say your daddy was in Ireland?'

Lucy nodded and swigged more juice. 'County Wicklow,' she said. 'Where the fairies and leprechauns play.'

This revealed a wealth of information to Simmy's eager ear. Lucy's father was an Irish poet, a romantic soul with a rich sense of humour. A man not so different from her own father, in fact.

48

Who now proved it, by singing the line back to the child, to the tune of 'Home on the Range'. Both females laughed delightedly.

Simmy broke her own rule by asking, 'Does Daddy live with you and Mummy?'

Lucy's eyes sparkled scornfully. 'Of course he does. Sometimes, anyway. When he isn't at his house.'

'Not in County Wicklow, by any chance?' Simmy's father put in.

'Cockermouth,' Lucy corrected. 'He had a flood and his chairs floated like boats. There was a fire engine.' She frowned.

'Should have been a flood engine, eh?'

'Yes.' Uttered with emphasis.

'That was years ago, petal. You must have been a baby.'

'I was five. That's not a baby.'

'Ah! Not the Great Flood, then. A special one, just for Daddy. Nasty.'

'There was mud on the walls and the garden was a wreck.' The quotes were vivid, the trauma plainly still very much in evidence. 'And . . .' the child's eyes widened with mimicked alarm, '. . . he *wasn't insured*.' This came in a horrified whisper, that was also an obvious quote, probably from her mother.

'Dreadful,' sympathised the man who cared little for such mundane aspects of modern life. 'Very bad luck.'

Lucy shook her shoulders as if discarding the whole episode. 'Is there any pudding?' she asked. 'Please?'

'An apple,' suggested Simmy.

A repressed grimace greeted this idea. 'No, thank you.'

'Heavens, Sim, we've got ice cream, haven't we?' her father expostulated.

'I don't know, Dad. I don't live here, remember. Mum

said apples, so that's what I thought we were meant to have.'

The doorbell pealed loudly before the matter could be decided. 'People,' said Russell. 'I seem to recall mention of small boys. Might be someone to play with,' he told Lucy.

Something about this puzzled the child. 'Are they visitors?' she asked.

'Not exactly. They've come here for bed and breakfast. That's what this house is – a B&B.'

'B&B,' repeated Lucy. 'Oh. But it isn't bedtime,' she objected. 'And not time for breakfast.'

He laughed ruefully. 'Perfectly true. Usually people don't come until after they've had dinner somewhere. These are outrageously early. I don't know why. There's probably a very good reason.'

Ten minutes later, Angie arrived with an explanation. 'The little child has to have a nap at precisely three-thirty,' she told them, with an exaggerated sigh. 'They're following some inflexible schedule that seems insane to me. They're putting it in the cot now. The other one is allowed to come and play with Lucy, in the sitting room.'

Lucy looked wary. 'Is it a boy?'

'William. He's three and a half.'

'Oh.'

Simmy felt weary and resentful. How had all this happened, anyway? She had been exploited, seized as a convenient solution to a problem that had nothing to do with her. She had been flagged down by a youth who was shortly to be murdered, spoken to in a wholly inconsequential fashion, and thereby embroiled in the biggest local scandal for many a year. Lucy was easy enough, but that was beside the point. Detective Inspector

Moxon had been the brightest spot in the day, surprisingly. A human being amongst the peacocks and prattlers that were the local gentry. One of them had killed their bright young hope, and the house of cards had deservedly collapsed about their ears.

'She doesn't want to play with a three-year-old boy,' she said, with unwarranted force. 'Do you?'

Lucy considered. 'I don't mind,' she said. 'After I've had pudding.'

'Ange – do we have ice cream?' asked Russell. 'Under the circumstances . . .'

'In the freezer. Some of that honeycomb stuff you like,' said Angie automatically.

'Honeycomb?' Lucy's eyes sparkled. 'Like Markie has? That's my favourite.'

Simmy's parents had not registered the identity of the murdered boy; they did not react to the mention of his name. But Simmy was unprepared for it, and it sent a shard of ice through her guts.

'Markie?' she repeated. 'Is that what you call him?'

Lucy gave her a withering look. 'Yes,' she said shortly. 'He's called Markie.'

So Lucy knew the murdered boy, shared his ice cream, counted him amongst her intimates. The tragedy of his loss could not leave her unaffected. Whoever had killed him had damaged an innocent child, and who knew how many others, in the process.

# Chapter Four

She took Lucy out for a walk when the three-year-old B&B guest turned out to be an impossible playmate. The prospect of a holiday in the Lake District appalled and enraged him. The car journey had made him feel sick; his small brother had received unfair quantities of attention. His very natural response was to pull Lucy's hair and scratch her cheek. In reply, she had pushed him hard, sending him reeling into the bookshelves, where a sharp edge had caught his brow and raised a spectacular bruise.

Simmy had grabbed her charge and removed her from the house entirely.

'It wasn't my fault,' Lucy repeated, as they walked blindly down the hill towards Bowness.

'No it wasn't. He's a little beast.'

This surprised Lucy into silence for a moment. 'A little beast,' she murmured in wonder. 'Yes.'

'That's the trouble with B&B – you never know what the people might be like. Nearly all of them are very nice, but sometimes there's trouble.'

'Sometimes there's a little beast.'

Dimly it occurred to Simmy that in the current era of universal approval and respect, such pejorative descriptions were taboo. Everybody was intrinsically virtuous. It had all been taking root during her own schooldays, she supposed – clumsy efforts to remove all tendencies towards exclusion of the thick or the malignant. Since then it had been perfected to the point where such care had to be taken over language that it might as well have been Soviet Russia in the 1950s.

'That's right,' she affirmed. 'Although we must admit that he's probably had a difficult day.'

'Like me,' suggested Lucy diffidently. 'Mummy says a wedding is always very stressful.'

*And this one more than most*, thought Simmy, with a pang. That poor young Markie – how could it be possible? What in the world could he have ever done to deserve the ultimate violence?

'Your day has been *much* more difficult,' Simmy said. 'And you're being very brave and good. I must say I'm very impressed.'

'Oh – it's the Baddeley clock!' came the unexpected response. 'Daddy and I *love* the Baddeley clock.'

Simmy experienced for a second time a sense that her and Lucy's fathers had much in common. The clock tower stood on the point where the old Lake Road joined the more recent New Road, and was generally agreed to mark the border between Windermere and Bowness. Russell Straw had been enchanted by it on his first day in Windermere and had researched the man it memorialised. It was a fairy-tale construction with four little turrets guarding a spire topped with a weathervane. A tiny wooden door stood on the north side, with the clock and inscription to the south. It had windows to the east and west, the whole edifice decorated with crenellations on the corners and around the windows. It was easy to imagine a family of elves or trolls living inside it. 'Baddeley conducted campaigns against stone quarries,' Russell discovered. 'And here's this crazy folly made of the very stone he disliked so much.'

'But it's lovely!' Simmy had protested. 'It's been made so carefully, as a pure act of love.'

'I know,' Russell had chuckled. 'That's what's so delightful about it.'

'We have to walk round it three times and make a wish,' said Lucy. 'That's what they do in Mongolia, and it always works.'

'So what are we going to wish?'

'I'm going to wish for Bridget, not me,' said the child, suddenly serious. 'Bridget's going to need all the luck she can get.' Once again, it was obvious that she was quoting from an adult, even before she added, 'That's what Daddy says,' in confirmation.

Trying not to think about probable watchers from the Victorian villas on either side of the road, not to mention passing traffic, Simmy allowed Lucy to lead her three times around the tower, pausing to bow at the completion of each circuit. By the end of the second, she had lost much of her self-consciousness and was aware of following an ancient ritual that had a certain power, even now. The October leaves on nearby trees held a magic of their own, with the intimations of endings and hardships to come. When the killing of a princely young man was factored in, there was certainly some additional dimension to be acknowledged. *Good luck, Bridget*, she whispered, as the third circuit ended.

They walked as far as Rayrigg Wood, scuffing leaves and watching two frantic squirrels chasing through the branches. Conversation was sporadic, but Simmy learnt that Lucy and her mother lived in Ambleside, with her father an inconstant presence. Lucy went to school at an establishment known as 'St Clare's' where her teacher was Miss Hamble. She had been assessed as 'gifted and talented' because she had a reading age of ten. 'And I'm not even seven yet,' she boasted.

Bridget lived in the same house, but she had been going to college in Carlisle for a long time, and didn't come home so much any more. Peter was nice. Mr Baxter smelt funny, but not exactly in a nice way. Markie was sad because his girlfriend dumped him.

'Oh?'

'Bridget said it broke his heart. She said it was Mr Baxter's fault. They shouted a lot.'

'So Bridget and Markie . . .' She didn't know how to frame the question. They were half-brother and -sister – very possibly they would be close friends, sharing emotional confidences and watching out for each other. She changed tack. 'Where does Markie live?'

'Don't know.'

'You haven't been to his house?'

Lucy shook her head. 'He comes to us. He stays sometimes. There's a room. There's lots of rooms.'

Under the trees, the light was fading, the chill of evening starting to make itself felt. 'It's nearly five o'clock,' Simmy said. 'We'd better go back and wait for your mother to collect you.'

'Am I staying at the hotel again tonight? They said it would be two nights.'

'I don't know.'

The chaotic consequences for the wedding would be reverberating still. It seemed obvious that there could be no carefree disco, as planned. After what had happened, guests would have the discretion to stay in their rooms, or to quietly leave again, if they had arrived for the dance unaware of events. Bridget and Peter were married – that was the main thing. But rooms remained booked, the hotel kitchen would be devoted to supplying provisions throughout the evening to the remaining company, who hung on for whatever reason. Some had probably flown over from foreign parts and could not readily make alternative arrangements.

How, she wondered, could poor Inspector Moxon ever hope to untangle it all? How could he make sense of such a ghastly crime? The cast of suspects must run into the dozens, with all the dogged sifting of means and motives and alibis and witnesses ahead of him. Simmy marvelled at her own urgent wish to help him. She wanted vengeance for Markie, who had, she slowly admitted to herself, singled her out for some opaque sort of appeal. She had failed him, as it turned out. He had been trying to tell her something, perhaps somehow hoping she would gather him into her van and drive him off to a place of safety. And yet their exchange had concluded with a piece of optimism about the weather; a prediction that had proved miraculously accurate. She hoped, foolishly, that he had lived long enough to see the cessation of the rain, while knowing that he almost certainly had not.

\* \* \*

She thought over the timing, while walking back towards Lake Road, hand-in-hand with young Lucy – half-sister of Markie's half-sister; a relationship that only the aborigines of Australia were likely to have a word for. If the killer had been among the wedding party, then he would have been in the hotel, witnessing the couple's vows, at the moment when the rain stopped. And that meant that the deed had been done at an earlier point. Sometime between nine-thirty and eleven, then, and more likely at the earlier end of that period, to leave time for changing into topcoat and tails; to insert the buttonhole and square the shoulders. What monster could behave like that? And why?

'I need a wee,' said Lucy, apologetically. Simmy remembered the two large glasses of pineapple juice and was not surprised.

'Can you wait till we get back to the house? It'll be ten minutes or so.'

'I don't know.'

Simmy looked around. There were shady trees and shrubs that would conceal a squatting child. 'You could go behind a bush,' she suggested, totally ignorant of the protocols of such an idea.

'A bush?'

'Yes. Pull your trousers and pants down and wee on the ground. I'll stand guard and make sure nobody sees you.'

'I can't,' said Lucy flatly.

'Okay. We'd better get back to the house quick, then.'

Probably a narrow escape, Simmy decided, as they marched briskly back up the hill. She'd be accused of abuse if anyone saw her handling the naked nether regions of a strange child. What did people do these days, anyway? She remembered that peeing behind a bush had been an integral part of most family walks, thirty years ago.

They reached Beck View without accident, and Simmy rushed Lucy through the house to the downstairs toilet without pausing to announce their presence. The side door was never locked during daylight hours, so access was easily gained. Only as she stood outside the loo did she become aware of an unusual silence: no radio or TV, no voices, no footsteps overhead. Had the B&B people all gone to bed for some peculiar afternoon nap? Had her parents remained quietly in the kitchen, drinking tea and thinking their own thoughts? Before she could go to investigate, her mother appeared from the dining room, her face pale and drawn.

'Mum? What's the matter? You look awful.'

'They've gone. They said they'll be suing us for the damage to their kid. They called an ambulance for him, because he seemed drowsy.'

'What? But that's ridiculous. It was just a bruise.'

'Yes, I know. But they wouldn't listen. They're completely paranoid, both of them. I've never seen anything like it.'

'But they can't sue *you*. It was Lucy who did it.'

'And it was *you* who brought her here. And the law still hasn't fully decided whether a B&B is a public place or a private home. In this case, they were paying me for accommodation, with the implication that I would protect their children from attack. I keep telling myself not to worry, but I have to say it was extremely unpleasant.'

'It'll be fine, Mum. The hospital will tell them they're overreacting, and they'll drop the whole thing.'

'Including their holiday. They might want compensation for that.'

'And *you* might want compensation for loss of earnings for no good reason.'

Angie sighed. 'Why is life always so unpredictable? Just one thing after another, and I never see it coming. I'm too old for this sort of thing.'

'You're sixty-one, Mother. That's not old, by about twenty years. Even Dad isn't really old, and he's seventy.'

'I *want* to be old. I want to put my feet up and go on cruises and let the young people do the worrying.'

'Don't be ridiculous,' Simmy laughed. The notion of her mother on a cruise was almost surreal. 'You haven't got the right clothes, and you'd probably murder three or four of the other passengers.'

The word *murder* hovered uncomfortably in the air, dissipated only by the front doorbell ringing.

'Oh, God – they've come back,' Angie shuddered. 'Save me!'

But the people at the door were not outraged parents, but traumatised wedding guests. At least, Eleanor and George Baxter should have been traumatised, but both looked disconcertingly normal. Simmy recognised him from pictures in the local paper and had to straighten her thoughts before she remembered that these two people were no longer a couple. They had been divorced at least eight years ago, when Bridget was ten, and George had remarried before Lucy was born. And yet there was plainly an amicable connection between them. If not, George should not have been there at all. Where was his current wife? And, more urgently, where was Markie's mother?

'Lucy!' she called, wondering where the child had wandered off to. 'Your mother's here.'

'Has she been all right?' asked Eleanor, without visible concern.

'Fine. She's good company.'

'She is, isn't she? We're not sure quite how it happened, but she seems to be turning out rather well. Bridget was monstrous by comparison.'

'Come in. I'll go and find her.'

Angie was in the back room with Lucy, the discarded bridesmaid's dress in her hands. 'I suppose you'll have to change back into this,' she said dubiously.

'You don't need what she's wearing, surely?' Simmy objected. 'They'll give it back in a day or two.'

'How do you know?'

It was a good question. There could be no guarantee that Eleanor would follow any of the known rules about such things. Lucy saw her doubt. 'Yes, we will,' she said. 'I don't want to wear *that* again.' She eyed the pink-peach satin with disgust.

'It is horrible, isn't it,' said Simmy reflectively. 'Amazingly nasty.'

'A kindred spirit,' came Eleanor's voice from the doorway. 'Don't you think there's a sort of wicked conspiracy that prevents us from saying how vile the whole wedding business is? I never realised quite how awful they are until now.'

'Well . . .' Simmy ventured, thinking today's wedding had hardly been representative.

'Oh, I know what you're going to say. They've cancelled the whole evening business. Sent everybody away. Bridget and Peter are up in their suite, with Glenn and the others. I think they're playing cards. George is all in pieces, of course, so I said he could come with me. He likes Lucy.'

'I thought Markie might come for me,' said Lucy, her voice ringing clear in the room. She looked hard at her mother, with a challenge to disclose the truth.

Eleanor scooped the child to her, in a rush of protective emotion that struck Simmy as oddly unpractised. Lucy accepted the demonstration with equanimity, but did not hug or cling. 'Oh, baby,' moaned the mother, 'you'll have to understand that Markie's gone. We won't see him any more.'

It had been a long day. Nerves were strained by the awareness of a lurking malice and suspicion, and the uncertainty of what might happen next. George Baxter hovered behind the women, in his fabulously expensive suit and glowing silk tie, his face blotched with red patches. Of everyone in the room, his loss was by far the deepest, and the awareness of this gave him an aura that went beyond the charisma he was said to display as a matter of course. Simmy recalled that Markie had seemed to be apprehensive about his arrival at the wedding.

Lucy reacted badly to her mother's words. She opened her mouth and wailed, the sound too loud in the crowded room. Eleanor hugged her tightly and made soothing noises, looking round blindly for a place to sit. She chose a battered leather couch and flopped inelegantly onto it. Everyone else stood uselessly around, until Russell appeared, peering around the door. 'Ructions?' he ventured.

George Baxter seemed disproportionately relieved to see another man. 'The news about Markie's just got through,' he said tightly. 'Poor little thing.'

'Oh, indeed – tragic. Fancy a gin or something?'

Baxter seized the offer like a man dying of dehydration. 'Good man,' he accepted. Russell led the way to the kitchen, leaving the women to cope with the distraught child.

Simmy watched Eleanor, comparing the woman before her with the scraps of gossip she had gleaned over the past months, and the impression she had gained from the interview about wedding flowers, back in August. There was a well-guarded core of dignity that seemed to take precedence over everything else. She kept her chin up, whatever might be happening around her. She was not impulsive or emotional. Simmy thought her strength came from somewhere chilly and controlled. She treated her little girl more as a close acquaintance to be enjoyed than a child to be protected. The woman had her ex-husband with her, apparently because he had nowhere else to go and nobody else to be with. This implied that she held no permanent grudge against him for his part in the collapse of their marriage. Simmy always marvelled at women who forgave their men; who recovered from the shattering damage that separation and divorce wreaked on them. Sometimes she wondered whether she would have been less annihilated herself if her own parents had not remained together so steadfastly. She had grown up with the assumption that marriage was for ever, and Tony had initially endorsed this with such fervour that it had never occurred to her to doubt him. She still could barely understand what had failed, apart from the death of their baby. Of course that was the whole and complete explanation, and it had not been Tony's fault. Why, then, did she hate him so deeply, even now, two years later? Why could she not recover from that appalling year in which they could find no way to share their grief and console each other?

Still she looked at Eleanor. She had her two daughters, alive and well. She had a poetic Irish partner who taught magic to their little girl, and was apparently nothing more than a fey boyfriend who wandered off to Ireland when there was a wedding going on.

Lucy's sobs were fading, and she lifted a wet face to her mother. 'I don't want Markie to be gone,' she whimpered. 'Markie's going to marry me when I'm eighteen, just like Peter and Bridget.'

'I know, darling, I know,' murmured Eleanor. 'It's very very sad.'

Simmy was struck by the impossibility of understanding the currents and traditions of anyone's family other than your own. These people were solidly affluent, secure, well connected, admired, and yet not invulnerable. They could die, like anybody else. They had to get through the day without too much pain, year after year. There seemed a chance that Eleanor understood this and had developed her own means of addressing it; not least in the production of a very fine little girl.

The father of the bride was a much more obscure subject for scrutiny. His reputation inevitably coloured any direct assessment. The pathos of his volatile emotions was real, but said little about his basic personality. Any man would react with shock, rage, accusation, confusion when confronted with the murder of his only son. And many a woman, having been once married to the man, would abandon resentment and take him to her breast. Simmy's tentative conclusion was therefore that these two people were really almost normal. And Eleanor at least might yet turn out to be likeable.

Indeed, Bridget, their daughter, had been more than likeable. She was a sparklingly lovely laughing creature. Bright, beautiful, beloved. Eleanor made nice daughters, it seemed. And Markie too had been very pleasant in the brief moments in which she had encountered him.

'Well, we must go,' Eleanor announced. 'Home. I've got your gubbins in the car. Let's get back to normality.'

*Huh*, Simmy inwardly snorted. *Not much chance of that.*

'I'll go and tell Mr Baxter,' she offered.

'Thank you. Actually, Miss . . . Mrs . . .'

'Simmy. Call me Simmy.'

'Yes, well, actually, we hoped you'd come back with us for a chat. There's some talk that you met Markie this morning, and we rather hoped you might tell us about it. George, you see . . . his last words to the boy weren't very nice.' She interrupted herself, conscious of the child on her lap. 'Are you free this evening? We would run you home afterwards. It wouldn't be late. Then we could give you back the clothes – unless you'd like them washed first?'

Simmy dismissed this with a quick shake of her head. She had no reason to refuse the request. Her curiosity as to how these people lived had been growing all day. She was almost flattered to be asked. But there was a thread of resistance, alongside the instinct to accept. They were only interested in her because of Markie. They would pick her up and drop her again without a second thought. She might be seduced into regarding them as friends, only to find herself rejected within days.

Since moving to the area she had found it difficult to characterise the local attitude to incomers. There was no overt sense of closed ranks, perhaps because almost everyone she knew, other than Melanie, was also an incomer. Windermere was at the softer end of the Lake District, the fells covered with trees and the climate benign. A few miles north and the trees disappeared, the winds blew more harshly and human habitation dwindled to a smattering. Windermere saw the families and the retired, those more interested in a cruise on the lake than scrambling up High Pike or Scandale Fell. The handsome Victorian villas that filled the little town maintained an atmosphere of elegance and comfort, even now. The persistent presence of Shirley C Lingerie in the prime commercial position was an inevitable metaphor for the town. Without doubt, Eleanor Baxter bought her underwear there.

'Okay, then,' she said, with dubious grace.

The car was a roomy BMW, which had a child booster seat in the back. George automatically took the front passenger seat, so Simmy sat with Lucy. The interior smelt of money: a luxurious mixture of clean leather and a spicy perfume that emanated from a dangling freshener attached to the rear-view mirror. No hint of dog or mud or accidental spills, which filled her mother's old Renault. Angie had befriended a local dairy farm and bought illegal milk there from time to time, transporting it in unreliable containers that often slopped. The resulting smell could be dreadful on a warm day.

The lake was in shadow, the sun having almost disappeared behind High Wray and his neighbouring hilltops. The autumn colours deepened into dark chestnut and liver red, reflected in the calm water. 'Isn't it lovely?' Simmy breathed, her admiration all the more genuine for being involuntary.

'Mmm,' said Eleanor from the driver's seat.

The woods of Rayrigg passed on the right, before Simmy's own home turn towards Troutbeck. She had yet to experience the challenges of steep winter roads, snow and ice making the journey to and from the shop impossible without diligent attentions from the council gritting men. She had arrived in the last week of January, having missed by a few days the five weeks of serious winter that Cumbria had suffered that year. Nobody could quite convince her that all would be well in the coming months. Much more credible was a much-repeated tale of locals getting lost in a blizzard and freezing to death. Her cottage was on the winding road through Troutbeck, all the ways out being equally steep and down which a car would inevitably slide out of control, standing no chance of getting up again until a thaw arrived. Melanie, Angie and others all laughed at her fears, pointing out that a system of salting the road was well established, and she was far from being the only person needing to travel back and forth every day.

Ambleside was only a few minutes further on, with the sudden looming fells embracing it on every side. Sandwiched between the river Rothay to the west, and Wansfell to the east, the town had a tighter, more chaotic feel to it than Windermere. Charming, historic – Simmy felt there was a lot more to discover about Ambleside, when she had the time.

They turned to the right, climbing up towards the mountains, before stopping at a building that Simmy would have designated a mansion, if asked. Gables and wings, three floors and a generous parking area filled her view with a jumble of impressions. No wonder various relatives could stake a claim to their own permanent room here. At a rough estimate, there had to be at least eight bedrooms.

Constructed of the same dark stone as so many other nineteenth-century edifices, this was a villa on a significantly grand scale. 'Wow!' she breathed. 'What a fabulous house!'

'I'd like to pretend it's been in the family since it was

built, but the truth is much less glamorous,' Eleanor said. 'George and I bought it when we were first married. His father died the week of our wedding, and there was lots of money sloshing about.'

The parallel was too stark to be ignored. 'Sounds a bit like a jinx,' Simmy suggested.

'What?'

'Deaths and weddings,' Simmy explained, thinking of the famous Curtis movie. 'Although—'

'God! I never thought of that! You realise you've just ensured that nobody in the family will ever get married again, don't you?'

The tone was lighter than might have been expected. Eleanor, Simmy suspected, was not so very profoundly affected by the death of Markie, despite his regular presence in her life and her little girl's affection for him. After all – why should she be, if the story Melanie had told was true? Markie had been born to a . . . what? Paramour? Concubine? . . . of George's, while he was married to Eleanor and fathering Bridget. Effectively a bigamist, conducting the two families with little effort to conceal the truth, he had a reputation for getting away with it. At least Eleanor had retained the handsome house, when they finally divorced. By that time, George Baxter had been making money by the truckload, with his hedge funds and offshore dealings. He could afford to be generous, in the feckless nineties. Since then, the world had turned against him and his kind, but his money was safe and, until this day, his serenity unruffled, as far as Simmy could gather.

'Shame about the flowers,' said Eleanor.

Simmy was getting out of the car, as these words were

uttered, and wasn't sure she had heard them properly. Lucy had extracted herself from her safety harness and was waiting like royalty for release from the car. George was unmoving in the front. 'Pardon?' said Simmy.

'I mean – what happens to them now? All those lovely swags and sheaves and whatnot. The girls will take their bouquets home, but all the rest of them just go to waste. It seems so awful.'

'The hotel will use a lot of them, I think. That's quite usual. They might put some of the big arrangements in the foyer. But the swags have to come down in the morning. I'll have to go and do that.'

'Do you take them away with you?'

It was an awkward question, at least potentially. 'Some of them, yes. They don't get sold again,' she added defensively.

'I wasn't imagining they did. It just seemed sad, that's all. So much discussion and work, getting them done, and then just over in a flash.'

'Ephemeral,' said Simmy. 'That's the whole thing about flowers, though, isn't it? That's why they have them at funerals – to symbolise the brevity of life.'

'Is it? I thought it was to mask the smell of the corpse.'

'Nell – for Christ's sake!' George had got himself out of the car and was leaning one hand on the warm bonnet, apparently in serious need of the support.

'Sorry. Take no notice of me. Come on, Luce . . .' She opened the rear door of the car and the little girl scrambled out. Nobody seemed to want to go into the house. The sky in the west was streaked with reds and pinks, mirroring the turning leaves on the hillsides. A puddle on the edge of the sweeping approach to the front door caught the same hues. Ambleside lay below them, and the lake stretched away to their left. It was an almost outrageous place to live.

'Welcome, anyway,' Eleanor added awkwardly to Simmy. 'Come inside and we can have a drink.'

They went in through the front door, opened with a simple Yale key. Simmy waited for elaborate disabling of alarms to happen, but there was no suggestion of such precautions. The spacious entrance hall was gloomy and chilly, its stone floor uncovered by any mitigating carpet or rugs. There were doors on both sides, as well as straight ahead. Most of them stood open.

'It's a rambling old place,' Eleanor said, half apologetic. 'Impossible to keep warm, of course. We tend to huddle in the family room all winter.'

She led the way into a big square room with a high ceiling and a window taking up a fair proportion of the rear wall. It looked eastward onto fells rising into the distant twilight, beyond a large garden. Eleanor pulled the heavy red velvet curtains across before Simmy could properly admire the view. This, it seemed, was not the family room. It contained a baby grand piano, richly patterned Turkish carpet and a set of bronze statuettes on plinths that were pure art deco. The wallpaper should have been William Morris, but was something rather more muted, in the same autumn colours that had been haunting Simmy all day.

'Lucy, are you hungry?' Eleanor asked, as if the thought had only just occurred to her.

'We fed her,' Simmy interposed. 'But it wasn't much. We've been on a long walk since then.'

'Thank you. I was rather awful, wasn't I – expecting you to

take charge of her like that, with no warning? I just assumed you'd have little ones of your own, for some reason.'

Simmy merely shook her head. Lucy flopped down on the carpet, beside an antique revolving bookcase, and slowly sent the thing twirling round and round. The house was silent, with no hint of a cook or nanny or lady's maid poised to fulfil such needs as might arise. George Baxter went to the piano and sat down on its stool, looking as unlike a pianist as anyone could.

He was a solid man, the flesh of his jaw and neck somehow dense and unyielding. His mouth was a thin line, his small hands a pale beige colour. He moved stiffly, as if wearing a corset.

Who *were* these people? Simmy found herself wondering. Why was she there? What did they want of her? If ever there was a case of intruding on private grief, this had to be it.

'That police inspector seemed a decent chap,' Eleanor began yet another new tack. 'Surprisingly sensitive, I thought. Dealt with George very professionally.'

George glowered. Simmy remembered that Melanie's Joe had reported Mr Baxter as throwing wild accusations around, in the first moments following the discovery of Markie's body. He had, apparently, leapt straight to the conclusion that the boy had been murdered. What, she wondered, had DI Moxon made of that?

'I do want some supper,' Lucy interrupted. 'Please.' She glanced at Simmy, as if to assure her that the earlier nudge towards politeness had been noted.

'Right, then. Soup, boiled egg and the rest of that crumble we had yesterday – okay?' Eleanor, who had remained standing near the window, made decisively for the door. The child got up and followed.

Simmy felt a sharp panic at the prospect of being left alone with George. Was she supposed to just blurt out her conversation with Markie, the moment Lucy was out of the way? Or should it wait until the child was fed and put to bed? That could take hours. She herself had yet to find a place to sit. There were upright chairs against the wall, but no sofa or easy chair. 'Oh, sorry,' said Eleanor, before disappearing. 'The sofa's away being reupholstered, that's why it seems so uninviting. Grab one of those chairs – they're not as bad as they look.'

There was something odd about the decision to use this formal room, Simmy felt. Did Eleanor want to keep the family room free of the taint of death? Or did she never take visitors there? Simmy's head felt swollen with the need to concentrate, whilst not appearing too inquisitive or intrusive.

'I'll get us a drink,' said George heavily. He went to a mahogany sideboard and opened one of the doors. 'What would you like?'

It was the first time he had looked directly at Simmy, and he seemed to have to force himself. She glimpsed an array of bottles in the cupboard and wondered wildly what she ought to say. 'Oh – sherry, thanks.'

'Dry, sweet or Amontillado?' he asked automatically.

'Amontillado, please, if that's all right.'

He extracted a bottle and opened the other door to find glasses. Everything was accomplished deftly, as if for the thousandth time. He poured himself an inch of neat whisky and carried the drinks across the room to where Simmy was perched on a chair that she was fairly sure must be a Chippendale. She considered a host of possible conversation openers:

*Did it take you long to get here this morning?*

*Have you other children?*

*Eleanor seems to have interesting ideas about home decorating.*

*I understand that Bridget and Peter have known each other a long time.*

*I hope Lucy isn't going to be too badly upset by all this.*

And more along similar lines; all of them, except perhaps the first, impossible to utter, for fear of where they might lead. It was equally unacceptable to refer to Markie's death and *not* to refer to it. She knew, vaguely, where Baxter lived. There had been a prominent magazine feature about the house he and his present wife had created somewhere in Lancashire. Melanie had shown it to her, when the approach about the wedding flowers first happened. The new wife had evidently remained aloof from the wedding, or perhaps not been invited. The only thing Simmy could recall about her was that she was a landscape gardener and had wrought something miraculous on the exposed coast somewhere north of Fleetwood. Perhaps this would be a safe opener.

But before she could find the breath to speak, George himself was cracking the conversational ice and turning it to steam. 'One of those cronies of the Harrison-Wests did this,' he exploded, eyes bulging, fists clenched. 'The lad was in too deep. I *told* him, years ago, to stay clear of them. But no – he had to follow Bridget wherever she went, whatever cesspit he might fall into because of her.'

Simmy's insides fluttered at the crazy violence of his words.

She thought of the fresh-faced Bridget, so blithe and carefree. *Cesspit?* she queried silently. Then 'Cronies?' she said aloud.

'That Spaniard, for one. And Harrison-West himself, come to that. The golden boy with his easy money. Not so smug after that accident on the mountain, was he? Nearly finished him, that did. If it hadn't been for Glenn Adams and Bridget, he'd have landed up in the funny farm. And Markie – my Markie – worrying himself to a shadow over it all. "Not your business, boy," I told him. But he wouldn't listen. Just kept saying Peter and Bridget needed him.'

He wasn't really talking to her, she realised, but more to some invisible controller of destiny, who might just possibly help him to make sense of the calamity that had befallen him.

She could make little of his remarks, other than gleaning a hazy picture of five men – if Markie were included – and one girl, friends for years, with their own secrets and passions impenetrable to an outsider. None of the men was married, as far as she was aware. Had Peter spoilt some sort of pattern by entering into matrimony? Had Markie made trouble somehow? Felix was also planning to marry, according to Melanie. The old bonds would loosen and change, inevitably. Baxter seemed so sure that one of the 'cronies' killed the boy, but the thought was deeply repugnant.

'Surely,' she protested, 'none of them would do such a terrible thing to Bridget? Markie was her *brother*.'

Baxter took a breath and stared at a point above her head. 'I'm sorry,' he muttered. 'You don't know any of us, do you? You can't begin to understand. I'm not sure I do myself. I just keep remembering an incident, when Markie was about fifteen. He fell off a horse. We all blamed Harrison-West for it. Just like when Mainwaring fell off the mountain.'

'What happened?' Simmy prompted.

He spoke in fragments. 'It was the summer. They wanted to go camping near Ennerdale. It's wild country up there. Nell said Bridget could go, but Markie's mother put her foot down. He went anyway. Ran off and joined them.'

'And fell off a horse while they were there?'

'Trekking,' he nodded. 'Broke his arm.'

'And they all went? Pablo, Glenn – all of them?'

Baxter nodded. 'Penny was furious. Almost scratched his eyes out.'

'Whose eyes?'

'Harrison-West's. He paid for it all. It was always down to him, when they did those trips. Buying popularity, as I saw it.'

'You let Bridget go, though. You trusted them?'

'Safety in numbers,' he shrugged. 'Nell said it would be all right. They went off every summer, playing *Swallows and Amazons*. But Markie was the interloper. He never fitted in. Never had friends of his own age.' He trailed off, with a deep sigh.

Simmy couldn't let it end there. 'But you *trusted* them? With your young daughter?' she repeated, unable to get to grips with the story she was hearing. 'All those men so much older than her.'

He smiled grimly. 'Never too sure about the Spanish bloke,' he admitted. 'He's in insurance, for God's sake.'

Simmy wanted to ask whether that was better or worse than being a financial advisor or a fund manager. And whether any of them automatically qualified a person for homicide.

She wanted to enquire into the background of everyone at the wedding, for the satisfaction of her own curiosity. Who was Glenn Adams, the shaven-headed best man, for example? And how did Bridget's parents really feel about their girl marrying a man scarcely younger than themselves? She realised that her image of Peter Harrison-West was of an overripe bachelor, too long living alone to readily adapt to the married state. Would his young bride have to fall in with his foibles and routines? Or did she know them already, from earliest childhood? Was the marriage really something very sweet and wholesome, as most people seemed to think?

'Have you known him long?' she ventured.

'Who – the Spaniard? No, I don't know him at all. I never even spoke to him until last week when we had that stupid pre-wedding party. That was a fiasco, I can tell you. Waste of money on a grand scale.'

Simmy had some acquaintance with the habit of very rich people to watch closely over their pennies. 'Well, of course,' Melanie had said when Simmy remarked on the frugality of a funeral of a man known to be well heeled. 'That's how they get to be rich in the first place.'

It made sense, but Simmy suspected there was more to it than that. They wanted to escape opprobrium from people less well favoured than themselves. And they wanted to avoid the sheer bad taste of excessively flashy demonstrations. Celebrities, made rich overnight, might indulge in the scattering of their wealth – easy come, easy go – but if you really worked for it, then you didn't throw it around.

'Fiasco?' she echoed.

'Peter was in a foul mood, for some reason. Nerves,

probably. Or somebody said something to him. I don't know. Bridget was upset, which put a damper on everything. That girl is *never* upset. She's like some sainted angel, the way she breezes through life, always smiling and thinking of others. Even when her mother and I . . . well, even then, she sailed through without taking sides or complaining. She gets on with Wanda; she's besotted with Lucy. And Markie was her best friend,' he concluded wretchedly.

'Wanda?'

'My wife.'

'Of course.' *Of course.* She knew that. *Keep up, Sim,* she ordered herself. So why wasn't Wanda at the wedding, at her husband's side, supporting him in his loss?

He answered the silent question. 'She was meaning to be there, obviously. She thinks the world of Bridget. But she's ill. Something she ate. Can't keep anything down. Doctors think it must be e-Coli, which would make it a serious business. She's thin enough as it is.'

'Worrying,' she sympathised.

'Yes.'

'That police detective seems to be quite . . . well, he seems to know what he's doing.'

George shook his head angrily. 'Wasting time, asking all those stupid questions. Needs to cut to the chase, before the trail goes cold.' The hunting metaphor wasn't surprising, she supposed, but it sat very awkwardly with her impression of DI Moxon.

'They'll be doing a lot of forensic stuff,' she said vaguely. 'It's probably much more proactive than it looks.'

'I *told* him it had to be one of the gang – most likely

the Spaniard. He was in a real state through the ceremony, dancing about, eyes everywhere. A picture of guilt, if we'd only realised at the time what he'd done. I *told* that detective bloke all about it. There were money issues, damn it. Markie's got a lot coming to him, it needs to be managed properly—' He stopped on a choking breath, as he heard himself. 'What'll happen to it now?' he whimpered.

*Give it to Bridget*, Simmy thought. Wasn't she just as fitting an heir as Markie?

'Pablo handled Markie's money?' she queried. 'But you said he was in insurance.'

'Life insurance. Covering his back. It's complicated.'

She threw caution out of the window. 'But how would he benefit from Markie's death?' she asked.

'Benefit?' The man blinked at her, mastering his anguish with an effort. 'He'll be given merry hell, if there's a payout. The boy's life was insured for millions.'

'So he'd be more likely to do everything in his power to keep him alive, then – wouldn't he? Why would he murder him?'

She tried hard to keep abreast of the flying shards of information. If Markie's life was insured, wouldn't his parents get the payout when he died?

Baxter closed his eyes. 'He's quite liable to have taken out a counter policy, a gamble if you like, betting the lad would die young.'

'What? That can't be legal, surely?' The murky practices of high finance were no less obscure to her than to any other ordinary person, its language so alienating that she preferred to ignore it completely. 'And if he did do that, the police will discover it.'

He nodded with a brief smile, suggestive of a cunning satisfaction. 'They will now I've spoken to them,' he said.

'But you don't know for certain. You're just guessing.'

'It's what I would have done,' said the City financier, without a shadow of shame.

'You would have killed another man's son? The brother of your friend's fiancée?' She gave herself a mental gold star for getting the relationships right first time.

'No, of course not. I mean I'd have tried to cover all the bases. Make sure it was win-win. It's second nature.'

Simmy felt a quiver of fear at the effortless power these men could wield. Nothing could break their hold on the purse strings; as soon as the rules changed or tightened, they found a loophole, like rats shut out of the food store, making an alternative entrance overnight. The comparison with rats seemed to hold good in other ways, once she began to think about it. Ruthless, sharp, hungry and with no sense of moderation – both groups fitted these epithets quite neatly.

'But—' She wanted to shout at him, to accuse his entire breed of inhumanity and wholesale lack of integrity. She wanted to tell him his way of behaving was sick and corrupt and small wonder it ended up with the death of an innocent boy. And yet he had just lost his only son, and was therefore not to be shouted at. She wondered how gently DI Moxon had treated him. Had the detective taken Baxter's accusation against Pablo and the others seriously? Perhaps, by now, the whole business had been settled, the Spaniard in custody making a tearful confession.

Baxter interrupted whatever she might have said, with a flapping gesture in front of his face. The sort of gesture people made when they were choking and did not want to be slapped on the back or given water. His face darkened, and his eyes were different. She watched him as the actual irreversible truth of Markie's death hit him for the first time. She watched inner defences crumble, and waves of horror replace the all-too-easy anger and intellectualising. She watched him blunder across the room, push back a curtain and stare blindly out at the uncaring lake and mountains outside, now dotted with lights as night took hold. He was shaking, his teeth chattering. Simmy considered fetching Eleanor to deal with him, but remembered the child, who might come as well and be traumatised by the sight of a man collapsing in front of her.

Murkily, she wondered what the last words between father and son might have been. Had they been exactly the sort of thing you would never forgive yourself for? From what she had seen of Baxter, that felt all too likely. He would be haunted by them for the rest of his life, blocked by the impossibility of putting it right. She made a brief resolution never to say anything to anybody that would linger poisonously if that person died unexpectedly.

The man had his back to her, the shoulders sagging in the expensive wedding suit. He was pathetic and she was tempted to go to him and let him sob on her breast, if that was what he needed. She glimpsed the dissolution of a whole castle of plans and assumptions, projected far into the future.

And then a new thought hit her, bringing with it amazement that it had not occurred before. 'His mother?' she asked. 'Where's Markie's mother?' Shouldn't George be huddled together with the one other person in the world with equal reason to be in emotional meltdown?

'What?' His voice was thick. 'What did you say?'

She knew he had heard the first time, so did not repeat the question. It was not her business. If he wanted to ignore it, that was his right. She was occupied in trying to recall what Melanie had said about Markie's parentage. Another woman, another household, running parallel to that containing Eleanor and Bridget, in the very house where Simmy now lived. So what had happened? Where was that other woman now?

He turned towards her, his face grey. 'She married a man with a bigger yacht than mine.' It was plainly an old joke, habitually told in bluff male company, with the rueful laugh that would go with the acceptance of female gold-digging as a fact of life. 'But it didn't last. She's in very reduced circumstances these days, working in a public school somewhere down south. Positioning herself to snap up one of the well-heeled dads, I shouldn't wonder.'

Simmy nodded wordlessly, redrawing her image of a quiet little woman settled in a remote Lakeland cottage with her little boy, like something out of *The Forsyte Saga*. Instead it morphed into a mixture of James Bond and Evelyn Waugh. A jet-set couple, carelessly creating a child between other relationships, the mother virtually forgetting about him, or so the implication appeared to be.

# Chapter Five

Her sherry long since finished, she began to think about going home. Eleanor had blithely undertaken to drive her back, but that now felt like an unreliable promise. Baxter would have to babysit, and he might not be regarded as fit for that task. Neither was he likely to act as chauffeur in his current condition. Old associations of being stranded at children's parties when her mother forgot to collect her at the appointed hour came back to her, along with a wholly irrational resentment. If it came to the crunch, she could probably walk home. Troutbeck was surely less than four miles from Eleanor's house, even going back the way they had come. It would be shorter if there was a more direct route, but that was unlikely to be a proper road. And she did require an actual road; attempting a steep muddy footpath in the dark was not enticing, especially as she was still hazy about the precise geography.

Eleanor swept back into the room like a force of nature. 'God, I'm sorry,' she cried, as if late for a royal command. 'I had to read *five pages* to her before she'd let me go. I'm too old for this game, let's face it.' She threw a smile at Simmy.

'I was forty-five when I had her, you know. It seemed rather clever at the time, but don't let anybody ever tell you it's a good idea.'

Simmy endured the familiar stab with habitual stoicism. On average, somebody said something of this sort once a day. Today, though, was turning out to be unusually painful.

'Here are the clothes your mother wants back,' Eleanor remembered, proffering a plastic supermarket bag.

Simmy took it just as Eleanor belatedly noticed Baxter's disintegration. 'George? Are you all right?'

'I think it finally hit him,' Simmy explained awkwardly.

'So it would seem. Well, old man, it had to happen sooner or later. You can't avoid it for ever.' The brisk tone had no discernible effect on him. He leant his brow on the windowpane, half hidden behind the long curtain. Less of an old man than an anguished little boy, desperate in his lonely suffering.

'I should go home,' said Simmy.

'Right. Well . . . Um . . .'

'I suppose I could phone for a taxi.'

'No, no. Don't be silly. I'll take you. Where did you say you lived?'

'Troutbeck. It's not very far.'

'Pity it's dark – you could have gone on foot along Nanny Lane and been there in forty minutes. We'll have to go back the way we came, as it is.'

Simmy refrained from reminding the woman that this entire exercise had been at her insistence. 'Nanny Lane?' she repeated.

'Right. It's a footpath, the other side of Wansfell. Impossible at night, obviously. We'd never see you again.'

She laughed. 'Curses – another boy has fallen into the abyss.'

'Pardon?'

'Oh, sorry. It's a family thing. We had an old phrasebook – German, I think. That was one of the phrases. My sister and I say it to each other rather a lot, even now. It's surprising how often it seems to crop up.'

The joke was in alarmingly bad taste, given the events of the day, and Simmy forced the tightest of smiles.

'George,' said Eleanor in the loud clear tones of a nurse addressing a distracted elderly patient. 'I'm taking Persimmon home now. You're in charge of Lucy. I'll be half an hour. All right?'

'Persimmon?' He stared at them. 'Is that what you said?'

'Come on, George. It's her *name*. Get a grip of yourself. I want you to stay here and listen out for Lucy. She's very tired, so you shouldn't have any trouble. But stay in the house, all right?'

'Persimmon,' he repeated. 'Lovely orange things. Make your mouth dry, though. There was a tree in that garden – remember? In France, where we stayed that summer. Goudargues.' He sighed. 'You were a bitch because I was pining for Pasquale.'

'You make it sound like a thousand years ago.'

'It was.'

'Bridget was eight. Ten years, that's all.'

Simmy listened reluctantly to this piece of intimacy. She could detect no bitterness or animosity in either of them, and could not prevent herself from making a comparison with her own abiding rage against Tony. These two seemed relaxed to the point of nonchalance about past betrayals. They had both moved on to other people, with little discernible harm done. Would they be equally nonchalant about the disappearance of these partners in a few years' time? Was it routinely expected that no relationships endured for long in the circles they inhabited?

It was an alien mindset that she found confusing and irritating. Other people's morality was often disturbing, of course. They committed acts that you'd been taught to regard as entirely wrong, and received no retribution for it. Except that in this instance, retribution had fallen catastrophically onto the Baxter man, and if Simmy was not mistaken, there was a large dose of guilt mixed in with his grief and anger.

In the car it turned out that Eleanor was less carefree than she might have seemed. 'I'm so sorry,' she repeated, driving too fast down the winding lane. 'We were going to have a proper talk with you about this morning, weren't we? I should have realised it would be too much for George. He's never had anything like this happen before.'

'No,' said Simmy. 'Not many people have.'

'Of course not. Listen to me! What a stupid thing to say. I meant, hardly anything has ever gone wrong for him. Money just sticks to him, women chase after him, he's never been ill.'

'He thinks Peter's friend, Pablo, killed Mark. Something to do with insurance.'

Eleanor gave a little cry, half horrified laugh, half protest. 'No! Does he? Oh dear.'

'He told the inspector, apparently.'

'Poor Pablo. Peter's very fond of him. They've known each other for ever. They were at Repton together.'

Simmy guessed this must be a school, but had never heard

of it. 'He was outside with Markie and Peter and that best man chap. They were waiting for Mr Baxter.'

'Right.'

'I thought that was what you wanted to talk to me about?' She felt some faint obligation to unburden herself, as if that might be a way to shake free of these people. In those final minutes in the house, she had understood that she had no wish to involve herself with them any further.

'Yes, it was. Sort of. I hoped you might be able to reassure George somehow. Tell him that Markie was in good spirits, looking forward to seeing him again, happy about the wedding. They parted under a cloud you see, last time they met.'

'Oh. How long ago was that?'

'A month or so. Markie and Bridget had been reminiscing about their childhood, and laughing about the freedom they'd had, and George heard it as critical of him, for some reason. They were pure *Swallows and Amazons*, for years, growing up here.'

'So I gather. You were rather famous in the area, apparently. My assistant has told me about it. You sounded like a cross between the Bloomsbury Group and *Dynasty*. All that money!'

'Never as much as people think, of course. But we were peculiar for the times, I admit. There's nowhere as good as the Lakes for being peculiar. It's easy to transport yourself back to the thirties, or even further. William Morris, Ruskin, that Bolton man at Storrs, all leaving their traces behind. You can just *feel* their ghosts, especially at this time of year. Another month, and it'll be day-long mists, with everything dripping wet, and sheep looming at you without warning. I can't tell you how much I love it,' she finished with a contented sigh.

'And now there's Lucy to start it all over again. I have to say I'm amazingly lucky. I know I am.'

It was a very odd speech for the member of a family violently bereaved that very day.

'But—' Simmy started, wanting to suggest that if Markie could be murdered, then was there not cause for concern about Lucy, or Bridget?

'You'll have to navigate me from here,' Eleanor interrupted. 'Which end of Troutbeck are you?'

The potential awkwardness in the fact that she was now inhabiting the house in which Baxter's other woman and child once lived made her deliberately vague. 'The other end. Between the hotel and the pub. You can drop me outside the hotel, if you like.'

'Right. Sorry, again. We must seem outrageous to you, dumping Lucy on you, and then spiriting you away for no good reason. I don't expect we've been very rational, at least in the eyes of a normal person.'

'No problem,' Simmy assured her, heartily. Did anybody relish being called 'normal', she wondered. The word came packed with patronage and a disingenuous hint that the speaker really quite valued being abnormal herself. 'Thank you for the lift.'

Eleanor gave a brief chirp of farewell, and turned the car around with a flourish. Simmy walked the few yards to her little house, and let herself in. Her car, she remembered with a jolt, was still down in Windermere, three miles away. Why hadn't she asked Eleanor to take her there, instead? She'd have to walk down in the morning, and it was sure to be raining.

* * *

It was still not quite eight o'clock, but it felt a lot later. The chilly little house held no welcoming cat or dog; no flicker of life at all. She was used to it by this time; all the fears of intruders or evil spirits long since despatched by routine and custom. Although the past week had seen no fewer than four large spiders invading her home, as they detected the onset of winter and sought out a cosy spot for hibernation, and these she did fear. Hypersensitive to them, Simmy saw them the moment they ventured into the open, crossing the floor with a terrifying purpose. Her irrational self beat them to death, even as she felt guilty at doing so. Spiders didn't hurt you – she knew that. But there was no way she could sleep, once she had seen one in the house with her. One day, she promised herself, she would grow out of it, and be a properly sensible person.

In Worcester, she and Tony had lived in a flat, with other people both above and below, and on one side too. It had been like a hive, the cells nestled neatly together, and everyone in their own allotted space. Shops, pubs, cinema had all been within an easy walk. She had never consciously assessed the relative merits of town and country, adapting readily to each in turn. The market garden job she had mentioned to DI Moxon had turned up by accident, never intended to be permanent. It had been a speculative venture on the part of a friend of Tony's – ten acres of ordinary field transformed within weeks to a riot of soft fruit and vegetables, which had to be tended, picked, packed and transported. It had suited her almost miraculously, for reasons she still had not troubled to analyse. From there to establishing her own floristry business had seemed a small step. Everybody liked flowers, after all. To be the source of fragrance and beauty and a symbolism redolent of love and attention seemed to her the best of all possible jobs.

The house opposite was the holiday home of a London couple. They made the long drive perhaps eight times a year, bringing huge quantities of possessions, which they unloaded noisily right outside Simmy's front gate on arrival and reloaded again on departure. However hard she tried, she could not avoid disliking them. They could see into her front rooms, through windows she seldom bothered to cover with curtains. They made comments on her garden and treated her like a close friend. They had not been since late August and she was sure they would be back again at any moment.

She went to bed early, weary from the long day, which had begun at six-thirty that morning. The news of Mark Baxter's death would be everywhere by this time, the story highly likely to make national headlines, with its high-society background and the compelling mix of romance and murder. It was a classic, a *Lorna Doone* or *Wuthering Heights*, forcing violent horror onto the peachy-pink happiness of a wedding.

She thought about Bridget and what the girl might be feeling, on this wedding night. Julie the hairdresser had insisted that it was a love match, with nothing beneath the surface to spoil the joy. Obviously, Julie had been wrong.

# Chapter Six

Sunday was damp again, but on nothing like the scale of the day before. Simmy had dreamt about a funeral, the coffin piled high with ostentatious wreaths that were deep purple in colour, except for one that glowed a ghastly neon orange, clashing grotesquely. *So much for wondering whether we dream in colour*, she thought, as she remembered it. The horrible combination remained clear in her mind as she dressed and went downstairs. One of the worst aspects of being christened Persimmon was an active dislike of all shades of orange. Or apricot, come to that. Her preferred colour was a rich blood red, that made her hair and skin look darker. Somewhere in the past there had been Celtic ancestry, to which Simmy's colouring was testament. Russell sometimes hinted that his wife might have a drop of something even darker in the mix. A shipwrecked Spaniard, perhaps – a possibly mythical source of swarthy colouring all along the western coasts of the British Isles.

Russell himself was an unremarkable mongrel assortment of Saxon and Scots with a dash of French. His sister Jeanne had researched it all in the hope of unearthing some surprises. The most startling revelation was that their great-grandmother had been born in Paris, and had deep black eyes that people noticed. She married a blue-eyed Londoner and gave birth to a batch of colourless shopkeepers and clerks. There had, though, been a daughter, Norma, who retained the dark eyes and full lips of her mother. Norma had died under the wheels of a coal truck, when she was eighteen.

Aunt Jeanne was dead now, as well. She had been sixty-six and there was still a sense that she had never enjoyed her natural span. There had been worlds yet to explore and she was in the full swing of her explorations when an aneurysm felled her, a week after Simmy's dead baby had been delivered. For months, the survivors held their breath, waiting for the third calamity to befall them.

A grey Cumbrian Sunday created an irresistible backdrop for gloomy musings about death. Nothing to look forward to but darker days and weather-related frustrations for several months to come. The stoical take-it-or-leave-it character of the local people reflected the climate and the landscape. There could be snow to interrupt Christmas plans, and ice to send people and their vehicles slithering down the steep winding lanes when they were forced to venture out. Business would go into hibernation, with nobody sending flowers until the insanity of St Valentine's Day reawakened them all. The irritating poinsettias and holly wreaths that symbolised Christmas were pretty much all that would sell between now and then, except for a wedding in the New Year – a far less flamboyant one than that of Bridget and Peter. In the quieter spell, she would take the opportunity to experiment with new designs, using ideas from Jane Packer and others.

Inevitably her thoughts veered back to Storrs and the truncated wedding party. Those who had stayed overnight would be taking their leave. Even the new couple would be packing up for their honeymoon – assuming DI Moxon permitted them to leave. What a terrible shadow had been cast over them, to taint every anniversary of their wedding day, for the rest of their lives. How would they manage the strain of it?

The silence in the house did not disturb her. She had quickly grown to treasure the complete darkness and the absolute quiet of nights in Troutbeck. Her bedroom looked over the slopes of Wansfell, which stood between her and the lake, with no human habitation in sight. The rarity of such an undisturbed existence made her value it all the more. Planes might pass overhead, and traffic from the A592 might divert through the village for a look, but not in the small hours of the night. She had come rushing north to get away from all associations with Tony, blindly following her parents, and had never regretted it. She often found herself envying those who had been born there and spent their whole lives amongst the stunning lakes and fells.

The business would grow and develop into a solid foundation for a full life. She understood that she was only in the first toe-deep shallows of the ocean of learning ahead. Flowers contained unlimited potential, in every aspect of life. She had scarcely begun to approach restaurants, for example, with a view to establishing regular contracts for table decoration. There were issues around available time – the Storrs wedding had kept her busy for weeks, with the final few days exclusively devoted to it. The resulting payment would cover rent on the shop for months. Weddings were the cash cow, no doubt about it. But a big funeral, coming without warning, could boost the coffers quite handsomely too, at times.

Her mobile broke into her quiet disjointed musings, just after nine o'clock. She answered it carelessly, while spreading marmalade on her morning toast. It would be her mother, she supposed.

'Miss . . . Mrs . . . Brown? I'm sorry to trouble you again, but I'd like to see you today. I'm afraid I lost the thread last night. There were things I wanted to ask you. Could we try again, do you think?'

'Mr Baxter,' she identified, after the first few words. 'I hope you managed to get some sleep?'

'Never mind that. Will you see me? And Peter. He wants to come along, as well.'

'Peter? The bridegroom, you mean?'

Baxter snorted at the word. 'If that's the way you view him, then yes. Harrison-West, new husband of my daughter. My son-in-law, come to that. He's three years younger than me.'

There was no actual disdain or criticism in his words, but the sentiment alone was enough to suggest something less than positive. An impatient breath reached her ear, and she tried to stick to the question. 'Well, I suppose I could. I've got things to do first, though. What time do you want me?'

'Could you be at the Old England for lunch?'

'The . . . ?'

'Old England pub – hotel, whatever they call it. It's in Bowness, Fallbarrow Road. You'll find it, if you don't know it already.'

'I expect I will. What time?'

'Let's say midday.'

'Could we make it half past?'

'If you say so.'

She bit back a *thank you*, unsure of whether it was apt. He made it feel as though she was the one doing the favour, which she supposed she was, when it came down to it. The prospect of meeting the new son-in-law was intriguing, pushing out insistent questions about why the family were being so attentive to her. What was it they wanted to extract from her? Something about her brief exchange with Markie, she assumed. A need she could just about understand: to revisit his last known words, the last expression on his face.

There were tasks to be done before she could consign the day to questions of murder, however pressing that might be. The week's accounts were refusing to balance, for one thing. She had brought all the till receipts home with her, all the card transactions and cash takings. Knowing that figures were her weakest point, she had allocated a strict Sunday morning session to keeping abreast of the finances, every week. She had learnt how to do spreadsheets on the course she had taken before buying the shop, but never felt comfortable with doing the work on a computer. It made far more sense to her to write it by hand in a big ledger, where nothing could get lost, and she could easily track it all, step by step. Melanie had been appalled when this failing came to light and had insisted on entering everything on a computer they kept at the shop, in addition to whatever method Simmy chose to employ. Orders were mostly done online, she pointed out. It took only a few more seconds to log the transaction on the database at the same time. Simmy struggled to cooperate, fully aware that she would never make a success of the business if she routinely messed up the accounts. One day, she promised herself, she would have a full-time employee dedicated to that whole side of things.

Meanwhile, she carefully inspected every scrap of paper, clipping each day's together and labelling it; listing the most popular items sold, for future analysis; keying all the totals into a calculator and writing down the results. VAT, business tax, and the vast welter of paperwork associated with employing somebody, all threatened to engulf her, when she only wanted to enjoy the flowers and develop some of her own ideas regarding design and new lines to sell.

She phoned Melanie to suggest they both go quickly to Storrs and retrieve the ribbons and wires and other reusable material from the swags in the room used for the wedding. The hotel would not see it as their task to take decorations down, even if they were happy to keep other displays for a few more days. Time would be tight, but with two of them, it should take under an hour. 'I'll get my car from Lake Road, and have a quick coffee. Then I'll pick you up at home at eleven or just after.'

'Okay,' Melanie agreed flatly. 'But you'll have to run.'

'I know.'

By nine-forty-five she had come as close to completion of her paperwork as she was likely to. She packed it all away in the capacious filing cabinet in the room that was intended for dining, and went upstairs to change into an outfit suitable for lunch with a millionaire whose son had been killed.

Sunday morning coffee with her parents was a sporadic commitment that they understood they could not depend on. To return to Beck View only a day after a previous visit was highly unusual, but after the events of the previous day, she expected they would want to talk over the implications of all that had happened. The disastrous guests would have to be discussed, in conjunction with the visitation from the Baxters. The fact of the lunch engagement would certainly interest them.

It was not raining, and the walk was all downhill. Despite a temptation to phone and ask her father to bring her car up to Troutbeck, she resolved to go on foot. It was good for her, and there was just time to get everything done if she hurried, before arriving in Bowness for the lunch appointment. She followed the Trout Beck, through Thickholme and down to the Bridge, from where it was pavement into town. Walking was an activity she had promised herself when she made the move, and she had trained herself to use her feet as a regular form of transport between the numerous settlements along the lakeside. It was the best way to discover the ancient byways in the area, and the profusion of wild flowers along the trackways gave the walks a pleasing association with her professional life. Now, as the leaves were starting to turn, and red berries appear on holly and hawthorn, it was a real pleasure. Her mind went blank as she simply absorbed the beauty of the day, her legs swinging energetically, and worries over accounts faded away completely.

Angie opened the door with a dramatic flourish, as soon as she saw Simmy approaching down the street. It was as if she had been watching for her from the window of the guests' dining room – which struck Simmy as unlikely. 'God, what a weekend!' were the first words she uttered.

'Why? What's happened now?' She edged past her mother into the house and pushed the door shut behind her.

'Those people with the kid – they're not going quietly. Your Lucy's going to be up for GBH, if they get their way.'

*Your Lucy* sounded rather sweet to Simmy's ears. Enough to make her bristle in defence of the child whose company she had enjoyed so much. 'Rubbish!' she said. 'She's five years old.'

'She's at least six,' Angie corrected. 'Trust you to be so vague about it.'

'So what have they said, exactly?'

'The husband phoned and said they'd had a terrible night in a hotel they can't afford, the kid awake and crying for hours, the baby not feeding properly with all the upset, dah-di-dah-di-dah. All sorts of nonsense. You do wonder, don't you, why God lets some people ever have children.'

Angie used 'God' as an umbrella term for fate, society, biology, luck. She meant it as a sort of witticism. Simmy supposed she should be glad that the topic of children was not taboo between them.

'So what are they going to do?'

'Oh, probably nothing when it comes to it. If they stop to think for a minute, they'll see how ridiculous they're being. But Daddy says there's so much litigation around these days they might find a lawyer who'll try and get something out of us.'

'Is he worried?'

'Cross.'

'Oh, well. I've got to have lunch with the Baxter man and Peter Harrison-West, after collecting all the bits and pieces from Storrs. I'll have to go in a minute. I'm collecting Melanie – we'll get it done quicker with her to help.'

'Lunch? Where?'

'That Old England hotel – in Fallbarrow Road. You know?'

Angie's face expressed an array of reactions: surprise,

amusement, curiosity. 'Fancy that! They've had some terrible comments on TripAdvisor in the past. The rooms are too hot, apparently.'

'Every hotel gets bad comments. It doesn't mean a thing.'

'I hope you're right, because we'll be getting one ourselves any minute now. That was one of the first things yesterday's man said to me. He's going to tell the world how dangerous and heartless we are.'

'Oh, well,' said Simmy again, thinking there were much more important matters to be focusing on. Somewhere she was nervous about meeting George Baxter again, and she wanted to examine precisely why. 'He talked to me for quite a long time last night, and then he got upset and Eleanor drove me home.' Her mother ought to have enquired, she felt, instead of moaning about her disgruntled guests. 'It hit him, all of a sudden, that his boy is dead.' She frowned. 'I'm not sure what else there is to say, actually. I guess he didn't let me say much about seeing Markie on Saturday. And he says he wants Peter to hear it.'

'What'll you tell him?' Angie was finally paying attention. They were in the kitchen, the room they automatically gravitated to, even with its semi-industrial atmosphere. 'Haven't you got time for coffee?'

Simmy shook her head. 'I'm not sure what I can safely say.' This, she realised, was at least part of the reason for her nerves. 'Markie seemed scared about seeing his father. They were all standing out there in the rain, waiting for him. He said something about his father needing moral support before he could face all the wedding people. That seems a bit funny now. I mean, Eleanor and he get along perfectly well, so who else would he be worried about seeing?'

'Who knows? Daft old aunts? Impoverished cousins? Families are riddled with tension, aren't they? Old arguments, unpaid debts, people thinking things are unfair. Ask your father – he's got at least two relatives he'd fly to Australia to avoid. And you know how he hates flying.'

The only surviving Straw relatives were Russell's two brothers, three nephews and one niece, and a very ancient aunt. Angie, like Simmy, was a single child. Relatives, in fact, were in painfully short supply. 'You exaggerate,' she accused her mother. 'You mean Cousin Harry, I suppose.'

'And Auntie Pauline. That woman's a monster.'

'Whatever – you're probably right about the wedding people. The police are going to have to unravel all that, I assume. If Mr Baxter was on bad terms with somebody, they'll probably think that person might have killed Markie, to get at his father.'

Angie shivered. 'That would be a *filthy* thing to do.'

'Monstrous,' Simmy agreed, deliberately echoing the careless epithet Angie had used about poor old Auntie Pauline, who had definitely never murdered anybody at all.

Melanie was waiting and they hastened in the van down the lakeside road to Storrs. Simmy conscientiously reported her visit to Eleanor Baxter's lavish mansion above Ambleside. 'It's a beautiful house,' she repeated. 'With all kinds of lovely furniture. I can't imagine growing up in a place like that.'

'You were privileged,' said Melanie tartly. 'Nobody gets invited up there.'

'Really? I got the feeling it was open house to a whole lot of people.'

'Just the inner circle. I bet it's got a ten-foot fence all round it.'

'You bet wrong. She hardly even bothers to lock the door. No burglar alarms or anything. What's the matter with you?' It had taken five minutes or more to grasp that her assistant was not in the cheeriest of moods.

'Nothing you can do anything about.'

'Try me.'

'There isn't time. We're there, look.'

Storrs Hall was waiting for them on its natural lakeside rostrum. The water lapped gently a few yards from the western wing. Simmy caught sight of blue police tape attached to posts, keeping everyone away from the place where Markie Baxter had been found. 'Spoils the view,' she murmured. 'It's going to have rotten connotations for years to come, after all this.'

'Nah,' Melanie argued. 'They'll make a virtue of it. It'll give them something to boast about.'

'Cynic,' said Simmy. The image of the boy's fresh rain-splashed face, in the last hour or two of his life, sent a sharp grief through her chest. The exact mechanics of how he had been killed were secondary to the simple fact that he was dead, sixty years before his time. No wonder his father could not avoid revisiting her encounter with Markie. Any parent would be obsessed with every little detail of that morning.

They were admitted to the handsome space where weddings were conducted, and quickly set about pulling down the carefully constructed swags of foliage. 'I don't suppose half the guests even noticed them,' Simmy sighed. 'People don't really look up much, do they?'

Melanie merely shrugged.

'Come on,' Simmy urged. 'Tell me what's bugging you.'

'It's my eye,' came the unexpected reply. 'They've decided to give me a different one. I've got to go and have it fitted next week.'

'So? Don't you want it? They can't make you, can they?'

The girl sighed in exasperation. 'You don't understand.'

It was true. Simmy could not imagine having a sightless eye, which had slowly clouded over throughout Melanie's childhood, until being removed when she was eleven and replaced with a prosthesis that was a fair match for the good one. But it was fixed immovably, and never had quite the same pupil size as its partner. On their first meeting, it had taken Simmy three minutes to work out what was odd about the girl's face. Within ten minutes, she had asked for the story of what had happened.

'I guess it's rather unpleasant, having people mess with you like that,' she ventured.

'It's not that. It's being *reminded*,' Melanie blurted. 'I can go weeks without even thinking about it, and then it all comes back, and I have to face it all over again. I have to admit I'm a freak.'

Simmy lowered her chin and gave the girl an old-fashioned look. 'Don't give me that,' she said. 'Because I'm not playing along with it. If every person with a little piece of themselves missing was a freak, then there'd be hardly any normal people, would there? I don't think that's what's bothering you at all.'

Melanie pouted, and tugged hard at a string of glossy chestnut-brown leaves. 'It *is*, more or less. I don't like people being sorry for me, asking me how I feel all the time. How do I *know* how I feel? I can't even remember having two eyes. I don't get why we all have to pretend it's no big deal.'

'So it *is* a big deal?'

'Sometimes it is, and sometimes it's not. And even I can't always tell the difference.'

Simmy laughed, and Melanie gave a tentative grin. 'So who killed Markie Baxter?' she asked, loud in the echoing empty room. 'That's the *really* big deal.'

Simmy experienced a very inappropriate relief. 'His father thinks it must have been one of the groom's "cronies". That's what he calls them. The best man and the ushers. He seems to favour the Spanish one – Pablo something. Probably because he's foreign.'

'But not the groom, then?'

'I guess not. I'm meant to be seeing him at lunchtime, as well as Bridget's dad. All a bit heavy, to be honest.' She had been doubtful about telling Melanie of her lunch appointment, feeling faintly that she might be seen as fraternising with gentry and thereby removing herself from such as her assistant. Now she understood that this was entirely in her own head, and that it said a lot about her attitude towards social class. All Melanie cared about was the murder investigation.

'But you saw him last night? What more does he want?'

'Search me. He seemed to have a thing about insurance.' Simmy chewed her lips for a minute. 'Would somebody do a murder to get hold of the insurance money, do you think?'

'Course they would,' said Melanie.

101

# Chapter Seven

Bowness was much quieter than it had been the previous day. Clear, dry days would become rarer as winter approached, and visitors were probably taking the opportunity to get into the fells while they still could. Only those wanting to cruise the lake still milled about waiting for the boat to collect them. Not all the shops had opened, as they did throughout the summer on a Sunday. Simmy had heard muttered complaints about this break with Christian teachings, in the few meetings she attended with other business people. For herself, she had decided from the start that Persimmon Petals would remain firmly closed on Sundays, come what may. 'It's all right for you,' the souvenir shop people said. 'We can't afford such a luxury.'

Melanie had questioned the decision, pointing out that the streets of Windermere were far from empty on a summer Sunday. 'I don't care,' Simmy had insisted. 'It wouldn't be worth the wear and tear on my temper. And when would I do the accounts if I had to be in the shop on Sunday mornings?'

'Saturday night – seeing as how you never go out,' said

Melanie with a disgusted look. Simmy's lack of a social life caused Melanie much annoyance. It was as if she was letting the side down in some way. She still made sure she invited her employer to the riotous evenings she and her friends engaged in at weekends, despite knowing she would never be accepted.

'I'm too old for all that,' Simmy always said. They both knew it was true.

She delivered the girl back to her house, and then managed to get to the Old England Hotel with four minutes to spare. She parked in the small street at right angles to Fallbarrow Road, where there were plenty of empty spaces, and remained in the van for a moment, gathering her thoughts. She was not eager to meet the bereaved father again, after his collapse of the previous evening. His son had been dead for little more than twenty-four hours, and she understood his desire to extract every detail of her encounter with him, in the final moments of his life. But why, she wondered, didn't he ask one of those men who had been standing in the rain with Markie? They knew the boy and would have been much better at judging his mood.

The answer was obvious, of course. There was every chance that one of those men had committed the murder, and would therefore tell lies at worst, or evade questions at best. Suspicion would cloud the conversation, in any case. How had she got herself embroiled in the business in the first place? She had been singled out, that was the truth of it. Markie had deliberately detached himself from his friends and spoken to her with an intimacy that had been entirely unjustified. Since then, his family had pursued the same determined connection. It wasn't fair of them, she whined to herself. Why didn't they stick to their own kind, their long-standing friends and relations?

The answer came back as before. Nobody in their own circle could be trusted. There was a pressing need for an outsider, who would be more likely to offer uncomplicated information and unclouded assistance. She ought to be flattered, she supposed, and in some ways she was. But the result of her brief inner musings was to increase a sensation of anxiety. Her insides were misbehaving in a clear indication of reluctance to get any more deeply involved.

She had her back to the hotel and the lake behind it. A man was standing to her left, a little way up the gentle slope towards the town centre. It was not George Baxter or Peter Harrison-West, and therefore not interesting. She looked at her watch – two minutes before the agreed meeting time. He had not said whether or not she should go inside and wait for them there. This was a further cause for anxiety – would they look for her in the bar, or dining room, or terrace, if she went in before them? The only option, then, was to remain outside until they came.

Being two of them, they would most likely separate and cover both inside and out, making it easy for her. A gentleman would be automatically aware that such situations could be awkward for a woman, regardless of equality. And George Baxter had struck her as quite a gentleman at heart. His son might have hinted at a tendency to bully, or judge, or enforce undue discipline, but Simmy had seen little of that. And she felt sorry for him. But she was still not eager to talk to him again.

She rummaged in her bag for a hairbrush, wishing she had washed her hair that morning. It hung inelegantly around her face, still suffering from the effects of the previous day's rain. On a good day it could gleam with natural chestnut highlights, springing energetically from her crown to add height and character. Tony had much admired her hair when they first met, and once even went with her to have it cut, which startled the hairdresser and made Simmy feel both cherished and patronised.

Using the van's wing mirror, which she tilted inwards, she did what she could to create a respectable image. When she nudged it back again, to something like its former position, she realised that she was looking directly at the hotel's entrance, framed squarely in the mirror. The distinctive white globe lights flanking the door caught her eye, and she wondered what effect they might have at night. A young woman wheeling a suitcase went in, and then a familiar man came into view. He paused and looked around, then glanced at his watch. It was Baxter, and Simmy took hold of her door handle, meaning to get out quickly and call to him. She was perhaps thirty yards from him and the street was quiet. He would hear her easily.

The *crack!* when it came was not especially alarming. If she thought about it at all, it was to assume the hinge mechanism of her van door had made the sound. They did that sometimes. She pushed the door further and swung herself out of the seat, taking a breath to call out.

But something had happened to George Baxter. His head had lurched sideways, and as she watched, he toppled horribly into the window to the left of the hotel's front door. The glass withstood the impact, and he sank to his knees, his arms inert, his head flopping ever more grotesquely. She thought nothing at all. A powerless spectator, she simply stood passively, frozen in place. Even when the man lay crumpled on the pavement, and nobody came to see to him, and somewhere deep in her brain something hinted that he must have been shot, she stayed where she was. No fear or pity or rage took hold of her. There was no narrative to explain things, no sense to be made, in those initial seconds.

Then a young man, a youth of sixteen or so, came up the street from the left, and headed straight for the prostrate man. Perhaps it was his tender age that galvanised Simmy; perhaps he reminded her of Markie, and she feared for his safety. Whatever the facts of it, she called out, 'Be careful!'

Just why she chose those words was deeply obscure. She had no mental image of a frenzied killer intent on slaughtering everyone in Bowness. Rather, it had something to do with Baxter himself, who surely needed the most expert of attentions. A callow lad with uncooordinated limbs and unpredictable assumptions was not likely to be a good first responder. She moved, somehow, closer to the scene. A woman appeared in the doorway of the hotel, apparently simply intending to go for a walk. She failed to observe the crumpled man on the pavement for some seconds. 'Look!' croaked Simmy, her voice obstructed by the rising wave of comprehension and bewildered panic. 'Look at him.'

The woman looked. 'Oh!' she gasped. 'What happened?'

'Shot. See,' said the boy, pointing a shaky finger at the side of Baxter's head. There was a bloodless hole in his temple, as if created by a sharp spike driven carefully through the bone. 'I heard it.'

'What?' Simmy stared stupidly at the youth. 'How?'

'Gun. Obviously.'

The woman from the hotel began to scream, a thin high sound not unlike the cry of a gull. Words began to form. 'Dead! He's *dead*. My God.' She clutched at her heart and all colour left her cheeks. She turned and stumbled back into the safety of the Old England.

'She'll phone the cops, then,' said the boy, already fingering his own mobile phone. 'Or d'you think I could do it?'

'You might as well,' said Simmy, finding a pool of calm within herself, prompted by the useless hotel guest. 'They'll want you to be a witness. First on the scene and all that.'

'Wow!' He paled. 'They won't think *I* did it, will they?'

Simmy laughed; an inappropriate laugh that quickly threatened to become hysterical. 'I'll vouch for you. I practically saw it happen.' She paused, trying to recapture the scene of a few minutes before. 'I heard the shot. I saw him fall. Did you?'

He nodded. 'Sort of. I was just there.' He pointed at a spot on the street that sloped down to the waterside. 'I was watching a squirrel,' he added inconsequentially.

'Funny there was only us in sight,' she said. Looking round, she realised that four or five other people were slowly approaching, from various directions. They could see the man on the ground, eyeing him warily, loathe to interfere if this was an embarrassing epileptic attack, or a drunk liable to vomit or curse. Where, Simmy wondered confusedly,

107

was Peter Harrison-West? Why was he not here at her side, handling the murder of his new father-in-law?

And then, as if impossibly accelerated, events took on a rush and bustle that involved shouted instructions, a hotel blanket, and a dramatically enlarged crowd of onlookers. Simmy retreated to her vehicle, unable to speak coherently to the officious hotel manager and a smart woman who claimed to be a doctor. Her fellow witness went with her, and got into the passenger seat without asking permission. 'We'd better wait for the police,' she said.

'My name's Ben,' he said, not holding out a hand for her to shake.

'I'm Simmy. Do you live locally?'

He nodded. 'My mum's doing a roast. I should go.'

'Phone her.'

He nodded again, but made no move. 'It's my birthday,' he added miserably. 'It's my birthday lunch.'

'Oh? Happy birthday. How old are you?'

'Seventeen. He *was* dead, wasn't he?'

''Fraid so. They've covered him up with that blanket. I don't think you're meant to do that, before the police get here. It messes up the evidence.'

'Yeah. I thought that.'

'You can't tell people, can you? Not unless you're a professional. They get arsy about it.'

Ben grinned, and she realised she was speaking lines more suited to him. He seemed a nice boy, she thought vaguely. Would this experience damage him for life? 'I know him. He was supposed to be meeting me here. We were going to have lunch.'

'Wow. Who is he, then?'

'Baxter. He's some sort of businessman. Rich. His son was killed yesterday.'

'You're joking!' The boy's head swivelled nervously, scanning the turmoil outside the hotel. 'I heard about that. At the wedding – right? Down at Storrs? So – somebody's bumping off the whole family, one by one? And you—' He gave her a careful look. 'Why's he seeing you, then? Have you been carrying on with him?'

'*Carrying on?*' she echoed sarcastically.

He flushed. 'That's what my mum calls it. You know what I mean.'

'Sorry. No, I haven't. I only met him yesterday.'

Ben nibbled the edge of a thumbnail. 'You were at the wedding, then?'

'Sort of. I did the flowers.'

'Right. My brother works at Storrs – in the kitchen. He wants to be a chef.'

'Was he there yesterday?' The host of shadowy personnel working invisibly in a hotel nudged at her thoughts. In theory, any of them might have murdered poor Markie. Ben and his brother would now feature in the police investigation, the fact of their relationship flagged as potentially significant – or so she supposed. A sense of menace descended on her, with this second death.

'No,' said Ben, shattering her assumptions. 'He's got glandular fever. Signed off for three weeks. His throat is awesome – covered in pus. He spits it up. Disgusting!'

'They're here,' she said, seeing a police car draw up opposite the hotel. 'At last.'

'Quick, really,' he argued. 'Ten minutes, give or take.'

'Is that all?'

'What do we do, then?' He looked at her pleadingly, almost plucking at her sleeve in his anxiety. 'You'll tell them, won't you – that I was just . . . you know.'

'I'm sure you can trust them to understand. I have a feeling you'll need somebody with you before they ask any questions. A parent, probably.'

'Fuck that!' he flashed. 'I don't need a nursemaid.'

She recoiled instinctively at the language, before reproaching herself. She even used it herself at moments of high stress.

'Sorry,' he said, noting her reaction.

'I might have got it wrong, anyway. I don't know anything about how the police operate. I saw a detective chap yesterday who seemed more or less human. It'll be him again, most likely.' Until that moment she had forgotten DI Moxon and his gentle questions. The prospect of seeing him again warmed her briefly, before an inner voice impishly mooted the possibility of this new motive for murder. A variation on stalking – murdering members of a family one by one simply to gain access to an attractive detective.

'Come on, then,' he said. 'Let's go and get it over. I want my dinner.'

# Chapter Eight

It was a further twenty minutes before Moxon himself put in an appearance. Simmy and Ben had been taken into the hotel and asked to wait. Somebody brought them cups of coffee. Ben phoned his mother and tried to make light of the experience of seeing a man killed in a quiet Sunday street. Simmy refrained from calling her own mother, who would not be missing her. Plenty of time for that, she thought ruefully.

'They'll be taking him away, then,' said Ben. 'Can't leave a body out there, can they?'

'Bad for business,' she smiled. 'But I have a feeling there's a whole lot of stuff to do before they can move him. Don't you watch police dramas on telly?'

He shook his head and then shrugged. 'I like *Bones*. But it's not on any more. Never bothered with any of the other stuff. Don't watch the box much, anyway.'

'Nor me. Never heard of *Bones*, to be honest.'

'American. Gory stuff. Maggots. The girl in it is a sort of geek, but pretty.' He smiled absently. 'They call her Bones.'

'What sort of gun do you think it was?'

'No idea. I've never even seen a gun.'

'Nor me. They shoot animals around here, though, I imagine. Foxes and things. Pheasants.'

'Squirrels. Rabbits.'

She winced. 'Poor little things. But those are just shotguns, aren't they? Would they kill a person?'

His shoulders lifted. 'Dunno.'

'Does this feel as unreal to you as it does to me?' she burst out. 'It's like a dream. There's no proper sense to it.'

The door opened as she uttered these words, and Moxon rushed in like a furious headmaster, followed by a younger man. Ben threw a panicked look at Simmy. She was focused entirely on the DI's features, which were shockingly changed from the day before. There were grey shadows under his eyes and grooves around his mouth. His hair looked greasy. His emotions seemed to be barely under control. She wondered briefly why she had ever thought she liked him.

He looked from one to the other and back again. 'You two know each other?' he barked.

They both shook their heads. 'But we both heard and saw what happened,' Simmy said hesitantly. 'This is Ben. He's seventeen.' She thought of adding that it was his birthday, but something about the maleness in the room restrained her. The boy wouldn't thank her, and the detective wouldn't be interested.

'I need to talk to you separately. Ms Brown – you were meeting Mr Baxter here for lunch – is that right?'

She nodded. 'And Peter Harrison-West. But he doesn't seem to be here.'

The detective gave his own forehead a light tap with a

forefinger, as if physically inserting an idea or mental note. 'All right. I'll talk to you first. Ben . . .' Moxon consulted a piece of paper in his hand '. . . Harkness. Seventeen? Leave us your address and we'll come and talk to you at home. Okay? It won't be a big deal, don't worry.' The man's voice was softening as he addressed the boy. 'Unless you saw the person with the firearm, and I'm guessing you'd have told somebody already if that was the case?'

'What? I can go, then?'

'That's right. After you've given the policeman outside your address. He's the one with the computer thingy. You can't miss him.'

Ben got up to leave. 'I didn't see anybody with a gun,' he said, with a hint of reproach. 'I saw a man with a hole in his head.'

'Happy Birthday, Ben,' Simmy threw after him, in a vague effort to restore normality.

He looked back at her, with a grim smile. 'Thanks,' he said.

'It's his birthday?' Moxon asked, when Ben had gone.

'His mum's doing a special roast. He phoned her to explain where he was. He's a nice decent boy.'

Moxon's brows lifted. 'I never said he wasn't.'

'I never said you did.'

His face relaxed somewhat, reminding her that they already had a connection, that she had disclosed her personal tragedy to him, and felt safe in doing so. What she had initially taken as anger against her and Ben was redefined as acute pressure brought about by two murders in as many days.

'So – you've progressed from wedding florist to lunch

113

companion since I last saw you,' he said. 'How did that happen?'

'I was dragooned into minding the bride's little sister, yesterday afternoon, and it sort of developed from there,' she summarised.

'Developed how?'

'Well, I was asked to Eleanor Baxter's house, so they could talk to me about Markie, but that never really got going, so Mr Baxter invited me to try again today, over lunch.'

'Did you talk to him at all?'

'Oh yes. For quite a while, actually. He thought his son was murdered by one of the wedding party. One of Peter's cronies, he said. Then he talked about insurance.' She frowned. 'I can't remember it properly now. It sounded like a sort of scam – insuring Markie twice over. At least . . . sort of gambling on him dying, it sounded like.' She heard her own garbled words and stopped.

'You expected Mr Harrison-West to be here today? Is that right?'

'Yes. I didn't quite understand why, though. I imagine Mr Baxter needed moral support or something. And his wife – sorry, *ex*-wife – is busy with Lucy.'

'So why exactly do you think he wanted to see you again today?'

She sighed. 'I've been thinking about that all morning. I can only guess that he wanted me to describe how Markie was when I talked to him. I can understand that, can't you? A final picture to carry with him. It makes me think again about the whole business of witnessing something. It's quite a complicated thing, isn't it? Quite profound.'

'The Quakers use it to describe what they do when someone stands up to speak in a Meeting,' he said. 'It means something rather different from the police definition, though.'

'Police witnesses are always unreliable, I guess.'

'Sadly so, I'm afraid. The human memory is a frustrating thing. But we've got to give it our best go. Let's get down to it. Did you see a man with a gun anywhere?'

'No. I *did* see a man, but there wasn't a gun – unless he had it in his pocket. I don't think it could have been him.'

'Could you tell where the shot came from?'

'No idea at all. I never dreamt it *was* a shot, until he collapsed. Even then, it took me a while. I'm not going to be of any use to you,' she concluded, with a sigh. 'I'm a hopeless witness by any standards.'

'I'm not so sure about that. You'll have picked up a whole lot of background, for a start. More than we can hope to glean from interviews. Without making hard and fast assumptions, we have to start with the theory that the two murders are connected.'

'At the very least,' she agreed.

'But you didn't see anybody this morning who was also at the wedding?'

She patted the arm of her chair with an open palm, in a gesture designed to slow him down. 'I should tell you that I was at Storrs again this morning, taking down some of the wedding decorations.'

'Oh? And did you see anyone you knew?'

'No. It's not important, really, but I wanted to make it clear.'

'All right,' he nodded, looking faintly frustrated. 'So – no gunman visible. No passers-by?'

'Not at that moment, no.' She shivered at the thought of a gunman hiding somewhere close by while she sat in her van brushing her hair. 'There's a big hedge across the road,' she remembered. 'Could he have been behind it?'

He sighed. 'It's possible. He might even have been in the hotel, leaning out of a window. I don't suppose you saw Mr Baxter bending down to tie a shoelace, or anything of that sort?'

'Sorry. He was just standing there, looking round a bit. We hadn't agreed a precise meeting place – inside or out, I mean. I got out of the van as soon as I saw him, and that's when it happened. I thought the noise was something to do with my vehicle, to begin with.'

'So it must have been very close?'

'I don't know. It was just one crack, not very loud. I don't know what guns sound like normally. I always thought they were quite loud.'

'You've never had anything to do with the police before – is that right?'

'Yes, that's right. I'm not sure I've ever even spoken to a policeman until now. Not since I took my cycling proficiency, anyway. That was when I was nine.'

'No officers in the family?'

She laughed. His face tightened, and she wondered if he had taken offence. 'No,' she clarified. 'We tend to avoid institutions as much as we can.'

'I see. Well, the police force is certainly an institution. I can't deny that.'

116

'I'm not trying to be difficult. I'll do whatever you need me to, to help. I still can't believe this is happening. I feel as though I must be dreaming. People don't kill each other in my world. I'm a *florist*, for God's sake.'

'Yes, I was thinking about that. Flowers are associated with the big moments, aren't they? Weddings, funerals, anniversaries, birthdays, new babies. They represent love, recognition, goodwill – that sort of thing? You're at the heart of all those rites of passage. People send flowers when they want to say sorry, as well. Sorry for a loss, as well as sorry for something they've done.'

She stared at him. 'Yes,' she said softly. 'That's more or less right.'

'Good.'

She waited, thinking about his analysis of her work. It had dawned on her quite gradually that she was frequently involved in moments of high emotion. When she had originally had the idea, she had been thinking of flowers as decoration, as statements of a mood, as a means of conveying congratulation. The first time a customer had ordered funeral flowers, she had been alarmed at the tears that came with the choice of message. A young woman, unable to attend the burial of her great-aunt, had actually *cried* as she composed the words to accompany the wreath. Simmy had reacted badly, feeling embarrassed and awkward. It had been her mother who counselled her to be ready for further similar experiences. 'What did you expect?' she had demanded. 'Obviously you'll get cried on.'

Moxon was consulting the notes made by the first officer on the scene. Simmy recognised them, and could even read a few words, despite their being upside down. 'What would you say are your chief skills?' he asked her, exactly as if he were conducting a job interview.

'Pardon? What's that got to do with anything?'

'Humour me, all right?'

'Well . . . um . . . focus, I suppose. Reliability. Organisation. I'm good at design – shape and colour. I'm reasonably decisive, I think.'

'You see the big picture?' he prompted.

She nodded doubtfully.

'Have you ever thought of joining the police?'

She huffed an astonished laugh. 'God, no. My mother would kill me.'

'She thinks we're the bad guys?'

'She was a hippy in the seventies. I grew up on lentils and there were no chairs in the house. She took me to Greenham Common six times.'

'I see. At least, I'm not sure I believe you about the chairs.'

'That was an exaggeration,' she admitted.

He leant back in the ornate seat provided by the hotel, and stretched his arms over his head. He appeared to have become considerably more relaxed over the last five minutes. She watched his long head tilt back, thinking he might improve his appearance if he let his hair grow a bit. It was fine and black and slightly greasy. His eyebrows were shapely, over deep-set brown eyes. She could not begin to imagine his ordinary daily routines; the things he had to confront, the people he had to deal with. 'I can hardly think of a more terrible job,' she said.

'It suits me,' he returned equably. 'So I take it you don't think Ben Harkness killed the Baxter man?'

'Of course he didn't.'

'No. He has nothing whatever to do with anything.'

'I'm glad you agree.'

'Now . . .' he brought his hands forward, clasped in a double fist, 'let's get serious. Two men are dead. What's going on? Who benefits? Why kill *both* of them? Any thoughts?'

'I have no idea, other than it has something to do with insurance. If that makes any kind of sense. But I don't know these people. They're rich, well connected. I don't move in the same circles as them – not by a million miles.'

'But they took to you, didn't they? Took you to their bosoms, in fact.'

'Only two of them. I don't know the two who got married – Bridget and Peter. I've never even *spoken* to Peter.' She was reminded then of a persistent impression at the back of her mind, a shadowy space where a missing man should be. 'And anyway – where *is* he? He was supposed to be here. That's quite odd, isn't it? You'll need to ask him about it.' Then she gave herself a small reproachful shake. 'Not that it's for me to tell you what to do. But it *must* have something to do with business deals, or legacies or something, if it isn't the insurance. Money. It's sure to be about money.'

She was speaking loudly, defiantly, trying to drown out the little voices inside her head that whispered about Markie and his nervous manner, the father in his grief, the little girl Lucy, and the chillingly confident Eleanor.

'You think so, do you?'

'I don't know. I've wandered into a nightmare and all I want is to get back to work tomorrow and forget the whole thing.'

119

'Really? Don't you want to help?'

She paused. 'I would if I could . . . I suppose. What did you have in mind?'

He puffed out his cheeks, and she wondered whether she was expected to show more deference towards him. The exact protocols involved had never formed part of her education, and the strange intimacy of the situation did nothing to make her feel subservient to him. 'Seems as if this is a new experience for us both,' he said.

'Haven't you investigated a murder before?' She blinked incredulously.

'Of course I have. But I haven't had a witness like you before. Not that I can recall, in any event.'

'Oh?'

'You seem completely unemotional about it. You're not scared or angry or upset or impatient.'

'I am quite impatient, actually. And I'm hungry. And shocked. I'm *very* shocked.'

'Are you? It doesn't show.'

'I'm numb. Paralysed. Why aren't you asking me some proper questions? I can't see where this is getting us. I really would like to leave, if that's all right.'

'Your car is outside, is it?'

'I told you – it's the shop van – I was in it just before Mr Baxter was shot.'

'On your own?'

'Of course.'

'And you feel all right to drive?'

She sighed. 'Completely.'

Still neither of them moved. The man was so totally

unlike any police detective she had seen on TV that she found herself with no means of assessing him. He was in no way attractive physically, apart from the steady brown eyes and understanding manner. He seemed intelligent, confident, authoritative, but also vulnerable to stress. She could imagine him manifesting bad temper – shouting at underlings, grabbing young offenders by their clothes – but not losing control of his own emotions. This man would not weep for a murder victim, or a child crushed on a motorway, she concluded. He would get angry and super-efficient.

'How come you've got so much time for me?' she asked. 'Shouldn't you be out there finding the murderer?'

'I think he'll have gone by now.'

It was a joke, a deadpan let's-see-how-long-before-you-get-it joke. She laughed with genuine merriment, before stopping abruptly, with a sense that it was wrong, when a man had just been killed.

'But you're right, of course,' he added. 'I'm telling myself that you are the prime witness, so far; that you have more to tell me than you might realise and that there has to be a way I can harness your usefulness.'

'Oh.' She shrank from him slightly. 'I don't think I like the sound of that very much.'

'Pity,' he smiled. 'But at least it's nice to know I can make you laugh.'

'But we shouldn't. Oh, God – that poor girl, the morning after her wedding. As if yesterday wasn't bad enough. Her brother *and* her father, both killed. It's an absolute nightmare for her. Has somebody gone to tell her? And the wife?'

'You know about his wife?'

'Only what they told me last night. Everything seems very amicable between all his women. Eleanor, Markie's mother, and this new one. I suppose there might have been others, along the way, as well. It's another world, isn't it?'

'Is it?'

'It is for me. My parents have been married for forty-three years. I don't think there's ever been a hint of another person disturbing things for them.'

'But most of us are not so lucky, are we?'

'No,' she said resentfully.

He got up then, and with a little flourish of his hand indicated that the interview was over. 'Thank you,' he said formally. 'I'm sorry to have taken up so much of your time. I'm afraid I can't promise that this is the end of it. When the forensics people have done their bit, not to mention ballistics as well, we might need to walk you through it. You *and* young Ben, probably. Funny that there was nobody else about. The season isn't over yet.'

'I imagine he waited for a quiet moment.'

He looked at her with a new expression, the two of them positioned awkwardly by the door. His look felt rather like respect. 'I imagine he did,' he nodded. 'I hadn't thought of that.'

'Except . . .' she felt momentarily foolish, 'he'd have to seize the moment when Mr Baxter was standing in the right spot, wouldn't he? So it was probably more luck than anything.'

'Mr Baxter didn't see you – is that right?'

'I don't think he did. I was sitting in the van, watching out for him. I should have been standing by the hotel entrance,

I know. It was just . . . I would have felt conspicuous. If I'd been there, he might still be alive.' It was the first time she had allowed herself to think events through in any detail, and this was certainly the first pang of guilt to strike her.

'Don't get into that,' he advised, opening the door for her. 'It's unprofitable, to say the least.'

'But . . . his family. They'll blame me, won't they?'

'I doubt it. There's a difference between being involved and being to blame.'

'Yes. Involved,' she repeated thoughtfully. 'I suppose that's what I am. And yet I never met any of these people before. They don't care about me – even the ones who know my name. Most of them have no idea who I am.'

'They will soon,' he said heavily. 'I'm surprised your ears aren't burning already. One more thing, before you go. I'd appreciate it if you didn't mention the gun to anybody. I know there are plenty of people around who'll spread the story, but we prefer to keep details quiet, as far as possible.'

They parted in the hotel's hallway, Moxon giving her his card and promising they would meet again.

'Involved,' she murmured to herself, as she started her car. Should she be afraid, excited, angry – or what? Suddenly she wanted her father, and his calm, old-fashioned take on things. She wanted to hold him close, because hadn't she just learnt that fathers could be killed, leaving a gaping hole in the lives of their children?

# Chapter Nine

Ben's mother met him on the doorstep with an expression of blank bewilderment. 'I thought you were just going round to see Jack,' she said. 'The meat's gone all dry now.' She looked around him. 'Are you by yourself?'

'Yeah, but they're coming to question me in a bit. I have to have you or Dad with me. I *was* just going to see Jack. I did go to see him, and was coming home. I was passing the Old England when this bloke was shot. Coincidence.'

'But he might have shot *you*,' she wailed. 'How close were you?'

'I don't know. Not very. I heard the shot and saw the man fall. That's it. End of.'

'It's not, though, is it? Wasn't there anybody else there?'

'A woman. She's a florist. She knows the man. She's cool.'

'Well, come and have your lunch. I've tried to keep it nice for you.'

'Did you go ahead without me?'

'Ben – it's half past two. They were hungry.'

'Half two? It can't be.' He stared at her.

'Well it is. You're in shock, love. Time does funny things. But listen – I've got a project I absolutely have to get finished. And Dad's got a mountain of marking, as usual. Do you think Wilf would count as a responsible adult, or whatever it is they need? He's nearly twenty. Would you mind?'

He sifted the churning emotions that this gave rise to: disappointment, abandonment, relief, resignation. 'No, that'll be fine, I guess. They already know I haven't got much to tell them. It probably won't take long.'

'So, have your lunch, and this evening we'll do the birthday stuff. What did Jack give you?'

'Computer game,' he shrugged as if it was obvious.

His brother Wilf emerged from the big square room at the back of the house that they called 'the playroom'. He was gaunt from his inability to swallow for over a week, and the sporadic aches and pains his illness had caused. The worst was over, apart from a constricted throat, and he was intending to return to work in another day or so. 'What's all this then?' he asked. 'Got yourself involved in a shooting? Doesn't look as if you were damaged.'

'Wilf – the police are going to be here soon, to interview him. Will you sit in with him? I've got that Gibson job. It's already late, and if I don't—'

'Okay, I get it,' he interrupted. 'We were lucky to see you at all today.'

'Not at all. It's Ben's birthday. That takes precedence. It's just—' she forced an anguished grin and spread her hands.

The brothers looked at each other with exaggeratedly raised eyebrows. For as long as they could remember, their mother had been distracted by the demands of her work –

most of which she did at home. She boasted to her friends that she was a stay-at-home mother – no childminders or day nurseries for *her* offspring. In reality, she left them to watch out for each other and disappeared for the greater part of every day into the converted attic, where her architect's business was conducted, doing remarkably well as it happened.

'Good old Gibson, I say,' croaked Wilf. 'If he pays for a car for me, I'll gladly do all I can to make it easy for you.'

'It's not the car – it's the damned insurance,' said his mother.

Ben heard the conversation as if through ear mufflers. Something was happening in his head, a sort of aural fog that made him think he might be ill. 'Um     ' he said, 'Can I go and sit somewhere?'

'Good God, the boy's going to faint,' said Wilf. 'Quick!'

'They shouldn't have let him come home by himself,' tutted their mother, as they took him between them into the dining room. 'It was irresponsible.'

'Where exactly did this happen?' Wilf asked.

'Outside the Old England, apparently.'

'Five minutes' walk, then. They probably thought he could manage that.'

'I *did* manage it,' protested Ben. 'I'm all right again now. It was just a thing . . . I might be hungry, actually.'

'Did you have any breakfast?'

He shook his head.

'Anything at Jack's?'

'Cup of tea.'

Briskly, she sat him down at the big table and fetched a

plate of roast pork and all the trimmings from the kitchen. 'Eat,' she ordered, and he obeyed with ready enthusiasm. Wilf picked at some crackling, chewing it thoroughly and forcing it down his sore throat. 'It's definitely better,' he reported.

The brothers, left on their own, were both unsure of what to say to each other. Ben wanted to tell his story and Wilf wanted to hear it, but the knowledge that a police interview was pending seemed to constrain them. It was too large an event to gossip over, and without their mother they were hesitant to start something that could lead into darker waters than they felt equal to. 'What was the computer game?' Wilf asked.

For answer, Ben pulled it from his pocket with an ironic grin. 'Just what I need if I'm to be a police witness,' he said. 'It's all about catching crims using forensics.'

Wilf laughed. 'That gunman should have waited till you were out of the way. You'll not rest till they've caught him, if I know you. Right up your street.'

'It never occurred to me until now. The real thing's a bit different. Nothing like a game. A woman screamed, real screaming. They threw a rug over him.'

'*Him*? Not *her*?'

Ben giggled. But despite the light moment, he could see that Wilf's imagination was incapable of sharing the experience. Always a prosaic character, his ambitions as a chef lay in technique rather than creativity. Other people could construct the menu – his skill lay in the mixing and searing, knowing the precise moment to turn down the heat, and always producing impeccable sauces and gravies without a hint of a lump. Wilf's mashed potato had been legendary since he was fourteen.

The police arrived five minutes later, and were formally escorted into the living room, where a young sibling had to be ejected from watching TV. It was not DI Moxon, but a detective sergeant and female constable. They gave Wilf a dubious examination, having been instructed to ensure a responsible parent was present.

'I'm an adult. They're both busy, I'm afraid,' Wilf explained.

'Are they here in the house?'

'Upstairs,' he nodded.

'Well, then, we must have one of them in here,' said the sergeant firmly. 'This is important.'

Ben groaned quietly. 'Can't we just get on with it?' he pleaded. 'I never saw anything that'll help, anyway. I've said it all already, when it first happened. This is a bit silly, if you ask me.'

The sergeant bristled alarmingly. He was in his late twenties, recently promoted, Ben suspected, and terrified of getting something wrong. With his natural inclination to imagine himself into the other person's shoes, Ben understood that here was a man who would make any simple thing as complicated as he possibly could. He would talk in jargon and dwell on small irrelevancies. 'Silly?' he repeated furiously. 'We're investigating a *murder*. *Two* murders, to be exact.'

Wilf held his ground. 'My mother asked me to sit with Ben. I promise you, I'm quite capable of doing the job. Unless you propose to charge him with homicide, I really do think I can cope.'

'He'll be fine, Keith,' said the constable patiently. 'Let's get on with it.'

Sergeant Keith reluctantly subsided, a tape recorder was produced, and questions posed. Ben described the scene in as much detail as he could, but was unable to indicate a direction for the gunshot. 'It just sort of echoed around the streets,' he said helplessly. 'It wasn't very loud.'

'And were there any other people at all in sight?'

'Not one. It's usually quiet down there, anyway.'

'What about the woman in the van? Mrs Brown?'

'I didn't see her until afterwards.'

'Do you go there regularly?'

'Not really. My mate Jack lives just along the street from the hotel. I go and see him sometimes.'

'And did you know the deceased? Mr George Baxter?'

'Not at all. Never heard of him. At least – not before yesterday. I heard what happened at the wedding, last night on the news.'

The questions rambled on, and Ben was careful to stay focused. He had no intention of offering any guesses or assumptions. But it struck him that it was a very inefficient interview; a real waste of time. The man had been shot. Somewhere there would be traces left by the firing of the gun, the gun itself. They should be concentrating on angles and distances and searching every building that overlooked the front of the Old England Hotel. Asking repetitive questions of a passer-by was ridiculous. But it cost him nothing, and at the end left him feeling superior, excited and purposeful. He was *involved*, the same as the florist lady was.

And lurking on the very edge of his memory was

something wordless and mysterious that he could not recapture. There had been a *sense*, a peculiar silence, in the second before the gunshot. He had been thinking about his new game, and the three episodes of *Bones* he had watched back-to-back last night, so that when a man was killed right in front of him, it had taken a while for him to grasp that this was actually happening, in real time. The same thing that people said about the Twin Towers collapsing. You assumed, at first, that you were in a movie. But had he somehow seen something, without knowing what it was, just before the gun was fired? He thought his head had been up, his gaze directed in a roughly easterly direction, away from the lake. He could remember seeing buildings, trees, overhead wires – nothing the least bit unusual. No flash of sunlight on gunmetal; no warning click as the safety catch was released. Had there been a pair of eyes on him, calculating that he was no threat, still twenty or thirty yards from the target? Almost certainly there had. He had been, by a fluke, the only person on the street at that moment. He had been about to cross over, away from the hotel, up the slope to his home in Helm Road. He had already checked for traffic, despite the absence of any engine noise. And perhaps he had seen something then? He *should* have seen something. He wished he had, so that now he could be a proper witness. But he hadn't. Whatever sly little atom of perception might have entered his head, it was too faint a trace ever to be recovered.

At much the same time as Ben was being questioned, Simmy was explaining the day's events to her parents, as concisely as she could. They had heard nothing about it, secure in their own preoccupations, nearly a mile away. A new booking had been telephoned through, and Angie was bustling about with pillowcases and checking her stock of fresh breakfast eggs. 'Four of them – two couples,' she said. 'They want to stay three nights.'

When Simmy managed to tell her story, Angie and Russell were both silenced. They exchanged looks of concern, frozen in place as the implications slowly became evident. 'Those poor people,' Simmy's father managed, after a minute or so. 'It's beyond imagining what they must be feeling.'

'Somebody murdered the boy and his father?' Angie repeated. 'Why in the world would they? And you *talked* to them both,' she accused Simmy.

'I'm involved,' she said. 'No getting away from it.'

And in confirmation, there came a knocking on the door that brooked no denial. Angie went to answer it, coming back with Eleanor Baxter at her shoulder. 'She wants you,' she told her daughter.

'You've got to come,' Eleanor ordered Simmy. 'Now. They all want to talk to you.'

'Who?'

'Bridget. Peter. Glenn. All of them. They're still at Storrs until tomorrow morning. They want to get to the bottom of what's going on, and they think you might be able to help.'

'I can't. How can I?' She was pleading, first with Eleanor, and then with her father, who was standing in the kitchen doorway holding the Sunday paper.

'I don't know. They want to meet you, anyway. After last night, you see. I told them you were at my place last night, and you were seeing George again today.'

'You can understand it, pet,' said her father.

Simmy shook her head. 'Not really. I can't *tell* them anything. I have no idea what's going on.'

'You might, though – without realising it,' Eleanor insisted. Her eyes were tragic, her skin blotchy with no make-up.

'Where's Lucy?' asked Simmy, instinctively. The little girl was the only member of this ramshackle family she could truly say she cared about.

'Never mind Lucy. Please come with me. We'd all appreciate it.'

'Did you get any lunch?' Angie put in.

'What?' Simmy looked at the clock on the hall wall. It said ten past three. 'No, just a cup of coffee. It doesn't matter.'

'We can have sandwiches or something at Storrs,' said Eleanor impatiently. 'Not that anybody's likely to feel much like eating.' The bags under her eyes seem to sag even further. 'Somebody killed *George*!' she burst out. 'How is that possible?'

'I don't know,' said Simmy helplessly. 'I really do not know.'

She went with Eleanor because to resist would have taken more energy than she possessed. She was still numb, her mental processes sluggish. The prospect of a large group of Baxters and others, all questioning her and trying to discover the special knowledge they seemed to think she carried, was daunting. They might be suspicious of her, since she had been so close to George when he died. They might shout and threaten. Even Eleanor might well feel no desire to protect her. She shrank into the car seat and let herself be carried along. She supposed she should be impressed by the woman at her side, and her ability to function so soon after hearing what had happened to her one-time husband.

'Poor Bridget,' Eleanor muttered. 'She's the one who's lost the most. I don't know whether she'll ever properly get over it. She's only eighteen, poor girl.'

Simmy said nothing, knowing that *getting over it* was a forlorn hope for most people finding themselves suddenly bereaved of someone they had taken for granted. Like her own baby, she thought with a sick pang.

The road down to the hotel was dappled with golden afternoon light, glimpses of the lake the same consoling little treat they always were.

'Don't you love the lake?' Simmy sighed without self-consciousness. 'I never stop thinking it's a special privilege to have a lake on my doorstep.'

'I know what you mean,' said Eleanor, as if she really did.

Storrs Hall lay ahead, and Simmy's chest began to feel tight. She had been entertaining increasingly dark thoughts about Peter, the bridegroom – and he was most likely to be in charge of the coming encounter. Her ambivalent role in the family catastrophe would make it impossible to establish a comfortable tone. Eleanor headed down the main drive with barely any change of speed, with no sign of nerves or hesitation.

'The hotel must be very shaken up,' said Simmy. 'After yesterday.'

'They'll wish they'd never heard of the Baxters or the Harrison-Wests. They'll be cursing the day they ever thought of having weddings here. They'll be counting the minutes until we all go away. But everybody's staying on another night, I think. That was the plan.'

Simmy thought of the brother of Ben Harkness, her fellow witness of that morning. The hotel was connected in more ways than it realised. *Involved*, came the word again. It conjured a bigger tangle than 'connected' did, something sticky and persistent. And very slightly culpable.

'They won't think I did it, will they?' she said, aiming for a jokey note.

'What – murdered Markie *and* George? I don't suppose so. Why – you didn't, did you?'

Young Ben's face floated before her eyes – asking whether the police might suspect him of shooting Baxter. 'Everybody feels irrational guilt at a time like this, apparently. It's such an enormous crime – such a dreadful thing to do – that we all feel we must have contributed to it somehow. Isn't that it? As if it's too much for one person to have done on his own.'

Eleanor pulled the handbrake violently, making the car lurch reproachfully. 'I disagree,' she snapped. 'There's only one guilty party in all this.'

Simmy stared at her. 'You sound as if you know who it is.'

Eleanor rolled her eyes. 'If I did, I'd have torn his arms off by now.' It was an imaginative revenge, which Simmy could all too horribly visualise. 'Come on, then. Let's get on with it.'

Four men and one young woman were assembled in a room overlooking the lake, in which half a dozen tables were laid as if for dinner. The people mostly occupied two dark-brown leather sofas placed at right angles to each other at one end of the room. 'Why have they put us in here?' asked Eleanor.

'Why not?' said one of the men crossly.

'It's handy for Felix,' said Bridget. The man in the wheelchair was positioned close to the end of one sofa. He was pale and ill-looking.

'Well, we're here now, anyway. This is Miss Brown. These are Peter, Glenn, Pablo and Felix,' she pointed them out in turn to Simmy. 'And Bridget, of course.'

The bride was also pale and solemn, sitting huddled between her husband and his best man. The wedding roles still clung to them, in Simmy's mind, despite the casual clothes and cheerless faces.

'Hello,' said Simmy. 'I'm so sorry for what's happened. It's absolutely terrible.' She looked from one to the next, hoping for some manifestation of warmth. But instead there was a collective gaze of mistrustful enquiry. Polite, yes, but very far from friendly.

'Gosh, this is worse than a job interview,' she said, in an effort to lighten things. 'I'm really not at all sure I'll be able to give you the right answers, though.'

'You witnessed Daddy's murder today. Is that right?' Bridget seemed even younger than her eighteen years, speaking up like a brave child.

For the first time, Simmy wondered how much the police had told the family about her. It struck her as rather questionable behaviour of them to mention her at all. She tried to think logically, to assemble all the information she had available to her. Hadn't Moxon asked her something about being able to see the big picture?

'I didn't really witness anything,' she corrected Bridget. 'Is that what the police told you?'

Eleanor made a small sound, drawing attention from the whole assembly. 'It wasn't the police,' she said. 'They just sent a couple of women to tell me George was dead. They didn't say how. They got his wife's contact details from me. I went down to the Old England, where it happened, and the manager said you had been there. Apparently he knows you.'

Simmy frowned. 'No, he doesn't.'

Eleanor nodded emphatically. 'He's been to your shop. He recognised you right away. And of course I knew you were having lunch with George. It's all quite straightforward.'

'The police didn't mention me?' It seemed an important detail.

'Of course not. They never tell anybody anything. Surely you know that?'

'Not really. I'm not sure I've ever spoken to a police detective before.' She remembered Moxon telling her how Markie had died, and wondered whether she had been favoured with special information.

'You saw Markie yesterday,' put in Peter, the bridegroom. 'He spoke to you. Glenn and the others saw you.' He looked at the other men, who nodded confirmation.

'He did,' Simmy agreed. 'I was appalled when I heard what had happened to him.'

'So were we all,' said Peter Harrison-West brusquely. Simmy began to think she disliked him, which in turn made her fearful for his new bride.

Boldly she faced him. 'Where were you today, anyway? I thought you wanted to talk to me, with Mr Baxter. That's what he told me. You were *both* going to have lunch with me.'

'What?' He blinked blankly at her. 'I have no idea what you're talking about.' He turned first to Glenn, then to Bridget. 'What does she mean?' he asked helplessly.

Bridget merely widened her eyes powerlessly, but Glenn reached out and patted his friend's hand. 'Must have been some idea the old man got hold of,' he said reassuringly. 'Maybe he couldn't find you. You did go off, remember?'

Peter's jaw tightened. 'I didn't *go off*. I've been here all bloody day, doing nothing.'

'Let's get back to Markie,' pleaded Bridget, looking hard at Simmy. 'How did he seem? I never saw him, you see. I hadn't seen him for weeks. And there we were, getting married, while he was cold and dead in the lake.' Her face crumpled into sudden sobs. 'Poor Markie. How am I going to get on without him? How could anybody possibly kill *Markie*?'

'Come on, Briddy. You've got Peter now.' The consolation came from Glenn, who threw a complicated look at his best friend over Bridget's head. The girl had leant her wet face into the best man's shoulder, while he patted her.

'It was gruesome timing, though. You have to admit that.' Pablo, the black-eyed Spaniard, spoke perfect English, and appeared to have a saturnine outlook to rival Peter's.

Simmy had begun an attempt to answer Bridget's question, before realising that nobody actually expected her to say anything. The precise reasons for summoning her were no clearer than they had been at the start. Perhaps they wanted to look at her, as if she might come trailing fragments of the two dead men, messages from beyond. Or did one of them have a nagging fear that she knew something that would incriminate him? Struggling to maintain a hold on the bigger picture, she entertained a theory that one of the people in this room, eyeing her with such severity, was a double murderer. There were other candidates, of course: Lucy's father and other relatives; various shadowy business associates; hotel staff – there might be hidden reasons for any of them to eradicate the two Baxter men. There was even an obvious theory that Baxter had killed his son, and then been avenged by one of the others. But here was the group that she had seen around Markie, with the addition of Bridget and Eleanor. Here were the men who had means and opportunity to kill the boy and drop his body into the lake before going to change into their smart wedding clothes and behave quite normally for the next hour or so.

*The men* repeated in her head. Had they hatched a ghastly plan between them, for some appalling motive and slaughtered Markie collectively? Even Felix might have played a part. And then the same again that morning, gathering inside one of the buildings near the hotel and firing from a window . . . she saw it like a sort of western film, the men jostling each other, egging each other on, the long-barrelled gun pointing unnoticed out of the window.

But why call Persimmon Brown to stand before them, in that case? To demonstrate their innocent concern to Bridget perhaps?

She thought of DI Moxon and his likely reactions to this particular Star Chamber. He would want to observe the dynamics between all the players: any body language suggesting guilt or anxiety; revealing snippets of information. Like it or not, she was at least partly his representative here.

He would have no such opportunity, even if he arranged a similar gathering. People behaved very differently when a police detective was in the room. Or so she supposed.

She wasn't standing, of course. Eleanor had positioned the two of them at a table facing the sofas. Pablo, next to Peter, rested languidly over the leather arm beside him, with Felix a few inches away. They made a pair, in some odd way she could not at first characterise. As Pablo spoke, Felix turned to him, watching his lips. He repeated, 'You have to admit,' softly, to nobody in particular. Then he said 'admit' again, as if tasting the word.

'What?' Glenn leant forward to peer past Pablo at the man in the wheelchair.

Felix snorted. 'Language,' he explained. 'The words people use at such a time. It's worth taking notice. Pablo said "admit". It's close to "confess", you see. And "confession" is what's needed. Somebody to admit they did these killings.'

'Shut up,' said Glenn in disgust. 'You're talking gibberish.'

'Oh, Glenn!' Bridget reproached. 'Don't be so nasty.'

'I can take it,' said Felix robustly. 'Don't worry about me.'

'Nobody was,' said Peter. 'We all know better than that.'

'Boys!' urged Eleanor, rather belatedly. 'Don't start arguing over nothing.'

They weren't boys, though, Simmy noted. Felix was probably the youngest, in his mid thirties. Glenn and Peter were both some years older than that, with Pablo apparently somewhere in between. Bridget was like a freshly cut lily amongst a clump of drying twigs. Or bullrushes, as Simmy had visualised them the day before. Bridget was the baby Moses in the thicket of brown reeds, given up by her terrified mother . . . Shaking herself, Simmy returned to her observations of what was there before her. Bridget was not conventionally pretty, except in the way that all eighteen-year-old girls were. Clear skin, glossy hair, crisp jawline and flawless neck. All the attributes that a woman almost forty ceased to take for granted.

How *brave* she must be, though, to enter into such a marriage. The two men either side of her were solid, powerful, settled. They might crush her slim body between them, without ever intending any harm. They would surely crush her spiritually, simply by forgetting how it was to be so young. Or perhaps they would form an impregnable wall of protection around her. Perhaps now she had no father or brother to fight for her, she could simply replace them with Peter and his friends.

Pablo, apparently irrepressible, stuck to his original point. 'Markie was out there with us waiting for his dad to turn up. He was in a perfectly good mood, joking about the rain. Then the old man drove right past us, ignoring us, and Markie just stood there staring after him. Later on, when we discovered what had happened, Baxter was beside himself, full of self-reproach, because the boy had died before he could speak to him. Am I right?'

'As far as it goes,' nodded Glenn. 'What's your point?'

'Poor Daddy!' mourned Bridget. 'He never meant to be nasty to Markie. He was late and wanted to come and talk to me before everything got going. He didn't want to get his clothes wet, that's all. He had no idea that Markie was waiting out there for him. He just saw a gaggle of men under big umbrellas and thought nothing of it.'

'That's what he told me,' confirmed Eleanor. 'It was silly of Markie to wait out in the rain like that.'

'But he wasn't there alone,' contributed Simmy, on the grounds that she could be back at Beck View eating cake with her mother, if they weren't going to ask her any proper questions. 'Why were you all standing out there like that?'

'Pablo wanted a smoke,' said Glenn. 'That's why we went out in the first place. And we got chatting, and watching the light on the lake, and arguing about some daft thing Felix said. Then we went in again,' he finished simply.

'Without Markie.' Bridget's tone held a flat fatalistic accusation. 'You left him out there to die.'

'We left him, and he died,' Glenn corrected her. 'None of us *knew* that was going to happen, did we? We'd have stayed and watched out for him, otherwise.'

There was pain somewhere in his eyes and his voice, Simmy thought. Glenn-the-best-man was suffering, and Bridget, his friend's new wife, was not slow to detect it.

'It's okay, Glenn,' she said gently. 'Nobody's blaming you.'

'*Blame* him? Glenn? Of course they bloody don't.' Peter's anger flared without warning.

'Sounded to me as if Bridget was reproaching all of us, just now,' said Felix. 'Even me. And it's true, we did leave him. We must have done, since none of us can remember him coming back inside with us. We all just assumed he was there somewhere.'

'And we went ahead with the wedding without him,' wailed Bridget. 'I'll never forgive myself for that. I knew he wasn't there. Everybody did, by then. And none of us had the decency to go and look for him.'

'Except George,' said Eleanor. 'George went out, before you'd got your rings exchanged.'

'Did he?' Peter frowned at her. 'I never knew that.'

'He didn't find him, though. It never occurred to him to look in . . . in the . . . you know.' Her voice faltered. 'Poor Markie. He was such a sweet boy.'

'Can we maybe try to stop saying that?' said Pablo, with a sigh. 'It's no more true of him than of any boy, after all. He was *young*. That's the terrible thing here. We don't have to beatify him to make the loss any greater than it already is. And the waste.' He pushed himself back into the comfort of the sofa, where Glenn could hardly see him.

'Oh, Pablo! You always say the wrong things, don't you?' Bridget chided him lightly, almost flirtatiously. Simmy could almost hear the added phrase *He's from Barcelona*, clamping her lips together against the smile that threatened. She savoured the word 'beatify' without being quite sure of its meaning. The deepening sense of being accidentally admitted into a long-established club made her uncomfortable. This was banter, welling up from a reserve of history and familiarity between the four men, that held only a limited place for women, and even less for girls. It appeared that Markie's death was bad, but not quite bad enough to flatten them. Again, Simmy wondered what Bridget thought she was doing, and whether she was actually in genuine danger. Despite the words and the solemn faces, she was beginning to detect a deficiency of genuine grief over Markie's death. Only Bridget seemed to understand what had been lost, and even she was distracted by her role as a new bride and her sandwiched situation, between Glenn and Peter. Eleanor was somehow fading from view, having delivered Simmy to the lions' den, her task was essentially done. She was sorry about Markie, shocked about George, but she still had her daughters and the mysterious poetical father of the younger one. Eleanor, in fact, had lost nothing.

Simmy had to ask twice before Eleanor pulled herself away from the peculiar interview. Glenn came to her assistance. 'I'll come out with you,' he said. 'My head needs clearing.'

He led the way, holding the door open for the women and looking back at the huddle on the sofa. 'Poor old Peter,' he said softly, when they were in the lobby. 'This has hit him terribly.'

'And Bridget,' said Simmy. 'What an impossible loss for her. She's going to need so much support.' She examined him, with his brutal haircut and impassive features. 'Which it looks as if she's getting,' she added. 'You're all being very solicitous.' The girl's own mother was showing nothing like the same concern, she realised. She hadn't kissed Bridget, either on arriving or leaving.

'We'll look after her,' said Glenn confidently.

'You are good, Glenn,' said Eleanor, formally. 'Where would we all be without you?'

He rolled his eyes amiably, and put a hand on her arm. 'Thanks, Nell. We'll get through it, if we all stick together. They'll catch the swine who did this, sooner or later. All those forensic people gathering invisible clues – they're sure to work it out.'

Outside, Simmy inevitably found herself looking towards the lake, with the police tape and the trampled grass. 'Where, exactly, was he?' she asked.

Glenn scanned the muddy bank beyond the landing stage, and waved an imprecise arm. 'Just over there.'

'And who found him first?'

'George, wasn't it?' Glenn looked to Eleanor for confirmation. 'I'm afraid I was almost last on the scene. I stayed in the hotel with young Lucy when people started shouting.'

'It was George and one of the hotel people,' said Eleanor. 'George went to pieces, ranting and raving. He wasn't making any sense.'

'He was throwing wild accusations about,' agreed Glenn ruefully. 'Not surprising, when you think that Markie was his only son. Anybody would be knocked sideways by a thing like that.'

Simmy remembered Melanie reporting a similar scene. George Baxter had made a great spectacle of himself, evidently. 'Who precisely did he accuse?'

'Everybody, I think. Peter, me, Pablo, the head waiter – the lot.'

'Not the head waiter, actually,' Eleanor corrected him. 'But I think he did include Peter's mother, poor old girl.'

Scrappy ideas flittered through Simmy's head at this elaboration of what had happened. Was it not reasonable to think that one of George's accusations had hit the mark, thereby sealing his own fate?

# *Chapter Ten*

Eleanor took her back to her parents, and drove away without a backward glance.

It was almost five o'clock and the hunger pangs of an hour before turned into a sort of sour nausea.

'Well?' said Angie, with a rare direct look, 'What happened?' She had been making scones and there was flour on her hands as well as down her front. She produced mugs of tea for them both, as an automatic response to Simmy's appearance.

'Nothing much. They weren't really very interested in me. They talked to each other, mostly.'

'Who are "they", exactly?'

'Peter Harrison-West, and his new wife. The best man, Glenn something, and two other men, who were ushers. Pablo and Felix. Felix is in a wheelchair. He fell off a mountain and broke his back. I think they've all been friends for decades. Went to some boarding school together.'

'I know Felix Mainwaring. Or I did. Before the accident, he worked for the council. Something to do with tourism. He was at a couple of meetings we went to. Of course it was in the papers – all very dramatic at the time.'

'Melanie told me about that,' she remembered. 'Surely the council didn't sack him?'

'Presumably not. But I don't think he's working at all now. I expect he's writing a book or something.'

'They were quite peculiar. It felt as if they were giving a performance, somehow.'

'Sounds as if they wanted you to witness them, in some way.'

'What do you mean?'

'Well – you're the main police witness, if I've understood it right. That must be how they think of you. They know they're all regarded as suspects, so they wanted to give you a demonstration of their innocence.'

It chimed uncannily with Simmy's own suspicions, and she raised her eyebrows encouragingly. 'I know it's a bit late,' Angie went on, 'but I wish you hadn't got involved in it all. I wish I'd stopped you going off with that woman last night. I was distracted, otherwise I would have done.'

'I wanted to go.'

'Did you? What in the world for?'

'It was Lucy, I think. Eleanor seemed so careless with her. I wanted to make sure she'd be all right.'

Angie sighed. 'Oh P'simmon, you'll have to let all that go. You can't go through life rescuing every little girl you meet.'

There were buttons that only a mother knew how to press. The tears flowed hot and prickly. Angie took her into a warm floury hug. 'What you need is to get out there and find a new boyfriend,' she murmured.

*Getting out there* was an adjuration Simmy heard regularly. She wasn't sure she knew where was meant or how

146

she should go about doing it. As she had tried to persuade Melanie, she was not conscious of any desire to figure it out. But her mother was doing her best and deserved a response.

'The policeman likes me,' she said, with a choked little laugh.

'Policeman?'

'He's called Moxon. He's CID.'

'Do you like him?'

'He's all right, except for his hair. It's too short and too greasy.'

'Well, he sounds highly unsuitable. Think of somebody else.'

'He said I'd make a good police officer, and I said you'd kill me if I did that.'

'He's right.'

'Anyway, I'd hate it. I like to think the best of people, and I don't suppose you can if you're in the police.'

'Precisely.' They pulled away from each other, and Angie returned to her scones. Simmy put the kettle on for a second mug of tea. 'So what happens now?' asked Angie.

'No idea. I hope they won't want anything else from me. I'm sick of it. Literally. I do feel quite sick.'

'That's because you missed your lunch. You need something hearty. I'll do a fry-up in a little while. Sausages, mushrooms, eggs, bread.'

'And cheese. Can we have fried cheese?'

'You're such a baby,' sighed her mother theatrically. 'And me with all those people due to show up at any moment.'

'And me with a shop to run,' Simmy flashed back, recovering from the weak moments. There was a strict limit on her mother's maternal resources, and it had evidently been reached. 'I'll go now, if you'd rather.'

147

'No, no. You have to eat. Your father's going to expect something. He's been in the shed all afternoon.'

Simmy laughed briefly. *The shed* was in fact a handsome summer house with elaborate fittings, positioned on the very edge of the beck. Russell would take magazines and newspapers out there, and listen to Radio Three. Once in a while he would smoke a pipe. He had a sketch pad and pencils, and sometimes brought a drawing of birds to show his wife. He entered them in the Windermere Summer Show from time to time, and had won a red rosette for a picture of a coal tit, a year before.

'He'll be getting a laptop to keep out there, before you know it – and then you'll have to worry.'

'Why? Do you think he'd get hooked on pornography?'

'Melanie says they all do, sooner or later.'

'Oh well,' shrugged Angie. 'Better later than sooner, I guess. Not so likely to corrupt him at his age. I must admit I don't like what it does to boys.'

'Right.' The association took her straight back to the dead Markie, who had been a boy and might have indulged in computer sex, for all she knew. And from Markie she moved to George Baxter and his daughter.

'I'm going out to talk to him,' she said.

Russell was sitting in a saggy armchair, close to the open doorway, a book upside down in his lap. His eyes were shut. Simmy felt a stab of sheer terror. 'Dad!' she shrilled, far too loud.

He shuddered awake, shock clear on his face. 'What? What's the matter?'

'Sorry. I didn't mean to. You looked . . . for a minute, I thought . . .'

'You thought I was dead?' His eyes widened. 'I was dreaming about an eagle, flying low over a river. I was on its back. It could have been the angel of death in disguise, I suppose.'

'I doubt it. I'm just being hysterical.'

'The Baxter man,' he nodded. 'You did say he was shot, didn't you? Seems hard to believe.'

Simmy nodded. 'I saw the hole in his head.'

'You don't expect gunslingers in Windermere, do you? What's the world coming to?'

'I suppose lots of people shoot pheasants and foxes and things around here. All the gentry must have guns.'

'As I understand it, they're meant to keep them registered and locked away in special cabinets. I'd be surprised if there were rogue guns this side of Manchester.'

'Or Glasgow.'

'Indeed. But that must be very naive of us. Where there's a will there's a way, as they say.' He watched the trickling beck for a moment. 'Only one hole in his head?'

'I think so.'

'Not a shotgun, then. If I remember rightly, they deliver a lot of little missiles. I remember we used to find it in the hares my old dad used to bring home. Little lead balls. It was a bit like finding the things in Christmas pudding. Must have been a pistol, then. Easier to hide, of course.'

'Oh, Dad.' She knelt beside him and nuzzled into his chest. 'It makes me so sad. And scared. Dying shouldn't be so easy. What if somebody shot *you*?'

'That isn't going to happen, is it? Don't be a child, Sim. You have to take the world as it is.'

'That can't be right. What would Mother say to that? She's spent her life trying to change it all.'

'And see where it's got her. Moronic guests suing her because one child pushes another. We're all helpless in the face of that sort of thing.'

Simmy had forgotten about the pushed child. She groaned and slowly detached from his chest. Two parental hugs within ten minutes of each other might actually be too much of a good thing. 'We're having a fry-up. Those people will probably turn up in the middle of it, but never mind. Funny day to arrive – a Sunday.'

'Sundays are no different from other days now.'

'They are for me,' she said stoutly. 'I like the idea of a Sabbath.'

'And you with such a pagan upbringing,' he teased. 'Just goes to show.'

It was a much needed interlude, with her reliable father keeping her anchored. Other people's families might be so dysfunctional as to permit two brutal murders in one weekend, but hers was nowhere near such disintegration. For them, it was nothing worse than a dead baby and moronic B&B guests.

'So what happens now?' asked Angie again, after the early supper and glasses of home-made wine. The guests had arrived, dumped their luggage and gone out again to find food. No matter how importunate they might be, Angie steadfastly refused to provide evening meals. 'That way madness lies,' she said. 'There are plenty of pubs out there.'

'I go home, make a list of this week's orders, watch

mindless telly and go to bed,' said Simmy. 'Same as usual.'

'You think they'll leave you alone now – those Baxters?'

'They've no reason not to. I've told them all I can, which is hardly anything. They weren't even interested, when it came to it.'

'And the police detective chap? What about him?'

Simmy hesitated. 'If they find the killer, I might have to be a witness at his trial. But that won't be for ages, if ever.'

'You think they might not catch him?' said her father. The concern on his face startled her. 'A madman out there with a gun, knowing you're a chief witness. I don't like the thought of that, Sim. That's going to keep me awake. Tell that detective he has to do his job. I insist on it.'

'I think he'll do his best, Dad. He seems quite conscientious.'

'And you didn't see anything, anyway, did you?' added Angie. 'So you're no threat to him, whoever he is.'

'That's right,' said Simmy with an emphasis that concealed a new line of thought. Almost all the talk had been about Markie, when she had been taken to see the people at Storrs. Nobody had asked her a thing about Baxter. And yet she had been much closer to the action the second time. With Markie, she had witnessed nothing but his apparent state of anxiety; with George she had seen him fall. She had been the reason he was there on the pavement in the first place. Why hadn't they been more curious to know how he died?

Because, she concluded, nobody but Bridget cared about him. Peter had lost a father-in-law, a man he had known for most of his life, even if he might not have particularly warm feelings for him. The others, presumably, were even less attached. Markie was their friend, even their mascot. The youngster who liked to hang out with the older men, admiring their maturity and worldly wisdom. And they had failed to keep him safe. One of them might even have been his killer.

And if that was true, was it not reasonable to think the same person killed George Baxter?

She went home just as it was getting dark. Her father's uncharacteristic worries about her safety had to be resisted and she kept them firmly under control. It would be only too easy to believe in a lurking gunman, his weapon trained on her bedroom window or front door. Her nearest neighbour was within easy shouting distance, and any stranger seen hanging about would be challenged to explain himself. Unless he was a clever actor, passing himself off as a tourist or rambler, a would-be murderer was unlikely to succeed in concealing himself for long. Even if he knew where Simmy lived, he couldn't possibly know when she would arrive home. She repeated such reassurances to herself as she parked as close as she could to the house, and ensured she had the door key ready to open the door in seconds.

It was with a rueful feeling that she had been foolish that she gained the sanctuary of her living room. Everything was exactly as she had left it, and there were no messages on her phone. Lights were coming on in the houses strung along the village street, lending a sense of comradeship and security when she looked out of her front window. It was a timeless scene, the little beacons of good cheer flickering from inside the cosy homes of friendly neighbours. She had loved it from the first night she moved in, conjuring stories of strangers being made welcome and meals being shared. Mrs Pepper, from a few houses away, had brought a tin of little cakes to mark her arrival and stayed to give a brief account of four or five local families who would all be glad to accept her into their midst.

One by one, they had made themselves known to her, eager to hear the details of her business and her plans for the future. Barely half of them had roots in the area, telling instead stories of how they had relocated from other parts of the country. They worked in towns, sometimes forty miles away and more, or they ran their own little enterprises, reliant on visitors as Simmy's parents were. 'Flowers?' they said thoughtfully, when she explained her own venture. 'That's nice.'

Flowers, it seemed, held no threat to anybody. The worst you could say was that they were frivolous. 'We'll come to you next time there's a funeral,' more than one person promised. 'We still have a custom of sending lots of flowers for a funeral – not like those nasty cremations they have down south, with hardly a flower to be seen.'

She concentrated on these friendly memories as she made coffee and idly watched a costume drama on TV. Winter was coming, in all its unpredictability. There could be snow, gales, floods, treacherous ice or all-pervading mud. It was essential to prepare for them all, ensuring the roof was sound and the log pile well stacked. Special tyres would be fitted to the cars, and thicker curtains hung across the windows. All the talk would be of previous years and how magnificently everyone had coped. Sheep would be kept alive, against all the odds, and only one or two dim-witted climbers would come to grief on snow-clad fells.

The fact of her parents offering a safety net down in the softer town environment where snow and ice were quickly despatched, had taken some adjustment. To return to even an arm's length daughterhood had felt like weakness, even failure, at first. The decision had been made during the anguish of loss, an instinct that brooked no argument. Angie and Russell had both held back, doubtful as to the wisdom of the move. 'Of course, it would be lovely to have you so close, but . . .' had been the message. The routine in which they saw each other barely once a week had been deliberately created to avoid any suggestion of undue dependence. This weekend had been an aberration not entirely caused by the Baxter murders.

The truth was that something somewhere had stalled. Melanie had been the one to point it out in undiplomatic terms, with her nagging about getting out there and making more of a life for herself. 'At least get yourself a dog, so you can go for long walks with it. Dogs are brilliant for meeting people.'

The thought of a dog was disconcerting. 'I can't leave it shut in all day, and I don't think it would be a good idea to have it in the shop.'

'A little one would be all right,' said Melanie blithely.

'I quite like the idea of a horse,' Simmy had conceded. 'But I couldn't possibly afford it.'

This was dismissed without a second thought. 'That's just silly,' said Melanie. 'You'd have to rent a field to keep it in, and they're ridiculously time-consuming.'

'I don't need an animal,' she said. *What I need is a baby*, she acknowledged silently. The need for a baby was like a lump of lead in her middle. Every passing month made it more likely that she would never achieve one. She told herself it was mere biology, irrational and misguided. A baby would be even more disconcerting than a dog, a nuisance, a complication, an unimaginable responsibility. Her body ignored such transparent rationalisations and continued to harass her.

The costume drama finished and was followed by the news. Shockingly, the day's events were the first headline, with lingering shots of the Old England Hotel, Lake Windermere, Storrs Hall and a lot of police tape. 'Thirty-five police officers from across the region are working on this tragic case of a double murder,' intoned the presenter. 'Although not officially confirmed, it seems that the victims were father and son.' A bluff police spokesman came on, asking for information, and stressing how rare and unusual such violence was in the serenity of the Lake District. 'We will not rest until the person or people involved have been apprehended,' he promised.

Thankfully, there were no references to witnesses, although names were given for the victims. No precious respite for the family, then.

She turned off the TV and forced her thoughts onto the next day's business. Halloween was coming, with the escalating nonsense that went with it. The opportunities for floristry were expanding as a result, with two people already asking if she could fashion decorations for their front gates. Apparently this was the norm in America, and it had begun to catch on here as well. Hurriedly consulting a few websites, she had wondered at the variety – cobwebs, skeletons, ghosts, witches and goblins all featured prominently, and had little connection with flowers, as far as she could see. The whole thing was a messy amalgam of the Day of the Dead, All Souls and even Guy Fawkes. In the southern states of America, she read, people decorated graves with autumnal seed pods and flowers, ribbons and bells. Any attempt to extract significant meaning from it was doomed to fail. Nobody cared about that. They just wanted to dress up and frighten themselves. Harmlessly silly, she concluded, feeling a trifle curmudgeonly, and making some sketches for suitable decorations.

The materials she planned to use were similar to those she had employed for the wedding on Saturday, the colours inevitably in the same range of oranges and browns, with splashes of red. She could weave sparkly silver thread to represent spider webs, and create sinister faces out of berries and nuts, peering through the lacquered leaves like a Jack in the Green.

The evening was concluded with several ideas captured on paper, the accompanying satisfaction a reassuring end to a gruelling day. Putting the ideas into practice would occupy a substantial part of the coming week, with a display in the shop window likely to attract further orders. Nobody could say she was slow to respond to a new retail opportunity, she congratulated herself. She could forget all about the weekend murders and return to being a simple florist.

# Chapter Eleven

But she had reckoned without Melanie. Monday morning had barely got started before Simmy's assistant turned up bursting with excitement at the events of the past two days. '*Two* murders!' she breathed. 'It was all on telly again last night – did you see? They gave their names and everything.'

Simmy shook her head, repressively. It had no effect. Melanie went on, 'I mean, the names of the victims. They don't normally do that, do they? Not so quickly?'

'Don't ask me,' Simmy sighed. 'I suppose they thought it was so obvious there wasn't any point in keeping them secret. It makes it sadder, though, somehow.'

'What does?'

'Telling the whole world that they're dead. I don't like it.'

Melanie managed a whole minute of sympathetic silence before bursting out again. 'George Baxter dead, though! It's incredible. Right here, in broad daylight. I tried to phone you to ask if you were there – was it before or after you had lunch with him? I mean . . .' she laughed '. . . obviously it wasn't before, because if he was dead, he wouldn't have had

157

the lunch. You know what I mean,' she finished with a flick of her hand. 'Tell me the whole thing.'

'Yes, I was there. But I didn't see anything,' she lied. The mood was all wrong for describing the sight of a man as he died. Melanie was too voracious, the chance of an interrupting customer too great. 'Sorry, Mel. That isn't entirely true, but I can't talk about it now, okay?'

'Not really,' the girl complained.

'Well, it'll have to be for now. Now, listen, I want to try something new for Halloween. I've made some sketches. We'll have to order a whole lot of stuff for them. It'll keep us busy.'

Melanie forced herself to pay attention. 'Flowers for Halloween? Are you sure?'

'Why not?'

Melanie simply raised her eyebrows and said nothing. As time went on, she and Simmy were equally persuaded that floristry was never going to be her thing. They both knew she would move on at the first opportunity.

'I googled him last night,' Melanie reverted to the more important issue.

'What? Who?'

'George Baxter, obviously. He was worth a hundred million pounds, at least. Gave money to the Tories, at the last election, and is patron of a charity that runs schools in Africa. There wasn't anything we didn't already know about his personal life.'

Simmy shivered at the idea of a dead man's life being exposed to the public gaze, with him helpless to prevent it. 'Poor man,' she sighed.

'Rich man, actually. And now Bridget is sure to benefit.

158

She'll inherit something – bound to. Nice for her new husband, don't you think?'

In spite of herself, Simmy was drawn in. 'That's a horrible thought,' she protested. 'And I think it's the wife who gets it, not the daughter. And what about Markie?' She wasn't even sure what she meant by the last question, except that the boy's life had been insured, and there was a great deal of money sloshing about, with nobody left to inherit it but two women – and one of them a mere half-sister, with very little legal claim.

Melanie gave her a bemused stare. 'Markie's dead,' she said. 'What's he got to do with it?'

Simmy squared her shoulders. 'I think this is the sort of speculation that we should try to avoid.'

'Ooh, Miss Pompous!' Melanie mocked. 'Nobody else is going to avoid it, believe me.'

'But it's like accusing Bridget and Peter of deliberately killing her brother and father. That's dreadful. You should have seen her yesterday. She was destroyed. And she's only eighteen.'

'You saw her yesterday?'

Too late, Simmy realised. Her intention to remain silent about her second Sunday visit to Storrs had evaporated at the first provocation. 'Yes,' she admitted.

'Just her? On her own?'

'No, the whole family, pretty much. I was there, you see. When Mr Baxter was sh— killed. So Eleanor took me back to the hotel so they could talk to me.'

'You're joking! My God!'

Melanie ignored the presence of a customer at the front of the shop, and put a hand on Simmy's upper arm. 'You've got to tell me the whole thing, from Saturday to last night.

You haven't told me anything properly. I knew you'd been interviewed by Moxo, but that's as far as I got.'

'Moxo?'

'That's what they call him. Was he all right with you? They say he's pretty savage.'

'He was all right. Rather kind, actually. Not the least bit savage. That all seems ages ago now. Look – see to the customer, and I'll tell you about it later.'

The elderly woman was dithering between three different bouquets that Simmy had made up that morning, with selections from the day's delivery. These speculative creations, positioned prominently on the threshold of the shop, would catch the eye of passing shoppers and almost always sell by lunchtime. They were never the same two days running, and several people made a point of inspecting them every morning.

She watched as Melanie stood impatiently waiting for the decision. The girl made no attempt to help, despite the customer's obvious desire for some conversation. 'I forget what these mauve ones are called,' she said.

'Alliums,' replied Melanie shortly.

'And will they last? I'd like them to stay nice all week.'

Simmy could endure it no longer. She marched forward, edging Melanie aside none too gently. 'They'll be fine for a week if you refresh the water every day. The alliums are nice, aren't they? I use them a lot. They go well with a lot of things.'

'Those leaves are eucalyptus,' said the old woman, with a triumphant smile. 'I recognise them.'

'That's right,' said Simmy like a primary school teacher.

'I never buy flowers just for myself. But . . . well, it is my birthday tomorrow. So I thought . . .'

Simmy's heart thumped in painful pity. 'Oh, gosh, of course you must, then. Look, I'll make a special price, as a birthday present. I really do want you to have them. Put them in a light place, where you'll see them first thing tomorrow. They'll brighten the day for you.'

The saggy chin lifted proudly. 'Of course, my son might send me some, as well. He does that sometimes.'

'You can never have too many flowers,' smiled Simmy.

'That's true. Well, thank you, dear. You've been ever so kind.'

When the woman had gone, Simmy gave Melanie a reproachful little pep talk. 'People often want to chat while they're buying. Especially old people. They remember a time when shopkeepers knew everybody and there was time for a bit of gossip. It's part of the service we're trying to offer them, don't you see? A personal touch. We should see it as an opportunity – they'll keep coming back if we treat them nicely.'

'I *was* nice,' protested Melanie.

'No, you weren't. You were impatient and dismissive. Close to intimidating, quite frankly.'

'Sorry,' mumbled the girl. 'I didn't know I was allowed to cut fifty per cent off the price.'

'You're not. That's strictly down to me. Forget I did that. I felt sorry for her. She's obviously going to be all on her own for her birthday, poor old thing.'

'Okay, okay. Now, what about the Baxters? Exactly how involved are you, would you say?'

Simmy began a brief summary of events from twelve-thirty onwards: witnessing the moment of George Baxter's death, being questioned, and then the return trip to Storrs.

'Blimey!' breathed Melanie. 'All because you did the flowers for the wedding. How crazy is that?'

'As I keep trying to tell you, a florist has a special place in the big events of people's lives. They're very likely to talk to us about a whole lot of personal stuff.'

'Right – but not *murder*. Why should a florist be a witness to a murder? That's not in any job description I've seen.'

Simmy laughed. 'I admit the murder – murders – were a long way beyond anything I expected.'

'You've probably spoken to the person who did it, without realising.' Melanie's eyes were bulging with the drama of it. 'It's *sure* to be one of the family.'

'Don't say that,' Simmy pleaded. 'I spent the whole of yesterday evening telling myself that couldn't possibly be true.'

The shop door opened again, and a familiar youngster came in. 'Ben!' Simmy greeted him. 'Why aren't you at school?'

'Free period. I needed to talk to you.' He eyed Melanie doubtfully. 'If that's okay.'

'Of course. Things are quiet this morning.' She made a shooing gesture at her assistant, who mulishly obeyed by disappearing into the cool room at the back where flowers were stored.

'Thanks.' He made a forlorn attempt at a smile.

'You look as if you haven't slept very well.'

'Right. I keep seeing that hole in his head. My dad says it must have been a rifle, like snipers use. I was scared to walk along the street just now, in case there was someone on a roof pointing a gun at me.'

'*My* dad says it might have been a pistol.'

'That would have been louder, wouldn't it?'

'I have no idea, Ben. I suppose a rifle would be easier to get hold of. But more difficult to keep hidden. I don't think you should worry about it. Nobody's going to know who you are or where you live, anyway.'

'They do, though. It's all round the school already. Everybody's whispering and pointing. One boy called "Hello, Ben Witness" at me, in the corridor. It sounds a bit like my real name, Harkness, see.'

'It was the first item on the news last night. I imagine Bowness is more or less paralysed today. I hadn't really thought about it until now. Not from that angle, I mean.'

He gave an impatient little shake. 'I can't face going back to school, with everybody looking at me. Can I stay here?'

'What – all day? No, of course you can't. If it's as bad as that, you should go home. Isn't your brother there, with his glandular fever?'

'I can be useful. I like flowers and gardening and all that. I grew some amazing dahlias this year, all my own work. They came second in the Show.'

She looked at him closely. He was hunched and pale, his hair untidy and the school uniform crumpled. 'I don't know,' she hesitated. 'We'll have to tell people where you are.'

'I was there for registration. Nobody's going to miss me. I'll just go home at the usual time.'

He *was* seventeen, Simmy reminded herself. Old enough to join the army and drive a car. He was unlikely to be posted up as a missing child. The dahlias had made an impression on her, too.

'You'll have to stay in the back. If we get any customers, they might wonder what you're doing here.'

His shoulders straightened and a half smile brightened his face. 'Okay,' he agreed eagerly. 'You won't be sorry. I'm a good worker. What do you want me to do?'

'You'd better ask Melanie. It's her department, out there. She's probably sorting out this morning's delivery, and throwing out the ones from last week that are past it. I've got to get onto the computer and see if there are any new orders.'

'Your window's looking a bit messy,' he said boldly. 'And that stuff out on the pavement. Do you want me to sort it?'

'Messy? What do you mean?'

'Sorry. Just – it could be better. There's no proper focal point, and the colours aren't right. Too much blue. It's depressing.'

'So what do you suggest?'

'Have you got something that's a really rich purple? Or deep red? That would give it depth, see.'

'Yes, Ben, I do know these things. I've just sold a bunch out of the display, which is why it looks unbalanced now. I can't let you do it – you'll be far too visible. But thanks for the comments. I admit I'm impressed.'

'Can I come out now?' Melanie sounded distinctly tetchy. 'What's going on?'

'Sorry, Mel. This is Ben. He was there yesterday, in Bowness, when Mr Baxter was killed. It was his birthday, as well. It's all been getting to him, so I said he could hang out here for a bit.'

Melanie gave the boy a long scrutiny. 'You're not Ben Harkness, are you? Brother of Wilf?'

'Yeah.'

'I know Wilf. He was in my drama group, with Mr Herbert. He was the year above me.'

'Yeah,' sighed Ben. 'You're Melanie Todd. He had a thing for you. I didn't know you worked here.'

Simmy knew she should be used to the close connections linking all the people in Windermere and its surroundings. They inevitably all went to the same school, bought their groceries in the same supermarket, ran into each other in the Chamber of Commerce meetings. The presence of thousands of visitors in the summer, and scores in the winter, sometimes obliterated the core community of permanent residents. 'Well, that's nice,' she said fatuously.

'I still don't get it,' persisted Melanie. 'Why do we have to look after him?'

'I told you. Be nice, will you? It's past coffee time. Let's get the kettle on and maybe there'll even be a few customers, if we're lucky.'

But the next person through the door was not seeking to buy flowers. Melanie saw him first. 'Don't look now, but I think it's the CID,' she hissed in a loud whisper.

Simmy looked, and met the eyes of DI Moxon. He nodded, unsmiling, and shifted his gaze to Ben, who had failed to remain out of sight in the back room. 'What are you doing here?' he demanded.

Ben's mouth opened and closed, once or twice, but no words emerged. 'He came here for sanctuary,' said Simmy. 'Word got round that he was . . . you know. On the spot, yesterday.'

'So? There's no shame in helping with police enquiries, is there?'

All three regarded him without speaking. The question contained too much angry frustration for any safe response.

'Okay,' he said. 'Let's start again. It's lucky, actually, that

165

you're both here.' He gave Melanie a speculative look. 'And you are . . . ?' he prompted.

'Melanie Todd. I was at Storrs on Saturday as well, for a bit. It was me who told Simmy you wanted to question her. My boyfriend is Constable Wheeler,' she added proudly.

'Pleased to meet you,' said Moxon politely. Melanie preened, and Simmy had a glimpse of how important a detective inspector might seem to a new police constable. She suspected that Moxon had no idea who PC Wheeler actually was.

He addressed Simmy with some severity. 'I understand you met with members of the family again yesterday afternoon?'

'That's right. Eleanor took me to talk to Bridget and Peter and the other three men—'

'Who were?' the detective interrupted.

'Oh, you know. Glenn – the best man, Felix something, in the wheelchair, and Pablo, the Spanish one.'

'All right. Carry on.'

'They wanted to talk to me, after they heard about Mr Baxter. Why? Is that a problem?'

'It could be, yes. As I understood it, you had no connections with the Baxter family before Saturday. And now you seem rather . . . intimate with them.'

'I did the flowers for the wedding, which means I met Bridget and her mother to discuss what they wanted, on two occasions. I'm not the least bit *intimate* with them.'

'And now you've forged a bond with the other witness from yesterday.' He cocked his head at Ben. 'Is this a habit with you?'

'Is what a habit?'

'Making such instant friendships. I have to say I find it very unusual.'

Simmy blinked, speechless. There was a definite accusation in his tone. She tried to order her thoughts, to understand what he was meaning to say.

Melanie was not so intimidated. 'There's nothing at all unusual about it,' she burst out. 'Simmy was approached by Bridget Baxter's mother, and asked to look after her little girl. And George Baxter wanted her to tell him about Markie, but before they could meet, he was murdered. What's so suspicious about that?'

He sighed. 'Thank you, Miss Todd. I'm sure Mrs Brown appreciates your loyalty, but it isn't very helpful.'

'Stop it,' Simmy ordered. 'This is ridiculous.'

'Si-i-i-im,' cautioned Melanie, suddenly deferential. 'I'm not sure—'

'It's all right,' Moxon interrupted. 'I must say it's quite refreshing to be told off like that. It looks as if we need to start again – again. Third time lucky. I wasn't trying to accuse you of anything. At least, I was hoping to get some sort of grasp of how things had developed since I last saw you. Less than twenty-four hours ago, that was. We've got most of the Cumbria force brought in, as you might imagine, nobody's getting any sleep, nobody's turned up any proper evidence. So I thought it might come back to you, somehow.'

'I'm a last resort,' nodded Simmy. 'I see.'

'You don't think she did it, then?' Ben ventured, his face paler than ever.

Moxon laughed sourly. 'Did you see her doing it, yesterday?'

'No, of course I didn't.'

'And she didn't see you, so you can provide excellent cover for each other, can't you?'

Melanie's intake of breath was impossible to ignore. All three looked at her. 'Sorry,' Moxon grimaced. 'There I go again.'

'Don't worry,' said Simmy. 'We're just not used to the way the police mind works. I for one haven't the slightest idea how you might go about finding the murderer – or murderers, I suppose.'

He grimaced again, and Simmy was reminded of the solid male phalanx at Storrs, the day before. So many broad shoulders and strong necks, revealing a muscular power that could kill and capture weaker mortals on a whim. Except that George Baxter must also have been one of these alpha males, with money and status in abundance. She realised she was thinking of young Bridget, who had taken on the character of a helpless pawn in Simmy's mind. And Lucy, even more so, another girl child at the mercy of unreliable adults.

'Evidence,' said Melanie. 'They have to look for evidence.'

'We have to protect the public – that's our chief role. That's why I'm here, basically. Not to alarm you, but there *is* a killer out there, and you do live alone.' He was speaking exclusively to Simmy, as he had tried to do since he arrived. Ben and Melanie were little more than irritants, it seemed.

'So? What do you want me to do?'

'Take sensible precautions. Lock doors and windows. Don't open the door to anyone you don't know.'

She shivered. 'If somebody wants to shoot me, I don't see how I can stop them. What if they're hiding under my bed when I get home? Or lying on the back seat of my car when I get in to drive home this evening?'

'Those things only happen in the movies,' said Ben stoutly. 'Not in real life.'

'I don't believe you. *He* thinks otherwise,' she tipped her chin at Moxon. 'Plus we know for a fact that there is someone out there with a gun.'

'Who is very unlikely to risk being found with it,' said the detective. 'He'll have thrown it into the lake by now. All the same, it might be wise for you to stay with your parents for a few days, just until we catch him.'

Simmy closed her eyes for a moment, and uttered a little moan. 'I can't do that. All the rooms are kept for the guests. They'd think it was a ludicrous overreaction on your part, or a total loss of nerve on mine.'

'She'd have been fine if you hadn't come along and scared her like this,' accused Melanie. 'Look, Sim – why don't I come and stay at yours for a night or two? We can do some of the paperwork together. And I can finish my assignment for college. It's bedlam at my house – I'd get it done much better somewhere quiet.'

Simmy groped for the shreds of her dignity. 'Thanks Mel. That's a great idea.'

'Good.' Moxon clapped his hands together lightly, as if a difficult task had been accomplished. 'Very good.' He turned to leave, and Simmy watched the stubbly back of his neck as he made for the door.

'Bye, then,' she called after him.

He gave a little wave, and pulled open the door. All three exhaled as he vanished from sight.

'He likes you,' said Mel.

'You were quite rude to him,' remarked Ben, with something close to admiration.

'He seemed to be floundering rather,' said Simmy thoughtfully. 'I've never seen a detective before. Not close to, anyway. It's as if he was from another planet. Are they all like that?'

'Like what?'

'I can't think of the words. Stolid, maybe. And careful. Unimaginative. Hidebound. He was actually quite nice on Saturday, but since then I've gone off him. I think they're all so hedged about with regulations and fear of criticism that they become robots.'

'My boyfriend isn't like that,' said Melanie huffily.

'Give him time,' said Ben. 'I know that Joe. You're too good for him, you know.'

'Oh yeah? I suppose you'd rather I took up with your precious brother?'

'He'd suit you better. He's going to have his own restaurant one of these days, you see. And if you're doing flowers, that'd work out just right.'

'I'm not doing flowers, I'm doing hotel management. This is just temporary.'

'Even better,' said Ben equably.

'Come on, you two,' said Simmy, unable to forget that she was almost old enough to be their mother. 'There's work to be done. I still haven't checked for new orders, or made a list for the next delivery. Melanie – is everything all right in the storeroom?'

'Everything's absolutely fine. It's nearly time for me to

knock off. I've got a tutorial this afternoon, remember?' She looked at Ben. 'Not that you need me here anyway, now you've got him.'

'Of course I need you. I'll see you on Wednesday.'

'No you won't. You'll see me tonight. I meant it about staying at yours, you know.'

'Sorry. I forgot.' The prospect was not entirely appealing. 'It's very nice of you. I'll cook us something, then. Thanks, Mel.'

A customer broke the awkward silence that followed. Simmy went to offer assistance and the others faded from sight.

Half an hour later, Melanie left for her tutorial, promising to be back at five-thirty when Simmy closed the shop. 'What happens for lunch?' Ben asked.

'I bring sandwiches.'

'I don't suppose there's enough to share?'

'Depends how hungry you are.'

'I'll go and get something from the bread shop, then. Won't be long.'

Alone for ten minutes, Simmy tried to assemble her thoughts. Despite the demands made by Ben and Melanie, the threats issued by DI Moxon, and the sadness over Markie and George Baxter, the face hovering persistently in her mind's eye was of Bridget, new bride of Peter Harrison-West.

# Chapter Twelve

Ben turned out to be good company in the few hours he remained at the shop. He recounted stories of school, and a family holiday that summer on Corsica. 'The mountains are incredible,' he enthused. 'They make the fells look like molehills. The roads are terrifying. Great big gorges you could easily fall into if you weren't careful. My mum was clinging to the door handle, convinced we were going to drive over the edge. And wild pigs all over the place. You'd never think it was Europe.'

It turned out that the Harkness family was a large one. In addition to the older brother, there were no fewer than three younger sisters. 'Zoe's fourteen and the twins are twelve.'

'Twins!'

'Yeah. Mum says she ordered them specially. It was amazing when they were little. Even I wasn't sure which was which. They're horrible now, of course, especially Tanya. She's a witch.'

'What's the other one called?'

'Natalie. She's clever. She's going to be a computer geek like me.'

'It sounds wonderful,' said Simmy wistfully. 'I've hardly got any family at all.'

'You've got all this, though,' he said, sweeping the shop with a widespread arm. 'This is really something. Like your own little empire.'

'You think?'

'Absolutely. You can do whatever you like with flowers. Have you ever been to the Botanical Garden in the Bronx?'

'Nope. Have you?'

'Last Christmas. They do this thing with model buildings, made out of sticks and leaves and seed pods and that. Real buildings from New York, they are. I went round it three times. Mum went off and left me, and I had to get the train back to Grand Central all by myself.' The pride was more than endearing. 'There was snow,' he added for good measure.

'Wow.'

'Anyway, the point is, you could try something like that. Make a model of the clock tower, or something. It's probably not too hard. Then you varnish it to make it keep, and bring it out every Christmas for your window display.'

'Gosh, Ben, that's a pretty fantastic idea. You *do* mean the Baddeley clock? Little Lucy Baxter and I stopped to have a good look at it on Saturday, actually.'

'Lucy Baxter?'

'I'm not sure that's her surname, come to think of it. She's Bridget Baxter's half-sister. Same mother. She was the flower girl at the wedding. They asked me to look after her,

173

when everything got chaotic, after they found Markie.'

He nodded carelessly, his mind no longer on the murders and the suffering Baxters. 'So – all you need to do is take a big basket with you to the woods and collect all the bits and pieces. It doesn't have to be exact, see. You can play about with it, so long as people recognise what it is.'

Simmy was having difficulty in visualising the exact process. 'You'd have to help me.'

'That's what I hoped you'd say,' he grinned.

'So what about the Baxter business?' she said with some difficulty. There was an inner resistance to returning to the subject that needed to be overcome. 'We can't carry on as if it never happened.'

'Hardly,' he agreed. 'Bowness is in lockdown, for one thing.'

'Everyone's going to be scared at the idea of a sniper picking people off from a top window somewhere. Don't they have a range of half a mile or something crazy like that?'

'More than scared. Wasn't there a thing in Florida, years ago, with two men doing that? Nobody went outside for about a month.'

'I do vaguely remember, yes. I imagine everyone's talking about it again now.'

'Silly, though. It's obviously about the Baxters – not just random.'

'You don't think it extends to you and me, then?'

'Not really,' he asserted uneasily. 'It must be obvious that we don't know anything.'

'Right. Except . . . I sort of *do* know them, now. They've drawn me in, so I'm involved with them.'

'Why would they do that? Sounds weird to me.'

'My mother thinks they wanted to persuade me of something – maybe that they're all perfectly innocent and none of them killed anybody.'

Ben mused on this. 'If that's true, then it means there's a conspiracy, doesn't it? That they really *aren't* innocent, so they got together to prove something to you. More likely, they wanted to find out how much you know.'

'But *that* suggests a conspiracy as well. That they're all in it together. It *did* rather feel like that. It was like a job interview, with a panel of board members all staring at me. And then they hardly asked me anything.'

'Who are *they*, exactly?'

She listed the remnants of the wedding party – the bride, groom, best man and two ushers. 'And Eleanor, of course. Bride's mother. She's got the little girl, Lucy, and a husband or partner or whatever, Lucy's father. He sounds intriguing, but I haven't met him.'

'And Baxter's got a wife somewhere, right?'

'Right. She's ill, apparently.'

'They weren't at the wedding, so they probably didn't kill Mark.'

'Markie. Everybody called him Markie. He was about your age.'

'Yeah, I know. He was in the cricket team at his posh school. We played them a few times.'

Simmy uttered a squeal, part amazement, part exasperation. 'God, Ben – does everybody know everybody around here? And you – exactly how many talents do you have?'

He ducked his head modestly. 'I'm a pretty good bowler. And I got a special certificate for languages, in Year Nine.'

She tried to calculate the near-forgotten system of school exams and tests. 'You're in Year Twelve now – is that right? AS level? How many GCSEs did you get?'

'Thirteen,' he mumbled.

'How many were A-star?'

'Only ten. I made a silly mistake in Russian, and had an off-day for drama. And I only got B for political geography. They couldn't fit it into the timetable, so I had to do it on my own.'

'Bloody hell, Ben. Most people are thrilled if they get nine passes. Melanie got seven, if I remember rightly.'

'Yeah, well. It comes easily to me, that's all. More luck than anything.'

'I assume you're brilliant with computers, too? And you've read all the English classics, and can quote *Hamlet* from start to finish?'

'Of course not. Don't tease.'

She laughed. 'Sorry. Are your parents teachers?'

'Dad is. Modern languages. Not at my school, though. My mum's an architect. She works from home.'

The third customer of the day put the conversation on hold. Flowers were required for a christening, which was a first for Simmy. The challenge absorbed her for twenty minutes, the baby's aunt and godmother delighted to be drawn into the decision-making and shown various options. Ben faded from sight, in a fashion that was starting to feel familiar. She suspected he was still within earshot, curious to follow the process. The required flowers were to be a centrepiece for the party after the church ceremony. The baby was a girl, but the two women agreed that pink was too obvious as the main colour. 'Creamy white and pale yellow,' said Simmy. 'With a few of the palest pink rosebuds scattered here and there. Lily of the valley, stephanotis, honeysuckle . . . maybe that's too many rich scents together. Cut the honeysuckle . . .' She scribbled notes, with a few sketched shapes, showing the customer what she was doing. At the end, they exchanged satisfied sighs.

'You're good!' congratulated the woman. 'Really good. It's going to be gorgeous.'

'I'll do my best,' promised Simmy. Without warning, the thought that she might have created something similar for her own baby if she had lived brought a tightness to her throat. She forced a smile and closed her sketch pad.

The afternoon meandered on, with Ben departing at half past three. He did not seem to be in any hurry. 'Are you sure you won't be in trouble for missing school?' she checked.

'Should be okay. I'll swing it somehow.'

'You must be their star pupil. They'll give you some leeway, thanks to your brilliant results. Must look great on the league table.'

He rolled his eyes, and hovered in the doorway. 'Of course,' he began, 'one sure-fire way of being safe from the killer is to get him caught and locked up where he can't do any harm.'

'Oh, yeah,' she scoffed. 'And how are we going to do that?'

'We'll have to think about it, won't we?' And he was gone.

\* \* \*

177

Melanie phoned at five with a change of plan. 'I'll come up to your place at about six,' she said. 'I'll need my wheels for tomorrow. There's a lecture at ten.'

'Look,' Simmy began. 'You really don't have to do this, you know.'

'Yes, I do. It'll be fun. You said you'd cook, remember.'

'I did. And I will. It's nice of you, Mel. You must have better things to do.'

'Shut up,' said Melanie.

By six-thirty they were both in Simmy's kitchen, circling each other attentively. Melanie had brought her laptop, with every intention of devoting the evening to her assignment. 'Where should I go? I don't want to be in your way.'

Simmy hesitated. 'There aren't many tables. Either in here or upstairs in the spare room, I suppose. There's nowhere in the living room that would work.'

'I'll go upstairs. Then you can watch telly in peace.'

The prospect of another person staying all night in the spare room was unsettling. Since coming to Cumbria, she had only entertained one guest, and that had been awkward. Tony's sister had foisted herself on Simmy, distraught at their break-up, eager to take Simmy's side and condemn all men as impossible. She had managed to say exactly the wrong thing at least a dozen times a day. After two nights, Simmy had used the demands of setting up a new business as an excuse to send her packing. 'I'm really sorry, Cat, but I can't spare any more time for you. I've got a list a mile long of jobs to be seen to. The shop opens in two weeks, and I'm nowhere near ready.'

The spare room was small and poorly furnished, but it

did boast a table big enough to hold a laptop and a few books, as well as a lamp and a vase of flowers. 'That'll do perfectly,' said Melanie, when they went to inspect it. 'And don't worry about making up the bed for me. I brought a sleeping bag.'

Simmy felt a surge of gratitude. 'You thought of everything,' she said. 'You are good.'

'Just organised,' said Melanie modestly. She busied herself setting up the computer and bringing an untidy sheaf of notes and worksheets from her bag. Simmy watched her fondly, drifting into nostalgic memories of her own student days. It was a few minutes before she recalled more immediate concerns.

'Do you know what Ben said, just as he was leaving?' she asked Mel. 'He said we should see if we can catch the murderer. That way we won't have to worry any more about more trouble.'

Melanie barely reacted. 'Obviously,' she shrugged. 'I could have worked that out.'

'So, how do you think we might go about it? You're the one with the policeman boyfriend. What's the procedure?'

It was like releasing a cork from a gassy bottle of wine. Melanie turned away from her homework and faced Simmy eagerly. 'The first thing is, we don't say a word to Joe. That'd just get us all into trouble, including him. We need to find a reason to talk to the family, and the people at the hotels – both of them. We have to make notes and test theories. Ben and I can do some more googling, and see what George Baxter was into, business-wise. We might be able to find out what was in his will, as well. Don't they publish them?'

'Not for a long time, I think. He's bound to have left a lot to Bridget, surely.'

'Which makes her a suspect.'

'No it doesn't. Don't be stupid. She couldn't possibly have killed Markie. Nor her father. You should see how upset she is.'

'The wife, then. She's his official next of kin.'

'I don't think this sort of speculating is very helpful,' Simmy said irritably. 'We need to be sensible about it.'

'And I suppose *Ben* is Mr Sensible, is he?'

'He's certainly clever.'

'Tell me about it. The head teacher went mad when Ben got that languages thing in Year Nine. He was in the top five in the country, or something. What d'you expect when his dad teaches German and Spanish and all the rest of it?'

'He told me about that. Don't you like him, then?'

Melanie puffed out her cheeks to express the range of complexities associated with this question. 'He's a geek. What's not to like?'

'Has he got friends?'

'One or two geeks like him. They go LARPing and that.'

'What?'

'You know – live action role play. Joe did it for a bit, before I was going with him. Said it was childish. It's what geeks do, basically.'

'Well, I like him. He seems very mature to me.'

Melanie merely laughed at that, and Simmy went to prepare a meal for them, wondering what on earth she had got herself into.

\* \* \*

Down in Bowness, Ben too was going over recent events. He had made somewhat too light of his absence from school and would undoubtedly have been missed from the afternoon classes, and the non-appearance noted in the register. But they wouldn't do anything about it until the next day. He would have to account for himself, and be treated like a much younger child for a while. While lip service might be paid to the increasing freedoms that came with maturity, a schoolboy was a schoolboy and the rules were implacable. Watching Wilf's autonomous lifestyle was both frustrating and inspiring. One day he too would be able to go where he liked, any time he wanted. He would be a student at Durham or Manchester and organise his time to his own satisfaction. Only another year to go. He found himself calculating the number of hours still to be spent at school, the number of 'Present!' responses he would have to make, before it was all over.

He had been unsettled by the florist woman, whose name, impossibly, turned out to be Persimmon. He was half in love with her already, for that detail alone. She was so direct, so engaged, so approachable. She had listened to everything he said, and replied easily, without first processing her thoughts into appropriate language, as teachers always did. She was transparent – that was it. She had no resistance to letting people see who she was. She was a proper grown-up, and yet felt like a contemporary. Melanie Todd must have had a shock when she first started working there, finding herself taken seriously for the first time in her life. Everyone knew the Todds were too scatterbrained to finish a sentence; too disorganised to get their kids to school on time. Melanie had always stood out as different, but it had been a battle. 'There but for the grace of God go we,' his mother said, more than once. Her own large family only escaped the same fate because they had a bigger house and more self-confidence. She had first encountered Mrs Todd outside the gates of the primary school, and used her as an object lesson ever since.

Wilf had liked Melanie a lot – more than he had ever admitted out loud. Ben had heard him sniffing back tears in their shared bedroom, when she had dumped him after one uncomfortable date. It seemed that she had forgotten it had ever happened, now she had Joe Wheeler. Wilf would be unsettled by his brother's sudden connection with her, just as he was over her, at last. Probably, Ben decided, it would be best not to say anything.

He had meant it when he said they should have a go at finding the Bowness Killer, as he was starting to think of the faceless gunman. The fact of Markie Baxter's death kept sliding away, as being of lesser significance, but he knew this was a mistake. Two murders provided far more traction than one. Assuming the same person committed both, there had to be a whole stack of logical deductions to be drawn and a lot of people eliminated as suspects. But *had* it been the same person? You weren't meant to make assumptions like that, with no evidence. The MOs had been completely different, which was always a strong signal that there were different killers. He felt the frustration of not knowing the individuals concerned. A bridegroom, his best man and two or three ushers, had all been on the spot for the first murder. So had about fifty other wedding guests and countless hotel staff. Markie had been killed at close quarters, according to the news report, and then pushed into the lake either to ensure he died, or to conceal the body. So the culprit must have been wet and muddy . . . He sighed at the surge of envy that flooded through him, picturing the forensic lab where clothes would be scrutinised, thread by thread, and the faintest marks on the body's skin magnified enormously to reveal a thumbprint or unexpected scratch. How could anybody expect to escape detection these days, when so much technological power could be used against them?

His Ace Attorney game – birthday present from Jack – had not yet been properly begun, given that real murders had happened under his nose. His accidental proximity to one killing, and his new friend Persimmon, gave him access to something both thrilling and terrifying, and he was not going to waste a minute of it, whatever the school might think.

## Chapter Thirteen

As the evening went on, the whole idea of Simmy needing the protective presence of her employee felt more and more ridiculous. What could possibly happen? The house was in good repair, all the windows had proper latches, and there were no cellars through which a marauder might creep, only to materialise through a hatch in the scullery. Melodramatic scenes from Stephen King stories bore no resemblance to the mundane reality of a small stone house in Troutbeck.

To her credit, Melanie was no trouble. She disappeared into the spare room for nearly two hours, emerging triumphant, having finished her assignment. 'Do you want to read it?' she asked diffidently. 'I've made a big deal of the part flowers can play.'

Simmy knew she should. The assignment had been going on for weeks, and she had heard a lot about it. The title was 'Adding Value to Hotel Services' with special reference to so-called 'boutique hotels'. Privately, she doubted that Melanie was temperamentally suited to hotel work in the first place. Her lack of patience would certainly disqualify her from working on reception, handling the impossible demands and complaints from guests with too much money and too few brains. But she might find a niche in administration or accounts or something, Simmy supposed.

'Go on, then,' she said, holding out both hands for the laptop. 'You must be glad it's finally finished.'

'Careful! It's hot underneath,' Melanie warned. 'Where shall I put it?'

They balanced it on the arm of a chair and Simmy scanned the screen. There were ten pages of it. She read quickly, increasingly impressed at the numerous ideas the girl had come up with, at the same time as being shocked at the poor grammar. It seemed that Melanie had yet to master the use of the full stop. One sentence went on for half a page. But she knew better than to criticise.

'Brilliant!' she enthused, at the end. 'You've really put some thought into it, haven't you?'

'I'm an ideas person,' boasted the girl. 'That's what I'm best at.'

'I can see,' Simmy agreed.

'So now can we talk about the murders? What time do you usually go to bed?'

It was almost ten. 'In another hour or so. But you can go when you like. You don't have to wait for me.'

'No, but I want to *talk* to you,' she insisted.

Simmy had spent the evening trying to read a novel set in Elizabethan times, featuring Tradescant the gardener. It was engaging, enlightening and entertaining – but she still wasn't able to concentrate on it. The faces of Bridget and Lucy, Eleanor and George kept intruding. She heard again

Lucy's prattle and Markie's brief disclosures outside Storrs Hall in the rain. She saw George crumple, and Bridget huddle miserably between Peter and Glenn. She admitted to herself that the horror and trauma of the two deaths could not be tidied away. Death didn't work like that. You needed to go over it a hundred times, telling yourself the story of what had happened. It had been like that with her baby. You owed it to the dead person, for one thing, not to forget them. The baby had lived, inside her. She had wriggled and turned, flicking a tiny hand down near Simmy's bladder, a special little trick that had gone on for months. They had known each other in that time. And then the baby had died, outrageously, just as poor young Markie had died. You couldn't let it go at that. There had to be an accounting. Baby Edith had died because the placenta had been defective and she was starved in those final hours. Markie had been killed by someone who had forfeited their right to a free and easy life by that vile act.

'All right,' she said.

Nothing remotely resembling a plan emerged from the next hour's talk. Melanie's talent for ideas threw up a number of propositions, nearly all of which Simmy rejected as either unrealistic or illegal. They compared observations of the people involved, despite Melanie's frustratingly brief glimpses of them. She knew a surprising amount of background information, gleaned from years of gossip about the prominent local families. But Simmy treated it all with scepticism. 'You can't believe the stuff they put in the papers,' she said.

'It's not papers,' Melanie argued. 'It's magazines. They

do articles about their gardens and show photos of them in their best outfits.'

'I saw Mr Baxter's picture in the paper,' Simmy remembered. 'That's how I recognised him. Didn't he take over some local business a few months ago?'

Melanie brushed this aside. 'It's Peter Harrison-West we're most interested in,' she said. 'And Bridget.'

'And the Spanish chap. Pablo. He's really rather lovely, you know. Amazing eyelashes. Don't you know anything about him?'

They were going over old ground, and Simmy felt weary of it all. 'We can't possibly hope to understand it all,' she groaned. 'We'll have to leave it to the police.'

'Don't be so defeatist. Hey – we've forgotten the most obvious thing of all.' Melanie clapped her hands together like a small child, in her glee. 'They'll have to include us, after all.'

'What do you mean?'

'Funerals, dummy. There'll be two funerals in a couple of weeks, once the police have finished with the bodies. Masses of flowers. Television people. Everybody talking. We'll be right in the thick of it.'

'A couple of weeks? Are you sure?'

Melanie hesitated. 'I think that's the usual thing. They do post mortems and take samples and photos and all that, then the undertakers collect them and do the coffins and embalming and whatever else they do. I can ask Joe if that's right.'

'It's a long time away. What do we do meanwhile?'

'I don't know,' Melanie confessed. 'Maybe something'll turn up.'

'And maybe it won't. Now I'm going to bed. Don't forget

you're supposed to be keeping me safe. If you hear any strange noises in the night, scream.'

'Better than that.' Melanie produced a metal whistle from her pocket. 'I'll blow this. It makes a tremendous noise. And I've got a torch as well. I wish I had a pepper spray, but nobody in Windermere sells them.'

'Did you try to buy one?'

'I did. Got a few funny looks, as well. I'll get Joe to find one for me.'

'I thought we weren't telling Joe what we're doing.'

'Since we don't seem to be doing anything, that doesn't look like a problem. I can tell him I'm scared, with a murderer running around loose. He'll go along with that.'

'Thanks again, Mel. I do feel better with you here. It's been a nice evening.'

'If I hadn't come, I'd never have finished the assignment. So we're both happy, right?'

'Right,' laughed Simmy.

She was mostly on her own in the shop throughout Tuesday. There were no visitations from the police, and not a great many customers. One of the people who wanted a Halloween decoration called in to see if Simmy had any new ideas. They discussed it for a while, concluding with a design that had substantially mutated from the first suggestion.

She drew up a careful order for the wholesalers, to include Chinese lanterns and mesembryanthemum, for use on the Halloween project. She tinkered with the window display, and the buckets of cut flowers on the pavement, bearing in mind Ben's comments. And all the while, her thoughts remained stubbornly on the Baxters, her inclination to go and find someone from the family increasingly urgent. She wanted to see for herself how they were behaving, who was in control, how they dealt with the fact of their victimhood. Because it was obvious to her that there were more victims than Markie and George. Bridget primarily, but also perhaps Peter, who was now landed with a bride very different from the cheerful excited girl he expected. And if Peter was upset, his friends might well be too.

Except, she found it hard to summon much sympathy for the man. What was he doing marrying a virtual child in the first place? Her image of the couple as a mismatch between a hard unyielding block of wood on the one hand, and a pretty soft unworldly flower on the other had only strengthened since Sunday. It felt wrong, and she was inclined to accuse both Eleanor and George of irresponsibility in having allowed it to happen. Peter was an enigma she worried at repeatedly. On both occasions when she'd seen him, he had struck her as half of a pair with Glenn, Bridget sandwiched between them. Glenn had done much of the talking for them both, which had evidently suited Peter well enough. There was a nagging weakness about him, which she could not make sense of.

And then, at half past two, Bridget herself came into the shop. She pushed the door closed behind her and stood beside the display of lilies, apparently frozen. 'Hi,' Simmy greeted her. 'I didn't expect to see you.'

'No. Well . . .' Her cheeks, which had been pink with excitement and mirth on the morning of the wedding, were now white and waxy. There had been a wholesome roundness to her face, the full lips and shining eyes adding to an image of health and good fortune. Now she looked fifteen years older and infinitely sad. 'Sorry. I was thinking about the last time I came here. Like ten million years ago.'

'I know.' Simmy waited.

'The thing is, I never got an answer, did I? On Sunday Peter and the others wouldn't really let you talk. So I've come to try again, that's all. I want your impressions. My mother says you've got insight, whatever that means. She likes you. So does Lucy. You were a friend. You *are* a friend.'

'I didn't do anything, really. I was just handy, that's all.'

'That's what Peter said. He's cross with Mummy for bringing you to Storrs. Well, he's cross, full stop, actually. They won't let us go on the honeymoon, you see, and he's lost thousands of pounds. The insurance won't cover murder, apparently.'

It should have raised a laugh, but Simmy could see there was no prospect of any merriment. 'Victims get compensation, don't they? There must be a fund or something.'

'Oh, it doesn't matter. He can afford it. His bonus last year was half a million pounds. Can you believe it?'

'So – are you still staying at Storrs?'

'Oh no. We're at the house now. Last night was the first proper night as a married couple. It didn't seem to count while we were still at the hotel. I thought it would all be okay, but it's horrible.' She shuddered. 'Cold, and miserable, and Peter all cross and silent. If Glenn hadn't come round, we'd have been a total disaster.'

'Where is the house? Here in Windermere?'

'Ambleside. Peter bought it six months ago. We've been doing it up since then. It's nice.'

They were still avoiding the subject of Markie and her

father, Simmy realised. 'Shall I make some tea?' she suggested. 'I would offer to close the shop, but I can't really . . .'

'God, no. Don't do that. If anybody comes I'll just sit quietly out of the way. Tea would be nice though. Thanks.'

They sat at the back of the shop, squashed into the area beside the till and the computer. 'Markie was the same age as you – is that right?' Simmy began, unsure of how to broach the subject without being too upsetting.

'Five months younger. It was a great scandal – which you probably know. Daddy shouldn't have been allowed to get away with it, but somehow he did. Mummy found out before I was a year old, and insisted we grow up as brother and sister as much as possible. She always liked Markie – everybody did. His mother was sensible enough to stay in the background. Poor woman – I've had her on the phone this morning. She's been talking to the police, of course, like all of us. She wants to come and see me and Peter. That'll be fun, won't it?' She grimaced. 'I can't imagine what I'll say to her.'

'Did he live with her, right up to . . . up to now?'

'No, no. After she sold the house in Troutbeck, he went to live with Daddy. Penny's got a live-in job at a boarding school, which is a bit weird, really. Daddy says she's on the lookout for a rich man, father of one of the boys.'

'They lived in my house,' Simmy said absently.

'Pardon?'

'That's what Markie said. He knew it was me. I think that's why he stopped me – to make the connection. On Saturday. Isn't that funny?'

'Is it?'

'One of those little coincidences that lead to much bigger things.'

Bridget eyed her doubtfully. 'What did it lead to?'

Simmy paused. 'Nothing important, I suppose. Just my involvement. If he hadn't waved me down, I'd have had no reason at all to ever see any of you again. The police wouldn't have bothered to question me, and I'd never have even met your parents.'

'Oh,' said Bridget carelessly. 'Well, I'm glad you did. You're so nice and sensible. It's refreshing.'

'Thanks,' said Simmy ruefully.

'Anyway, we were talking about our childhood,' Bridget pressed on, as if needing to get the story told before any further sidetracking could happen. 'I can't pretend it was a very normal family life. My mother never forgave Daddy, in her heart. She just pretended. The truth is, she was punishing him in the cleverest way imaginable. Never letting him forget what he'd done. She used Markie. I only came to understand that a little while ago. She insisted he got the same education and holidays and gadgets as I did. It looked like generosity to most people, but it was really a never-ending rubbing of his nose in what he'd done. Awful, really.'

'Gosh,' said Simmy faintly.

'I can't say I suffered at all. I gained a brother, after all. Then they divorced, when I was ten, and I didn't see Daddy much after that. Neither did Markie until he went to live with him.'

'But you still saw each other?' There was a discrepancy lurking somewhere, that kept slipping out of reach. Bridget's recital was obscuring a more recent detail.

'Not so much. There wasn't the same point to it after Daddy had gone. But we emailed and phoned all the time, and insisted on being together in the summer. We stayed at Peter's every year from when we were twelve.'

'Really?' Could it actually be as innocent and ordinary as Bridget seemed to be implying? Had Peter Harrison-West spent all those years grooming the little girl, biding his time until he could marry her? It was close enough to the stereotype of a paedophile to raise alarm, but far enough from it to subside into mere puzzlement.

'Was he a friend of the family, then?' she asked.

'Sort of. His mother was Mummy's aunt's foster sister.' She smiled faintly. 'It was years before I got that straight. We always just said we were cousins, when I was little. But there's no blood connection. It got important to say that. Of course, Adelaide is my mother-in-law now. That's a bit weird.'

'Was she at the wedding?'

'Oh yes. But she's quite old now, and deaf. She still doesn't really understand what's happened. She loved Markie,' she added sadly. 'He used to go and talk to her in her little house. They played canasta together sometimes. She always won, apparently.'

Simmy was slowly understanding that Bridget no more wanted her impressions of Markie than did Peter or Glenn or Felix or Pablo. She wanted to reminisce without argument or interruption. She had lost a beloved brother, and nobody could tell her anything about him that she didn't already know – or thought she knew.

'He was with all the other men,' she offered. 'They all seemed very chummy together.'

'What? Oh – on Saturday, you mean. Yes, I know. They were waiting for Daddy.'

'Hang on,' Simmy interrupted. 'If Markie was living with your father, how come they hadn't seen each other for weeks? Why didn't they go to the wedding together?'

Bridget waved an impatient hand. 'Markie was travelling. He was supposed to start school again this term, but he never showed up. That's why everybody was so cross with him.'

'I see,' lied Simmy.

Bridget inhaled sharply, and burst out: 'But what the hell *happened* out there? They all went back into the hotel to get changed, and Markie stayed outside. Then somebody killed him. And we had the wedding without him. It's just those facts that keep going round and round in my head.'

'And mine.'

'So who killed him? It must have been a man. All the women who knew him were upstairs with me. My mother, the bridesmaids, even Adelaide came in for a bit.'

'Peter's mother?' Simmy was valiantly keeping track of the family, hoping there wouldn't be any more new names to memorise.

Bridget nodded, with an exaggerated grimace. 'She insists I call her Mother now. She's an old witch most of the time, but you have to admire her.' Simmy heard this as a worn-out phrase, probably used about the old lady from Peter and others. She very much doubted that Bridget lost any sleep over what Adelaide Harrison-West thought of her.

'There are too many people,' she complained. 'Wanda. Penny – now Adelaide.'

'Wanda's got some bug – sounds quite bad. And Penny

wouldn't come to my wedding, would she? Not only would my mother kick up a fuss, but Penny hates Peter.'

'She hates Peter? Why?'

Bridget heaved a sigh. 'It was because he let Markie fall off a horse, when he was fifteen. That's how she saw it, anyway. He broke his arm in two places. She said he couldn't go to Peter's ever again, but she couldn't stop him. Markie just packed his rucksack and got the train by himself. She was absolutely furious when Peter refused to send him home again.'

It was, Simmy presumed, the same incident that George Baxter had told her about. It had plainly left quite an impression on the whole family. And it was in the comparatively recent past. The emotions involved would still be warm and raw. But the boy's own mother was surely unlikely to have killed him and his father for motives somehow associated with the story.

'Does Peter know you're here?' she wondered suddenly.

The girl bristled. 'Why should he? He's my husband, not my jailer. I'm free to see who I want to.'

'So that's a no,' nodded Simmy.

'What if he doesn't? He's been so foul to me, he doesn't deserve to be consulted.'

'He's probably worried.'

'I don't care.'

'I'm assuming you do love him? In spite of his being foul?'

'Worship him,' Bridget said simply. 'Always have. All he has to do is look into my eyes, and I turn to jelly. He created me, the person I am now. He always listened to me, and took me about with him, and read my mind. I read his, as well. We are totally soulmates. Nothing's ever going to change that.'

'Not even two murders?'

'I hope not,' whispered Bridget, tears running down her face.

Simmy was reaching for the box of tissues she had learnt to keep handy, when the door flew open, the bell above it clanging wildly. 'There you are!' cried a man. 'For God's sake, we've been going frantic.'

It was Pablo, the usher. His eyes were two black holes and his skin seemed several shades darker than before. He rushed at Bridget, and gripped her by the arm. 'You little fool. What do you think you're playing at?'

'Hey!' Simmy protested. 'Let go of her.'

'Get off me,' Bridget added, with a shake.

The man subsided and took a step back. He swept a hand across his brow. 'Sorry,' he muttered. 'But we thought . . . why didn't you say where you were going?'

'Why should I?'

'Because, you stupid girl, there have been two murders and nobody can assume they're safe. Somebody's got it in for your family, that's obvious. So what are we meant to think if you just disappear?'

'You're telling me that Peter's actually *worried*?' Bridget gave Simmy a quick complicit grin. 'That's amazing.'

'Glenn, Felix – all of us. It was Glenn who realised you were missing.'

'I'm *not* missing. How did you know to come here for me?'

'I didn't. I saw a woman I know, out in the street, and asked if she'd seen you. She said she had – that you'd come in here half an hour ago.'

Bridget shuddered. 'I must be famous, then, am I? Everybody recognising me. That's a horrible feeling.'

'So stay at home, damn it,' he snarled. 'Where they can't see you.'

'I bloody well won't.' The tears were returning, this time born more of frustration than grief, thought Simmy.

'You bloody well will, until the killer's caught. Peter's going to make you. You didn't even have your phone on,' he finished with a final fatal accusation.

'Well, she's perfectly safe,' Simmy pointed out. 'So you can calm down now.' For the first time he gave her a proper look, followed by a half smile.

'It's you,' he said. 'Sorry – that sounds stupid. But I didn't stop to think. Bridget's so precious, you see. "Peter's princess", we call her. Thanks for watching out for her. You seem to be a very useful person, one way and another.'

She returned his look, lingering on his long eyelashes and shadowed jaw. He appeared not to have shaved for a day or two. His clothes were rumpled. She tried to put herself in his place: the glamour of the wedding obliterated by violence and suspicion and shattered plans. His friendship with the others, which had probably been based on easy male jocularity spiced with a light competitiveness, had been thrown into something far deeper and darker. How were they managing it? Were they eyeing each other warily, conscious that one of them might be a killer? Even Felix could in theory have wielded a bludgeon of some sort on Saturday morning, despite his disability.

'I'm not sure I want to be "useful",' she demurred.

'Of course you do. Everybody does.'

'Hmm,' was all she could think to say to that. 'All I did was deliver the flowers. It seems as if I was just sucked in from there on. I don't even understand why, really.'

Bridget gave her a pat on the arm. 'You were useful to Mummy. You minded Lucy for her on Saturday. And she thinks you would have been useful to Daddy, as well, if only . . .' she faltered.

Simmy found herself thinking about George Baxter's death for the first time since Bridget had come into the shop. It had all been about Markie. 'Maybe,' she said. 'I doubt it, actually.'

'You're a brilliant listener, anyway.'

Pablo took charge. 'Come on then, Bridge. I'll have to take you back. Peter's calling the police about you being missing. It's going to be a bit of a mess. We'd better go and explain ourselves.'

'That's so *stupid*,' Bridget wailed. 'Nobody said I couldn't go out.'

'Nobody thought you'd be such a fool. At least you should have had your phone on.'

Simmy began wondering just how unusual the whole set-up was. Bridget was obviously a highly peculiar eighteen-year-old in more ways than she'd grasped so far. Wasn't it congenitally impossible for them to sever the lifeline of the mobile, even for five minutes?

'The phone's still at Mummy's. I left it there on Saturday. I didn't think I'd need it during the wedding.'

'Okay. That makes sense,' he conceded. 'We'll go and fetch it, now, on the way up to Ambleside.'

'I've got my car. I'm not coming with you.'

'What?' He frowned at her. 'What car?'

'The one Peter gave me as a wedding present. Remember?

It's up by the church. I was thinking I might take it down to Newby Bridge and back, to give myself some time to think.'

'But it's not insured yet. You weren't meant to drive it till after the honeymoon.'

'Well I did,' she defied him. 'Because the honeymoon's been cancelled, remember?'

They were spitting at each other like sparring cats, the man acting far younger than his actual age. Simmy felt her whole attention engaged by them, and by the challenge of understanding everything about them. She wanted to know the whole history, the way they fitted together, the assumptions they made about each other. It was impossible and imperative, all at the same time. She had no right to question them, or even to expect them to acknowledge her existence beyond this moment. And yet Bridget had sought her out, and begun an extensive explanation of her life and the people in it. They had been interrupted just as light had begun to fall on some of the more crucial aspects.

Pablo's shoulders slumped, and he shook his head helplessly. 'It's too much for us,' he sighed. 'For any of us. There are no rules for something like this. It's just panic and chaos for everyone. Come on, now. You can drive, and I'll sit in with you. I'll get my motor later on. But I've got to call Peter and tell him I've found you. I should have done it before now.'

With his phone clamped to his ear, he moved automatically to the front of the shop. Bridget followed him meekly, and they went outside together. 'Bye, then,' called Simmy, suppressing the flash of offence she felt at being so readily abandoned. Surely she hadn't been meant to report Bridget's presence, as if she'd been a lost child?

There were entirely too many of these young adults under her care, she felt. Ben Harkness was another one. And she wondered belatedly whether she ought to have checked with Melanie's mother before letting her stay overnight with her. Melanie was almost nineteen, but she did still live at home, and people did worry about daughters, whatever their age.

Except Eleanor, perhaps. Bridget's mother had expressed scarcely a flicker of anxiety for her older girl, in Simmy's hearing. There had been a distance between them each time Simmy had seen them together. Even in the bridal suite, before the wedding, Eleanor had been absent from her post, when the flowers were delivered.

Left on her own, she swung between thinking the entire collection of Baxters, Harrison-Wests and their entourage were beyond weird and then deciding that they were really quite normal. They were simply reacting to a situation that was far beyond anybody's experience. They were bound to be scared, stunned, irrational. And Pablo was undeniably beautiful. His image still shimmered before her eyes, startling her for a number of reasons. Since Tony had let her down, she had scarcely acknowledged the existence of men in the world. And now, here she was, suddenly feeling stirrings at the sight of a swarthy Spaniard who might very well be a murderer.

# Chapter Fourteen

Melanie had carelessly remarked that she would, of course, stay Tuesday night at Simmy's as well. 'After all, there's no point in only doing it for one night, is there?' she added.

'So when do we stop?'

'When they've caught the killer, of course.'

'But that might be *months*. You're not proposing to move in permanently, are you?'

'It's an incentive, then,' said Mel. 'For us to make sure it's all sorted quickly.'

'We'll talk about it properly this evening,' Simmy had said firmly.

Tuesday evening turned dramatically wet and windy, and Melanie phoned to say her car wouldn't start. 'It's the head gasket,' she reported mournfully. 'It won't be driveable until it's fixed. My brother's not happy. Says I've got to sort it, as if it was *my* fault.'

'And you can't use the bike in this weather.'

'Well, I *can*, but my mum isn't too happy about it.'

'No, Mel, I won't let you, either. I'll be absolutely fine here on my own. What self-respecting murderer is going to come up here with it like this? I'm locking all the windows and closing the curtains, and forgetting all about it.'

'Well, be careful, then,' said Mel reluctantly. 'You should get yourself a dog.'

'Don't you start,' said Simmy and put the phone down.

It rang again ten minutes later. 'Is that the right number for Ms Brown?' came a youthful voice.

'Is that you, Ben?'

'Right. Listen. Wilf – you remember Wilf?'

'Your brother, who works at Storrs. I remember.'

'Yeah. Well, he went back today, for the lunches, and he's just got home. The police forensics people only packed up this afternoon. Guess what – they've been going through the rooms of the groom and the best man and all the ushers. It's been a real pain, obviously, for the hotel, not being able to use those rooms. They must be collecting hair and skin and fingerprints. Like in those Jeffrey Deaver books – you know?'

'Sorry. Never heard of them.'

'It's all about forensics. Amazing what they can find. I might go in for that myself,' he added thoughtfully. 'Do you watch *Bones*?'

'No, Ben. You asked me that before.'

'Did I? Sorry. There's a character called Zack, in the early series—'

'Ben, don't tell me about it now. Get me the DVD and maybe I'll watch it, if it isn't too gruesome.'

'It's *very* gruesome. That's what's so good about it.'

'Storrs,' she prompted.

'Right. Yes. So the police obviously suspect one of the men in the wedding party. They haven't been nearly so thorough about the women. I guess there aren't proper alibis for the men. They all say they went back to their room to change for the ceremony, and as they were all in single rooms, nobody can vouch for them.'

'Is that what Wilf thinks?'

'It's what they *all* think. And get this – there's a rumour that Markie wasn't hit on the head at all. He was just held down in the lake until he drowned.'

'A rumour? Where did it come from?'

'I don't know. But it's bad, isn't it?'

'The person would be soaking wet. And there'd have been lots of noise and splashing.' She thought again of young Markie and his conspiratorial smile. 'It's horrible.'

'There wouldn't have been anybody out there in the rain to hear.'

'We don't know that for sure.'

'But if it was somebody from the wedding party who did it, it must have been well before the ceremony got going – the person would have had to go and get dry and then change, and be ready to do his ushering or whatever.'

'Do they think the same person killed Mr Baxter?'

'I dunno. It's a very different MO.'

'MO?'

'Modus operandi. Don't you *ever* watch crime stuff, or read the books?'

'Sadly not. I prefer chick lit or historical romances. I realise I'm being very disappointing.'

'You're not a very good amateur detective,' he told her kindly. 'But I'm sure you must have useful skills, all the same.'

'The Moxon man seems to think so. He said I see the big picture.'

'There you are then!' he crowed. 'That's great.'

'Is it? I'm not so sure. It just seems so terribly wicked and sad and cruel. Bridget came to see me in the shop today, and she's in an awful state. Then Pablo, one of the ushers, came and fetched her. It was all fairly weird.'

'What?' His voice shook with excitement. 'You've actually *seen* one of the main suspects. This *afternoon*?'

'You mean Pablo? Surely not. He's so . . .' she couldn't say *beautiful* to a boy of seventeen '. . . nice,' she finished weakly.

'Obviously he's a suspect. His room was being searched. He had the same opportunity as the others.'

'More than Felix you mean?'

'Who?'

'The one in the wheelchair. That really just leaves Peter and Glenn, doesn't it? Unless it was somebody else entirely. Some passing stranger. Someone on the hotel staff. We can't assume it was one of the wedding party.'

'Hmm,' he said. 'I think we probably can, you know.' A woman's voice could be heard calling Ben's name. 'Okay, Ma,' he shouted. 'Gotta go now. Feels like good progress to me. I can come in after school tomorrow, maybe? Around four. Bye now.'

*Good progress?* she repeated to herself. What were they actually doing? Was it any more than idle speculation, with no real involvement or input?

Outside, the weather was behaving with increasing

violence, tossing trees on all sides. Something near the top of the house was rattling. The capacity for the elements to dominate the lives and moods of every living creature, including human beings, was new to Simmy. She had always lived in comfortable huddles with other buildings, unnaturally warm and sheltered. This northern exposure was altogether different. The houses were certainly solid, darkly resisting the gales, but there was alarmingly little between one's naked body and the caprices of the climate. She found herself giving more and more thought to the subject, alternating between exhilaration at the challenge, and dread of finding herself out in the snow one night, quietly freezing to death.

Perhaps it was this perception of disproportion between what a single person might achieve, compared to the power of strong wind and lashing rain, that reduced any lurking fear of an attacker to almost zero. Even a bullet would be blown off course by such a gale as this.

There was work, as always, that she could be doing. The flowers for the christening were a priority, along with the need to put into practice her Halloween ideas. There had been a surprising realisation in the first few months in the shop of just how soothing and fulfilling floristry could be. Every job she was asked to do came wrapped in warm emotions. People sent flowers out of love, primarily. Even those ordered from feelings of guilt implied reconciliation and forgiveness. They were redolent of congratulation, welcome, sympathy and romance. The reality of this had quickly convinced Simmy that there was no better line of work she could have chosen. She sometimes wondered why everybody wasn't a florist.

All of which only made it more shockingly difficult to grasp the fact of two vicious murders. They could only have been born of hate, revenge, greed or insanity. Cimmerian emotions, bred below the ground, emerging maliciously to destroy people's lives. She, Simmy, whose name was close to that of the subterranean tribe, strove to remain in the light. The horror of Bridget's traumatic losses nagged at her insistently.

The rattling was starting to worry her – it seemed to come from the roof. Perhaps a gutter had come loose, she thought, despite the robust workmanship she had taken careful note of when she first acquired the house. Hard local experience had surely guaranteed that builders knew to anchor everything very firmly, from satellite dishes to ridge tiles. The noise of the wind in the trees dominated everything else, but there was definitely something knocking at irregular intervals, overhead. When she went upstairs it got louder, and she eventually tracked it down to a trapdoor into the roof space above the spare room where Melanie had slept the night before, which was lifting and dropping unnervingly, with a loud clatter, presumably as wind found its way inside the roof. That in itself was alarming. Was it meant to do that? If it went on all night, she'd never manage to sleep. Could she stick it down somehow? After some thought she decided to try parcel tape, which so often came in useful.

The ceiling was over eight feet high. She carried a dining chair upstairs to stand on, and just managed to reach far enough to unroll a length of tape and fasten it untidily across the wooden rectangle, fixing it to the wooden edges set into the ceiling. It was awkward, and she had cause to thank her luck that she was so tall. Anyone shorter than her five foot nine would have needed a ladder.

The noise did not recur, confirming that the trapdoor had been the source. When the gales died down, she decided, she would make a proper inspection of the roof space, to find the hole where the wind had come in. When she bought the house, a surveyor had assured her that everything was well made and unlikely to need any repairs for many years to come. She had never been up there herself. The confined space did not appeal to her in the least. But a quick look with a torch in her first week there had suggested a few boxes and cobwebby shapes left behind by the previous owner. Now, for the first time in many months, she remembered them again.

It had provided a useful little distraction from the murders, at least. The evening was passing easily enough, and soon she would take herself to bed with her Tudor romance and forget that she might in theory be the target of a crazed killer. You could get used to anything, she had discovered, and living alone was not particularly difficult to adapt to after a few months. Tony had not been especially talkative, after all, and the absence of the relentless sports commentary from TV and radio that he had listened to all the time was a blessing. One or two friends had asked her what was the most upsetting part of their break-up, and she had been hard-pressed to describe what she most missed. 'The idea of myself as half of a couple,' she said. Or 'Having another body in the bed for the warm company it provides.' Both were true, and important, and yet they sounded feeble when spoken aloud.

But she had got past all that. Now she simply carried inside her a hard nugget of rage against Tony for his betrayal and weakness. She still dreamt of attacking him, generally verbally, shouting until her throat was dry, but once, in a dream, she knifed him, plunging the razor-sharp stiletto between his ribs. She had never confessed this to a soul, and did her best to deny it even to herself. It had insistently crawled out of its hiding place in recent days, ever since her interview with DI Moxon. When asking herself who amongst the people she had met since then might have committed two murders, she could not avoid the conclusion that it could have been any one of them, because there was a shadow of a chance that she herself might be capable of such an act.

Anyone but Lucy, she amended, with a fond little smile.

Once in bed, however, she found it impossible to sleep. The wind was still raging outside, and her thoughts revolved endlessly around Markie and George, Eleanor and Bridget. Somebody had told her that Markie had been dumped by a girlfriend and been made unhappy as a result. Had anyone told DI Moxon that? Was it significant, anyway? Ben's eagerness to find evidence was preying on her mind. Surely there could be no prospect of unearthing any physical clues? Which meant they'd have to be content with piecing together items of information that could only be gleaned by talking to people. Or perhaps he envisaged following the main suspects around, scampering from bush to bush with a pair of binoculars. There was certainly no question of interfering with the police investigation, visiting the scenes of the crime and getting in the way.

Her mind was entirely blank when it came to understanding exactly how a self-appointed amateur detective could even begin to operate. And yet the need was there; the need to avenge poor Markie, and in the process restore to Bridget whatever vestiges of happiness were still possible. She was astonished at the strength of her desire to achieve this. Justice, revenge, morality – whatever word she might apply to her motives was irrelevant. There was something quite comforting in the realisation that her reaction was the same as that of society in general. Killers had to be caught. It was axiomatic. And if young Ben Harkness thought he knew how this might be done, then he was to be encouraged.

# *Chapter Fifteen*

The alarm woke her after a miserable three hours of sleep. The wind had abated, but there was still a light rain falling. The becks would be full at this rate, muddy water tumbling over the stones, and people pausing to watch with the eternal fascination that water always elicited.

Somewhere in the brief sleep, an idea had been born. More than an idea – a determination. She would take the initiative, telephoning Eleanor on some pretext, and after that Bridget. Both women had, after all, sought her out and used her for their own purposes. She would list every detail she could remember that might concern the family and help to construct an explanation of why two of them had been murdered. She would do her best to fathom the truth of Bridget and Peter's relationship. That, in particular, felt odd, almost to the point of wrongness. She recalled Lucy wailing that she had wanted to marry Markie when she grew up, just as Bridget had married Peter.

But Bridget seemed to have married *four* men, not just one. Did none of the others have wives or girlfriends, or did they exist solely to ensure that Peter's bride came up to expectations? Were they always in perfect harmony? Had any of them been involved when Felix fell off the mountain? The questions burgeoned like Japanese knotweed, new offshoots materialising effortlessly as she concentrated on everything she had learnt so far. Even the strong suspicion that DI Moxon and his enormous team of detectives would have been asking the same questions, and delving into every aspect of the Baxters and Harrison-Wests, did not deter her. Nobody would imagine that she and two teenagers were conducting their own surreptitious enquiries. The killer himself would be certain to dismiss them as being no threat, even if initially worried that Simmy or Ben might have seen something incriminating.

Melanie was scheduled to appear at two that afternoon, to sort the midweek delivery. She was very adamant about using flowers in rotation, reining Simmy in when she wanted to use a new arrival in a display or recent order. 'You won't waste so much my way,' Mel insisted. 'It's common sense.'

Simmy had to admit this was right. Melanie might be unmoved by flowers themselves, but she was miraculously useful when it came to systems and routines. Her very lack of creativity came to seem like a virtue.

The morning passed slowly. Two customers came in for birthday bouquets, and an Interflora order came through on the computer, which would involve driving to Kentmere. She would have to go the moment Melanie arrived, to meet the promised delivery time. Such commitments regularly proved difficult, especially on Melanie-free days – then she had to close the shop, with a notice saying when she'd be back. She had spent hours of her life weighing up the various options for resolving this difficulty, to no avail. A full-time assistant would be underoccupied, and cost too much. Cancelling her membership of the Interflora network would be commercial suicide. Once, when a bouquet had to be taken to a remote homestead in Grizedale, she had prevailed upon her mother to hold the fort for a couple of hours. Angie had been reluctant, and got into such a muddle with the minimal takings that they had both concluded it could not happen again. 'Ask your father next time,' said Angie. But Russell had been reluctant to cooperate, for reasons that remained opaque. 'Too much responsibility,' was all he would say.

Funeral flowers had threatened to be an even bigger problem until she realised that the local undertakers were fabulously well organised, and would supply names, times, special instructions, the day before the funeral. Simmy would make up the tributes at the end of the day, for delivery early next morning. There were purpose-built racks, close to the parking area for the hearse and limousines, with the names of the deceased pinned onto them for flowers to be left. Unless they were scheduled for late in the afternoon, or the weather was very hot, the flowers could be taken to the undertaker before the shop opened at 9.30am.

But today's order meant she would not get a chance to talk to Melanie until three or later. This felt like an unacceptably long time away. She wanted to get going on her plan before that. She could google Baxter and Harrison-West for herself, instead of leaving it to Melanie and Ben, but doubted whether she would find an actual address for the house that she felt it increasingly urgent to visit. She was conjuring visions of Bridget imprisoned in a luxurious room fit for a princess, whilst four men waited on her. She imagined herself rescuing the young bride from this cloying incarceration and restoring her to something closer to a normal life. It had felt very much as if Bridget were asking for help, the previous day. If she, Simmy Brown, simply turned up on the doorstep, as a casual visitor, would she be admitted? The more she thought about it, the more she wanted to give it a try.

Melanie was early, her cheeks flushed and eyes sparkling. 'It's cold out there,' she gasped. 'And there's a fallen tree across the Birthwaite road. They've only just moved it. It was *huge*.'

'Why were you over there?'

'Long story. All to do with my car. You don't want to know.'

'Okay.' Simmy explained about the Kentmere order. 'I'll be back by three, at the latest. You can trim the new delivery. Usual thing. I want to talk to you about Bridget Baxter – Harrison-West, I mean. Ben phoned me last night. Made me think.'

'Kentmere should be exciting after all that rain.'

'Oh?'

'You'll see what I mean. Have you ever been there before?'

'Once, in the summer. Fabulous scenery.'

'More so after a downpour. Now off you go, and I'll see you later.'

Simmy carefully gathered up the sheaf of flowers she had assembled during the morning, and put it in the back of the van. 'I hope I can find the place,' she said, before setting off. 'It's right in the middle of the village, so it should be easy enough.'

Melanie made no attempt to give advice. Simmy was nearly twenty years her senior, and therefore by definition more competent. She set off along the main road leading east, knowing she had to turn left at Staveley and follow the river, past Kentmere Tarn and on to the village. It was a long narrow valley, with impressive fells on both sides, and, as Melanie had hinted, frothy tumbling becks brought the recent rainwater from the hillsides down into the river Kent. There were puddles in the road in some places, the general impression of water on all sides very reminiscent of the Saturday wedding at Storrs, with the rain washing across the lake. You had to choose, she had come to understand, between making the water your enemy or your friend. You lived constantly with the risk of inundation, where your chairs might float and your home be uninsurable. You built of stone and waited for your house to shake itself dry again. You kept your books and photographs upstairs and made sure the drains were clear.

The recipient of the flowers lived in a prominent house with its name blessedly legible on the gate. Delight was expressed, and the familiar warm emotions once more reinforced Simmy's faith in her profession. She was on her way south again within twenty-five minutes of leaving the shop.

If there had been a roadway across the fell past Garburn and Sour Howes she would have taken it, for the views and the chance to learn a new route, but there was nothing that would take a car on a muddy October day. All she could do

214

was retrace the same journey back to Windermere. She was, after all, she reminded herself, eager to talk to Melanie.

But still she was glad to be out. Anybody would be, now the rain had stopped. The stretch from Kentmere to Staveley was beautiful by any standards, in any weather. But from there on, with the big soulless main road and the disappearance of the fells, it all changed. As far as she could tell, the whole of the English countryside was like this now. Pockets of glorious timeless landscape were encircled by man-made desecration of one sort or another, which had the effect of reducing one's pleasure considerably. You knew, if you drove just one more mile down a tiny meandering rural lane, you'd come to a major road or a railway or housing estate that would cloud your pleasure. Scotland and Wales made a better job of it, on the whole, although the alien giants that were wind farms went a fair way towards ruining a lot of their beauty spots.

But she couldn't dawdle. There would be plenty of opportunities for sightseeing ahead. Melanie would be expecting her, and she should behave responsibly.

She parked in the street a few yards past Persimmon Petals, noting how quiet Windermere town centre was that afternoon. The season was definitely drawing to a close, the visitors dwindling and the days shortening. There would be more time for socialising, if that was what people wanted to do. Simmy thought she might buy a pair of decent walking boots and watch the onset of autumn from the slopes of some of the bigger fells.

There was movement inside the shop, which she could see through the door. Something about it made her heart do a double thump. She pushed quickly inside and tried to make sense of the scene halfway down the main part of the shop. Melanie was pressed back against a rack of evergreens, a man, an inch or two shorter than her, standing aggressively close and waving a clenched fist.

'Hey!' shouted Simmy. 'What's happening?'

Melanie lurched towards her in a panic. 'He's only just come in. He was shouting before the door had shut. Wants to know what we've done with Bridget, or something.' She had seized Simmy's arm, and was trying to put her boss between herself and the angry man.

'Peter Harrison-West,' Simmy said loudly. 'This is a disgrace. What do you think you're doing?'

The man was obviously close to a complete loss of control, and Simmy had to swallow down a real fear. Was this what had happened to Markie – an enraged bridegroom thumping a fist down on him and then drowning him in the lake, out of a fit of sheer fury? Was Peter mentally ill?

'Melanie – go into the back room, will you? I'll be all right.'

Melanie made no move to obey. 'I'm not leaving you with him,' she said.

Peter's raised fist had already dropped to his side, and he was inhaling painfully deep breaths. 'It's all right,' he grated. 'I won't hurt either of you. Of course I won't.'

'I should hope not.' Since she was sixteen, Simmy had been taller than a great many people. She had grown accustomed to the automatic respect it brought her. Now she met this man's eyes from a slightly superior height, and despite knowing he possessed much greater strength, she made full use of the advantage it gave her. 'What's this about Bridget, anyway?'

'She's gone – again,' he said bitterly. 'Same as yesterday. Pablo thought she might have come back here for some reason. She seems to want to talk to you.'

Simmy forced herself not to overreact. 'And she didn't say where she was going? Didn't take her phone?'

He was shaking with the after-effects of his violent rage, scarcely able to speak. 'I don't know what's the matter with her. She's a different girl. Glenn says . . . never mind. So she's not here?' He looked around as if he might have failed to notice his runaway bride.

'I have no idea where she is. Have you tried her mother?'

'What? Eleanor? She wouldn't go there.'

'She might. Listen – you and I don't know each other at all. It's by sheer accident that I ever even met you. But I have seen Bridget a few times, as well as her mother. And not only is her brother dead, but her father is too. Can't you understand what that must be like for her? Don't you think she might need her mother, with things as they are?'

'She's got *me*. I should be enough for her.'

'Well,' she said rashly, 'it seems otherwise, doesn't it?'

He hovered visibly between a revival of his rage and an acceptance of this unarguable truth. 'But Glenn says—' he started again.

'Is this anything to do with Glenn?'

'He's my best friend. He knew Bridget before I did. We've always been a gang, with Pablo and Felix too, of course.'

'And Markie,' said Simmy, thinking of the group of them standing in the rain on Saturday morning.

'Sometimes,' he conceded. Something of the reality of his situation seemed to get through to him. 'It's all spoilt now. We had such brilliant times, every summer since the kids were twelve. All of us together for weeks at a time. We went camping and sailing and all that. Of course, we knew each other for years before those trips. It all goes back to when Briddy was about eight.'

Just like *Swallows and Amazons*, thought Simmy, wondering at the extraordinary privilege his words conveyed. Not just having the time and space for such summers, but the freedom from convention. Peter would have been in his mid-thirties when Bridget was eight, and lucky to have more than a few weeks to spare from demands of work. A single man, from a wealthy family, he could do whatever he liked. And it would appear that he had earmarked the little girl as his, from an unsuitably early age.

But then he had not abused her or frightened her; he had not despoiled her and cast her aside. Peter Harrison-West had waited patiently for her to grow up, and had then married her. And, as far as Simmy could see, Bridget had been more than happy to cooperate. If there had been exploitation or manipulation, it had been subtle, and the Baxter parents had willingly colluded with it. At this point, her thoughts slipped into a familiar track, and she gave a deep sigh.

She looked intently into the man's face. Whilst far from being a chinless wonder, there was a flickering weakness to be detected. He only met her eyes for a second at a time, before sliding away. His lips were full and loose. Bewilderment was lying close to the surface, as well as frustration. Events

218

had not gone as he had expected, and he was nowhere near mature enough to deal with the blow he'd been dealt.

'Go and see Eleanor,' she advised him firmly. 'Bridget will come back when she's ready. You've got to let her go where she wants.' She had been burning to utter these words, ever since the episode of the previous day. They came out with some force.

'That's right,' echoed Melanie, who had been silently attending to every word spoken since Simmy's return. 'She's not your prisoner.'

'Hush!' Simmy turned on her quickly. 'You fool.'

Peter's fist came up again, of its own accord, and both women took steps back. 'Go!' Simmy ordered him. 'Now!'

He slowly did as he was told, not pausing for any final words at the door, as Simmy had half expected.

'Phew!' Melanie blew out her cheeks with exaggerated relief. 'You were fantastic with him. What a headcase!'

'And you were an idiot,' said Simmy without rancour.

'Sorry.'

'I wonder where Bridget's gone, all the same.'

'As far away from him as she can, I should think. It's obvious now that he's the killer. He's liable to murder her as well. She's probably realised that for herself and she's hiding somewhere.'

'No-o,' said Simmy slowly. 'No. That can't be right. Why on earth would it be him?'

'He's crazy – simple as that. You saw him. I thought he was going to kill me. Honestly, I did. Just before you came in. I practically wet myself.'

'He *was* scary. But that doesn't make him a murderer.

219

Bridget loves him. She told me she did. She was so happy to be marrying him.' She thought back to the morning of the wedding. 'You should have seen her. She didn't care about the rain, or anything. She won't even have been bothered about Julie not doing her hair. She was *radiant*.'

Melanie held out a hand. 'Look – I'm still shaking. I've never had anything like that happen before. We should tell the police.'

'What?' The idea had not crossed her mind. 'Why?'

'It was threatening behaviour. It's against the law.'

'But . . .' It was new territory for her. 'What would we say to them?'

'Just tell them what he did. They should know what he's like.'

'He's under a lot of stress. They all are.'

'Pooh! That's no excuse. And what was that about him and Glenn being best friends for ever? Didn't you think there might be something a bit . . . you know . . . about that? Weird, I mean? More than just good friends?'

There had been times over the past months where Simmy had felt considerably less worldly-wise than her young assistant. Just how come Melanie had acquired so much insight into human behaviour remained obscure, unless it was avid attention to TV soap operas. 'But . . .' she began. 'Why would he marry Bridget if that was the way of things? Wouldn't she realise?'

Melanie shrugged. 'She'd be a smokescreen for him. And maybe she's not very into sex, so it would suit her as well. She gets a nice life in a big house. Makes a lot of sense, when you think about it.'

'And Markie? George?'

'They'd worked it out and were threatening to make it public. Or – more likely – they wanted to save Bridget from making an awful mistake and tackled Peter about it.'

'Glenn's not married, is he?'

'Absolutely not.'

'How can you be so sure?'

'Sim – they're all over the county magazines and the Internet, as well as the local papers. My mum talks about nothing else at the moment. "Bachelor friends close ranks in face of horrendous murders" or something like that. Haven't you seen any of that?'

Simmy grimaced helplessly. 'I never did get the habit of reading that sort of stuff.'

'You should.'

'Okay. I'll think about it. So what about Glenn? He knew Bridget first – that's what Peter just said.'

'I never knew that. I can't see that he has anything to lose, whatever happens. He's got Peter where he wants him, and Bridget's not going to start causing trouble now.'

'Isn't she? Looks as if she's doing exactly that, running away. Don't you think it means he loves her, the way he was just now? He's scared she'll be murdered as well.'

Melanie slapped a hand on the table holding the computer. 'I don't know,' she exploded. 'I just think we should report that man for the way he behaved. You're being far too cool and reasonable about it. How do we know he won't come back, angrier than ever? Never mind *him* being scared. It's us you should be worrying about.'

The shop door opened. 'Who's worrying about what?' asked Ben.

The two females fell over each other to relate the episode to him. He listened politely, asking one or two questions. 'Doesn't make him a killer,' he judged, when they'd finished.

'It makes him a lot more likely than Pablo or the others,' Melanie protested.

'Do you know Pablo?' Simmy asked her.

'No, of course not. But you told me he was nice.'

'She told me that as well,' said Ben with a grin.

'Do you want some tea?' Simmy asked him. 'It must be time.'

'If you like,' he shrugged. She told herself that politeness was bound to be sporadic in a boy his age. 'So – are you going to tell the police about the Harrison-West bloke?'

'I don't know. What do you think?'

'I think we need to sit down and make a proper list. I've started, actually. Look.' He pulled a new-looking notebook from his bag. 'All the things we know about the suspects and the victims. How they're related, and all that.'

Simmy was impressed, but also unnerved, by his application. Ben, she reminded herself, had reason to take the murders seriously. He had been there for one of them. He had seen a man with a hole in his head. 'Okay, then,' she said. 'Give me three minutes.'

She made the tea, and glanced at her computer to check for new orders. Melanie was going to have to stay late at this rate, to process the midday delivery. There were commissions due, and two big funerals looming, not counting those of Markie and George Baxter. Putting her mind to Ben's list was going to take some effort.

But they quickly got into it. 'Markie had a girlfriend who dumped him,' she contributed. 'He was upset.'

Ben and Melanie exchanged a look. 'Who would that be, then?' she asked.

He lifted his shoulders in plain bafflement. 'No idea.'

'Glenn knew Bridget before Peter did. He told us that just now. She was eight when he first met her. They spent the summers together, doing outdoorsy things.'

'Glenn was abroad for a bit. He came back a year or two ago,' offered Melanie. 'I think it was Dubai or somewhere like that.'

'George Baxter's got some business thing out there,' said Ben. 'Wilf told me that. He owns some massive hotel, I think.'

'Owned,' Simmy corrected him. 'Did Glenn work for Baxter, then?'

'Might have done. That'd make sense.'

'What about Felix and his accident?' Simmy asked. 'How exactly did that happen? And when?'

Melanie supplied the details proudly. 'It was last winter, before Christmas. He was climbing, with Peter and Glenn, and fell off. That's it, really. They took two days to rescue him, because it was foggy and freezing cold. He broke his back.'

'Two days? He'd have frozen to death in that time.'

'Glenn was a hero, apparently, and stayed with him, keeping him warm. Peter went for help, but then they couldn't find them for ages, in the dark and fog. It was a real drama. They hadn't taken mobiles with them.'

'And Glenn was a better rescuer than Peter, by the sound of it.' She could imagine Harrison-West blundering furiously around the fells, too unfocused to be effective in getting help. 'Funny they were so cross with Bridget yesterday for not having her phone. I guess it taught them a lesson.'

'The rescuers were scathing about it. They said Felix might have walked again, if only they'd got to him right away.'

'That's awful! They must feel so guilty.'

'For lack of a phone, walking was lost,' declaimed Ben. 'You know – that poem about a horseshoe nail.'

They ignored him. 'Actually, I've heard a lot of people say it's taken all the adventure out of fell climbing,' said Melanie. 'If you've got a phone all the time, you're not really getting away from it all. My dad says he can see their point. Everything's got so safe these days.'

'Even so,' Simmy demurred. 'Felix paid a pretty high price for it, didn't he?'

'They think they might be able to do something eventually. An operation, I guess.'

'What else do we know about Felix, then?' Simmy returned to Ben and his notebook. 'He seems to be the shadowy one.'

'He's younger than the others,' supplied Melanie. 'But I think he went to the same school. He's getting married next summer, but she's not local.'

'Shadowy,' affirmed Ben. 'But at least they're all still friends. That must mean he doesn't blame anybody for the accident.'

The phone rang, and Simmy spent several minutes taking down a detailed order for a funeral wreath. 'They want it to go to Coniston first thing tomorrow,' she groaned. 'It's that woman who was so pleased with the flowers we did for her five months ago – the one who gives lavish dinner parties. Says nobody else could do it as well as us.'

'Tomorrow!' Melanie was outraged. 'That's impossible.'

'No it isn't. I can get it done now, and take it first thing. I've done it before.' For the first time all day she remembered her sleepless night, and sagged at the sudden wave of weariness that came with the memory. The youngsters looked at her as if she'd let them down badly. 'Come on!' she shouted. 'I'm trying to run a business here. That's sixty pounds' worth of flowers she's just ordered. What do you want me to do?'

'Okay,' Melanie placated. 'We'll get on without you, then.'

'No you won't. I'm paying you to work, remember. Ben – this'll have to wait. We weren't really getting anywhere, were we? Real life is always going to get in the way. That's why there's a police force. We ought to leave it to them. You've probably got homework, anyway.'

'Nothing important.' He looked again to Melanie for support.

'Won't work, Sim,' said the girl. 'We're even more involved now, after being yelled at by that Peter. There's no escape.'

'Don't say that. It's past four o'clock, and there's work to be done. Forget the Baxters and their troubles. It's not our problem.'

Melanie smirked mutinously. 'Don't be too sure of that,' she said.

*Not my problem, not my problem*, Simmy repeated to herself as she drove home at six-thirty. Any further suggestion of being minded by Melanie seemed to have died away over the past day, in spite of Peter Harrison-West's aggression. The funeral tribute had taken her over an hour to construct, but it was now sitting proudly in the cool room behind the shop, ready for early delivery next day. She had an evening ahead in which she could eat a proper meal, read more of her novel and then have an early night. There would be no reason for anxiety. With every passing day the police must inevitably be closing in on the killer, without any need for assistance from a bunch of hopeless amateurs.

The house felt chilly when she went in, and unusually silent. A welcoming cat, or even pet bird, would have been nice. She put the lights on in the hallway and living room, and then went through to the kitchen. Something was different. The air was moving when it shouldn't. Puzzlement swamped any fear that might have been expected, as she looked around. Nothing was broken or misplaced. The window was still closed. She went quickly back to the passageway and into the living room.

'Hello,' came a small voice from a shadowy corner. 'I hope you won't be cross with me.'

# Chapter Sixteen

'Good God – Bridget! How did you get in?'

'I've got a key. It was lucky you told me Markie lived here when he was young. I never gave it back. It seemed sort of meant to be, when I wanted somewhere to hide. I knew you'd look after me. Good thing you didn't change the locks.'

'But I did. At least, there's an extra one.'

'Not at the back. It's a key to the back. The door makes a nasty scraping noise when you move it, so I left it open. It's got a bit cold now.' The girl spoke in a dreamy, stunned voice, as if from a great distance. 'Penny never shut the door, you know. I was pretending she and Markie were still here. I haven't damaged anything.'

'Peter's looking for you.' It was a rerun of the day before. 'He's really upset.'

'Poor Peter. He's very weak, you know. He depends on me for everything. Can you believe that?'

'Not really. He's got all those men friends.'

'They're no use. They just make him worse.' She looked up at Simmy with tragic eyes. 'What am I going to do?

227

Markie and Daddy were going to make it all all right. I can't manage him without them.'

'Oh dear.' Simmy sat down beside her on the sofa, and took a hand. It was cold. 'I thought you might have gone to your mother.'

Bridget uttered a harsh laugh. 'What could *she* do? She never had any time for me. She barely even knows who I am.'

Simmy thought about the wedding, and its less overt implications. An immature girl so willingly handed over to a man close to middle age; a mother who could scarcely be bothered with the fuss of it all; a father distracted by his business responsibilities and a life moved on. If Peter was not proving to be the stalwart partner she had presumably expected, then she was indeed bereft.

'I'm scared,' the girl confessed. 'I don't understand what's going on.'

'You can stay here,' Simmy heard herself offering. 'But we'll have to tell somebody where you are. There'll be a huge police hunt for you otherwise.'

'Then he'll come and fetch me again. Or send Pablo or Glenn, more likely. I'm *scared* to go back. Until I know who . . . which . . .' she raised her stricken face again, 'one of them killed Markie and Daddy. Do you see?'

Simmy was struck silent by this voicing of the obvious. She merely shook her head helplessly, while an even more awful idea formed itself. *What if it had been ALL of them, together?* Was that not a perfectly reasonable suspicion? And if true, would it not make a police investigation impossibly complicated? Forensic evidence pointing to them all separately – footprints on the lake shore, flecks of skin on their clothes, the pressure of many hands on Markie's drowning body – how could they ever unravel all that?

Bridget was weeping quietly, both hands across her face. Curled on the sofa like a ten-year-old, it was easy to imagine her a frequent visitor to her father's other woman and her half-brother, attracted by the more normal environment and Markie's fellowship. 'Did your mother know you came here?' she asked. 'Surely she wouldn't have liked it?'

'She didn't care. All she ever cared about was that house. I can't bear to go there, you know? It freaks me out. And now it's happening all over again with Lucy.'

Simmy had forgotten Lucy, the little half-sister. 'She seems okay,' she said. 'Her father sounds . . . interesting.'

'He's a wimp.'

*Like Peter?* Simmy wondered, bemusedly. Nobody, surely, could ever use such a word about that angry man. His weakness, if it was real, took a very unwimpy form.

'Look, we really will have to do something. What if I call that detective man? Moxon. He can head off any search parties, at least. I don't think he'll tell Peter where you are, if we ask him not to.'

'I don't know. How can we know what he'd do? Men stick together. I've discovered that, lately.'

'Peter can't force you to go back. You're an adult. Men don't own their wives any more.'

'Right,' said Bridget, sounding very unconvinced. 'Why has everything turned so horrible?' she moaned, turning her face into a cushion. From the heaving of her shoulders, it was clear that she was still crying.

Simmy gave her a minute, and then changed the subject.

'Are you hungry? Because I am. Starving, actually. I'll find something to eat, and then I'll phone him. He gave me a card with his number on it. We don't have to dial 999 or anything.'

'Thirsty,' said Bridget, in the exact same voice that her little sister had used, four days earlier. The echo brought a host of surging feelings to Simmy's throat, disabling her for a moment. She, then, was the universal nanny, the caring grown-up who sheltered waifs and strays. Had she got all the way to thirty-seven without noticing that this was her rightful role in life? She had watched with a mixture of envy and alarm as her mother welcomed a motley assortment of guests into her home. She had marvelled at the efficient provision of necessities, often awakening people to needs they didn't know they had. Books, games, jigsaws, as well as the soaring fells and sparkling lakes that would revive their spirits beyond all imagining. She restored a sense of proportion to jangled souls escaping from all manner of turbulence. If sometimes she failed, as with the people on Saturday, that was only to be expected. It did nothing to undermine the central message that Angie offered, simply by being who she was.

'I'll make some tea,' she said, without consultation. The tears had not fully abated, and there were times when tea was the only thing.

It took ten minutes of concentrated thought before she felt able to call DI Moxon. She went back to her single fateful encounter with Markie, and how he had already known she lived in his old house. That, she began to understand, was why he had flagged her down. He wanted to tell her of the link, because it was important to him. The house

230

had been sold when he was fourteen or fifteen – probably giving rise to all sorts of trauma. Houses, it seemed, were seriously important to these people. Bridget regarded it as a refuge, thanks to past experience and habit. Simmy herself was of lesser significance. She was so insignificant that it was possible for the girl to simply let herself in as if nothing had changed in the past three years. The present owner of the house was a minor nuisance – nothing more.

It should have made her angry, but instead it came as something like reassurance. She had no wish to be centre stage. If her entire involvement had been because of the accident of home ownership, that absolved her from anything like responsibility.

Except that Bridget was hiding here, in the house that was definitely now Simmy's. And if her husband found out, there would be noise and violence and an awful lot of trouble.

The card that Moxon had given her was inside her wallet, the wallet inside her shoulder bag. The bag lived permanently under the passenger seat of her car. That way, she never found herself without money when she went shopping. But it did mean she never had her mobile in the house, nor her credit card or chequebook. It meant she often had to go out to the area at the side of the house in all weather, to retrieve the bag.

She did it now, noticing that a drizzly rain had started, but that there was little or no wind. There was no sign of a waiting killer, patiently squatting behind the large escallonia hedge in the hope that his victim would eventually come outside. Such figures were patently absurd, Simmy knew. But the knowledge did not prevent her from turning on the bright outside light, and moving as briskly as she could to the car and back.

Rather to her surprise, Moxon answered on the first ring. He sounded alert and approachable. He knew immediately who she was.

'We're not sure we can trust you,' she began quickly, trying not to hear the impertinence in her own words. 'But I suppose we'll have to. Bridget Harrison-West is here. She's run away from her husband and his friends, and is frightened. I'm telling you in case he calls for a police search. She's quite safe.'

'Wait, wait,' he ordered. 'Why is she frightened?'

'Because—' What could she say? 'Well, obviously, because of the murders. She doesn't know who to trust.'

'She thinks her husband killed her brother and her father?' There was no discernible scorn or scepticism in his tone. He sounded as if he really wanted to know.

'No, no, I don't think so. Not really. But she can't be sure. Not until you've caught and charged somebody. Even then, it would have to be really convincing.'

'She's so unsure that she's hiding from him – is that right?'

'Him and the others. There are *four* of them.'

'Indeed there are,' he agreed heavily. 'All for one and one for all sort of set-up.'

'Right. But they can't all have fired the gun that killed Mr Baxter, can they?'

'Whoa!' His voice rose. 'That's a bit of a leap, isn't it?'

'Sorry. I suppose it is. I was thinking it through just now, and it just seemed . . .' she tailed off. 'Bridget sees them as a unit,' she added.

'The Spanish bloke's itching to get off to London tomorrow. Says he's indispensable and we can't stop him.'

'And can you?' She barely allowed herself the flash of

hope that Pablo would be forced to stay close by.

'Not easily. Sounds as if we'd best let him go, if he's such a problem for the little bride.'

'Um . . .' She had no idea where this was going, but there was a hint that he was telling her more than he really should. 'So you're still investigating?' she finished inanely.

'Exactly so. Mainly gun stuff. Guns are supposed to be traceable, you see. You'd be amazed at the things we know about the gun in question.'

'And?'

'And it's proving surprisingly elusive. They're not so very difficult to hide, of course.'

'And where Markie was killed – that's all churned up by the people pulling him out of the lake,' she suggested.

'To an extraordinary degree. At the last count, I think eighteen separate people got their feet muddy that morning.'

'Oh dear.'

'Now then.' He was suddenly businesslike. 'Have I got this right – you've called to tell me Mrs Harrison-West is with you, and doesn't want her husband to know?'

'That's it. I thought he might set some sort of police search in motion, and that would be an awful waste of time.'

'So if he does – what do we say to him?'

'Ah.' It was a good question. 'What about saying you're aware that she's safe, but that you've been asked to keep her whereabouts confidential?'

'That's a possibility,' he said slowly.

'So nobody's reported her missing up to now?' That seemed odd, on reflection. 'I think she's been gone quite a long time. She ran off yesterday, as well, and came to me in the shop.'

He was silent for several seconds. 'Pardon?'

'She—'

'Yes, all right. So don't you think it highly likely that they'll come to you to find her today? Do they know where you live?'

'I expect they do. Markie did, after all. I'm easy enough to find. It never even occurred to me . . .' She saw herself barring the doors, back and front, with heavy furniture and huddling in a corner with Bridget. 'They'd phone first, I expect,' she went on hopefully.

She could hear his sigh, suggestive of repressed exasperation and things generally going rather badly. 'Does she know you're speaking to me now?'

'I think not. She's in another room, crying, last I looked. I've given her a mug of tea and some biscuits.'

'And the doors are all locked?'

'Actually, no. The back one's open, I think. I'll go and shut it in a minute.'

'You don't sound worried,' he remarked. 'Most women in your position would be terrified.'

'Would they? Do many women find themselves in my position?'

He ducked that question. 'Keep a phone close by. Lock yourselves in. We can get people with you in ten minutes if we have to. Why don't I get somebody to go and see Mr Harrison-West and let him know we're aware that his wife is feeling nervous and that she prefers to be away from him for a little while?'

Simmy tried to think this through. 'Then he'd know that *you* know where she is, so he wouldn't dare come looking for her, to drag her home again. Yes – thank you very much. That should settle it. Then we'll be fine, won't we? Nothing to be scared about.'

He sighed again. '*If* he was the killer, and *if* he thinks you witnessed something, and *if* he doesn't trust his wife – then possibly there is. But those are all unwarranted assumptions at this stage. I hate to risk worrying you, but there's even a remote possibility that you have the killer right there in the house with you. Had you thought of that?'

'Of course not!' She almost laughed. 'She's the *victim* in all this. Nobody's suffering more than her. She's lost two crucial figures in her life, for heaven's sake.'

'I expect you're right,' he said, before repeating, 'But you'd be well advised not to make assumptions at this stage.'

How pompous he sounds, she thought. Was it the job, forcing him to utter platitudes to cover himself, or was it his nature? Didn't a person's nature eventually conform to the demands of the job, anyway? He had to be more harassed and stressed than he sounded, surely? Part of a huge team of detectives unpicking the lives of countless local people, exposing their secrets and casting doubt on their deeply held beliefs about each other – what sort of a man could comfortably do all that?

'All right, then. We'll have an early night, and hope for the best.' Again she remembered how tired she was, and how appealing the prospect of her bed. 'I've got to go to Coniston first thing tomorrow,' she added, for good measure.

'Any sign of trouble, call us,' he repeated.

Afterwards, she reproached herself for all the things she hadn't told him. Had he already mastered the network of friends and family and childhood romances that encircled everybody connected to the murder victims? Had it seemed clear to him from the outset that George Baxter had been killed because he knew who murdered Markie? Should this have been the central point that Simmy herself had focused on? She had spent time with him, on Saturday evening. Had he said anything to suggest an identity for the killer? As far as she could remember, he hadn't got beyond Peter and his cronies as a collective. But perhaps Eleanor had been given a clue? Or – more worrying – perhaps Eleanor had told people that she, Simmy, had been to the house and might well know more than was comfortable.

'Who were you talking to?' asked Bridget, when she finally went back into the living room.

'The detective inspector. It's all right. He won't tell Peter where you are.'

'You shouldn't have done that.' There was more resignation than anger in the voice. 'We can't trust the police.'

'I think we can.' A thought struck her. 'Where's your car? I didn't see it when I came home. If anybody's looking for you, they might see it.'

'I walked. It's only about five miles. I've done it about five million times before – from the Ambleside house, anyway. The new one's a bit further, but no big deal.'

'I'm impressed,' said Simmy sincerely. 'I'd be lost after ten minutes.'

'Peter showed me all the tracks, when I was about ten.'

'So – won't he guess where you are? If you used to come here all the time? He'll know I live here now. He'll make the connection.' In spite of herself, she felt a burgeoning fear, speeding her breathing and churning her insides. Peter Harrison-West was an unpredictable character, as she had already discovered. 'He can be quite . . . violent,' she pointed out.

'I left him a note, actually, saying I was going down to see Penny in Wiltshire. Then I hid the car on the other side of Rydal Water. I was quite clever, you see.'

*Clever enough to kill two men and get away with it?* wondered Simmy.

'Why didn't you tell me that before I phoned the police?' she demanded, feeling that she'd been foolishly precipitate.

'Why should I? Anyway, I didn't think you'd sneak off and do it without telling me first. I should be cross with you, but I'm too tired.'

'That makes two of us. Look – we need some supper. I'll do scrambled eggs or something. We can watch a bit of telly and then go to bed.'

Wasn't this too much of a repeat of Monday night, when Melanie had stayed? Was she fated to act hostess to a succession of young women with assorted reasons for wanting to use her spare room? Who was it going to be next?

'You don't approve of me, do you?' Bridget's expression was defiant. 'No job, no A-levels, a childhood spent roaming around the fells. Marrying a man more than twice my age. I'm not your idea of a success, am I?'

Simmy's mouth opened and closed three times before she constructed a response. 'I don't *disapprove*,' she protested. 'It's not for me to judge. I'm curious, I admit. It's a long way outside anything I've come across before. But I absolutely don't disapprove. You've got me all wrong, if that's what you think.'

'I liked you when we came about the flowers. You were great. That seems *years* ago now.'

'Does disapproval bother you, then? Is that what you expect everyone to feel?'

'More or less. Everyone except Markie and my father, really. I've lost the only two men I could fully trust.'

There was just a shade too much self-dramatization in this speech for Simmy to be convinced that the girl was entirely pitiable.

'And Peter's friends,' she prompted.

'They don't count. They only see it from his point of view, don't they?' She heaved a pitiful sigh. 'The thing is – I thought that if somehow it *did* go wrong, I'd always have Markie to run to. And if he couldn't cope, then Daddy would save the day. He'd send me off to some friend in Singapore or somewhere and everything would be all right. And I know that makes me sound like a spoilt little rich girl.'

'It does a bit,' Simmy agreed. 'At least it sounds as if life's been just a game for you up to now.'

Bridget frowned doubtfully. 'Not a *game*, exactly. Marrying Peter was quite serious, believe it or not. He wanted it so badly, and was so lovely about it, I never thought there'd be any problems. We've only been sleeping together for a year, you know. He wanted to wait until I was properly grown up. He said I had to pass my driving test first,' she giggled.

'But not the A-levels,' Simmy could not resist adding.

'There! I *knew* you disapproved of that part.'

'I didn't even know you hadn't done them until just now. It never crossed my mind to wonder what exams you'd passed. I'm nothing like as conventional as you seem to think.'

'Aren't you?'

They both examined the subject in silence for a minute. It had never before occurred to Simmy to assess her own rating in terms of conventionality. She wondered how DI Moxon regarded her in that respect. 'My mother's a complete rebel,' she said at last. 'I suppose she thinks I'm boringly ordinary compared to her. It depends where you start from, doesn't it? I can't see myself getting arrested for any of the thought crimes that exist these days, but I might well go on a march to protest against the abandonment of proper planning laws.'

'Planning laws!' Bridget's mockery was gentle, but real. 'Wow!'

'And,' Simmy pressed on, 'I can see there's not a lot of sense in ploughing through years of education with hardly any prospect of a decent job at the end of it, if you're not interested in it for its own sake.'

'I did quite like school, as it happens. I was extremely good at languages, and art. I can draw brilliantly.'

'Well, I guess that means you'll find a job easily enough if it comes to the crunch.'

'Don't you think the crunch might be rather horribly close?' The giggles had rapidly died away, to be replaced by pathos. 'I don't feel old enough to deal with it, that's what it is. I'm a little lamb lost in the wood, and there's nobody I trust to look after me. They've all turned into wolves.'

'Even Peter?'

'Even Peter,' she confirmed miserably.

# *Chapter Seventeen*

Melanie was in the shop promptly at noon next day, eager to report everything Joe had said the night before. Of course – Simmy remembered – Wednesday nights were always nights out with Joe, as well as Fridays and Saturdays. That would be why there'd been no further mention of staying at Simmy's in a protective role.

'He says there's scarcely any evidence for either of the killings. They've been doing door-to-door stuff in Bowness, but nobody's said anything useful. The people at Storrs just want to get back to work as usual, as quick as they can. You can't blame them, can you?'

Simmy had debated with herself, on the drive back from Coniston, whether or not to tell Melanie that she had a new lodger. If there was to be any reality to the idea that they might work together to identify the murderer, she obviously had to mention it. But Bridget would certainly have forbidden any such disclosure, if she had been consulted. As it was, Simmy had crept out of the house at seven-thirty, leaving the girl asleep in the spare room. The undisturbed night had been a great relief, once she had satisfied herself that it really had been undisturbed. She had slept so well, there was every chance that Bridget had been abducted at 2 a.m., without Simmy waking. But no. When she peeped into the room, there was her guest peacefully curled under the duvet, evidently far from the point of natural awakening. Simmy left a note with her phone number, and a suggestion she have a long serious think about what she ought to do next.

'Listen, Mel – something happened last night, at my house.'

'My God! Don't tell me somebody tried to break in? Did you keep them out? Are you okay?'

'I'm fine. Somebody *did* break in, sort of. Well, she had a key—'

'She? Who? I don't get it.'

'Bridget. She used to go in and out all the time, when Markie lived there, and kept a key, apparently. I called the police to tell them where she was, in case Peter reported her missing.'

Melanie went into deep thought, her prosthetic eye staring fixedly, while the other one flickered to and fro. It gave her a look both robotic and vulnerable. 'That's very weird,' she said, finally. 'Does she think Peter did the murders, then? She's run away from him twice now, after all. And he *is* pretty aggressive. I suppose I'd be scared of him, as well, if I was her.'

'She doesn't know who she can trust. I think there was a lot she wasn't telling me.'

'But she let you call the cops. What did they say?'

'I spoke to the Moxon man. And Bridget didn't actually

*let* me. I went off into the kitchen and did it of my own accord. He was interested. Said I shouldn't assume she was as innocent as she seems. Something like that, anyway.'

'He thinks *she* killed them? But she was up in that bridal room, wasn't she – the whole time? So she couldn't have drowned Markie. She wouldn't be strong enough, anyway.'

'I know. He's probably thinking the whole lot of them conspired together to do it. That they're all lying their heads off, to keep him from guessing what really happened.'

'Could be he's right.'

'I don't think so. They all seem much too edgy for that. All scared of each other, because nobody knows who – if any of them – did it. Glenn followed me and Eleanor outside, on Sunday, for a private word. Pablo comes here on his own looking for Bridget, then Peter the same. It doesn't feel to me like a gang working together.'

'The big picture!' Melanie congratulated her. 'Isn't that what you're meant to be good at? Looks to me as if you really are. It's a great skill.'

'Seems like plain common sense to me,' said Simmy modestly.

'So what happens next? How long is Bridget staying at yours? Is she in the same bed I was in?'

'Of course. I made it up fresh for her, like a good hostess. My mother would be proud of me. One thing she's really conscientious about is the sheets.'

'You'd have to be,' Melanie agreed absently. 'They'll find her, won't they? They might be there already, for all we know.'

'She'll be all right. She's very clever. She hid her car

242

somewhere near Rydal Water and walked all the way to Troutbeck, over the fells. That's pretty intrepid, with everything so muddy.'

'Or desperate. It must be six miles, at least.'

'She said five. Made very light of it.'

'But Peter knows she's capable of that sort of thing. He'll follow her trail.'

'She left a note saying she's gone to Wiltshire to see Markie's mother. Penny, she's called.'

'He'll find out with a phone call that she's not there, won't he?'

'Probably. Unless she's already got Penny to tell him she *is* there. She might have thought of that.'

'Dodgy,' said Melanie, but she seemed impressed. 'Meanwhile she's camping out at your place for how long?'

'No idea,' sighed Simmy. 'I imagine she's waiting for something to happen, like the rest of us.'

The next thing to happen was a not entirely unexpected visit from DI Moxon. He came in as before, deliberately, looking all around. His hair, Simmy noted, was greasier than ever. His dark eyes seemed smaller, with pouches beneath them. 'You look tired,' she said, without thinking.

'Mm.' He waved away the comment. 'I thought I should see you in person, make sure you're all right. Have to look after the witnesses, you know.' It was a feeble attempt at jocularity and she shook her head in protest.

'I never actually witnessed anything, did I? I can't have been the slightest bit of help with either of the murders. I'm probably a complete waste of time. A red herring.'

'No, no. You're very far from that. I told you before – your involvement is extremely useful. Possibly dangerous, as well.'

'Yes, you told me that before, too. I actually believed you on Monday. Since then I've got a lot braver. It's not looking as if I'm seen as a threat, after all.'

'Too soon to say,' he warned her. 'Much too soon.'

'Especially now she's got Bridget under her wing,' said Melanie. 'That might upset whoever-he-is quite a lot.'

'But if he doesn't want to get caught, he's going to steer clear, isn't he?' Simmy responded. 'He's going to carry on as normal, and hope the police don't find any evidence. Every passing day must be making him feel more and more confident.'

'Girls, girls,' pleaded the detective. 'This isn't how it's supposed to go. All this guesswork only clouds the issue. Somebody somewhere is playing a very nasty, dangerous, cruel game, and everyone needs to be very, very careful.'

'Be afraid. Be *very* afraid,' teased Simmy.

The others both gazed at her as if she had very definitely overstepped a mark. 'Sorry,' she mumbled. 'I don't know what came over me. I'm usually quite a serious person. It was just . . . well, you *did* sound awfully doomy,' she told the man. 'I guess I wanted to put a more female perspective on it. Life goes on, the flowers keep blooming – that sort of thing.'

He blinked at her. His eyes looked dry and sore behind his glasses. 'Last night you shouted at me for saying we can't be sure of Mrs Harrison-West. You said she was a victim, and I was all wrong for treating her with suspicion. Is that still true?'

244

Melanie and Simmy exchanged a glance. 'She *is* very clever,' Simmy admitted. 'But she's definitely confused and scared. She doesn't trust her husband, and that must be horrible. She says he's weak, which I think is a whole new perception for her. It makes her feel alone, I assume. And she's terribly sad about Markie.'

'Not to mention her dad,' contributed Melanie.

'Exactly,' Simmy agreed.

'She thinks Harrison-West is weak? Was that your impression?' Moxon asked Simmy.

'Not exactly. We didn't tell you, did we, that he came in here yesterday, when Mel was on her own, and behaved very threateningly.'

'You did not,' he said heavily. 'When was this?'

'After lunch. I had to take flowers up to a house in Kentmere, and when I got back he was waving a fist in Mel's face.'

'And you didn't report it?' His disbelief came close to eliciting another flippant response, but she clamped her lips together firmly.

'We did think about it,' defended Melanie. 'But the idea seemed a bit . . . inappropriate.'

'Disproportionate, she means,' said Simmy. 'He's got enough to worry about, after all. At least, that's what we thought at the time.'

'We almost felt sorry for him.'

'We did,' Simmy realised. 'And that suggests he might be a bit weak, after all. All bluster and bluff, hiding who knows what. And he's quite short, isn't he?' she added inconsequentially.

Moxon peered from under his dark brows. 'What bearing does that have?'

She guessed he himself was about five feet ten. 'When you're as tall as me and Melanie, short men can be difficult. They feel as if they're at a disadvantage. It's quite natural, but it's sometimes irritating. It makes them louder than they might be otherwise. Thinking about it now, I'd say that's all it was with Peter.'

'Throwing his weight around? But don't you think a man with so much money, all those loyal friends, and a lovely new young wife would be confident enough to stand up to you, even if you are an inch or so taller than him?'

'The new young wife had just run away from him – for the second time. Two people closely connected to her are dead. The loyal friends are itching to get back to their normal lives somewhere else. I imagine all that might have shaken whatever confidence he had on Saturday . . .' Simmy paused, rather proud of herself.

'So do you or don't you think he's weak?' persisted Moxon.

'I don't know, to be honest. On the whole, I think he's much the same as anybody else would be in the same situation.' She hesitated. 'Except for something that still bothers me – why didn't he show up on Sunday, with Mr Baxter? I asked him and he said he knew nothing about it.'

'But Baxter told you he was definitely coming? Harrison-West, I mean.'

'As far as I can recall, yes. I kept thinking he'd appear at any moment.'

'I've got a note of it,' he said, distractedly, before taking a deep breath and looking at his watch. 'I'll have to go. Just one more thing. You said Bridget ran away twice?'

'Oh. Yes. On Tuesday. She came here, and Pablo caught her and took her back.' Every time she spoke the name *Pablo*, something warm trickled down her spine. She noticed it more strongly with each repetition.

'Like rounding up an escaped captive,' he said thoughtfully.

'Exactly like that, yes. And now she's hiding at my house so they can't round her up again.'

'Is she afraid for her life?'

The stark question hung in the air. Was it possible for everything to change for Bridget so quickly and so totally? 'I'm not sure,' she answered. 'She's known Glenn and Peter since she was a little girl, and the others for nearly as long. She must think there's a good reason to lose trust in them, but I wouldn't say she's actually terrified. More defiant than that. There's quite a lot to her. And she's massively upset about Markie.'

'Not to mention her dad,' repeated Melanie loudly. 'He was shot, remember.'

'And we need to find the gun,' Moxon said. 'Except it's probably at the bottom of the lake, or under a rock up on Wansfell or Kentmere Pike.'

Simmy and Melanie murmured sympathetically. The detective went on, 'Although it is quite a special piece, according to the lab. Not something you'd throw away lightly. So the hope is that it'll show up again one of these days.'

'Just like that?' queried Melanie sceptically.

He sighed tiredly. 'No, not just like that. Every gun attack anywhere in the world from here on will be compared with this one, by computers.'

'But that presupposes it'll be used to kill someone else,' objected Simmy. 'Do you think that's likely?'

'Who can say?' He was almost through the door. Before leaving, he looked around the shop again. 'Don't get many customers, do you?'

'Enough,' she snapped. 'A lot of the business is done on the computer and phone, anyway.'

He looked at the window display and raised his eyebrows disparagingly. Before Simmy could react, he was gone.

As if to confound his remarks, two customers materialised over the next twenty minutes. A man wanted red roses – always a worrying sign – and a smart woman wearing leather gloves was looking for a canna lily. 'A canna lucifer, if possible. They're red, with yellow edges.' She spoke with determination, as if able to conjure the flower by sheer willpower. Simmy's failure to supply it was a major personal insult, it seemed, and she stomped out with a toss of her head. 'I had some last week,' mourned Simmy to Melanie. 'And nobody wanted them.'

'That's life,' said Melanie, with scant sympathy. 'Get a whole lot next week and put them in the window.'

When the door opened again, both Simmy and Melanie were in the cool room, constructing an order for the following day, trying to anticipate weekend demand. 'Shop!' came a familiar voice.

'It's your mum,' said Melanie, superfluously.

Angie was not a regular caller at Persimmon Petals,

although she liked to keep a display of fresh flowers in the hallway, and would insist on paying the full price for them when she got them from Simmy. Russell did his best to keep her supplied from the garden, but there were inevitable lean times when nothing presented itself.

'All right?' Simmy asked automatically, trying to remember which day it had been when she last saw her parents. The week was passing jerkily, leaping from crisis to crisis. Sunday – it had been Sunday. Of course.

'Not entirely,' said Angie.

'Why? What's the matter?'

'Those bloody people, of course. The ones with the kid on Saturday. They won't shut up about it. They're pressing charges against us. I need to get a solicitor. We'll have to provide name and address for Lucy, I expect. You'll have to tell her parents what happened.'

'Oh, for heaven's sake! I thought children banged their heads all the time. Aren't they designed to cope with it?'

'This one's different, apparently. There's a subcranial haematoma and he's got to have surgery to relieve the pressure. It could be serious, actually. It can cause epilepsy and a whole lot of things, if the pressure gets too bad. He *did* hit the fireplace quite hard, I suppose.'

'He was a little beast. It served him right.'

'I'm not sure that's the sensible line to take. I'm going to have to grovel and abase myself and plead guilty. The fact that Lucy's brother, or whatever he was, had just been murdered might count as a mitigating factor, if I'm lucky.'

'Eleanor's not going to be very cooperative. She'll blame me.'

'It's your fault, technically. You were *in loco parentis*.'

'Was I? I had no idea.'

'Just give me the address, will you? And phone number if you've got it.' Angie stood tall and unyielding, a stoical Englishwoman facing up to her responsibilities. 'I don't suppose it'll come to anything too ghastly. I've got liability insurance, thank goodness.'

'I don't know the phone number. And I can't remember the name of the house. I'll have to ask Bridget.'

Melanie was yet again at her elbow, listening to everything that was being said. 'You have got them, Sim,' she said. 'You did the flowers at the wedding, remember? Eleanor Baxter was paying for them. You've got her on your database.'

Simmy smacked herself lightly on the forehead. 'Gosh, yes. What an idiot. I wasn't thinking.' The wedding seemed impossibly long ago. She went to the computer, and copied down Eleanor's address and phone number onto a card. 'I'm sorry, Mum. I've been so distracted this week, I can't think straight any more. The detective man's been here again. They don't seem to be getting anywhere at all.'

Angie took the card, with a little frown. 'You said just now you'd ask Bridget. How could you do that? Isn't she off with her new husband somewhere?'

Simmy realised how much of the story her parents had missed and felt a strong resistance to bringing them up to date. She threw a warning glance at Melanie, before saying, 'No, actually. They had to cancel the honeymoon. Bridget's been in here once or twice since the weekend. She seems to want me to be her friend.'

'You'd think she'd want to stay as far away from you as

possible. You must be associated with two very nasty deaths, in her mind, surely? What does she want from you?'

'She seems rather short of female friends. Her mother's too busy with Lucy to be much use. And I do find her intriguing.'

'Well, good luck to you. Although I'd have thought Melanie would be more suited as a friend than you. Closer in age, I mean.'

Melanie smirked gently, and said nothing.

Simmy bit back any further half-truths and self-justifications. 'Sorry, Mum, but we've got quite a bit still to do before closing time. I'm extremely sorry about the trouble Lucy and I seem to have caused.'

'Oh well. Some people just attract trouble. There's not much anybody can do about it.'

'Do you mean me?'

'Of course not. The Tomkinses, obviously. They do everything they can think of to keep the dark side away, and see what happens. A small girl fells their kid in a perfectly safe bed and breakfast house and the only response they can come up with is to sue us. They think that's the normal way to react – that's the worst part of it. They'll go through life blaming other people for every little misfortune that befalls them. They don't deserve to live.'

'You don't mean that,' said Simmy, with a faint smile. Her mother had quite a lengthy list of people who she felt had no rightful place in the world.

'I do, actually.'

'Somebody felt the same about Markie and George Baxter,' Melanie reminded her, forcefully. 'And look what they went and did.'

Angie laughed uneasily. 'Well, I never said I wanted to *kill* them,' she defended. 'I just think they're rather a waste of space.'

'I don't think there's really a shortage of space,' Melanie came back, stiffly.

'Stop it!' begged Simmy. 'This is one you're never going to win. Mum's had decades of practice. And if you'd met the bloody Tomkins family, you'd probably agree with her.'

'Huh!' sniffed Melanie. 'I doubt it.'

They were saved further animosity by the arrival of Ben, thus making the shop feel rather crowded. Simmy introduced him minimally to her mother, who kinked a questioning eyebrow at him. 'I won't even ask what the basis of your relationship might be,' she said. 'I'm going home now. If you get a customer, there won't be enough space for all of us.'

Ben had a raised abrasion on the side of his face. 'What happened?' Simmy asked him, when Angie had gone.

'Peter Harrison-West punched me,' said the boy. 'Ten minutes ago.'

# Chapter Eighteen

'Where? Why? Does he *know* you?' Simmy fired the questions at the bemused youngster.

Ben delicately fingered his injury. 'It does hurt,' he whined. 'Is it broken, do you think?'

'The upper jaw doesn't break easily,' Melanie assured him. 'You were lucky it wasn't further down. Or up,' she added bitterly, indicating her own ruined eye.

'Answers!' Simmy ordered him. 'Tell us the whole story.'

'I was with Wilf, and he recognised HW, as he calls him. We followed him, just for a bit of fun, really. He was up by the station, just sort of wandering about. It looked a bit crazy to us.'

'Searching for Bridget, presumably,' said Melanie.

'Why? Is she lost?' Ben's eyes widened.

'*He* thinks so. Did he look as if he was searching?'

'Not at all. He looked out of it – drunk or drugged. And *wild*. He reminded me of Raskolnikov – you know?'

'No,' said Simmy and Melanie in unison.

'In *Crime and Punishment*. He wanders about with

staring eyes, after he's done the murder. You should read it. It's amazing how it stays in your mind, every detail.'

'Peter,' Simmy prompted him.

'Okay. Well, that's more or less it. We thought we should try to help him. He looked as if he might get run over if he went on like that. So we caught up with him, and asked him if he needed anything. He snarled at us like a mad dog and told us to leave him alone. "Haven't I got enough trouble?" he said. So I said, "Is it something to do with the death of your brother-in-law and father-in-law?" and he just hit me, with no warning. Wilf pulled me away, and we left him to get on with it. I hope he does get run over, the pig.'

Melanie was breathless with excitement. 'So he *must* be the killer? And the guilt has sent him mad? You know, I often think that must happen to people, once they realise what they've done. They can't bear the reality. It's so *final*, isn't it? You can never undo it again.'

'That's pure Raskolnikov,' muttered Ben.

'Where did Wilf go?' asked Simmy.

'He came as far as your door, and left me here. He's working this evening.'

'We should tell the police,' said Simmy slowly. 'We absolutely have to, this time.'

'What? That he hit me?' Ben said dubiously. 'I'm not sure—'

'Not just that, but how he was behaving generally.'

'I wouldn't bother. Somebody else will have spotted him by now and called the cops. He was really acting very strange.'

'Poor man,' said Simmy, surprising herself.

'What? Why is he poor?' Melanie demanded. 'However upset he is, there's no call to hit an innocent bystander like that.'

'I know. But he's lost everything he's wanted for all these years, hasn't he? He waited so patiently for Bridget to grow up, and now she's scared of him and hiding away from him.'

'With good reason, if he killed her brother and father.'

'I don't get it. Why would he do that? What possible reason could there be? It's completely illogical to think it was him.'

'We don't know enough about him. Maybe he's been psychotic all along, and kept it well hidden. Markie might have said something to him that made him see red, and before he knew what he'd done, the boy was drowned. Then George might have suspected him, so he had to go as well. That's quite logical, if you ask me.'

'Maybe.' Simmy's doubts were strengthening, the more she thought about it.

'Ben thinks he's a murderer, don't you?' Melanie nudged the boy.

'I don't know. There's definitely something wrong with him. You know – I think Simmy has the right idea, feeling sorry for him.'

'What? You said he was a pig just now.'

'Yes, I know. But he's sort of pathetic as well. Tell me about Bridget. What's been happening that I don't know about?'

Simmy gave a brief summary of the previous evening. 'I left her there this morning, but I don't know if she'll stay. She seems to be a law unto herself.'

'She's a user,' said Ben.

'A *drug* user?'

'No, no. She uses *people*. She's spoilt and pampered and rich, and just does whatever she likes.'

'I don't think so. Not exactly. She has had a very free life, admittedly. And everything went right for her until now. But she's clever and strong, as well. She's had two gigantic shocks, all at the same time, but she's still functioning. She told me Peter was weak. That's another shock. And she's so *young*.'

Ben and Melanie said nothing to this, seemingly aware of their own youthful ignorance as well as Bridget's.

'Anyway,' Simmy went on, 'let's find something for that face. I've got some witch hazel in the back room. It works wonders on bruises.'

'I always think that's because of its fabulous name,' laughed Melanie. 'I wrote a story when I was little about a witch called Hazel.'

Simmy went out to her first-aid kit, and when she got back a third youngster was in the shop. At first she assumed it was Ben's brother Wilf, but on closer inspection, he seemed to be more closely linked to Melanie. 'This is Joe,' the girl explained. 'He wanted to come and meet you.'

Joe the police constable was sandy-haired, with a wide loose smile. For reasons she could not immediately explain, Simmy was not glad to see him. He was a complication, a rogue link in a twisted chain. He would be eager to extract information from her about the Baxters and Harrison-Wests, in an effort to earn himself some gold stars with the CID. He would distract Melanie, and interrogate Ben.

'Hello,' she said. 'I'm afraid it's all rather busy just now. We're closing in a few minutes, and I've got to tally up the takings and a whole lot else.'

Melanie gave her a reproachful look. 'He only came to say hello,' she said.

'That's fine. No problem,' Simmy lied. 'Ben, you'd better come through to the back for a minute. Make a bit of space.' She could not have explained her resistance to telling Joe the story of Peter's attack on Ben. Melanie would tell him anyway, she supposed. She herself had wanted to report it to Moxon.

'What happened to your face, mate?' Joe asked, thereby destroying any lingering hope that it might go unnoticed.

Ben, however, was ahead of her. 'Bit of bother in the playground,' he said, staring hard at Melanie. 'Had to separate a pair of Year Nines that were trying to kill each other. Got in the way of a fist in the process.'

Simmy closed her eyes for two long seconds. The lie would be sure to get out, sooner rather than later, and Ben would have to explain himself. But for the moment she was profoundly grateful to him. 'Come on, then,' she said warmly. 'We'll soon have the sting taken off it.'

'Just wanted to say,' Joe began, with some effort, 'that I know you've got the Harrison-West lady at your house. I've been driving past all day, checking to make sure there's no bother.'

Simmy halted in her tracks. 'Oh?' she gulped, wondering why she felt so guilty. 'Does the whole police force know where she is? Because if they do, I imagine it won't stay a secret for long.'

'Just me and a couple of others. I thought she needed protection?'

'I don't know what she needs,' Simmy flashed crossly. 'The whole thing is a bloody mess.'

Joe, she remembered, had been at Storrs on Saturday. He had told Melanie about Markie Baxter's murder, and Melanie had immediately rushed to summon her. Joe probably felt himself to be in a special role. Perhaps with some justification, if Moxon had selected him as Bridget's guardian.

'Sorry,' she said. 'It's just getting a bit too much for me, that's all. Come on, Ben.' She almost dragged him into the back room.

'We'll be off, then,' called Melanie after them, her voice full of anger. 'If you don't need me any more.'

'Okay. Thanks, Mel. I'll see you on Saturday morning.'

'If not before.' It sounded like a threat. The doorbell pinged as they departed, and Simmy let out a long breath.

'We've upset her,' she said.

'It's the boyfriend's fault. Why did she have to take up with him, anyway? He's got no more brains than a mollusc.'

'It probably won't last. But why did we do that? It was awful of us.'

'It was me, more than you. I guess we just weren't ready. We need to process everything first.'

'You're right,' she realised. 'Completely and absolutely right.'

'Nobody's ever hit me before. It's very unpleasant.'

She laughed. 'I think it's meant to be.'

'No,' he said seriously. 'It's more than that. It steps

over a line, changes how you see things. It's a failure.'

'Failure?'

'It shows the limitations of reason and argument and language.' He was groping for words. 'It puts us back with the animals.'

'My husband hit me once,' she said. 'That's when I knew we were finished. I think that might be why he did it – to show me. It wasn't very hard. I don't think I minded it as much as you do. My baby had died – being hit didn't seem so terrible after that.'

He examined her face, rather as DI Moxon had done. She felt under scrutiny from someone much more mature than a schoolboy. 'You didn't think he might kill you if you stayed with him?'

'It never entered my head.'

'No.'

'Why?'

'Because I can't really see HW as a killer, either. Hitting and killing aren't the same thing.'

'Except you can kill someone if you hit them too hard.' She thought of the child Lucy, doing such damage to the annoying little boy.

'That's different. These killings were planned, and the person escaped. It's someone cunning and full of hate. HW isn't like that.'

'He came here, you know. Yesterday.'

'You told me. He was angry. Now he's wild and half mad.'

'Could it be that something's happened?' Simmy wondered why this hadn't struck her sooner. 'Has he found Bridget? She might have phoned him, at least. She might have told him she wasn't going back to him. Or Eleanor might have spoken to him for some reason.'

'Bridget's mother? His mother-in-law.'

'Right.'

'Do they like each other?'

'Good question. She's less than ten years older than him. It's bound to be a bit peculiar for both of them. But she seemed happy enough about the marriage, even if she doesn't like weddings. She's paid for the flowers, anyhow. It showed up on the computer this morning. How's that for efficiency?'

'Cold-blooded, if you ask me.'

'Maybe so,' nodded Simmy.

'What'll you do if Bridget isn't there when you get home?' he wondered. Then he grinned and added, 'And what'll you do if she *is*?'

'Get on with it, either way, I suppose. You know, I *do* feel a bit used, now you've drawn my attention to it. She should definitely have gone to her mother for protection, not me.'

He was still fingering his face, pressing the edges of the contusion experimentally. 'I'll have to tell my mum something. And then tell Wilf what the story is.'

'Is the truth out of the question?'

He pulled a face. 'It seems to be, yeah. Don't you think?'

'I'm not sure. Won't Peter expect you to report him, at least to your parents?'

'He was past caring. And he doesn't know who they are.'

'There's something very primitive about all this. Men fighting and killing each other, while the women stand back and take the consequences.'

'I prefer my violence to be virtual,' he grumbled. 'It doesn't hurt that way.'

She gave herself a shake. 'This is all very bad for business. I've got a lot to do yet before I can go home.'

He looked around, peering into the window display. 'Still not quite right,' he said critically. 'I could come and do it for you on Saturday, if you like. And we'll make some sketches for the model of the clock tower. You *are* up for that, aren't you?' He squinted anxiously at her, as if expecting disappointment.

She responded with an effort. 'There's nothing wrong with the display. I don't know what you mean. But yes, I like the idea of the model, if we can find a way to make it stay up.'

He grinned. 'Just let me at it. I won't break anything, I promise.'

'We'll see. Saturday still seems rather a long way off, at the moment. I've got a mountain of work lined up for tomorrow, first.'

'See you, then,' he chirped, and was away before she could say another word.

It was seven o'clock when she got back to Troutbeck. There were no lights in the front windows, and she found herself hoping that Bridget had taken herself off somewhere, to leave her in peace. The thought of the girl making free with her house was less disturbing than she would have anticipated, but it was still mildly disagreeable. She had no desire to act as nursemaid to another Baxter daughter, despite being curious as to Bridget's personality. She let herself in cautiously, braced for almost anything.

Bridget was sitting in darkness, in the living room, a cushion clutched to her chest. She jerked violently as Simmy entered the room, putting the light on automatically. 'Oh, it's you. Thank God,' she breathed. 'Put the light off.'

Simmy did as instructed. 'Why? What's been happening?' Everything looked normal at first glance.

'Pablo. He was here, shouting for me, banging on the door. Your neighbours heard him and came out to see what he wanted. They told him you were at work, and they were sure there was nobody in the house. I was down there, hiding.' She pointed at the floor under the window. 'He peered in, but he couldn't see me. He went round the back, as well. I thought he was going to break in, but luckily he didn't.'

'When? What time was it?'

'This afternoon. About four, I think. It wasn't dark.'

'There's been a policeman patrolling past all day. Have you seen him? I suppose he didn't see Pablo by any chance?'

She shook her head. 'It wouldn't be difficult to wait until he was out of the way. I never saw anybody, anyway. Was the policeman on foot?'

'In a car, I think. Useless, really. But Pablo went away?'

'Yes. But I can't stay here, can I? Not now. Someone's sure to see me.' She was huddled down on the sofa, as if afraid of being spotted from the window. 'I should have closed the curtains, but then I thought the neighbours might notice, and know someone was here.'

Simmy groaned. 'This is ridiculous, isn't it? What are you so scared of? There must be more than you've told me.'

'No, there isn't. But you can't understand how they've all

262

changed. *All* of them. They know something, and it's made them strange and horrible.'

Simmy thought of the wild-eyed Peter throwing punches in the streets of Windermere, and ruefully agreed. 'You think they know who the murderer is?'

'Must do. But it can't have been one of them – can it? Poor sweet Markie, he never hurt anybody, never did anything nasty. What monster could kill him? I've been sitting here all day thinking about him. He was just one of *us*, they all loved him.'

'I saw them together, on Saturday morning. I told you, didn't I? Standing in a group outside the hotel in the rain. They all looked very *together*, if that makes sense. Relaxed, even.' She caught herself up. 'Well, not relaxed exactly. There might have been an undercurrent of tension. They didn't quite like it when Markie came to talk to me. One of them – Glenn, I think – called to him, wanting to know what he was doing.'

'It probably seemed a bit odd to them. Markie didn't usually act of his own accord. He'd wait for somebody else to take the lead.'

They were barely able to see each other in the murky room, and Simmy felt a reluctance to conjure the murdered Markie too vividly. He had, after all, grown up in this very house. She changed the subject determinedly. 'Have you had anything to eat?'

'A bit of bread and some ham that was in the fridge. Is that okay?'

'Of course.' Simmy went to the window and pulled the curtains across. Then she turned the light on again. 'We're going to have to decide what to do. You can't go on like this, can you?'

'No. I know I can't. I've been thinking about it and I remembered your mum runs a B&B. Would she have me for a bit, do you think? As a properly paying guest? You could take me in your car, and nobody would guess where I was.'

Simmy laughed sceptically. 'She might have done, but she's a bit off your family, I'm afraid. All thanks to your little sister.'

'Lucy? What on earth do you mean?'

The story was quickly told. Bridget clearly found it hard to take the matter seriously. 'Oh well, if it comes to the crunch, my mother will pay up. She always thinks money can put things right – and most of the time it does, actually. With that sort of stuff, anyway.'

'I'm going to get us something to eat. Then we have to have a serious talk. I really don't like being so involved, you know.' It wasn't strictly true, she admitted to herself. She had long since passed the point where non-involvement felt like any sort of an option.

'Okay,' said Bridget in a very small voice. The second syllable was drowned by a thunderous knocking on the front door.

# *Chapter Nineteen*

Pablo and Glenn both stood there, solidly shoulder to shoulder, when Simmy opened the door. Glenn carried a bulky bag. 'Can we come in?' he said, with an air of urgency. 'We know Bridget's here.'

'She doesn't want to see you.'

'We understand that. We've left it till now, so she'll have you to look out for her. We're not going to hurt her. She's got nothing to fear from us.' The emphasis was odd, implying that she might well have something to fear from another quarter.

Grudgingly, she held the door just open enough for them to get in, glancing along the quiet street in the vain hope of seeing a friendly police car gliding past. 'She isn't going to like it,' she warned them.

'Don't worry,' Pablo smiled at her. 'It'll be fine, you see. Bridget's not in any danger at all. She never should have gone off like this.'

'She had her reasons,' Simmy defended, already feeling undermined by his charm. No man should be so beautiful. It wasn't fair.

'Well, maybe she has,' growled Glenn, who was so totally unprepossessing next to his friend that it was almost grotesque. His cropped head and thick neck gave him the look of a creature made for sweeping through cold northern waters. A seal, she thought. He's like a seal.

Subtly they had got themselves into the hallway, before Simmy had quite noticed what was happening. The front door was firmly closed, cutting off any prospect of passing policemen seeing anything unusual. 'Bridget!' Glenn called with authority. 'Come on, girl. We know you're there.'

This was met with silence. Simmy knew herself to be a traitor for letting them in. It was quite possible that the young bride had already vanished through the back door and out over the dark fells at the first sound of Glenn's gravelly voice.

'Where is she?' asked Pablo. 'I know she was here this afternoon. I could see her bag in the kitchen.'

*So that was it*, thought Simmy. Bridget's distinctive purple bag, in which she had brought minimal necessities for herself, ought to have been safely out of sight upstairs, but she must have brought it down for some reason.

'Damn you, Glenn,' came a sulky voice. 'What do you want?'

'I've got a whole lot to tell you,' he replied, following the voice. 'I can't pretend it's good news, but there's no danger to you. I'm not even going to try and take you away from here. It's actually quite a clever place to be for a little while.'

They all moved into the living room and encircled Bridget where she remained crouched on the sofa. Pablo hung back

266

slightly, obviously meaning to leave all the talking to his friend. He was planning to go back to London, Simmy remembered. She had assumed he would be already gone, from what Moxon had said. Something must have happened to stop him.

'Something's happened,' she said aloud. 'Hasn't it? Something to do with Peter?'

'Peter's gone a bit off the rails, yes,' Glenn agreed. 'I'm afraid it was Bridget disappearing the way she did that finished him. He's been out there searching all day.'

'He hit Ben Harkness in the face,' said Simmy. 'This afternoon. Ben said he's liable to get arrested, the way he's behaving.'

'Who the hell is Ben Harkness?' Glenn demanded, plainly displeased at this intervention.

'The boy who was there when George Baxter was shot on Sunday. He's another witness.'

'Never heard of him,' Glenn dismissed. 'Why did he have to provoke Peter? Wasn't that rather stupid? Unless . . .' he paused meaningfully, as if a highly alarming thought had just struck him.

'Unless what?' asked Bridget.

'Never mind for a minute. Let me start at the beginning. It might fit together later on.' Again his pause was full of heavy significance. 'The thing is, Peter has admitted to me that it was him.'

They all stared at him, Pablo included. 'Him what?' said Bridget. 'What are you talking about?'

Glenn reached into his sturdy leather bag and carefully brought forth a gun, gleaming with menace, to Simmy's eyes.

'This is what killed George,' he said softly. 'It's Peter's. He asked me to hide it for him.'

'You're joking!' Bridget sat up straight, then leant forward for a better look. Simmy caught Pablo glancing at the window, as if to be sure they could not be observed. 'I never saw it before. Peter has never had a gun like that.'

'I promise you, it's his. It used to be his father's. It's rather special, actually. A fine old Mk I Lee Enfield.'

'Is it registered?' asked Simmy.

Glenn laughed. 'I think not. The old man had it from *his* father, back in the dark ages. The story goes that it was abandoned at Dunkirk and Peter's grandpa "rescued" it. It should have been returned to munitions but he stashed it away and kept it ever since. It works, though. It works a treat.' He stroked the shining wooden stock, as if it were the neck of a beloved horse. 'Straight as a die. Quiet, accurate and lethal.'

Pablo was shifting uneasily from foot to foot. 'I didn't know . . .' he began. 'I had no idea.'

'Before your time, old chum. It must have been twenty-five years ago it last saw the light of day. Peter's old dad took him and me out into the woods for a bit of target practice a few times. But even he was worried about the damage it could do. So he locked it away again and warned us never to touch it. I think he meant to give it to a museum or something, but never got around to it.'

Simmy had lost any sense of a role in this startling turn of events. All she could do was watch and listen until the misty implications took on a clearer form. The gun that had killed George Baxter was there in front of them – that was the only fact she could yet grasp. Bridget did not appear to be doing much better.

'Why have *you* got it?' she managed, after a lengthy silence.

'It's bad news, Brid,' Glenn said with exquisite gentleness. 'We need to hide this beauty for a bit, while we think things through. I'm going to dismantle it first, so it'll be less obvious.'

'Why? You've got to explain it properly, Glenn. Pablo – what's he trying to say?'

Pablo put his hands up and shook his head. 'This is down to Glenn,' he said.

Glenn went on speaking. 'Peter's not thinking straight. You know what he was like, just before the wedding. If you ask me, Markie must have said something to him, out there in the rain, and he just lost control. You've seen the way that can happen sometimes.'

Bridget's eyes bulged with horror. 'No!' she screamed. 'Not Peter! It can't be. You're saying *Peter* killed Markie? My lovely brother? How could that be true?'

'It is, though. He told me, last night. He was in pieces, because he thinks you suspect him, and that's why you ran away. He says he did it so he could be sure of having you all to himself, just as he's wanted for so long.'

'Where is he now? I must go to him.' Then she slumped back. 'No, I can't. I can't bear to touch him, if it's true. But it *isn't* true. Glenn, you must have got it wrong. Peter must have lent the gun to somebody else, and they did it. That's it! You haven't been listening properly. You don't listen very well, do you? Not usually. You always think you know what people are thinking, without asking them. That's how it is now. You've completely misunderstood. Pablo?' she appealed to the other man, who was sitting on the arm of a chair, his face white.

'I think it's right, Briddy,' he said softly. 'Peter's been really wild for days now. He's got something terrible on his mind. Anybody can see that. But we want to protect him – and you. Don't we, Glenn?'

'Of course we do. Thanks, Pablo – I knew you'd see how it should be.'

Simmy continued to watch the handsome Spaniard closely. She was certain he had no prior knowledge of Glenn's bombshell. But his instinctive reaction was obviously pleasing to Glenn, who looked as if something had fallen neatly into place for him.

'Protect?' repeated Bridget. 'What does that mean?'

'We hide the gun, close ranks, get Peter to calm down, and say nothing,' Glenn summarised. 'There's no evidence, nothing to justify charging him.'

Bridget's face brightened slightly, as she pondered on this. Then she posed a very pertinent question: 'But – what about Simmy? She's already told the police I'm here and now she's in on it all.'

Both men focused unblinking stares onto Simmy. 'It's my belief she'll see the natural justice in what I'm saying,' Glenn murmured, his voice hypnotic. 'What good can it do now to drag the whole family through a ghastly murder trial? Peter will suffer agonies of remorse, for the rest of his life. He acted out of love. But of course it's all in ruins now. He never expected you to find out, you see. He assumed the two of you would have a happy married life together, with nobody getting between you.'

'Does he know you're here now, telling me?'

Simmy was examining the rising terror inside her own body. However pleasant and calm Glenn might be, he could quite easily force her physically to do whatever he chose. Pablo would help him. Pablo was a henchman to the core, loyal and dependent. They were discussing a double murder as if it were a minor financial oversight, a small transgression that was best forgotten. Bridget was functioning remarkably well, too. Was this simply the result of her spoilt, lawless childhood, where she always did whatever she liked? Was she so far from normal social ethics that she really could believe that Glenn was right?

Glenn answered her question carelessly. 'No, he doesn't. He thinks I've gone up into the fells to hide the gun. He told me to wrap it in oilcloth, and keep it in this bag. He loves it, I think. You can see why, can't you?' Again he stroked the old wooden stock.

'Looks to me as if you love it, as well,' Bridget snapped. 'You're all as bad as each other.'

Glenn chuckled, and looked towards Pablo. 'One for all and all for one, eh?'

Simmy remembered DI Moxon saying the exact same thing. Had he got the measure of these men already? Was he actually a step ahead of them, waiting for one of them to break rank, to drop his guard and give himself away? Was he outside at this very moment, listening with some electronic gadget to all that was being said? That would be too much to hope for, she supposed. But it made her feel better, just to imagine it.

Fear was slowly being diluted by sadness. Peter

Harrison-West had become a tragic figure over the past day or so, in an inexorable process reminiscent of a Shakespearean drama. 'He can't get away with it,' she said reluctantly, knowing she should remain quiet and pretend to agree with them. 'He's dangerous. He could do it again at any moment, if he's as off the rails as you say.' Where Bridget was already starting to collude with the impossible plan, Simmy still clung to ordinary reasonableness, the rules of society without which chaos would reign. 'He can't just be left to roam free.'

Bridget met her eyes, with a maturity that Simmy had not expected. 'He won't do it again,' she said. 'And he won't get away with it. But there are different kinds of punishment. That's what Glenn means. Peter's going to lose everything now, without having to go to prison for the rest of his life. I told you he was weak – remember? He kept it well hidden all this time, and I pretended not to see it. Markie saw it, though. He tried to tell me that marrying Peter was a horrible mistake, and I told Peter about it. I shouldn't have done that.'

'Because it got him killed?'

'Yes. No. Wait a minute. I need to think.'

'You don't need to think,' Simmy argued. 'You need to act responsibly and tell these two that there's no choice. They have to go to the police. From the sound of it, Peter's likely to hand himself in, anyway – but we can't rely on that.'

'Unlikely,' Glenn contradicted. 'Unthinkable. He wouldn't bring so much shame on Bridget.'

'We would have been all right,' Bridget spoke with the force of conviction. 'Peter and I would have been perfectly all right, if Markie had kept quiet. I could have helped him get more confident. I'd have been a good wife to him. I *loved* him.' Tears began to drop slowly down her face. 'And now it's all a dreadful mess.'

'We can sort it,' Glenn urged her. 'We really can. Pablo's going back to London tomorrow. Felix doesn't know what's been happening today, so he's in the clear. It'll be just you and me still here, making sure all the tracks are covered.'

'And Simmy,' Bridget reminded him. 'I don't see how you can be sure about Simmy.'

'I don't think she can cause any real trouble. If she goes to the police with what she's heard, it will only be hearsay evidence. I can make sure the gun is spirited away before anyone can even get here. I took the risk deliberately of letting her share in my news, partly so you'd have someone to take care of you, and partly because I wanted a witness, strange as that might seem.'

A witness! Again! Simmy felt defeated by this recurring role, for which she had not asked, and to which she was not equal.

'Did Peter *say* he killed them? Both of them? In so many words?' Bridget asked.

Glenn inclined his head in a silent confirmation.

'Really? You wouldn't lie about it?'

'I'm afraid he really did. He thought you'd already worked it out, and that there was nothing more to lose. That's why he told me.'

Pablo cleared his throat and everyone looked at him. 'I saw them talking,' he said. 'I couldn't hear all they said, but it looked just as Glenn's telling you. Peter was in an awful state. I've never seen anybody like it in my life. He was tearing his own hair out at one point.'

'I did my best to calm him down. I told him you'd always loved him, and that you'd very likely forgive him in time.'

'Did you? I can't even imagine what that would be like. I'm not sure I understand what forgiveness is, when it comes to it. Do you think we could just go on as normal, after all this?'

'People do,' he said. 'All the time. They get over things.'

'Rubbish,' said Simmy. 'That's complete rubbish. There are some kinds of damage you can't ever hope to repair.'

'For you, perhaps,' he flashed back. 'But Bridget's young and strong. She's not stupid or bitter or . . .' He seemed lost for another word, or perhaps aware that he was saying too much. 'She'll get over it,' he asserted. 'Of course she will.'

'It seems to matter an awful lot to you that she should,' Simmy observed.

'Of course it does. Why should her young life be wrecked by something that's in no way her fault?' He gave his head and shoulders a little shake, as if to throw off any such idea.

'But what about Peter?' Bridget asked. 'He's the one it all depends on. He's the one I married. I *married* him, Glenn. I should never have run away from him. It was a cowardly thing to do. Pablo fetched me back once, and I did it again. What must he think of me? If he did those terrible things out of love for me, that puts me in his debt, somehow. Do you see? It makes it all my fault. He must have thought I agreed with the things Markie said – or that I would, if I listened to him. He didn't trust me enough. But why kill my father as well? What did he have to fear from him?'

'You were very close to him,' Glenn said neutrally. 'Perhaps he thought you'd play them off against each other, if you lost faith in Peter. I'm just guessing. I don't really know.'

'I would never have done that.'

'Glenn,' Pablo's voice contained a sudden urgency. 'There's a cop car outside. I think they're coming to the door.'

Glenn moved liked lightning, pushing the Lee Enfield back into its bag and dropping it behind the sofa. 'Let them in,' he ordered Simmy. 'And then let me do the talking.'

She had half a minute, at most, to decide what to do.

# Chapter Twenty

It was Pablo who clinched it. He gently caught her arm before she left the room to go to the door, met her eyes with a smile, and whispered, 'Trust us.'

She opened the door in a confused haze and stared speechlessly at the two uniformed officers in front of her. 'Mrs Brown?' one of them said.

'That's right.'

'We're just checking that everything's all right. You asked for a police presence, I believe?'

'That was yesterday,' she said, feeling daft. 'Yes, it's all fine now. Thank you very much.'

'Are you here alone?'

'What? Oh . . . no. I've got visitors, actually.'

He cocked his head speculatively, while his colleague looked back across the street as if wanting to go. Simmy felt passive and useless. Women in films found clever ways of conveying a message in this sort of situation that would be undetected by the criminals inside the house. But Pablo and Glenn were not criminals – they were simply trying to shield a wretched man who was. What message did she have to convey? What would they do to her if she simply told the truth? *Peter Harrison-West is the murderer. His gun is here in my house.* She could say that – and then what would happen? Glenn would hear her and be out of the back door with the weapon before the policemen could gather themselves for action. If they thought there was a gun on the premises, they would probably retreat to their car and call for backup. There'd be a siege, with megaphones and an armed response team, or whatever they called it. Everything would escalate, confusion would reign supreme and nothing good could possibly come of it.

'All right, then,' said the man. He was plainly the more conscientious of the two, and probably more intelligent. He was uneasy about something.

'Thank you very much,' she repeated. 'I really am all right.'

'So it seems. We'll come by again later on, all the same. Nobody's been caught yet. Can't be too careful.'

'You're very kind,' she said, with a smile, and they went back to their car.


'Thank you,' said Pablo, when she rejoined the threesome. 'You did absolutely the right thing.'

'I'm sure I didn't,' she said wearily. 'It was just that I couldn't see there was much choice. The police have a tendency to overreact, don't they? Not that I know much about it. They get very excited about guns, though. I'm fairly sure I've got that much right. Is it loaded?'

Glenn laughed scornfully. 'Of course it isn't. Do you think I'm such a fool as that?'

'You might be,' she snapped. 'For all I know, you're a bunch of lunatics, the whole damned lot of you. Including you,' she snarled at Bridget. 'Dragging me into your ludicrous lives, where nothing makes sense and you've got no respect for decency and law and people's basic rights.'

'Phew!' whistled Glenn. 'Listen to you!'

'You can't really blame her,' Bridget defended. 'We have rather descended on her, haven't we? Don't worry, Simmy. We'll go soon. One more night, okay?'

'All of you?'

Glenn's scornful laugh was starting to grate on her. 'We've got homes to go to, you know.'

'Have you?' She looked at Pablo. 'I thought you lived in London.'

He lengthened his neck, almost preening, and she remembered that these were solid, respectable businessmen, with money and property and a barely imaginable lifestyle. 'I do, but I've got a little place up here as well,' he said.

She grimaced. 'I might have known.'

'He's got a wife as well,' said Bridget, with a shrewd look. 'Not that he ever sees her, but she does exist.'

'Shut up, Brid,' he snapped. 'Doozy and I have been separated for years now. It would take five minutes to get a divorce.'

'So why haven't you?'

'Can't be bothered,' he shrugged. Simmy, watching his face, suspected there was more to it than that. He was probably Roman Catholic, which would make divorce a much messier business than he claimed.

'Same here,' she said, in a vague attempt to keep her end up.

'Oh?'

'Well, we've done the nisi bit. It's going through rather slowly.' She flushed, unhappy at revealing anything so personal. However hard she tried, the word 'divorce' still stabbed painfully.

'Bummer,' said Pablo, with a warm smile. Was he simply keeping her compliant with his melting looks and careful understanding? These were men who could bribe and bully their way out of almost any tight hole. They were skilled manipulators, self-satisfied and sleek with affluence. She would barely register with them as an autonomous individual with the ability to argue or even betray. She was a humble florist, a faceless servant. At best, a useful witness.

'Well, can you go now, please?' she said firmly. 'I've had enough of this. Take your bloody gun and go.'

'We will, in a minute,' said Glenn. 'But not the gun. The gun stays here. It's the safest place we can think of. There's no possible reason why this house would be searched, after all.'

'You're that sure I won't just hand it to the police?' Simmy was thunderstruck at the casual insolence behind his words.

Glenn sighed theatrically. 'I thought we'd been through all that. We'll come back for it when things have settled down. It won't be for long.'

'I know exactly where to put it,' said Bridget. 'Don't forget I know this house from top to bottom. Especially top.'

Simmy knew immediately that Bridget meant the roof space, with the rattling trapdoor that she had taped shut. *Oh well,* she said to herself. *It can't do any harm up there, I suppose.* She watched as Glenn retrieved the rifle from behind

279

the sofa, and realised that she was far less afraid of it than she would have anticipated. It looked almost benign, cradled in the man's arms like a heavy metal baby. A chainsaw or even a long sharp knife would be much more frightening. Guns made holes in people's heads, but knives sliced and severed and made a lot of blood. And chainsaws could cut your head right off.

'I must be mad,' she groaned. 'You've made me mad, between you.'

'You'll get used to it,' soothed Bridget. 'It's just a different way of seeing things.'

'I hope not. I hope . . .' but she couldn't tell them she had every intention of rejoining the ordinary normal human race, first thing in the morning. She might well phone DI Moxon and tell him everything, after an uneventful night in which good sense was resumed. If indeed such a night were granted to her.

'That police car's going to be back again before long,' Pablo said. 'We should be gone before then. Don't forget the neighbours saw me here this afternoon. I did make a bit of noise. If there's any ructions now, they might make the connection.'

'Noise?' Glenn frowned at him.

'I was calling Bridget. I knew she must be here. The naughty girl hid from me.'

It was too sinister to ignore. The terror, which had faded into abeyance, flared again. This was no game, despite the relaxed manner of the two men. Their friend had committed two cold-blooded murders. There were no protocols for dealing with such extreme acts, which must be why she felt

280

so completely at sea. Was Bridget being enormously clever by behaving as if nothing too serious was going on? Was she in fact every bit as terrified as Simmy, but knew, far better than Simmy did, that the only hope was to cooperate and remain calm? How could anybody do that after what she had just been told? Years of practice, perhaps. She had been trained in manipulation and concealment, probably, during her long association with these men. Could it be that she knew, in her heart, what Peter was capable of – and had married him anyway?

'Sorry,' said Bridget easily.

'No, you're not. But all is forgiven now.' Glenn patted her head. 'It's all going to work out. Things always do, don't they?'

Bridget said nothing, but Simmy detected an involuntary flinch at Glenn's touch. She hoped he hadn't seen it, and spoke quickly in an attempt to distract him. 'You're going, then?'

'All right, don't be in such a rush. It's a big risk, obviously, leaving the two of you like this. But we need to keep everything normal, for the cops. They know she's here, which is good. They won't be worrying about anything except their forensics and computer databases. And about a thousand witness statements, by this time. That rifle's got a range of five hundred yards or more. They'll have to ask everyone in Bowness whether they saw anything.'

'Where was he, then?' asked Simmy, genuinely wanting to know. 'When he shot Mr Baxter?'

Glenn opened his mouth, and quickly closed it again. 'Don't ask me,' he snapped. 'How should *I* know?'

'Poor old Daddy,' sighed Bridget. 'I still can't believe it. Not that I saw him much, I suppose. I can pretend he's in Turkey or somewhere, and not really dead at all.'

Simmy looked at her in surprise. It hadn't occurred to her that Bridget might be coping so well because she was in complete denial. But the girl's expression assured her that it was otherwise. She knew well enough what had really happened. She was still deliberately making light of it as a way of deflecting Glenn.

It evidently worked, because he ruffled her hair with a sympathetic smile. 'Give it time, old girl,' he said.

'I'm hungry,' Bridget whined, suddenly acting the child. 'I had hardly anything for lunch.'

'So am I,' lied Simmy, thinking she might choke on any food. The effort required to remain passive was consuming her. She was acting a part, almost without knowing it, taking the line of least resistance for her own survival. If Glenn and Pablo believed her to be a genuine threat to their friend, there was no knowing what they might do. They could bundle her into the boot of their car and take her up to Kentmere and throw her in the reservoir, where she wouldn't be found for months.

'Okay then,' said Glenn, briskly decisive. 'You fry up some sausages' – looking at Simmy – 'and you, Briddy, get an early night. Hide the gun, have some supper and go to bed. We'll go and make sure Peter's safely back at home. I bet you anything he is already. We can give him some Valium and knock him out for the night. If you want to talk to him tomorrow, we can organise something. Come on, Pablo. That's enough for one day.'

They went without a backward glance. At least, Glenn

did. Pablo did pause on the threshold and look over his shoulder at Simmy. His smile was fleeting and she thought she saw confusion in his eyes. Was he wondering whether she and Bridget would really remain silent after the terrible news they'd been given? They were being left perfectly free to go and say whatever they liked. Had Glenn's assurances been enough for Pablo the henchman? And if not, how could they hope to convince Bridget and Simmy?

A car door slammed and its engine started up. Neither woman spoke until it had driven away. Then Simmy blew out her cheeks, and almost fell into the armchair. 'Well,' she said. 'Did any of that really happen?'

'No, it was all a dream. I hope.'

'It's not like in the movies, is it? Or on *Crimewatch*. Men with guns are supposed to shout a lot and bark orders and get terribly stressed out. And their victims are meant to cower in the corner and bleat helplessly. We didn't follow a single line of the script.'

'Because *they* weren't the baddies. Glenn and Pablo are just trying to save Peter. They've been friends for most of their lives. They couldn't ever give each other away.'

'Bridget – how much do you really love Peter? That's what it all comes down to.'

'I told you before. I barely even exist without him. I haven't thought of another man since I was ten. All this now – it's not the Peter I know. I think it really must be a dream, everything's so strange.'

'But you said he behaved weirdly. You ran away from him – twice. You must have thought there was something horribly wrong.'

283

Bridget gave this some serious thought. 'He was all right the night after the wedding. With me, anyway. He was angry and shocked and sad about Markie, and worried about how I'd take it. But he was sweet and gentle and reassuring. We consummated the marriage,' she added with a giggle. 'That bed in the hotel is fabulous. Like being in a cloud. We just locked the door and shut the world out.'

'He didn't seem guilty or scared?'

'Not a bit.'

'And did he go out on Sunday morning?'

'We all did. The police were there right after breakfast, still interviewing people. Pablo and Felix said they wanted to go over to Belle Isle in a rowing boat. Felix can row pretty well, even now, and he likes doing it. I went to the station with Jenny and Sally – the bridesmaids. They had to get back. I thought Glenn and Peter were together somewhere, but they can't have been. They came back in time for lunch at one o'clock, and then the police marched in and told us about Daddy. Everything went crazy after that – like Saturday only worse. They told us to stay in the hotel, and somebody must have told my mother, because she turned up with you. It's all a complete blur until that evening. We stayed another night in the bridal suite, because of the honeymoon being cancelled, and then just crawled back to the house, not knowing what to think.'

'And was Peter strange on Sunday night?'

'A bit,' she said slowly. 'Much more panicked. He hardly spoke to me. But it never occurred to me to think he was guilty. I never thought it was anybody I knew who'd done either of the murders. It seemed to me it must have been some business person that Daddy knew – or some stupid hitman who killed Markie by mistake, because he was called Baxter. I still think that might be it, and Glenn's got it all wrong. He *does* get things wrong, you know. It's never very easy to get through to Glenn.'

Simmy considered this for a moment. 'What's with his hair?' she blurted.

Bridget hooted a single note of derision. 'That was my fault. I told him I wanted the best man to look as if he'd gone to some trouble over how he looked. He'd been fooling about over it all, calling us the odd couple and other names. I yelled at him and told him he had to take it seriously and smarten up. So he had that haircut just to spite me.'

'He looks like a seal.'

'Or a bullet,' chuckled Bridget.

'Well, I think it was brave of him to come and tell you about Peter. People shoot messengers, don't they? You might have turned the blasted gun on him.'

'Brave.' Bridget savoured the word. 'I suppose it was, if you look at it a certain way. Poor Glenn. He worked so hard on the best man's speech, even though he pretended it would be a doddle. He makes speeches all the time, of course. But he was very pale about it.'

'Did he ever actually make it? Hadn't you found Markie by then?'

'Ironically, no, he didn't. How could we carry on with all that? Everything just fell apart. Peter even joked that at least it had got him out of having to make his own speech. That sounds awful, doesn't it? But he always makes jokes when he's stressed. It's nice, actually. He did it when my mother nearly died having Lucy and everyone had to sit in a corridor for hours. Peter just kept coming with the jokes.'

'I haven't heard this story. Was Markie there?'

'No, of course not. She's not *his* mother. There was me, Peter, Lucy's father, and Felix.'

'Why Felix?'

'He was just around, I think, and came to lend support. Her uterus ruptured halfway through the labour. It was a real drama. Nobody expected Lucy to survive. She went ages without oxygen, or something. But it doesn't seem to have done her any harm. She's abnormally bright, if anything.'

'She's a lovely little thing.'

'How do *you* know?' Bridget flashed, before checking herself. 'Oh yes, I remember – you had to look after her on Saturday afternoon.'

'That's right. We went for a walk. Her father sounds like a real character.'

'Oh, he's perfectly mad. You never know where he is or what he's doing. My mother won't let him move into her house, not permanently. He stays for a week or two at a time and then she packs him off again. She says she doesn't want to give him any legal grounds for claiming it if they separate. She's left everything to Lucy, if she dies.'

'Not you?'

'Nobody leaves anything to me, not even my grandparents. They think Peter will look after me.' Her eyes grew large and wet as she remembered all over again what Peter had done. 'Which he can't if he's in prison, can he? Simmy, we *must* stop that from happening. What would I do? Where would I go? How would I manage? I can't deal with bills and mortgages and insurance and stuff like that.'

'I'm afraid those aren't good enough reasons to ignore the law. The trouble is – I can't see any guarantee that he won't do it again. If he thinks he's losing you, especially. What if he blames Glenn and decides to kill him as well?'

'He'd never do that. He loves Glenn. They're like brothers, only more so.'

'But you *do* see, don't you? In the end, they'll catch him. After what he did this afternoon, they might have already done so.'

'Why? What did he do?'

'He punched Ben Harkness. You must have heard me telling Glenn about it.'

'I didn't take it in. Was it really hard?'

'Hard enough to hurt him. And Glenn just flapped it away as unimportant. Actually, I think it's very important. It shows Peter's dangerous.'

'Ohhh,' Bridget drew a shuddering sigh. 'I can't believe that. I'll go back tomorrow and see for myself. I might be able to make it all right.'

'You won't. Nobody can. But we'll leave it for tonight. I'll make a milky drink and some sandwiches, shall I? Are you really hungry?'

'I think so. I *should* be. Thanks, Simmy. You're being ever so good.'

'Don't mention it,' said Simmy wryly, relieved that Bridget couldn't read her thoughts.

Because her thoughts were rapidly clarifying now that Glenn and Pablo had gone. Scattered elements were coalescing into an increasingly coherent picture. The police were coming back before long. They might have seen the car that the men had used, and checked its ownership. If so, they'd realise that things had not been so unworrying as she had made them think. She carried a terrible knowledge that she would have to share, whatever the consequences. She could not understand why Glenn couldn't see that. He knew she was a witness to the killing of George Baxter, and therefore acquainted with a senior detective. Was he perhaps simply buying time, during which he would spirit Peter away to some distant country where nobody would find him? Would Peter be content to live in hiding for the rest of his life, presumably without Bridget? Or was Glenn so clever that he really did have full confidence that there would never be enough evidence to prosecute Peter, regardless of what Simmy might say?

Was there a tremendous urgency to convey the truth or could it wait till morning? That was the major burning question she now wrestled with. If the men drove through the night, they could get to Aberdeen or Harwich and find a boat to take them to Stavanger or Rotterdam or wherever. Unless the police had warned every port not to allow Peter Harrison-West out of the country. That was quite likely, surely? And would Peter go without Bridget? Would that not be too high a price to pay for freedom? Far more likely that he would wait until he had seen her again, hoping to persuade her to join him in a hideaway on a sunny island on the far side of the world. How much planning had gone into the murders, anyway? Most people seemed to think it was impulsive where Markie was concerned. And George Baxter had somehow got in the way, calling for a more careful execution.

If she phoned Moxon now, Bridget might hear her and react badly. There would be screaming and hair-pulling and aggravated neighbours. Shameful as it might be, Simmy was profoundly reluctant to upset Malcolm and Sharon Jamieson. She wanted them to like her and approve of her, but progress towards that end was painfully slow. She was still hoping for some sort of alliance against the holiday-home people, but so far the Jamiesons seemed to find little to object to in the noisy comings and goings.

It was bad enough having a very obvious police car pass every hour or two, slowing outside her house and even stopping to knock on the door. That alone signalled something sinister and worrying. Sharon was from Essex and had yet to adapt to the ways of the local people. She believed in locks and Neighbourhood Watch and paedophiles behind every gatepost. She had two girl children who caught the school bus every morning, with their anxious mother hovering as they disappeared from view. They had moved north, apparently, because Malcolm had a breakdown one day on the M25 and needed a quieter life from then on. He worked from home now, designing websites or something of the sort. Sharon made the beds in the huge hotel in the middle of Bowness.

There were other considerations, none of them worthy of comparison with a murderer on the loose, but nonetheless compelling. The christening flowers had to be ready for Sunday morning, and were not yet started, or even fully planned. Saturday was supposed to be the first proper day for Halloween ideas to take shape. A complete overhaul of the window display would have been performed, even without Ben's critical comments. There was the never-ending paperwork. And people she needed to speak to – including Julie the hairdresser with the broken fingers.

Paradoxically, the fact of such mundane preoccupations made the murder investigation seem more real. As if she had applied some sort of test to it, by comparing it to the demands of her work, and it had come through triumphant. *Yes*, it claimed, *I really am very important indeed*. She couldn't brush it aside or even put it in a 'pending' tray. It came first, took priority and had to be acted upon.

Bridget had reverted to passivity while Simmy prepared their scanty supper. 'Come and eat it in here,' Simmy ordered. 'You've hardly moved all day, as far as I can see.'

'What's the point? It's even worse now that Glenn's told me about Peter. I just feel heavy and scared.'

'You'll have to hide that gun. What if those policemen ask to come in next time they call by?' She looked at the kitchen clock. 'They'll be here any minute, I expect.'

'Before or after I eat my sandwich?' There was a hint of mocking insolence in her voice that made Simmy feel like a schoolteacher. People did that to her a lot, and she had worked out that it was an instinctive response to her height. Even she could see that she was a bit like a caricature schoolmarm at times, the way she looked down her long nose at people and asked them to make themselves clear.

'Before might be sensible,' she snapped. 'Am I allowed to know where you're going to put it?'

'In the roof space, above the room you've put me in. Markie and I used to go up there when we were little. I'm not sure I could squeeze through the hatch now.'

'You don't need to, do you? Just push it through and stick the thing shut again. I had to tape it when it was windy, to stop it rattling.'

'I'll go and do it, then. Won't be long.'

The police rang at the door while Bridget was upstairs, causing Simmy a violent attack of terror. Being in possession of the gun that could be proved to have killed George Baxter would involve them both in an unimaginable abyss of suspicion and trouble. Inhaling deeply, she opened the door.

The same two men stood there, the talkative one looking as if he was beginning to agree with his colleague that this was all a big waste of time. Simmy wondered, as before, what she was going to say to them. 'Hello, again,' she greeted them.

'Everything all right, madam?'

'Yes, thanks.' A thought rose to the surface. 'You found somewhere to park, then?' she asked, peering into the dark street. 'It was a bit crowded last time you came.'

'No problem,' he said with a small frown. 'It's not exactly double yellow line territory, is it?'

'No, but there was a car – just there.' She tried to indicate that this was more meaningful than it sounded. Behind her, she could hear Bridget coming down the stairs, making no attempt to remain quiet or out of sight.

'That's your visitor, is it?'

'That's right.'

'And everything's all right?' he repeated.

'Yes,' she sighed. 'We're fine. We'll go to bed early. You don't have to check us again now. It's probably all been a waste of time.'

Again, she hoped he would be sharp enough to understand

that she was not as relaxed and reassuring as she might seem on the surface. But it was obviously far too much to expect. What you saw was what you got, and he saw two women in a quiet house, who answered the door promptly and spoke with relative coherence.

'Night, then,' he said, and the two officers walked briskly back to their car. They were plainly ready for the end of their boring shift.

Bridget was waiting for her at the foot of the stairs. 'There's some stuff up there,' she began. 'At the back, near the chimney breast. Is it yours?'

Simmy shook her head. 'It must have been there when I moved in. Junk, obviously.'

'Sure to be,' Bridget agreed, unable to suppress the sparkle in her eyes. 'But it's probably *my* junk. And Markie's. Can I go up there tomorrow for a proper look?'

'If you want. Why not? It'll keep you occupied while I'm at work – if you want to stay here. I thought you'd be off to see Peter, first thing?'

'I might. I'm going to sleep on it. I might dream something that'll help me work out what to do.' At Simmy's sceptical look, she went on, 'Don't you have meaningful dreams that help when you've got a problem? It's magic sometimes. The person you're worrying about appears to you, absolutely real-seeming, and tells you what you should think or do,'

'No,' said Simmy, thinking of her own tragic nightmares where her baby was alive and chuckling at her, and Tony a doting father, and she woke to a tear-soaked pillow and a world of grey depression. 'It never works like that for me.'

'I had one this year, when Peter was wanting to fix a date for the wedding. He and Glenn were both there, telling me it was my destiny, and I'd be bound to have a wonderful life if I let them take charge. I could take any courses I wanted, or travel, or keep a boat or a horse, at the same time as being Mrs Harrison-West. I could hear their voices, just as if they were there in the room. So I said yes, we'd get married in October.'

'And you still think it was the right thing to do?'

'Ouch! You shouldn't ask me that. But yes, I do. I think.' She averted her face, staring into the living room and the curtained window, deep in thought. 'I think I'll have to trust Glenn and the others to make it all right. If anybody can do it, they can. And whatever we might think about justice and that stuff, it won't bring Markie and my father back to life, will it?'

# Chapter Twenty-One

Ben never even showed up for registration on Friday morning. He was sure things were happening that he needed to keep abreast of, that this was the day when it would all become clear. His mother had made a token fuss of his bruised face, but with Wilf's help he had convinced her that the playground fight story was true, and that there was no need for any further action. As far as the school was concerned, of course, nothing at all had actually happened. Which meant he would have to come up with another fabrication to explain his absence. He was tempted to ask Wilf to phone the secretary and say he thought Ben was starting glandular fever as well, but good sense restrained him. Such stories had a habit of bouncing back at you, bringing more trouble than they were worth.

He headed straight for Persimmon Petals, taking the road that branched away from the lakeside and into the centre of Windermere. It was a ten-minute walk from his house. Neither of his parents' cars was on the garth at the front. Wilf was still in bed and his sisters had taken themselves to school in their usual jostling female group that had no place for him. There were many more police cars on the road than usual, and he felt again the importance of being connected to such a famous crime. How brilliant it would be if he could help solve it – it would take him halfway to a job with a forensics lab the moment he graduated.

But when he surveyed the scanty material he had to go on, his optimism faded. The only hope was that Simmy had learnt more since he last saw her, and between them they could devise a plan.

She was working with utter concentration when he found her at the back of the shop. A cloud of cream-coloured flowers was being constructed with the help of slender wires, a pile of yellower blooms close by, as well as ribbon and a clump of tiny white stuff. He watched her twisting and tweaking, weaving and tying. 'What's that for?' he asked her, eventually.

'A christening on Sunday.'

'Will they keep till then?'

She nodded. 'In the cool room they will. Just. I daren't risk leaving it any longer, in case something crops up and leaves me with no time.'

'Did anything crop up last night, by any chance?'

'You could say that.' For the first time she looked at him properly. 'Why aren't you at school?'

He gave the ceiling a so-help-me glance, and waved a finger at her. 'Just leave it, okay? I want to be here, is all. I want to talk about murder.'

'So do I, actually. Although I absolutely ought not to encourage you.'

'Is Bridget still at yours?'

'Oh yes. She had a dream that told her to stay another day. We had visitors last night, which answered a lot of questions, but raised a few others.'

'Who? Tell me.'

'I definitely shouldn't. You've got to promise not to say a single word to anybody else at all. Not Melanie or Wilf or the police. Not until I've decided what to do. My dreams are nothing like as helpful as Bridget's.' She summarised the visitation from Glenn and Pablo, while she finished the christening flowers. Ben asked a lot of questions. She kept back any mention of the Lee Enfield, with difficulty. The less said about that the better, she felt.

'I get it,' he said at last, with an intelligent look. 'You're scared of those men, which is why you haven't told the police already that we know who the killer is.'

'I'm not scared of Pablo. I like him. I'm scared of making things worse. There's a lot I don't understand, and that makes it feel dangerous.'

'But he can't get away with it, can he.' This was not a question. 'Now we know it's him, we can get evidence and present it to the police. His friends can't save him, however much they want to. He might do it again.'

'I know.'

'I wish I'd known this when he hit me. I'd have made a massive fuss, called the cops, accused him of assault, and then told the Moxo bloke everything I knew. Too late now.'

'Is it?'

'For a start, we don't know where he is. Do we?'

'At his house, I imagine.'

296

'What a nerve he's got! Sitting tight, right under the noses of the police and everybody he's ruined the lives of, as if nothing can get him. I've a good mind to go there and tell him what I think of him.'

'He'll hit you again.'

He fingered his bruises. 'Yeah. He might. I could take Melanie,' he added hopefully.

'She wouldn't go. He was in here yelling at her on Wednesday and she didn't like it.'

'He's a menace. I don't believe you're just letting him get away with it.'

'Me neither. But I still need to have a think. It's not just being scared, it's knowing I could make things worse. What if the police go charging up there and he hangs himself or something? Or takes a hostage.'

'Like who?'

She grinned ruefully. 'Like Pablo. Or Glenn.'

'They'd be two against one. They wouldn't let him do that.'

'Or Bridget. She's quite likely to change her mind and turn up there to see for herself what he thinks he's doing.'

'That'd be *three* against one. Even better.'

'I know I'm being ridiculous. I think it's something to do with my mother and how I was brought up. She'd never shop anybody to the police if she could avoid it.'

'Even for *murder*? It's a bit different from fiddling a tax return, you know.'

He could tell she felt hassled, her hands faltering on the final stages of the christening flowers. He wondered at his own temerity, urging someone so much older than himself into a course of action that she surely knew was inevitable.

He was still trying to absorb the implications of the story she'd told him, and wondering what she had left out. Something to do with Bridget? Or Pablo? Or what?

'Probably not,' she admitted. 'But I can't ask her, can I? I can't say anything to anybody. I shouldn't be telling you.'

'But there's still no actual evidence, is there?' he realised. 'Somebody telling somebody else, and you overhearing it, isn't good enough to make a prosecution.'

'That's what Glenn said. I suppose the police would soon find evidence, once they were sure they knew who to investigate.'

A customer interrupted them, and before any further conversation could take place, two more turned up. Ben had almost forgotten they were in a shop until then. Now he could see it was going to turn busy, with Friday shoppers calling in for weekend flowers. 'Is Melanie coming in today?'

'Tomorrow.'

'I'll get out of the way, then,' he said, with a dawning idea of where he might go next. A reckless urgency was gripping him, and he almost trotted out into the street.

Transport was a problem. He did have a bike, but wasn't eager to go home and collect it. A glance at the sky confirmed an instinctive expectation of rain at any moment. Standing indecisively in the street, he was aware of a labouring engine coming up the hill. A number 599 bus! What an idiot he'd been not to think of it – it went up to Ambleside. Without another thought he headed for the stop, fifty yards away, and waved it down.

Settled into a seat at the back, he tried to work out what he thought he was doing. He had only the vaguest idea of where Peter Harrison-West's house was. Somewhere on the northern edge of Ambleside, he thought. The prominence of the wedding had produced endless columns of gossip in the papers and on Facebook about the couple and their families, with scant respect for privacy. Since the murders there had been a massive escalation in publicity, and Ben suspected there might even be a gaggle of reporters outside the house. That would be a mixed blessing – what he gained in ease of identification would be lost in the impossibility of access. For the time being he might simply have to be content with being on the scene, ready to focus in on anything of interest that might happen.

At the stop for Troutbeck, a girl boarded the bus. At first Ben took little notice of her, but then a sudden recognition shocked through him. Wasn't it Bridget Harrison-West herself? He had seen pictures of her, but never met her in person. The reality was oddly faded – *reduced* – presumably by the events of the past week. She was pale and seemed to be dragging herself wearily up the steps and into a seat behind the driver. She ignored the meagre scattering of other passengers.

Heart beating furiously, he tried to work out his strategy. If she got off in Ambleside, he would follow her, in the hope that she would lead him straight to the murderous Peter. A minute later he remembered that this was the local bus that only went as far as Ambleside anyway, so she was bound to get off there. His thoughts fizzed in a panic at this incredible piece of luck. The other people on the bus were all old and half asleep. Little could they imagine what might be about to happen, when Bridget confronted her new husband with his crimes. Even if they'd seen the news about the murders – and how could anybody have missed it? – they'd think themselves immune from anything so dramatic and alien. They didn't recognise the young woman at the centre of the story. People like the Harrison-Wests and Baxters didn't use buses.

The journey was almost too brief. Loss of nerve threatened to abort the whole project when Bridget got off at the last stop and Ben had no option but to follow her. The upper portion of the little town was dominated by fells on three sides, the scenic road to Rydal and Grasmere a favourite with tourists as it left the comfort of Lake Windermere and climbed into serious upland country. He hung back, pretending to be sending a text, waiting to see where Bridget would go next. The tops of the fells were hidden by dark clouds – rain was due at any moment.

He felt alone and exposed, the object of curious glances. *Why isn't that boy at school?* he could hear people wondering. *He must be up to no good.* Gazing unseeingly at his phone, he realised he couldn't text Simmy or Melanie, even if he wanted to. He had neglected to ascertain their numbers when he had the chance. There was nobody he could share his adventure with; nobody to summon in an emergency. This acquired the dimension of a very major oversight, as he tried to think through his next moves. A possible chain of information suggested itself: he might call Wilf and ask if he still knew Melanie's number. But he would have to explain, if he did that. And it wasn't Melanie he wanted. It was the older and wiser Simmy, who could come in her van and rescue him, if things went sour. It would take her fifteen minutes at most. Nothing too dreadful could happen in that time – could it?

Bridget was walking purposefully along the road, already passing the last of the houses, with the police station on her left. For a moment he thought she might be going in to betray her husband. When she kept on walking, he even considered going in himself. He might ask the person on the front desk to put him through to DI Moxon, who had spoken to him briefly on Sunday. He might leave a message vague enough to avoid immediate police response, but urgent enough to offer a sense of a lifeline. He could say he thought he'd remembered something else about the shooting of Mr Baxter, and would be in touch soon. But nobody would pass on a message like that. They'd ask a hundred questions, including his precise whereabouts. They would treat him like an unreliable child, and call his parents to come and take him home.

Still Bridget was walking, trudging along towards Rydal, where there was little more than a hotel and Wordsworth's house and a farm. She wore a light jacket without a hood – when the rain started, she was going to get seriously wet. The views were dramatic as they approached Scandale Bridge, clouds lowering over the lake, making the water look solid, trees looming on the western bank of Windermere, no more than a sinister black stain.

Ben stayed well back, praying that his quarry didn't look behind her for any reason. He was being drawn after her, regardless of his own will. Having come this far, he could see no alternative. Almost he began to see himself as a protector of a traumatised girl less than two years his senior. She was not, he concluded, going to her husband's house, after all.

Unless he'd got it badly wrong, the Harrison-West mansion was nearly half a mile behind them.

There was plenty of traffic on the road, adding to his feeling of vulnerability. Somebody he knew might well drive past. Somebody might even recognise Bridget, although it would be hard to connect this tired-looking creature in crumpled clothes with the beautiful bride of the glossy magazines. Would it look obvious to anybody passing that he was following her? If he hung back any more, he might miss seeing her turn off the road down some invisible track and disappear. If he closed the gap slightly, people might think they were a couple who had had a disagreement. Or, he thought bravely, he could simply catch her up and tell her he knew who she was. What could she do? She would hardly scream and shout for help. She might even be glad of his company.

So he did it. Twenty seconds' brisk trot was all it took to catch her up. 'Hi!' he said, from just behind her shoulder. 'Aren't you Bridget?'

She spun round, eyes bulging. 'Who the hell are you?'

'My name's Ben Harkness. I—'

'The boy Peter punched yesterday?' She was looking intently at his bruise. 'What do you want from me?'

'Nothing. I was on the bus, when you got on. I . . . um . . .'

'You followed me! What for?' She looked past him, back the way they'd come. 'Are you on your own?'

'Yes. You know my name? Did somebody tell you about me?'

'Simmy told Glenn when he came to her house. You know Simmy, then.' She shook her head, eyes closed tight for a few seconds. 'I can't take all this. I'm going away.' She had a purple bag slung over her shoulder, and she hefted it as she spoke. 'I've got something in here I need to think about before I talk to anybody.'

'Going away?' He stared at the road ahead, the Pikes soaring before them. 'Where?'

'Anywhere.'

His alarm made him breathless. 'Not up there?' Was she planning to sleep out in the cold, hoping to die of exposure? 'It's just about to rain.'

'No, you fool. I'm going to fetch my car. I left it at Pelter Bridge. Another half a mile or so, I guess.' She started walking again, not looking to see if he was keeping pace.

'Oh.' He followed automatically, the conversation unfinished.

'So what are you going to do?' she demanded, unfeelingly.

'Go home, I s'pose.'

She frowned at him impatiently. 'What did you think you were doing, following me like that? Where did you think we were going?'

He tried to straighten his shoulders, to stand tall and confident. 'I thought you were going to your husband's place, to confront him about what he did. I thought that might be dangerous, and it would make sense to stick around in case it turned nasty.'

'"What he did",' she repeated. 'You think you know what he did, do you?'

'Simmy told me,' he nodded, hoping she wouldn't react badly.

'How dare she? That's a total betrayal.' She seemed young

303

to him at that moment, and helpless in the face of the things people did. 'Why would she do that?'

'We were both there when your father was killed. We want to catch the man who did it. That's all.'

'She hasn't told the police, has she?'

He bit down on his natural inclination to give an honest answer. *Careful*, an inner voice cautioned him. 'I don't know,' he said. 'She might have done by now. She can't just do nothing, can she?'

Then a car drew up beside them. 'Briddy! It's Briddy!' squealed a child's voice.

'Bugger and shit,' muttered Bridget. Then she hissed at Ben, 'This is all *your* fault.'

'Sorry,' he muttered back.

A woman was peering across the child at them. 'Bridget? What the hell are you doing here? Who's this? It's starting to rain – you'll both get soaked.'

'He's called Ben. What do you want?'

'I don't want anything. I'm taking Lucy to a party in Grasmere. She said it was you, so I stopped.'

'You mean you didn't recognise me?'

'I was driving. And we're late. We were meant to be there for eleven.'

'Well, go on then. Everything's all right. Have a great time, Luce.' Bridget bent down and kissed the little face through the car window. 'See you sometime.' Her voice was sufficiently forced for the child to give her a worried look. 'I'm all right, honestly. I've got a cagoule in the bag, and we won't be out long anyway.'

Her mother sighed loudly and put the car into gear.

'Phone me,' she ordered. 'Later today. I need to talk to you.'

Bridget nodded and the car moved away.

'Shouldn't that child be at school? Not to mention the others who'll be at this party,' asked Ben, very aware of his own truancy. 'How old is she?'

'She's six. They all go to a weird little school that doesn't have normal hours. And actually I think it's half term this week.'

'Funny time for a party.'

'It'll be something to do with mushrooms or berries. Woodcraft Folk, probably.'

Ben struggled with this drastic mismatch between the woman in the car and this rustic image. 'Your mother didn't look to be dressed for anything like that. And it's raining.'

'What do you mean? What should she be wearing?'

'Never mind.' He thought wistfully of the missed chance of a lift back to Windermere. Even the chastening reproaches from Mr Piper, the maths teacher whose lesson he was missing, might be preferable to this confusing girl and her even more extraordinary mother. 'You don't get on too well, then? You and your mum?'

'I'm a married woman,' said Bridget, lifting her chin haughtily. 'And she's never been very maternal. She doesn't want to get involved.'

Involved in the murder of her one-time husband and his only son, he supposed Bridget meant. 'She's trying to keep things normal for your sister, I guess,' he ventured. 'That's what mothers do.'

They were walking again, Rydal Bridge, spanning the Rothay, visible ahead. Sharp spots of rain were making themselves felt on his face. He had been here with his family innumerable times, but only in the last year or so had he come to appreciate the drama of the uncompromising landscape; the enriching effect it had on the human spirit. It had been near this spot that he first understood something of the complex interactions between humanity and nature. The fells existed regardless of people and their sheep, and yet they were imbued with an abundant layer of meaning, accorded to it by human observation. The symmetry, the symbolism, the challenges and ultimate indifference all burst upon him on one April afternoon, earlier that year. Privately, he called it his epiphany, and wrote no fewer than eighteen poems on the subject, embarrassing himself in the process.

Like every local, he had heard tourists complain at the narrow twisting roads that gave no sign of having improved for a century or more. He had listened to their fearful shudderings about the absence of signs and steps and shelters up on the tops of the fells. Like most locals he knew his way up Loughrigg and Great Rigg and Scandale. He could predict the weather and identify which stone wall led back down to the shelter of the valleys.

'There it is,' said Bridget, pointing down to her left. 'We'll just make it before we get really wet.' The big car park contained a scattering of vehicles. They had to cross Pelter Bridge and take a footpath to the edge of the steep scarp that was Brant Brows. Rydal Hall was visible on the other side of the road, and people milled about in groups, many of them carrying rucksacks. 'I hope it'll start.'

'How long has it been here?'

'Since Wednesday. I decided the best place to hide it was

in full view, so I left it in the middle. There are always some other cars here at this time of year. People take a tent and go off for the night.'

'Yes, I know.' He gazed wonderingly at the vehicle, as they drew closer. It was a brand-new BMW. 'This is yours?'

She giggled. 'It was a wedding present from Peter. I didn't give him anything. I didn't know you were meant to. I think his feelings were a bit hurt.' She bit her lower lip in sudden pain. 'Oh God. I forgot for a minute. I've got to go and see him. Now. Come on. I can't leave it another minute.' She met his eyes, her own swimming with tears. 'Poor Peter,' she moaned. 'Poor, dear Peter.'

Simmy's day continued to be taken up with customers. All the flowers from that morning's consignment would disappear by teatime at this rate, she realised. And that would leave Saturday understocked. Quickly, she sent a new order to the wholesalers, mindful of the possibilities for Halloween and the nagging feeling that the window display required some urgent attention.

It would have been helpful to have Melanie's assistance, she thought. The girl never came in on a Friday, however. In the strange world of her college, the whole day was consumed with tutorials and lectures. She would show up next day, leaving Simmy free to have the christening flowers prepared as promised, and to make any trips that might arise. Interflora orders very often came through in the middle of a Friday, for a Saturday delivery.

But by far the larger part of her thoughts concerned Bridget Harrison-West and her husband. The more she mused on them, the more unlikely it seemed that the girl would remain passively in Troutbeck for another whole day. She would be impelled to act in some way, and that made Simmy nervous. Shortly after eleven, she decided to check, and phoned her house.

No reply. Where had she gone? Why had Simmy not had the sense to ask for Bridget's mobile number? Or Ben's, come to that? She had been hopelessly dim not to think of it sooner. The fact of Bridget's disappearance brought Ben to mind, illogically but insistently. They were both out there somewhere, two youngsters with the same urge to resolve the mystery of who killed the Baxter men. Simmy felt alarmed and responsible. She had let foolish sentiment distract her from the obvious and sensible course of action. There was danger out there, and she had to make up for her inaction somehow.

Melanie would be having her mid-morning break, in all probability. It might be safe to phone her and see if she could help.

Her assistant answered promptly. 'Mel? Are you in a lecture?'

'What? No, of course not. You can't use your phone in a lecture. Duh!'

'Listen. Have you got Ben Harkness's mobile number, by any chance?'

'What? No, of course I haven't. Why would I?'

'Have you got his brother's, then? Wilf's.'

'I doubt it. Hang on. Give me a second.' Silence ensued, and then Melanie came back. 'How about that? It's still here.' There was wonderment in her voice. 'It's more than a year ago. Must be time I got a new phone.' She recited the number and Simmy wrote it down.

'So what's going on?' Melanie demanded. 'What's the big panic?'

'No panic,' she fibbed, thinking that was exactly the word for it. 'I just thought it would be useful to have it. It's been busy here this morning,' she added, as a diversion.

'And here. I've got to go. See you tomorrow.'

'Thanks, Mel.'

She phoned the number for Wilf, wondering whether he might have got a new phone and a new number during the past year. Was it possible that he would answer? Wasn't he back at work at Storrs by this time?

'Hello?' came a wary voice. Evidently a strange number had popped up on his screen. Equally evidently, he and his contemporaries all answered their phones wherever they were and whatever they might be doing. Unless they were in a lecture, of course.

'Wilf? Hello. You don't know me, but I know your brother. I was with him on Sunday when George Baxter was shot.'

'The cool florist lady,' he supplied.

'Right. Simmy Brown. Listen – do you have his mobile number?'

'Yeah, course I do. Why d'you want it?'

'No specific reason. I just thought it might be useful to have it over the weekend. I feel sort of responsible for him. Daft, I know.'

'How did you get *my* number?'

'Melanie,' she said without thinking. 'She's still got it in her phone.'

'Has she?' he said softly. 'I'm amazed.'

'So . . .' she prompted.

'I'm not sure,' he prevaricated. 'Wouldn't he have given it you if he'd wanted you to have it?'

'We just forgot,' she said, trying in vain to be patient. 'Come on, Wilf. What harm can it do?'

'None, I guess. All right, then.' He gave her the number, after an even longer hiatus than Melanie had subjected her to. A man had come into the shop and was staring at some lilies near the door.

'Thanks,' she said quickly. 'Thanks a lot.' She turned to the customer, for a moment thinking it might be Peter Harrison-West, returning for another bout of aggression. Something about the hairline and the set of the ear seemed familiar. But when he faced her, he was a complete stranger, and she sighed her relief. He took five long minutes to choose a bunch of flowers for his wife and departed unhurriedly.

Then a new order pinged up on her computer. A *big* new order, comparable to the funeral tribute she had taken to Coniston the previous day. When all outlays and expenses had been deducted, she would still make a handsome profit. But it was required by five that afternoon, and would take well over an hour to create. In normal circumstances it would be readily achievable. As it was, she felt little but annoyance at the distraction.

Then she gave herself a shake. If Ben needed her, he could easily find the shop phone number and call it. He was old enough to be out on his own, as she had already told herself, earlier in the week. Without a car, he could not go far or get into much trouble. Her concern for him was irrational. It stemmed, she finally realised, from her reckless revelation of Peter Harrison-West's guilt. The knowledge made Ben vulnerable. Why had she not seen that sooner?

The respite from worry had lasted all of thirty seconds. She needed to know the boy was safe, because if he wasn't, it would be largely her fault.

She phoned the number, but got a message saying he was unavailable and to leave a message. 'Hi, Ben,' she chirped, trying to sound casual. 'Just wanted to say I've got your number now. I should have asked for it before. Here's mine, in case you need it.' She recited her own mobile number, and finished the call with a sense of having accomplished some small achievement.

When the shop phone rang ten minutes later, she was in the cool room selecting blooms for the new order. 'Simmy? It's Eleanor Baxter. Do you know a boy called Ben?'

'Yes I do,' she said. 'Why?'

'I've just seen him up at Rydal with Bridget. They were walking along the main road. I've no idea what was going on, but I thought you might.'

'Me? Why?'

'Just a hunch. I know Bridget likes you, and I know she hasn't been where she ought to be for the past two days. I just phoned Peter, and he said she's run off somewhere. What's going on?' She didn't sound especially concerned. Idle curiosity was closer to describing the languid tone.

'Why didn't you ask her?'

'I was in a rush. And she wouldn't have told me.'

*How did he sound?* She burned to ask, but didn't dare risk raising further suspicions. 'Did you tell Peter you'd seen her?' she asked instead.

'Of course. Why wouldn't I?'

Simmy bit back the snappy response that could force Eleanor to manifest some genuine alarm. If Peter was able to conduct a civilised conversation with his mother-in-law without raising anxieties, nothing too dreadful could be happening. 'I suppose because she isn't likely to want him to know,' she said. 'If she's run off, that's probably a fair assumption, don't you think?'

'Except she hasn't gone far, has she? I saw her on the road to Rydal, about two miles from where she and Peter now live. He might easily have stumbled on her himself.'

Rydal. Suddenly, Simmy knew what Bridget was doing. The question was – where would she go once she had retrieved her car? 'Did Peter say if he's there on his own?'

'He didn't exactly, but I could hear voices in the background. Glenn and Pablo, I assumed. And Felix, probably.'

'No, he's gone home – wherever it is he lives.' She caught herself up, wondering if she'd got that right. Glenn had only said that Felix didn't know about Peter's guilt. 'At least – that's what I thought they said.'

'It doesn't matter, does it? I also rang you to say your mother contacted me last night. I understand that Lucy's liable to be charged with grievous bodily harm. Why didn't you say anything on Saturday?'

Simmy had to think. 'Oh, that. It was such a stupid thing. But the people are idiots, unfortunately. I don't expect it'll come to anything.'

'That isn't what your mother said.'

'Oh.'

'Lucy isn't an aggressive child. I can't imagine what was going on.'

'Mrs Baxter – I really think the important thing is Bridget, just at the moment, don't you?' She felt proud of her assertive tone, her refusal to be diverted. It made her feel pleasingly grown-up.

'I really do *not* think it's for you to tell me what's important,' came the crushing reply. Eleanor Baxter, it seemed, was even more grown-up and assertive, if it came to a contest.

'All right. But that's what I think, whether you agree or not. You might not realise that I've been quite closely involved over the past few days.' She wanted to shout *Murder!* at the woman in an attempt to force her to admit the seriousness of what had happened, and was perhaps still happening. But she managed to maintain a reasonably calm tone, as she went on, 'I'm not sure that Bridget is safe. Two people have been killed, after all.'

'I don't need you to remind me of that,' was the frosty response, before the line was disconnected.

Simmy sorted the implications methodically. Peter knew that Bridget was in the vicinity, accompanied by a teenaged boy. Pablo and Glenn were probably still in the house with him. The gun was – she hoped – safely hidden in the attic of her house. Peter was at least rational enough to hold a coherent conversation with his mother-in-law, without raising any alarm in her. Mind you, Simmy thought to herself, it would probably take a large nuclear explosion to alarm Eleanor. The police were conspicuously absent. Wilf was still soft about Melanie . . . she gave herself a shake at this point. Those two could wait. The chief concern was for Bridget, and if Ben was with her, then that was a major new worry. A worry large enough to justify contacting DI Moxon, came the unavoidable conclusion.

Outside the sky was darkening under thick pewter-grey clouds, but the rain was as yet still quite tentative. Another wet weekend was in prospect, it seemed. It would mark the closing days of the tourist season, with only the real stalwarts still taking to the fells for their masochistic hikes. The rivers and becks would be running full and fast. The chunky slate houses would start sending woodsmoke up their chimneys and evening lights would appear earlier and earlier with every passing day. Simmy tried to think of it as an adventure, getting through her first Lakeland winter without losing her nerve. All around her were people who knew what to do about snow and ice and rising river waters. All she had to do was slot into their routines and take it a day at a time.

Meanwhile, she had to decide on the next level of interference in the lives of the Harrison-Wests. Fear of making things worse had assailed her ever since the previous evening – a fear sown by Best-Man-Glenn. He had appeared to be so completely in charge, and so confident that he could put everything to rights that Simmy's own assessment of right and wrong became unsteady. Viewed logically, this was entirely absurd. Logic, she felt, was gaining ground, here in her familiar shop where the conventions all held good.

She phoned Moxon. He answered promptly, which she took to be a good omen. She floundered initially, unsure where to start and what, if anything, to withhold. He gave her no assistance, but waited in silence for the story to emerge.

'Bridget and I had visitors last night. They told us that the killer was Peter Harrison-West, and asked us not to call you. When your men came to the door I told them everything was all right. It was, in a way. We weren't in danger. Glenn wouldn't hurt Bridget. Now she's with Ben and I think they might be going to Peter's house. I think that might be dangerous, especially for Ben. He's not answering his phone.'

Was that as garbled to him as it was to her, she wondered?

'They said Harrison-West committed both murders?'

'Yes.'

'And you believed them?'

'Yes.'

'Did Bridget believe them?'

'I think so. She was very upset at first, but she recovered quickly, and agreed that Peter shouldn't be handed in to the police. Glenn said there was no evidence.'

'Glenn Adams, that would be?'

'Right Peter's old friend. The best man at the wedding.'

'Do you know where he is now?'

'At Peter's house, I think. With Pablo. I don't know his surname. Plus Felix Mainwaring, who is Peter's cousin. The one in the wheelchair. They said he didn't know about Peter's confession, but he might be there with them.'

'At the Harrison-Wests' house in Ambleside?'

'Yes.'

'My God,' he muttered angrily. 'I've never known anything like this.'

'Neither have I,' she agreed with feeling.

'We'll have to go and see. Is there any suggestion of a weapon?'

She grimaced to herself, having hoped to keep that detail back. 'I think it's at my house. But there could be others, I suppose. I don't really know.'

'It makes a very big difference.'

'I expect it does. Are you going to arrest Peter?'

'Take him in for further questioning, probably.'

'Did you hear about him hitting Ben yesterday? He was wandering round Windermere in a very volatile state. We thought somebody might have reported him.'

His silence was plainly reproachful. 'No,' he said. 'Nobody thought to report him.'

'I expect he calmed down and went home, then.'

'Mrs Brown, there are fifty police officers working on this case. They are showing a strong presence in both Bowness and Windermere, in an attempt to reassure a frightened public. The chances of a man "wandering round" hitting people without being apprehended are really quite small.'

'Well, it happened, all the same. Up by the station, Ben said. I suppose it didn't cause much of a stir. Ben's brother Wilf was with him, and brought him down here to my shop. He wasn't badly hurt. I put witch hazel on it. And if anybody saw it happen, they wouldn't worry that it had anything to do with the murders, would they?'

'They might if they recognised Harrison-West. I gather he's quite well known locally.'

'By name, mostly, I think. And more in Ambleside than here.'

'All right.' He cut her off impatiently. 'So the situation is this – tell me if I go wrong. Mrs Harrison-West is returning to her rightful home, having spent two nights with you.

She believes that the husband to whom she is returning is the killer of her father and her brother, but she is not afraid of him. The bearer of this news, the best friend of her husband, is also likely to be there. She is accompanied by a seventeen-year-old boy who was an actual witness to the murder of her father. Right so far?'

'Yes.'

'You see – I have to make a report to my superior. I have to decide whether an armed response is appropriate. I have to devise a strategy – admittedly with substantial help from colleagues – as to how to manage this new development.'

'That sounds like quite a slow process.'

'Not really. You think we should hurry, do you?'

'I don't know. I am worried about Ben, I must admit.'

'Your worry is a significant factor. We have learnt, rather painfully, to take the worries of the public more seriously than we used to.'

'Good. That's good. Because there's a chance that Peter has already shot Ben, if there's another gun at the house. People like that tend to have guns, don't they? They shoot pheasants and things with them.'

'There are no firearms registered to Mr Harrison-West or his friends. Not a single one.'

'Good,' she said again.

'You think so? I thought I heard you mention a weapon being at your house. Did I dream that?'

'It's an old rifle, from the Second World War.'

'Oh, God,' he groaned.

She pressed on, hoping to reassure him. 'Bridget was going to hide it in my attic.'

'You didn't see her do it, I suppose?'

'I'm afraid not. But she'd have no reason to take it back to the Ambleside house. She wouldn't do that. She's got more sense.'

Another weighty silence made Simmy wonder if he was in fact issuing inaudible instructions to his team, instead of wasting time asking irrelevant questions. Then he spoke again. 'So we can at least go to Troutbeck, and instigate a search of your attic. If you give your permission, we can avoid applying for a warrant. You really need to be there, though.'

'I need to be here, actually. I've got a business to run. I've done my bit by phoning you and telling you everything. It's up to you now.'

'Yes, and I'm asking you to assist us with the next step in our investigations by being present when we make a search for a firearm that you believe to be inside your house. It would save time and damage. I don't think you have any real basis for objection, under the circumstances. We can come and collect you if that would help.'

'No, I want to have my car where I can reach it. Can I have half an hour to get there? I'll try to get hold of my assistant and see if she can cover for me.'

'I expect to see you at twelve-thirty, then, and not a minute later.'

The shop door pinged as she put the phone down. For a moment she couldn't think who the newcomer was. Then it clicked. 'Julie! Gosh – how are you? I heard about your fingers.'

The hairdresser held up her right hand, where three

fingers were taped together. 'Immobile,' she said. 'But what about *you*? All this business about murders and runaway brides. She didn't really run away, did she? Have you seen her?'

'Yes, I've seen her,' Simmy confirmed hollowly. 'And now I've got to go and let the police into my house. It's a really long story, Jules, and I can't stop.' She gave her friend a speculative look as a thought struck her. 'Can you use that hand at all?'

'The thumb's all right, and the little finger. I'm learning a few tricks.'

'Are you busy this afternoon?'

'What? How could I be busy like this? I can't even get it wet.'

'Will you mind the shop for me? Just take orders – make people write it all down. I might be back again by two. I'll try and get Melanie to skip a lecture and come in, if I can't make it.'

'Gosh! I have no idea how it all works, Sim. I'll make a terrible mess of it.'

'The flowers have all got prices on – that's the most likely thing you'll have to cope with. Just wrap paper round them and take the money. You might not get anybody, anyway.'

'Well—'

'Thanks a million. I wouldn't ask, except it's Friday, and you never know—'

'This is about Bridget Harrison-West, I take it? That little baggage. I had such plans for her hair. I spent hours practising kiss-curls. And then it all fell apart.' She sighed. 'Just goes to show.'

319

'At least they did get married.' Simmy thought yet again of young Markie being held down in the cold lake until he drowned. 'Although I'm not sure that's anything to celebrate, the way it's going.'

'Why? What's going on? You have to tell me, Sim. It's only fair.'

'Honestly, I can't. But I think there might be an arrest before long. The police are closing in, as they say. Not very rapidly, admittedly, but I think it's not far off now.' An image of Peter replaced that of Markie, his face red with rage and his fist clenched in Melanie's face. Whatever it might mean for Bridget, it would surely be a good thing if he could be caught and locked up.

Julie was a sensible person, in Simmy's experience. They had first met at an earlier wedding – a much smaller affair than the one at Storrs. The bride had been a farmer's daughter in her early thirties, accustomed to wearing wellingtons rather than heels, with hair that actually did contain hayseeds for much of the winter. Julie had patiently created a simple style that flattered the healthy outdoor face without a hint of the ridiculous. Simmy had met her at the house, when delivering buttonholes and bouquets, and they had admired each other's handiwork with genuine approval. The sweetness of the whole event stayed with Simmy for some weeks.

'Listen – if I'm not back by two, call me on my mobile. It'll be good to know you're here watching out for things. There's a chance somebody might come in – somebody to do with the murders, I mean.'

Julie's eyes widened. 'Not the murderer himself, I hope!'

'Unlikely. My mother's also in a bit of a state about

something else, so you might get her to cope with.'

'Don't tell me any more,' Julie begged. 'Just go and do whatever it is you have to do. And don't get yourself shot, for God's sake.'

'Thanks. I'll do my best.'

She took the van and headed for Ambleside, aware of having wasted more time than was comfortable. Eleanor had seen Ben and Bridget over an hour before – since then they might easily have got to Peter's house and challenged him. But surely he wouldn't hurt his beloved bride? Of course he wouldn't. There was really nothing too much to worry about.

Except the major worry of not knowing the precise location of the house. Nobody had told her the actual address, other than that it was on the northern edge of the town. Why she thought she could find it on such flimsy information now seemed unfathomable. She would have to go to the house she *did* know, instead. The big, beloved house belonging to Eleanor Baxter. That she could find, after being taken there on Saturday. And Eleanor would tell her how to reach the other one. She might even go with her. Two women on hand to offer consolation and shelter after whatever climactic events might be unfolding would be surely better than one – however deficient Eleanor Baxter might be in maternal instincts.

A police car overtook her on a bend, in heavy rain, its lights beaming aggressively at anybody in its way. No sirens or blue flashers, but it was obviously speeding urgently towards Ambleside. She was painfully reminded that she had agreed to supervise a search of her home for a gun, and that she might be in trouble for failing to do as promised. But that felt like a minor distraction compared to the need to find Ben and Bridget. She contemplated following the police car, assuming it was heading for the Harrison-West house. Before she could decide, it was out of sight. But it had very much changed her thinking, in those few seconds. Something bad was happening. Ben Harkness was going to find himself in the middle of violence and trauma. It was Ben, she realised, she had been most concerned about from the start.

When another fast-moving car came up behind her, waiting impatiently for a gap in the oncoming traffic, she resolved to chase after it. If she lost it, that would be too bad – at least she'd have done her best. It never occurred to her that DI Moxon might disapprove of her interference. She had not asked to be embroiled in the great family confusion that circled around Bridget and her husband, but it was by this time far too late to retreat.

The police car dodged past her, and she accelerated after it. There was only a mile to go before they reached the tangled streets that formed the centre of Ambleside. She easily kept pace for that distance, with no further overtakings, which would have proved difficult. In the rain, which had intensified in the past few minutes, the pavements were almost empty. A lorry was obstructing their progress and the police car hooted at it. It moved reluctantly out of the way, and Simmy followed the officious vehicle through the resulting space.

The town was more compact than Windermere, tucked into a tight valley between Loughrigg and Wansfell, with little scope for expansion. The Kirkstone Road kinked away to the east before shooting northwards to the famous pass.

Residential streets lay straight ahead, only to peter out into footpaths and tracks unfit for motor vehicles, following the course of the Scandale Beck. Peter Harrison-West's house had to lie on one of those roads, none of which Simmy knew at all. But she continued her pursuit, barely noticing that there were signs of affluence on both sides – detached houses with stone gateposts and large trees shielding them from public view; open areas behind stone walls where town met country in a dramatic alteration of terrain. They were on a straight road with houses on the left-hand side. She had no idea of its name, no time for any real observations other than the car ahead.

Suddenly there was a very obvious centre of activity and Simmy found herself in the heart of it with scarcely any warning. Cars had overflowed into the road from the driveway of a big house. The vehicle she had been following pulled up in the road and two men got out. Without a glance at her – for which she was both sorry and glad – they trotted into the approach to the house. Simmy drove past carefully, craning round to see what might be going on. Apart from a lot of cars, it was impossible to draw any conclusions. She crawled onwards, to a point only fifty yards further on where the road simply finished. There she sat, arguing with herself, for two minutes. She could not just turn round and go back to the shop. Nor could she casually walk up to the house where she was a stranger and see for herself what was going on. She could not make any useful or relevant phone calls. She had got herself into a pickle, she admitted ruefully. The pickle had been ripening and proliferating like a rising lump of bread dough ever since last Saturday. It had overspilt its bowl and was engulfing everything. There was no escape.

But what was there, really, to worry about? In the core of herself, she was not afraid. There might be shouting and punching, tears and broken hearts. But nobody else would die. DI Moxon wouldn't let them. Nobody would die. But if they did, please God don't let it be Ben Harkness.

## Chapter Twenty-Two

Ben could think of no sensible questions to ask, as Bridget negotiated the one-way system through the town centre, heading for the higher ground towards Scandale. He knew roughly where they were, and what lay ahead. The lane she turned into had stone walls on either side, which he knew closed in further up until the track became almost too narrow for motor vehicles. He remembered a ruined tower up here somewhere that his mother was especially fond of. The houses were handsome and discreetly tucked away, so that all you saw was walls and trees if you climbed only a quarter of a mile up the lane and looked back.

But they did not go as far as that. Instead, Bridget took them into a driveway that already contained three cars, and pulled up under a large cedar, from which rain dripped down aggressively. Over the past ten minutes it had gained considerably in force. Ben tried to imagine the scene in bright June sunshine, how infinitely less sinister it would seem under such conditions. He began to think of questions.

'Why are we here? You said you wanted to get away and

think about whatever it is you've got in your bag. I thought you could just take me home and—'

'That was before my mother saw me.' Her voice was firm, decisive. 'I can't risk her interfering. She's liable to call Peter and say she's seen me. It might set him off again.'

'Set him off?' echoed Ben, fingering his bruise. 'What makes you think he's not set off already? He might be ballistic by now.'

'We'll have to risk it.'

'*We?*' he muttered.

'Serves you right for following me. That was a daft thing to do.'

'I agree.'

'How old are you, exactly?'

'Seventeen and five days. Why?'

'No reason.'

He heard a wobble in the voice that had been so firm half a minute earlier. 'Come on, then,' she said. 'Now or never.'

He wanted to ask if he could stay in the car, and just wait for her to sort things out. She surely didn't need his protection?

'Come on,' she said again and he saw that he had no choice.

Then a man appeared in front of the car, stooping to peer through the rain-streaked windscreen at them. 'Bridget!' he shouted, somewhat too loudly.

'Uh-oh,' said Ben. It was the man who had hit him. Bridget's husband. Who still had all the signs of being a murderer. He still looked like Raskolnikov.

Bridget opened her door and threw herself at the man.

They embraced in a damp hug. The man was by far the wetter of the two, as if he'd been standing outside since the rain started. His hair was plastered over his skull. Ben felt fully justified in remaining where he was, but he compromised by lowering the window, so as to hear what was said.

'Bridget, how could you?' demanded the man, when they pulled apart. 'You don't know . . . you had no reason . . .' He choked on the words, his mouth shapeless with emotion.

'What?' She looked hard into his face.

'You think *I* killed Markie and George. That's why you ran away.'

'Sort of. But Glenn says we can save you. There's no evidence.'

'Because I didn't do it, Brid. How could you think I did? If you think that, how can we live together as a married couple? That would be . . . grotesque. Your own father and brother, murdered by your husband. You couldn't live with that. Can't you see how obvious that is?'

She held his arm, putting one hand flat on his chest. 'Don't say that. If you tell me you didn't do it, I'll believe you.'

'Will you? Really? Then who will we decide *did* do it? How can we relax, knowing there's a killer with an eye on us, all the time? We'd need to know why, and whether we were safe.' He seemed hysterical, the words tumbling out at almost incoherent speed.

Ben heard every word, but the couple appeared to have forgotten he was there. He was concentrating hard, assessing implications. If Bridget said the wrong thing, the man might throttle her, right there, before his very eyes.

'Glenn said it was because you wanted me all to yourself.

327

Markie must have said something stupid and you just lost it. And Daddy – I guess he worked it out, maybe? I've got the gun safe, Peter. Nobody's going to find it. And . . .' She looked back at the car, seeming to focus on the back seat, where she'd thrown her shoulder bag. 'I found something,' she finished.

Peter barely heard the last words. His face had collapsed even further at the earlier attempt to explain his motives. 'You really do think I did it,' he groaned. 'You've got it all worked out.'

'So convince me otherwise,' she challenged, putting both hands on his shoulders and shaking him. 'Pull yourself together and tell me the whole thing.'

'There's nothing to tell. You know everything that I know. More, if you've seen a gun. I never saw a gun. I don't know what you're talking about.'

'It was your grandfather's, from the war.'

'The Lee Enfield? But that's locked away in the pantry. I saw it when we moved, and made sure it was safely out of anybody's reach.' He shook his head. 'Who told you . . . why have you got it?' He frowned down at her, his face shiny with rain, his eyes red-rimmed.

'Are Glenn and Pablo here?' she changed the subject. 'And Felix?' She looked along the line of cars in the drive. 'Seems as if they are.'

'Not Felix. The others are leaving this afternoon, I think. They haven't really spoken to me for a day or two.'

'Why on earth not?'

'I've been in my room, trying to understand why you ran off. Trying to get hold of you. I went out searching yesterday, in a total panic. And the day before . . . was it? I went to that florist shop. You've got pally with her, haven't you? Pablo said something. He likes her. And a boy. There's a boy, who saw George being shot. I hit him.' He smacked the side of his own head, as if to order his thoughts.

'That boy's here. In the car, look.'

Peter looked. 'Yes, that's him,' he agreed dully. 'Is he setting the cops on me?'

'Of course not. Peter, let's go into the house. Let's see if we can put it all right, somehow. I'm completely soaked. I want to wash and change.'

'Do what you like. It's finished, Brid. I can't fight it any more. I expect I've been a fool about you, all along. Markie was right. I'm too old for you. It's not wholesome.'

'Is that what he said?'

'According to Glenn, it is.'

'But he didn't say it to you?'

Peter shook his head. 'Markie and I were mates, you know that. I never had any idea he was thinking that sort of stuff.'

'Nor me,' said Bridget slowly.

Two more men came walking from the house. Ben saw them first. 'Um . . .' he called out of the window. 'Company.'

'What?' Bridget whirled round, looking in the wrong direction.

'Hey, Briddy!' called one of them. 'Good to see you.' He trotted up to her and flung an arm around her shoulders. 'You're terribly wet. What's going on? Come indoors, for God's sake. And who's that?' He eyed Ben with exaggerated interest, a half smile on his face.

'Glenn,' said Bridget, pushing his arm away. 'That's Ben.'

'Ben Harkness?' Glenn's eyebrows rose. 'We meet at last.'

The sodden group stood in an accidental line, from tallest to shortest, each step an inch or two. Glenn was easily six feet, Pablo next, then Peter, barely five feet eight. Bridget herself was far from short. Ben scrutinised them carefully, wondering whether there was a suppressed violence just below the surface. There should be signs, if so, but detecting subtle signals was not his strong point. It was a family joke the way he never knew when to keep quiet, or respect someone's damaged feelings.

Peter was the most obviously disturbed. He had stepped away from Bridget as soon as Glenn and Pablo appeared, as if to leave them access to her. He seemed to dwindle in status and confidence. His gaze remained fixed on the ground. He looked, thought Ben, like a man waiting for his fate to strike, hopeless and defeated. He looked like a man who had done something dreadful and now hung his head ready for his punishment.

'Hey, Pete,' Glenn chided him boisterously. 'Chin up. Let's get inside. This is stupid, standing out in the rain.'

'You've done it before, haven't you?' said Bridget, sounding angry. 'At the wedding, you all stood outside the hotel in the rain, waiting for my father. *All* of you. Markie and Felix as well. And *then* what happened? What bloody happened? You all went in different directions, and one of you pushed Markie into the lake – right? You all know who it was, don't you? Or maybe it was a joint effort? You did it together, maybe?'

'Shut up, Brid. Don't be ridiculous.' Glenn spoke lightly, but his face was flushed.

'I *won't*. The really ridiculous thing is that you think you can get away with it. That's just boys' stuff. Even Ben's got more sense than that. Where are the wet clothes? The muddy patches? Didn't Markie fight back? You'd have scratches or bruises. You've all been telling stories, like you always have. You're just like silly children.'

'More company,' Ben warned, feeling he'd been given the role of a sort of guard dog. He'd have got the same reaction if he'd barked. He hadn't liked the *even Ben* remark much.

Two cars were coming down the drive, one behind the other. 'Police,' added Ben, superfluously.

Things became complicated after that. DI Moxon focused first on Ben, pulling him out of the car and demanding to know whether he was all right. He then asked the same of Bridget, before marching everyone down to the house for what he promised would be a seriously intensive set of interviews. 'New information has come to light,' he said severely.

Glenn and Pablo led the way, heads up, shoulders relaxed. Peter shambled after them, his face grey and crumpled. Moxon and a policewoman followed behind, leaving two further officers sitting in the second car. Ben was impressed at this foresight. *Backup*, he thought to himself. *Must be serious, then.*

He found himself walking with Bridget, surrounded on all sides by people a lot older and bigger than him. Moxon himself was plainly well muscled and light on his feet. The policewoman was in uniform, and had long hair tied back, sticking out from under her cap. She looked to be well over thirty. He felt lonely and scared, completely out of his depth.

How had he got himself into this, anyway? He hadn't done a single thing to deserve it.

Except follow Bridget, of course. That was his really big mistake.

He thought about the muddled accusations she had just been making to Glenn, implying that all the men in the wedding party had conspired to murder Markie. That was obviously stupid. It ignored the shooting of Mr Baxter, apart from anything else. He had been about to say something to this effect when the police arrived. He looked at the backs of Peter, Pablo and Glenn as they stamped their way into the house, shaking off their wet coats and brushing dripping hair out of their eyes. Except Glenn, whose hair was so minimal that it would dry instantly, like a dog. Ben wanted to go home, but he wanted even more to observe what would happen next. If he could just hide away quietly in a corner, and make everybody forget he was there, then he thought he might cope.

There was a muddled milling about in a big square room boasting a glorious view of Lake Windermere, with nobody too sure of what they were supposed to do. Bridget became shrill with impatience. 'What is this all about? What new information are you talking about? There's no reason for you to come here ordering us about. This is my house, mine and Peter's. These are all my friends.'

Moxon gave a small smile. 'It's my understanding that you have not spent much time here since your wedding,' he said. 'That alone makes me think there could be a lot more you can tell me.'

'Calm down, Brid,' said Glenn, interrupting her before

332

she could make another outburst. 'Let's get it over with, and not spin it out by making a fuss. Okay?' His voice was calm, affectionate, patient. It occurred to Ben that this man sounded more like her husband than Peter did. Peter, who had stuffed himself into a narrow wing chair near the empty fireplace, was taking little apparent notice of anything.

'We'd like, for the moment, to concentrate on the shooting of Mr Baxter on Sunday,' said Moxon, looking round at each face in turn, including Ben's. 'Since we have young Mr Harkness here.'

Everyone looked at him then, including Peter. 'But I didn't see anything,' he stammered.

'We can't be too sure about that,' said the detective. 'Let me run a few of our latest findings past you.'

'What – in front of everybody?' It seemed an alarming breach of protocol. Wasn't the normal routine to interview everybody individually?

'Why not? Now sit down, please. We'll just go through it all, and check we've got it right.'

They all found somewhere to sit – Pablo and Glenn on a sofa, Bridget on a large pouffe and the police officers on upright chairs that had been standing against the wall. Ben took a broad armchair that made him feel small and childlike.

'All right,' Moxon began, tugging a thick notebook out of his pocket. 'We've spent all week refining the examination of the scene of the shooting. Without going into every detail, we feel confident we've narrowed down the point from which the shot was fired. There's a stone wall to the south of the Old England Hotel, which would be good cover. There are certain marks on it which suggest it was the point we were looking for. Do you know the one I mean?'

Ben tried to visualise Fallbarrow Road and its neighbours. 'Not really,' he admitted. 'I was south of the hotel, wasn't I?'

'You were crossing the road. If you'd looked to your right, down towards the centre of the town for any reason, you'd have seen the wall. I know it's a lot to expect, but if there was just some small detail lodged in your memory, that might make a big difference.'

Ben felt hot under the collective stares from around the room. 'Well . . .' he began. 'I suppose I would have looked both ways before crossing. Even though it was obviously very quiet, with no traffic.' He closed his eyes, trying to recapture the whole scene. He had done the same thing a hundred times since Sunday. There *was* some detail peeping from the edge of his memory. He had known from the first that some silly little thing had fleetingly snagged his attention, and then hidden itself away again.

He opened his eyes again. 'How far along was the wall? I mean, how far from Mr Baxter?'

Moxon consulted his pad. 'Twenty-five metres, that's all. Close range for a rifle. Rather a waste of such a fine weapon, some might say. They're accurate for about twenty times that distance.'

Bridget made a wordless murmur and earned herself a sharp look from Glenn.

'I didn't see a gun, nor sunlight glinting on metal. Nothing like that. I can't picture the wall you mean. How high is it?'

'Four feet or so. The gunman would have to crouch right down. There's a very wide stretch of pavement between it and the road.'

'A squirrel! I saw a squirrel,' Ben crowed, disproportionately triumphant. 'It got halfway across the road, and then stopped. Then a little stone or something appeared from nowhere and hit it, so it ran back again. I thought nothing of it, really.'

'You must have wondered where the missile came from,' Moxon said gently. 'You didn't see anyone who could have thrown it?'

'No. I suppose I just assumed there was a boy in a garden somewhere. Then there was the shot, and I forgot the whole thing.'

Moxon was looking doubtful, working his shoulders as if rehearsing some complicated action. Ben was still glowing from the successful recovery of his memory. Another little squawk from Bridget made everyone turn towards her.

'Glenn!' she gasped. 'My God, it was *you*! You've never been able to resist throwing stones at squirrels. I've seen you do it five hundred times. *You* were hiding behind that wall, and shot my father! But *why*?'

The smile on Glenn's face was a clown's unnatural grimace. 'Of course I didn't,' he said, throatily. 'How could you ever think such a thing? This is *me*, Briddy, remember. Have a bit of sense.'

'Evidence,' muttered Pablo, looking pale. 'That's not evidence, is it? Lots of people throw things at squirrels.'

Moxon met the eyes of his female colleague. 'We could see if we could find the stone,' he said with a sigh. She blinked disbelievingly at him.

'There's no need,' shouted Bridget. 'I *know* it was Glenn. He's been trying to put it onto Peter, all along.

Peter – say something! Pablo – *you* know, don't you?'

Ben shrank into his chair, anticipating something unpleasant. Glenn was big and strong – and could hit a squirrel from halfway down a street. The incriminating compulsion to do so struck him as both comical and fatalistic. What self-respecting sniper would let a little rodent distract him at such a crucial moment? Where had he found the stone? Why hadn't Ben seen the arcing arm that must have appeared over the wall for the throw? He mentally practised, and realised a strong wrist could probably fire it without much visible movement. Did Glenn have strong wrists, he wondered, trying to get a glimpse.

Bridget was on her feet, facing Glenn with ferocity. 'It all makes sense now. You know us all so well, don't you? You know Peter's weak points and you jabbed away at them. You've probably got him thinking it really was him all along. But *why*, Glenn? What were you thinking?'

Ben watched in fascinated horror. *I did this*, he realised, with a feeling of power.

Moxon was also on his feet, but making no move to stop Bridget's attack. Pablo, next to Glenn, was looking from face to face in bewilderment. Peter had done little more than raise his head.

Glenn said nothing. Bridget raised two clenched fists and waved them in his face. '*Glenn!*' she yelled. 'You shot my father. You owe me an explanation. You told me it was Peter. I would have gone through my whole life thinking it was him. Was that what you wanted?'

'You'd have left him,' he muttered, barely audible. 'And come to me.'

Silence fell like a thick wool blanket. Then, 'What?' Bridget whispered. 'What did you say?'

Glenn merely shook his head. Bridget backed away, then turned towards her husband. 'Peter? Do you understand what's happening? Do you see what he's been doing?'

Harrison-West put out his hands, not to embrace her, but to fend her off. 'Not Glenn,' he choked. 'Glenn loves me.'

With a warbling scream of appalled exasperation, Bridget smacked at one of his hands and left the room at a run.

Before the front door slammed shut, Pablo was on his feet, and bending over Glenn, delivered a crunching blow to the middle of his face. Blood spattered from his nose, and Moxon sprang into action.

Simmy peered through the rain at the house, past the long line of cars. There was nothing to hear or see. Was Moxon in there, sorting everything out – or was he still waiting in vain for her to show up in Troutbeck? Had there been a second gun after all, with Peter holding everybody at bay, including Ben and Bridget? Might she manage to look in through a window and discover for herself? Slowly she approached the front door, debating worriedly with herself.

The house was square and dark, with decorated windows and high-pitched roof. It looked proudly over Lake Windermere, perfectly situated for maximum sunlight and minimal gales. Even in her anxiety, she had time to think *Lucky Bridget, marrying into such a handsome property.*

'Madam?' came a male voice behind her. 'I'm sorry, but we're not letting anybody in just now.'

It was a uniformed policeman, standing by one of the marked

cars that she had passed without realising it was occupied.

'Oh,' she said, irritably. 'I wasn't going in, anyway. I was just—'

And then Bridget herself was there, running out of the house without a coat, heading for one of the cars that Simmy had already passed. 'Hey!' she shouted, and made a grab for the girl. 'Where are you going? Where's Ben?'

As if punctured, Bridget simply collapsed into her arms. 'It was Glenn,' she wept indistinctly. 'Glenn killed them. And Peter won't believe it.'

A second policeman materialised from the far side of the car and stood passively watching.

Simmy ignored both the men. 'Come on,' she said to the weeping girl. 'Come and sit in my car and tell me about it.' Rather to her surprise, Bridget willingly agreed, and they began to slosh their way back to the lane and Simmy's waiting vehicle.

'Er . . .' started the first officer. 'Nobody's allowed to leave, either.'

'What?' Simmy glared at him. 'Why?'

'Orders,' he mumbled.

Simmy held steady. 'It'll be all right,' she said. 'Tell DI Moxon we've gone to my van, which is just over there.' She pointed. 'We want to talk.'

He hesitated, and Simmy lost patience. 'For heaven's sake. It's raining. She's upset. The police know where to find me. We can't do any harm. Write a report saying I refused to cooperate and you gave me a stern warning. What else can you do?' Her mother would be proud of her, she thought fleetingly. All her life she had been reminded of the limits of police powers, despite their inexorable increase over the years. They relied on obedience, and when it was withheld, there were few options left to them. 'Arrest me?' she answered her own question. 'For what?'

He hung on to his dignity, and waved her away without another word.

Once in Simmy's van, Bridget sat sideways in the seat, holding Simmy's eye as she brokenly told her story. 'He wanted me to himself. He must have thought Markie and Daddy were in his way – and if he made me think Peter killed them, that would separate me from him as well. It's all so simple, and so foul and horrible. He must have *planned* it.'

Simmy went blank with amazement. She could not even frame a question. 'Glenn,' she repeated stupidly. 'He's in love with you?'

Tears smudged the girl's features, her lips swelled and her nose went red. 'It's so horrible. I've always been Peter's girl, right from the start. Glenn never said a word. We were all friends together, with Pablo and Felix and Markie. It was like a story, you know? The Splendid Six we called ourselves sometimes, for a joke. They called me Timmy when I was little, like the dog in the Famous Five.'

'Did Glenn ever have a girlfriend?'

'Loads of them. But he kept them at a distance. Only one or two ever came walking or boating with us.'

'How . . . ? I mean, did he just confess, or what?'

'It was Ben. He saw someone throw a stone at a squirrel, just before Daddy was shot. I knew right away – that could only be Glenn. He always does that. He hates squirrels.'

Simmy forced her brain to function. 'And *then* he confessed?'

339

'Sort of. He didn't have to, really, because I knew and he understood that it had all gone wrong.'

'They still might need evidence, then?'

Bridget just blinked. 'I don't know.'

'Listen. We'll have to go and fetch that gun. I'm already supposed to be there while they search my house. They'll be able to match it with the bullet, for a start.'

'What good will that do?'

'Well . . . they might find powder marks or something, on his clothes. Or flecks of his skin where he was when he fired.'

'In this rain? Everything will be washed away.'

'He was outside, then?' Simmy's need to know exactly where the gunman had been positioned was surprising, even to herself.

'Yes. Behind a wall by the hotel.'

'How near?'

'Pretty near, apparently. What does it *matter*?'

'No – you're right. It doesn't now. Except . . .' Her skin was crawling with the knowledge that she had been almost face-to-face with a murderous gunman. 'No, go on,' she added.

'I keep seeing that poor little squirrel . . .' Bridget's voice tailed away and she closed her eyes. 'Stupid, I know, when there are much more important things to worry about.'

'He said something about a squirrel,' Simmy remembered. 'Almost the first thing he said to me. Gosh. So what happens now?'

'He'll give himself up,' said Bridget. 'Pablo and Peter are going to force him.' She heaved a long tragic sigh. 'Poor Peter.'

'Are they arresting Glenn, then? Is the Moxon man there?'

'Who? Oh, yes. The inspector. Yes, he's there. I think he had an idea all along that it must have been Glenn. He didn't seem surprised.'

'Didn't he?' Simmy tried to remember exactly what she had told him. Had he assumed all along that it wasn't Peter? 'He hasn't been much in evidence all week, has he? Though I did see him yesterday.'

'Doing background stuff,' said Bridget vaguely. 'I suppose.'

'Is Glenn under arrest?' Simmy asked again.

'I don't know. I left them before much could happen. I couldn't face Peter. He didn't really want me at all. He wants Glenn. Do you know what he said?'

'What?'

'That Glenn loves him. There was so much in those little words. The *betrayal* was what really hurt him. Not losing me. The real couple – that he really cares most about is him and Glenn, not him and me.' Tears flowed again.

'No. You're wrong,' Simmy tried to say, but Bridget drowned her out.

'I want my mother,' she wailed, like a small child. 'Take me home. Please.'

Simmy started the engine obediently, but made no attempt to turn the van around. The word *betrayal* echoed in her mind, with all the sinking feelings that went with it. Like walking onto a surface you think is solid, and find yourself falling into a quagmire. She had felt it herself when Tony had failed her. She thought about Peter Harrison-West and his inadequacies. 'No,' she said again, more loudly. 'You've got it wrong. Peter loves you the most.'

'How d'you work that out?'

She paused before trying to explain. 'He was flattened when he thought you believed he was the killer. He lost all hope, went crazy with the injustice of it. He expected you'd stand by him, whatever happened. But he believed Glenn implicitly. Glenn told him that you'd lost faith in him. He was left all alone.'

'He wasn't. He had Glenn and Pablo.'

'He didn't want them. Glenn was acting all solicitous and brotherly, sympathising and promising to make it right – really acting the part, and Peter could only think of you.'

'You make Glenn sound monstrous.'

Simmy waited for this thought to gain ground. She saw Glenn as an Iago figure, separating the lovers by finding their vulnerabilities. Having known them for most of their lives it was an easy task. But unlike Iago, Glenn's motive seemed transparently clear – he wanted Bridget for himself.

'He must be a psychopath,' Bridget went on. 'We always did wonder about him. He loves killing things – birds, especially.'

'And squirrels.'

The girl heaved a tragic sigh. 'Right. But he was never rough or violent with *people*. Markie idolised him. Poor Markie. What a ghastly waste. Simmy – let's get the gun and take it to the police. We can't let him get away with it.'

'You said he'd confess. And I thought we were going to your mother's.'

'Later. Now I'm angry. I'd like to shoot Glenn myself for what he's done.'

'We'll go back, then. But we're not fetching the gun. It's safe where it is.'

Bridget appeared to accept this, but Simmy saw a new thought fill her mind. 'Oh – I forgot!' she spluttered. 'My bag. There's something in my bag, in my car. We'll have to get it.'

'What are you talking about?'

Bridget said nothing, but shoved open her door and jumped out into the muddy puddle that had formed while they talked. Simmy was tempted to stay where she was, and perhaps make a few phone calls. She felt as if she were overflowing with new developments that should be conveyed to somebody. Precisely who, she wasn't entirely sure. Instead, she switched off the engine and opened her own door.

They both peered down the drive as they reached it, expecting to see police escorting Glenn in handcuffs, or pushing Ben into a car. Instead there was nothing but the two police officers once more inside their steamed-up vehicle.

'We came back,' Simmy shouted to them as they drew level. 'We need to go into the house.'

Both men responded eagerly. 'We'll have to escort you,' said the officious one.

'That's fine. But first Bridget wants to get something from her car.'

Bridget had run ahead, and was already pulling the shoulder bag from the back seat. She opened it and peered in. 'Do that indoors,' said Simmy. 'Whatever it is will get wet out here.'

Wet had become an intrinsic element to the whole experience. Rain ran down her neck, muddy water seeped through her shoes, her hands were slippery and cold. It had the effect of blurring everything, including her thoughts.

The foursome trotted along to the house and let themselves in without fuss. Simmy took a moment to admire the big square hallway, with fabulous Arts and Crafts tiles and impressive staircase. A house fit for John Ruskin, she thought irrelevantly.

Voices came from a room on the left, and the dominant policeman knocked gently before pushing the door open. Simmy was close behind him, and glimpsed a man lying full length on the floor with something white and red pushed into his face. 'What's happening?' she asked, her voice rather shrill. 'Who's that?' She was still afraid for Ben, she realised. If Ben was hurt, it would obviously be all her fault.

Before she knew it, Pablo had leapt forward and was holding her back. His hands were on her upper arms, in a gentle grip that felt pleasantly protective. 'It's all over,' he said. 'Everything's in the open now.'

Bridget pushed through the doorway, scanning the room. 'What do you mean?' she shouted. 'You don't know. None of you can know.' She flourished a black object in Pablo's face. 'We have to read this, before we know anything.'

Peter and Ben had been standing together near the window, like corralled sheep. They looked drained, but oddly relaxed, like enemies who have finally made peace after a long battle.

Moxon had been squatting beside Glenn, who turned out to be the body on the floor. Across from the detective was a woman in police uniform, who was applying the white towel to a bleeding nose. Now Moxon looked at Simmy with a very complicated expression.

'Sorry,' she said. 'I promised I'd be in Troutbeck, didn't I?'

'Doesn't matter,' he said, and switched his gaze to Bridget, and raised an eyebrow. 'What's that, then?' he asked.

'Markie's old laptop. He left it behind when they moved. It was in the attic in Simmy's house. All his emails will still be on it. He used to mail us all, all the time, before he got his Smartphone. It's *evidence*,' she finished sternly.

'Of what?' Moxon asked, his voice low and controlled.

'Glenn's . . . wickedness. We all ignored it, you see. He was our *friend*. But he has a cruel streak, too. He makes people do things they don't want to. Markie told me about it, in a lot of messages he sent to me and Felix. Felix most of all.' She looked around. 'Where *is* Felix, anyway?'

'He's gone,' said Pablo. 'The London Hospital called. They've got some results for him. It sounded quite encouraging.'

'Glenn made Peter think Felix's accident was all his fault. He made it sound like that in the papers. Felix can explain it. He kept trying to put it straight. He's Peter's *cousin*. He didn't want things spoilt between them.'

Simmy gently shook herself free of Pablo and stepped sideways around the room until she reached Ben. 'Are you all right?' she muttered.

'Fine,' he said. 'It was me, you know, who solved it. I remembered about the squirrel.' Then he frowned. 'Except I guess that laptop would have done it, anyway, without me.' His frown deepened. 'But I'm not sure it will really count as evidence. Old emails – what good will they be?'

Peter Harrison-West rubbed a hand down one cheek. 'He didn't use my granddad's gun, you know,' he said blearily.

'He couldn't have done. It lost its firing pin ten years ago. He'll have used the Mauser, which *his* grandfather brought back from the war. And I know exactly where he will have hidden it.'

Moxon looked up, not catching the whole remark. 'Did you say Mauser?'

Peter nodded.

'And you know where it is?'

Another nod.

'Then we're clear and free,' said the detective with a sigh of satisfaction.

# Chapter Twenty-Three

Simmy was not unduly surprised to get a phone call from Eleanor Baxter at eight that evening. 'Could you possibly come over?' she asked.

'What – now?'

'If that's all right.'

'No. Sorry,' said Simmy firmly. 'I've got too much work to do. Perhaps in a day or two I might manage it.'

'I wanted to thank you. I have no idea how you did it, but I feel sure you were the crucial element in the whole miserable business.'

'No, I wasn't, I assure you. If it was anyone, it was Ben.'

'That boy I saw with Bridget in the rain. So he's the hero of the hour, is he? Perhaps we'll be able to think of a way to reward him, then.'

Simmy was too shocked and exhausted to take the suggestion further. 'Just tell me one thing,' she said.

'What?'

'How could you let your daughter marry a man so much older than herself? How could you possibly think it was all right?'

'How do you think I could have stopped her?' The voice was ragged with sudden pain. 'Anything I could have said to her would have had the opposite result to that intended. There has never been a more stubborn girl than Bridget. She got what was coming to her, if you ask me. Besides,' she added, more softly, 'I think it's all going to be all right, in the end. Now they both know they can trust each other, what's to stop them making a go of it?'

Simmy had no reply to that. There were still too many questions, and too many stark betrayals for any seeds of optimism to take root.

Melanie was furious when she heard the story on Saturday morning. 'You left me out,' she accused, almost tearfully. 'I missed the whole thing.'

'I know,' Simmy sympathised. 'But there wasn't anything I could do.'

'So, it's all settled, is it? Just like that?'

Simmy hesitated. The speed at which it had all happened had left her with a sense of anticlimax. The main thing she remembered was Pablo's hands on her arms. 'I assume so,' she nodded. 'If they can find the gun.'

'I thought the gun was in your attic?'

'There's another one. The one in my attic doesn't work. They just kept it for sentimental reasons. Something about Glenn's grandfather being best mates with Peter's, and them both bringing rifles back with them after the war. It makes it all much worse, knowing the families have been such friends for generations. And then Glenn turns psycho on them.'

Melanie made a wise face. 'They all pretended he was normal, then. Wouldn't even consider that he might have killed the Baxter men.'

'Something like that. He convinced them all it was Peter who did it – even Peter himself, very nearly.'

'And *Ben* was there? That's the bit I can't get over. Why did *he* get all the fun?'

Simmy gave her a look and Mel changed tack. 'What does your mother say about it all?'

'I don't know. I haven't seen her. I did speak to Eleanor Baxter briefly, that's all.'

'But *Ben*,' Melanie said again. 'And *Wilf*. He phoned me last night, you know. I told him to get lost. Joe would have a fit if he knew.' But Simmy could see a wisp of indecision in her assistant's eye.

'Ben was the trump card, in the end,' said Simmy. 'The ace witness. The best of the bunch. That boy will go far.'

As if conjured from thin air, the boy himself came into the shop at that moment. He spread his arms wide in a dramatic self-introduction. 'Ta-da!' he crowed. 'Here I am as promised. Are you busy?'

Simmy laughed. 'Not as busy as I thought I'd be. Why?'

'Don't you remember? We're going to collect sticks and leaves and seed pods for our model.'

'No, Ben, we're not. It's much too early for that. For dry leaves we need to wait at least until the middle of November.'

'Aww,' he whined, childishly.

To cheer him up, Simmy told him what Eleanor had said about him. 'You were the hero of the hour, according to her.'

He preened, and fingered the fading bruise on his cheek.

'Well, if this ever happens again, *I* want to be included,' said Melanie.

'Not a chance,' Simmy told her, with great emphasis. 'We're none of us ever going to witness a murder again.'

To discover more great books and to
place an order visit our website at
**allisonandbusby.com**

Don't forget to sign up to our free newsletter at
**allisonandbusby.com/newsletter**
for latest releases, events and exclusive offers

**Allison & Busby Books**
**@AllisonandBusby**

You can also call us on
**0203 950 7834**
for orders, queries
and reading recommendations